The Savannah Stories

Cooking Up Trouble

The Savannah Stories

Cooking Up Trouble

J.L. Lemon

This book is a work of fiction. Names, character, places and incidents are products of the author's imagination or are used fictitiously. Any resemblance to actual events or locales or persons, living or dead, is entirely coincidental.

ISBN-13: 978-0-9796117-9-7
ISBN-10: 0-9796117-9-2

Published 2014

My Parents

In your eyes I've seen God's love. In your words I've heard His wisdom. Through your life I've found His grace.

For Dad-For your love, support and strength. You are my hero and my buddy.

In memory of my mom. I love you and will always miss you.

And Jude Gorman. For being you and for being there. You are a blessing to all who know you.

May those who love us love us.
And those that don't love us,
May God turn their hearts.
And if He doesn't turn their hearts,
May he turn their ankles,
So we'll know them by their limping.

Irish Blessing

Or Savannah's choice might be this quote by Oscar Wilde:

"Some cause happiness wherever they go; others whenever they go."

1

Pregnancy was not for the faint of heart. Books, TV and well-meaning relatives neglected to inform women that the first trimester is a Biblical trial unto itself. Between the peeing, nausea and swelling, a woman questions her common sense for not better preparing for such a massive, labor intensive undertaking. The nausea eased up with my second trimester but the swelling and peeing ravaged me as wholly as Sherman marching through Atlanta. Though I'd never confide it to my husband – relieving myself felt better than sex at times. Then came the third trimester. Baby grew, Mama grew, Mama's feet continued to grow (or so it seemed). I wore size ten shoes anyway so finding footwear was harder than locating the Titanic. It could be done but with lots of time and effort. All this occurred while my bladder simultaneously shrunk to the size of a gnat's eyeball. Yes, pregnancy tested a woman's stamina, nerves and sanity. So why did a woman put up with it all? Because she couldn't wait to see her adorable, soft, pink blessing from God. To hold that little piece of immortality in her arms, knowing that no matter how screwed up her life was, that chubby-cheeked cherub represented a new life and a new beginning.

My husband Ennis and I already knew our blessing was a girl.

We decided on the name Lily Christine. We named her after no one in particular, partly to avoid the sticky familial situation of namesakes and partly because we fell in love with the names Lily and Christine.

Ennis watched me approach the desk. Sitting in my chair, I rolled forward but once past my knees everything went to hell again. They said insanity is doing the same thing over and over and expecting a different outcome. Well, whoever said it never tried to shoe spoon their body behind a desk or they'd have called it *pregnancy*.

"Turn sideways," Ennis suggested. "You'll fit better."

"Why?" I asked, my tone slightly indignant. "So everyone can call me the U.S.S. Savannah? No thanks." Cue the first reference to retirement, I thought, because it's coming. Ennis and my older sister Georgia insisted I retire and be a full-time mom. A chorus I'd grown mighty weary of lately. I knew the words by heart, heard them in my dreams and arose each morning to them – because I slept next to the choirmaster. I didn't care that I waddled when I walked nor did I care that my daily trips to the restroom far outnumbered the stars in the sky. I still managed to do my job, a job I loved and until this whale beached herself or couldn't perform my duties, I would clock in for my shift.

But for now I fumed, "What idiot designed these tiny desks? Anyone with a few extra pounds is screwed."

"You've put on more than a few extra, sugar."

Oh, so he *enjoyed* sleeping on the couch. He'd take it for a test drive tonight if he didn't retract that statement, shred it, burn it and bury it. My expression said as much.

He backed off, "I meant you're looking mighty healthy for eight months."

And that comment was any better? Whatever, I thought. He'd get his when diaper duty arrived because Mama tolerated enough shit during her pregnancy.

My brave hubby suggested, "Well, you *could* go on maternity leave. Or you could retire from the job, have the baby and be a mom. Now that sounds reasonable."

"Now's not a great time to mention motherhood. I'm swimming in hormones. I fight the urge to cry, scream and break people in half all at the same time. You can't tell me that doesn't come in handy for at least seventy percent of the job. Just face the facts. I'm Sybil for the next few weeks."

"She had what, thirteen personalities? You only have five," Ennis winked.

Good thing he winked. I couldn't outrun a snail but he sure couldn't outrun a flying phone.

A knock on my door shattered wild notions of chucking things at my smart-alecky spouse. It was our captain, Josh Hunter. "They found a body at Lake Acworth," he said.

"And they called you?" Acworth, a community located thirty miles north of Atlanta, had their own police department. Why'd they need ours? So I stated the obvious, "They have their own police department. Why do they need us?"

"They said it might be Bob Davenport, the restaurateur."

Davenport's restaurant Blackstone sat square in the middle of Zone 2, our precinct. His house sat in Zone 5 so when his daughter filed a missing persons report, Zone 5 Detectives Mike Ramos and Darren Metcalf took the case. I'd met Metcalf once and equated the event to having a thousand paper cuts. "I still don't understand," I said. "There are detectives working the missing persons case. Do they not have homicide detectives in Zone 5?"

Truthfully, I tended to run my boss bonkers. I always ruffled his feathers, mostly without intending to. This time I had a valid question. The original detectives on the case were responsible for pretty much anything Davenport-related.

Captain Hunter bristled slightly, "Their investigation bled into our Zone. Literally. They think they've found evidence at Blackstone restaurant and that, Detective Prince, is our jurisdiction." He crossed his arms, "Is this pregnancy thing getting in the way of your job – or your thinking?"

"Oh shit," Ennis recoiled, probably because he recognized my expression. The one vowing grievous bodily harm for such a verbal blunder.

I felt big enough to orbit the Sun, my feet and I visually divorced around last month and I saw them only when I made an effort to lift them to ensure they were still there. I peed all the time so close proximity to restrooms was a must. My moods swung back and forth but not as often as they had during my teen years which was a miracle considering the level of hormones coursing through my system.

I stared at Josh Hunter with curious wonder. This man knew my temper. Even incurred it several times. Poking sticks at this expectant mother was as intelligent as juggling nitroglycerin with his feet. Take a deep breath and remain calm, I told myself. "This *pregnancy thing* is fine. My brain is in perfect working order which is why I fear for the safety of mother and child when Ramos and Metcalf blast through my office door, demanding to know why we stole their case. Because it will happen."

According to Hunter's expression, he read the murder in my eyes if he furthered the pregnancy/insanity angle. "I'll, uh, call Zone 5 and find out the details of the case. I'll see if they'll work with you. Or something."

My wicked glare faded to a smile, "See? When Sybil's happy, everybody's happy."

O O O

By and large, March in Atlanta meant afternoon temperatures in the sixties and chilly nights in the forties. I hadn't noticed much of the colder temps because of the pregnancy. At night I kicked off bedcovers, leaving Ennis buried in a mountain of sheets. For work I dressed for late Spring and early Summer temps but the moment I stepped into the cold damp air surrounding the two hundred sixty acre Lake Acworth, I regretted not bringing a heavier jacket. I made do with my lightweight suit jacket and steeled myself against the chilly breeze wafting across the water.

"You cold?" Ennis asked.

"Nope." I said, rubbing my arms anyway. He'd already begun shrugging from his suit coat and I stopped him, "I appreciate it but I'm fine, really." Actually I was freezing but letting other cops see me babied by my partner only evoked images of helpless females. Not a favorable image since I was already knocked up and all.

We crossed the road to an area of thick tall grass. They located the body on the back side of the lake that was more trouble to get to than the moon. We faced grass and weeds as tall as small trees and God only knew what lurked *in* that mess. Our only hope: a makeshift trail blazed through the overgrowth, its width about the span of two adults – which meant I alone could fit through there. Poor Ennis would have to follow me but at least that area's weeds grew about knee high.

Before spelunking our way in, we met the uniform guarding the outer perimeter of the scene. "Body's down that way," he pointed to an abyss of thicket and limbs. "Crime scene's already tagging potential evidence and taking shoe impressions."

In other words, you're late. Neither Ennis nor I said a word. That unnerved the cop who toned down his attitude, "Be careful of the evidence markers when you're walking. They got 'em hanging on limbs too."

"Thank you, officer," I used my sister's molasses Georgian drawl. "You might want to stay close by in case we get lost in there." You blockhead, I nearly finished.

"Let's go, partner," Ennis physically guided me away from the moron before I furthered my comment.

We tromped through the overgrowth leading to the body located near the lake's shore. The densely packed trees and tall grass we traversed through made *me* question our sanity now. A nice concrete pathway stood no more than thirty feet away and here we were squishing through a muddy forest to reach our destination.

"Can you believe Josh?" I asked Ennis. To keep my mind occupied, I mentioned our boss whose wife was also expecting, like, their twentieth kid. He should have known not to harass the knocked-up woman under his command.

Ennis's hand circled my elbow to steady me as we walked, "I can't believe he was that reckless. He's seen you mad. You being pregnant only gives him two pissed off females to contend with."

Our little girl did have Mama's demeanor at times. She loved punishing Mama by jamming her foot in my ribs or using those ribs as a trapeze. She used my body as either a jungle gym or Gold's Gym, depending on her mood.

We ducked into a gap where limbs barely gave breathing room, much less walking room. We sidestepped yellow evidence markers on the ground and tags hanging from a couple of limbs. The fit was so tight it forced us to walk one behind the other. The further we ventured, the more my claustrophobia crept in. Limbs protruded like fingers, poking and scraping as we went. The ones overhead closed in, shrinking our room – along with my lungs and sanity – until I finally spied freedom. Another uniform officer stood at the clearing ahead.

Displaying my badge, I asked the officer, "Is there no other way to this body? There was a perfectly good walkway back there."

"Sorry, Detective. Whoever tossed the body either used the lake to get here or squeezed through that tunnel you're in. The concrete pathway leads east, not west like you need it to."

"So we have to crawl back through the rabbit hole?"

He glanced at my belly and gave a contrite wince, "'Fraid so." He pointed to our right, "The body's over there about twenty feet. At least you get to stretch your back now."

Hmm, I thought. Someone had a wife and a kid. The officer's expression matched what a new father's should. Whether honest or bogus, the miserable pregnant detective appreciated the empathetic nod.

Ennis and I plodded through the muck and wet soggy grass until bright sunlight beamed from the vast, clear sky. I shielded my eyes as my body relaxed. My uneasiness and pounding heart settled out, allowing me to collect my mental marbles before getting on with business.

As we approached a small group of men, I noticed a few uniformed officers along with three other men. One wore a suit like Ennis, the other two wore black jumpsuits with "CORONER" emblazoned across their backs. Suit was the man we needed to see. He glanced up, excused himself and headed toward us. The man was Hispanic, black hair slicked back and judging by his physique, regularly visited a gym. In the clinical sense, he was nice looking, save for the grim nature of his expression but he fell short of Ennis's height. Most men did since my husband was six feet two. Suit thrust his hand out, "Detective Mike Ramos and you're Prince and Rutherford from Zone 2, right?"

"Right," Ennis replied, giving Mike's hand a solid shake. "Ennis Rutherford," he hitched his thumb at me, "Savannah Prince."

A wily grin crossed Mike's features when he smiled at me and shook my hand, "Mamacita, eh? When are you due?"

"Not soon enough," Mamacita replied without the requisite

smile. If this was the best Zone 5 found for detectives, no wonder they called us in. And I really hated cops who treated me like I was the help. Mr. Ramos would learn fast about a pregnant lady's inability to stifle brutal honesty if he didn't shut up quick. I searched the premises for Darren Metcalf. "Where's Metcalf?" Because the last thing I needed was a crazy man tackling me in front of everyone.

Ramos ignored my question, "You're about ready for maternity leave. You got twins cooking in there?"

"Nope, just one big happy baby. Metcalf. Where is he?"

Mike started back where he came from. Ennis and I followed while he continued his campaign, "The daddy must have some elephant size huevos on him."

Looking at Ennis, he was about to blow. I touched his arm to calm him down. He wanted Ramos to zip it too. "Where the hell is Metcalf? Peeing in the bushes?" I demanded a little too loudly. Great, I thought, seeing the uniforms turn in my direction. Now they all think I'm hormonal – which I was but eating glass sounded better than admitting it.

Ramos motioned for us to keep following so we did. He finally answered, "He's out on a family emergency. Just you guys and me today."

I couldn't think of a better way to spend a March afternoon. In the cool wind, next to a lake with a dead body and Mr. Suave with his silver tongue. Ech.

The crime scene techs pulled the plastic-wrapped body further out of the water near the weed line. I'd say grass but it was mostly weeds.

As we approached, the more I noticed that body looked pretty small. So small it gave me a shiver because it could easily have been a toddler inside the plastic sack. "There's an adult male in there?" I asked, just to be sure.

Without turning, Ramos nodded, "Yup and it's all hacked up."

Ennis curled his lip, "If someone chopped it up, chances are the killer made sure we can't identi —"

My husband's rant stopped cold and an instant later I found out why. The most putrid stench wafted into my nose, forcing me to breathe through my mouth to save my breakfast.

"Oh shit," Ennis pinched his nose shut. "And it's aged like a month."

"Stop talking," I snapped at him. My pancakes already used my stomach as a trampoline. I didn't need a play-by-play on visuals or the other senses. It was hard enough to swallow without heaving.

Somehow my spouse either failed to hear me or daringly chose to ignore me, "Only thing worse is if it's soup."

"Ennis Rutherford," I growled through clenched teeth, "if you do not shut up this very minute, you'll be wearing my sausage and pancakes. My constitution is exceptionally frail lately and my patience is thinner than the ice you're skatin' on."

"Shuttin' up," he said, still trudging through the muck.

It was Ramos who stoked my temper when he stood over the opened black trash bag with a smile, "You like beef stew, Detective Prince?"

Ennis's hand immediately tightened on my arm. He considered it his special little warning against jumping idiots. He whispered to calm down. At that point, he stood a better chance of stopping a tornado from spinning. As Ramos flashed those pearly whites, I narrowed my vision, "You're not married, are you, Ramos? I can tell you're not."

His brow lifted in surprise, "How?"

"You're still alive. Don't poke at me today. Expectant mothers get cranky around dead bodies, especially smelly, dismembered ones."

He slipped on latex gloves and his hand disappeared into the duct tape fortified plastic bag. Ramos leaned in to study something. Ennis and I ventured closer. Mike Ramos held a forearm in his hand. A very distinguishable Army insignia tattoo shined out from the decaying flesh. Ramos grinned up at me, "Well, Detective, looks like this is yours."

"My what?" Because I wanted nothing to do with the meat puzzle forensics managed to fish out of the lake.

"Your case. Metcalf and I were investigating a missing person and he ain't missing no more."

From the corner of my eye I saw Ennis shake his head. I voiced my skepticism, "How can you prove this is Bob Davenport?"

Ramos smirked, "That tattoo matches the one the wife said he had. Army insignia. If that don't convince you, this should." He pointed to the dissected arm.

I bent forward to see what he aimed at. The army insignia consisted of what originally looked like a red shield with a gold lightning bolt in the middle. What I saw beneath it made me groan. In big ol' block letters, read "Davenport". Great. Just great.

Mike gingerly placed the arm back in the bag, stripped off his gloves, "I'll get the files to you later today. Congratulations, it's a

murder." He thrust his hand out to Ennis who handily ignored it as did
I.

O   O   O

Ennis and I leaned back in bed after our long day. The Hawks were
playing and, like our Braves, our basketball team played well but lacked
the stamina to reach the big game. I snorted as the Miami Heat threw a
three point shot, lifting them to a twenty-two point advantage. With one
minute left in the game the Hawks were toast, just like Ennis and I were
once Metcalf discovered we owned his case. I spent most of the evening
fuming over that fact and Mike Ramos' stupid-happy way of rubbing it
in.

 "We're gonna get killed," I groaned. "Metcalf is a grumpy
middle-aged bastard with a bad comb-over."

 "You've dealt with him before?"

 "No, only a brief introduction and believe me, he's not a nice
person." I dreaded the moment he heard about us taking the case. The
city would see the mother of all mushroom clouds. And as usual Baby
Lily gave me enough worries so adding a battle with a fellow detective
shouldn't have bothered me but it did. I only prayed Metcalf wouldn't
hit a pregnant woman... "Metcalf chewed out one detective because the
poor guy questioned a witness involved in his case."

 Ennis frowned as I continued, "Metcalf didn't realize that the
other guy's investigation overlapped his. Darren's bitchy and jumps to
conclusions too quick."

Ennis sighed, "Yep. We're dead. I hope he doesn't have a heart attack or something when he finds out. That would be awkward."

I temporarily entertained calling in sick the next day just to avoid Darren's impending tirade but I refused to leave Ennis as a sacrificial lamb. I felt tense all over and nearly a little nauseous. Lily moved a bit then bounced a fist against my tummy. I winced, "This is even bothering Lily. She's punching me."

"It's 'cause you're tense. She feels it." Ennis positioned himself at the foot of the bed and brought my right foot into his lap.

Ah, a foot rub. I loved his foot rubs, especially since I got pregnant. "Oh," I countered, "so her answer is to go three rounds on my ribs? Such a sweet girl we have."

"If you'll relax, she'll relax."

"You sound like Georgia, which is to say, you sound like my mother." I settled back in bed while he positioned himself to rub my feet while watching TV. The Miami Heat players slapped each other's backs, high-fived one another and generally celebrated as if they'd won the Finals. I felt kinda sorry for the Hawks. They'd been bullied by a bigger, stronger team then squashed like bugs. Sorta the way Ennis and I would feel after enduring Darren Metcalf.

Ennis's thumbs pressed into a particularly sore spot on my foot. They tenderly massaged until I groaned. My husband possessed very large hands which was good because I had very large feet. Even larger now thanks to Lily. But what he did with those very large hands was magical. Truthfully it was really hard to concentrate on our imminent demise with all the blissful sensations rolling from my weary, sore and swollen feet all the way up my legs. Magical.

"Are you going to sleep?"

My eyes snapped open. "No," I lied, "I was staring at the backs of my eyelids."

He smiled, "Such a savvy liar. Try this one. Did you see today's mail? And before you lie again, remember I noticed a definite change in your mood after you thumbed through the mail."

He tightened his hold on my foot – probably fearing I'd kick him for mentioning *the mail.* Instead I sighed, "Yes and I got a cheery phone call from Georgia reminding me of it too."

As if I needed a reminder. My cousins Linda and Teresa couldn't cook their way out of a paper bag yet they invited family and friends and other various innocents to a cooking contest. They challenged each other to this culinary duel for bragging rights. In my opinion neither of 'em had a reason to brag unless it was about how much takeout they usually buy. Anyway, the two sisters always suffered jealous fits with one another but when faced with me and Georgia, it turned into a war. *Their* mother could cook better than ours, they said. Without fail, they concluded with their belief that their cooking skills far outshined mine or Georgia's. I always chalked it up to idiocy but inevitably Georgia took offense in the highest degree. That afternoon on the phone I told my sister to relax. As long as no one died, the contest would prove neither woman could cook. But still, "I dread the hell out of it."

Lily lodged a foot beneath my ribs and commenced pushing with all her might. My child hated me at times, I just knew it. I rubbed at the pain while sweet-talking the baby through clenched teeth.

"You know how she feels about your cussin'," Ennis hinted.

Yeah, I did since every time I uttered a cussword she kicked my gall bladder between the goal posts. "Then she shouldn't use my liver as a footrest. That tends to make me grumpy." I put some English on my wrist as I rubbed, "Come on, baby, lighten up on Mama."

The phone rang and Ennis, realizing Lily was in a fierce mood, decided he would answer instead of me. No need to scare off the caller. I heard him say I was busy which was the understatement of the day. Then he asked who was calling. As the pain in my ribs ebbed a micro-degree, he extended the phone, "Your cousin Grace?"

Ennis presented it as a question because he'd never met my mother's side of the family – and for a good reason. Most of them were nuts. Grace wasn't and how she managed to escape the Culberson lunacy amazed me. I took the phone, cleared my throat and tried to sound normal, "Hi Grace."

"Savannah? Is that you? You sound different."

"Oh," I kept rubbing, "that's because my baby is playing kick-boxer on my ribs."

"I didn't know you were pregnant. Congratulations."

"Thanks," I replied, noticing Grace didn't sound exactly right either. "Gracie, is something wrong?"

"It's Mama. She collapsed and I called an ambulance. While they're doing tests, I wanted to contact everyone."

Aunt Emma and my mother were sisters. They had another sister Katherine who spawned Linda and Teresa and two not-as-loony sons Talmadge and Dean, who sounded more like a figure skating team than two brothers.

Aunt Emma had Gracie and Abby. My mother Charlene had Seth, Georgia and me. Of all the cousins I was the youngest – or cow's tail as Ennis said – at six years younger than Georgia and at least two years younger than any Culberson cousin. Gracie and I were closest growing up. Now that we were full-fledged adults, we hadn't seen each other in six or seven years. With the news of Aunt Emma's emergency, I wasn't sure what to say except, "I'm sorry, Grace. Is there anything I can do?"

She paused. When she spoke the emotion caught in her throat, "No, not right now. Thank you for asking. If you'll just let Georgia and Seth know, I'd appreciate it."

"What hospital are you at?"

"Grady."

"I'll tell the brood and we'll come to the hospital tomorrow."

2

Prior commitments prevented Seth from going to the hospital the next day and Georgia had obligations with her publicist until around two-thirty. Meanwhile Ennis and I worked the case until I needed to leave and meet Georgia at Grady Memorial.

I repeatedly stretched my back, trying to loosen the knots the whole Davenport thing produced. Stretching without irritating the Little One proved a challenge. Lily felt fine, according to her lazy movements and Mama kept pushing her around. She tapped at my belly as a warning to stop now or pay the price.

When I looked up, Josh Hunter was staring at me. I tried to explain my strange calisthenics, "Growing pains. Hers *and* mine."

Hunter was around ten years older than me. His hair grayed out slowly in a sprinkling of salt and pepper. He was tall, attractive, kept in shape and managed to stay in a reasonable mood for a man with humpteen kids and an angry wife. Five months ago his wife Michelle ended up pregnant again and one day she arrived at the station armed with a suitcase and a warning. No more kids, she said, or he'd live out of his Samsonite until he got that vasectomy. I didn't know – and didn't care to ask – if my boss got that vasectomy but I was willing to bet if he didn't, some night his wife would give him the discount rate with a rusty kitchen knife.

After that public fiasco with his wife, Hunter approached his pregnant detective rather cautiously. He used kid gloves most times – except for the previous day – probably because of my constant hormonal upheaval. Today he reverted back to the kinder, gentler approach, "How are you and the baby doing?"

I removed my reading glasses, "Fine except when the baby lodges that foot in my ribs and makes me look like I'm in the throes of satanic possession. My last doctor's appointment went pretty good. I'm just grateful she's not twins."

"The baby or the doctor?" he asked then retreated verbally. "I mean, good, *good*. The due date's still next month?"

"Still next month."

"So no maternity leave yet." He kind of stammered, "I – I mean whenever you need it, of course. Michelle reminded me that the Davenport case might be a little much for you at, uh," he motioned to my stomach, "this stage of your pregnancy. Clark and Nesbitt are free to take it."

Don't tease me, I wanted to say. But having a case reassigned because I was knocked up? Never. And especially not to the new detectives in the station. "I'm fine, really." I decided to turn the tables, "Josh, are you okay?" Because anyone who knew Josh Hunter knew when Josh Hunter was not okay.

"Michelle and I argued last night. About baby names of all things. She's wanting Careen for a girl and Lyndon for a boy. I mean, I hear the word careen, I think –"

"A car careening off the road into a tree," I finished.

Josh sighed, "Exactly. And Lyndon only brings me to –"

"Lyndon Johnson, the president."

Frowning, he nodded, "And I'm a Republican. I can't have my

boy named after a Democrat. I won't. Did you and Ennis have this much trouble naming Lily?"

That answer came easily, "No, but then we don't have as many kids as you do. Eventually you'll run out of alphabet if you keep on this timetable."

Hunter's lips tightened. I admitted the comment served as minor payback for his *pregnancy thing* remark the day before. He loved kids but considering he didn't suffer the pains and miseries of giving birth, he needed to temper his enthusiasm. No woman in the sweaty rigors of childbirth, including his wife, says *yes, let's have ten more.* Plus, my boss disliked the female take on pregnancy. The simple things men took for granted. Things like the fact we ladies would, at some point, enjoy seeing our feet again without bending double. We would love to have an hour or two where the bathroom didn't see us for our regularly scheduled pee. I refused to mention the bloating, leg cramps or backache or other issues. Women just wanted to be normal again. To relieve him of any further conversation, I smiled sheepishly, "Well, gotta head for my favorite hangout. We really should splurge on repainting that bathroom. It would brighten it up a bit."

Ennis and I made a deal. No more than two kids. If he broke that rule, I reserved the right to toss his luggage at him Michelle Hunter-style. I realized getting pregnant was a two-way street but I could close *my* way down pretty damn quick. Ennis didn't strike me as a foolhardy soul. I could not tolerate more children than I had arms, legs or even kidneys. God gave me two of each so why not apply that logic to having children too?

I returned from my pilgrimage to find Ennis planted in the chair facing my desk. I suspected he ducked Hunter's visit earlier for fear our boss might hit a hot button with me. Ennis hated my temper worse than anyone except Georgia – and Lily.

He treaded carefully with his inquiry, "What'd the boss want?"

"Asking about maternity leave. I told him not to worry." I glanced at my watch. If I left right then, I'd squeak by on time to meet Georgia at the hospital. My sister ran twenty minutes fast which meant I was late if I was on time. She was almost always the first one to arrive anywhere while I brought up the rear. "Gotta go."

Ennis checked his watch, "But you've got at least thirty minutes."

"And to Georgia that means I'm probably late."

"Want me to go with you?"

"God no," I blurted. My panic widened his eyes in surprise. Then they narrowed at me. I kinda figured what he mulled over in his mind. "Ennis, there's a reason you haven't met part of my family. A very good reason."

"And that is?"

"Besides the fact they're nuts, they're also vicious. Remember Linda called me after I was diagnosed? Remember the comment about me getting a –"

"A will, I remember, but they'd restrain their maliciousness if I was with you."

The poor dear. Growing up in a large, loving family must have been wonderful. However the Cleaver-esque environment also shielded him from the likes of the Culberson clan. The Prince side possessed its own crazies but the Culbersons took *crazy* from hobby to obsession. The truth was, "Honey, if you show up, it will spur them on. Ask Georgia or Seth."

Ennis bristled at the rejection. I tried to soften it but the last thing I wanted to him to do was meet my familial fruitcakes. "I don't see how," he argued. "If they say anything rude, I'll just pound 'em into the ground."

"That should help. Then I can use our daughter's meager college fund to bail you out of jail. Sound good?"

He sighed again, "You're not lettin' me go, are you?"

"Nope," I said then smiled. "Take heart, babe. You'll meet 'em soon enough and when you do, you'll wish you hadn't."

3

Founded in 1892, Grady Memorial Hospital was Atlanta's only level one trauma center, had over ten floors, a whopping nine hundred fifty-three beds and over the years helped some of the nation's most notable people such as Margaret Mitchell and James Brown. I certainly didn't count as notable but I'd seen the innards of Grady a few times myself. Being a cop meant cuts, scrapes and stopping an occasional bullet when some moron refused to drop his gun.

My sister-in-law Leah worked at Grady as a trauma nurse. Because of that – and my frequenting the place due to mishaps and stupids – I knew the hospital pretty well. I could guide anyone to the bathrooms, tell them where to find the surgical units and most importantly where to find the cafeteria.

I arrived on time according to Georgia. She'd waited only five minutes for me to circle the lot for a parking place which ended up in northern Alabama (or at least felt like it).

My sister and I traversed our way through the busy halls until finally ending up at the elevator. With my claustrophobia, elevators were probably the biggest nemesis in my job. Every damn building had them and everyone wanted to use them – everyone except me. My condition meant any space smaller than the Georgia Dome practically gave me a heart attack. I couldn't breathe because my lungs shrank to the size of peas and I perspired as if I'd run the Boston Marathon. And being pregnant had not helped one little bit.

"Can you ride the elevator?" Georgia asked. One thing about my sister. Most times she *could* read my mind.

I stared down at my jutting belly then back up at Georgia. Pregnancy sucked the energy from me and climbing four flights of stairs seemed rather insurmountable but so did locking myself in a moving metal box but I'd tried developing a coping mechanism while inside elevators. Close my eyes and pretend it wasn't happening. Sometimes it kinda worked. Other times, well, it didn't. I nodded, telling myself I could do it.

The ride up to the fourth floor took forever. The elevator stopped at every floor to let passengers on or off. Each time the doors closed, the air felt heavy and sparse. Six people in a tiny box. I began to sweat, my heart sped up and I closed my eyes to the rising panic. A hand wrapped tight around mine. My eyes opened to see Georgia's composed, supportive smile. My sister might have been bossy but she had a heart of gold.

Immense relief washed over me when the bell chimed for the fourth floor. We ambled down the hallway toward the nurse's kiosk when my sister not-so-subtly cautioned, "Please don't start anything."

And there was the bossy trait again. I pulled back, coming to a complete stop. I crossed my arms in protest, "Name one argument I started with them. Just one."

Georgia's silence spoke volumes. She knew who the ringleaders were and none were named Savannah. Her tone softened, "I know how they are. Remember, I grew up with them too but try to ignore their idiotic ramblings about Mama and Daddy. Grace needs us. They're ganging up on her the way they did us. It's their nature to pick on the ones in distress so keep your cool and don't spur their lunacy."

"Yes, Mama."

She furnished her well-cultivated, often used motherly frown, "Try to behave."

Eh, I'd try despite the fact I considered two of my cousins an accidentally omitted plague in the Bible. Somewhere between the frogs, boils and locusts were Abby and Linda.

We got no farther than the waiting room when, "My, my. Looks like Savannah swallered a watermelon seed."

Oh good God. Just when life was complicated enough. The voice belonged to Linda. Four years my senior, her once pretty features hardened over the years due to a bitter divorce and generally sour attitude. She wore her black hair in a bob and dressed for comfort which meant she hoarded tank tops by the gross and adored her Wranglers as much as Brett Favre and Dale Earnhardt the Second. The most impressive trait – her sheer nerve. I stood five feet nine inches without my size ten shoes. She stood an even five feet *with* shoes. Most people recognized the danger of picking on people bigger than them – but not my cousin.

The baby tapped Morse Code on my belly. My interpretation: *Who is this moron?* Lily voiced her opinion about everything which warned me that my child and I would butt heads as often as I had with my parents.   When Baby expressed discontent, she grabbed my sciatic nerve and swung it like a dead cat. No, Lily Christine Rutherford wasn't coming quietly into the world, she was roaring in exactly the way her mama did thirty-something years ago.   Now I knew what *my* mama meant by *someday you'll have the daughter you deserve.* Yikes.

Linda approached with a half-sympathetic, half-smug grin, "Gettin' as fat as a whale, aren't you, honey? When I had Gene, thought I was gonna pop."

My sister took my hand again – I'd hoped as a supportive gesture. Then I remembered since my pregnancy, her method of keeping me in line changed from flat-out elbowing me to gently restraining me in a polite way.

"Savannah is not a whale," Georgia shot back. "She's beautiful pregnant or not. And she's certainly not going to *pop.*"

"No," I whispered, "but she might if my hands fit around that fat head of hers." I cringed as Georgia squeezed my hand as a warning. *Lord, woman, ease up…* I said as much, "Between you and the baby, I'll be permanently crippled before April. Cut it out."

Linda evidently didn't notice my sister's brutality, "Is it a boy or girl?"

"Neither," I replied, hoping to end the stupid, needless conversation. I waited for Georgia's ninja grip to relent. And waited. And waited.

Linda rolled her eyes at my answer, "Are you having it naturally or in a hospital?"

"I'm lettin' the kid decide. Seems as though she makes all the decisions lately anyway." Well, shit, I groused to myself. I just kicked Pandora's Box wide open. My private berating took a back seat when Georgia's grip tightened harder than bark on a tree. I slung at my hand, "Last warning. Let go or lose it." Magically, my sister let go.

"Oh, a girl," Linda gave a mournful shake of her head. "You've got your work cut out for you, honey. Parents of girls have all the stress. Keepin' 'em away from predators, hoping they won't get pregnant in high school, hoping they don't –"

"I get it, Linda. Good parenting is hard." Like she would know. "Love to stay and chat but we're looking for Aunt Emma's room." I took Georgia by the arm and headed to the nurse's desk.

"That was rude," Georgia harrumphed.

"You wanted me to behave. That was me behaving."

"*Let go or lose it?*" She sighed, "No wonder Mama went gray before thirty."

Yeah, right. Blame me. "And I bet you were a real peach to raise too."

"Well, if it isn't the Dark Prince side of the family. It's been a month of Sundays since our paths crossed."

I stiffened at the new voice. Cousin Teresa arrived to complete the unholy trinity. Georgia's hand migrated to my elbow and I aimed my glare at her, "Do it and you're first and she's second."

Her hand returned to her side. Teresa made the brave move of approaching us. Unlike her sister, she dressed only in skirts or dresses of Southern belle tradition, only not so billowy. She fancied herself a beauty queen contestant since developing a fascination with Delta Burke and her days of winning umpteen pageants.

To me, Teresa favored Kathleen Turner à la Romancing the Stone but her personality screamed right out of War of the Roses. My lovely cousin's finest talent consisted of steamrolling innocents the way Barbara Rose's monster truck flattened her husband's car – with him still in it. Somehow I doubted beauty pageants allowed mugging as a talent. She sure mugged her now ex-husband out of untold hundreds of thousands of dollars in their divorce and never let anyone forget it.

I surprised everyone by presenting a genuine smile, "Hello, Teresa. Nice to see you too. You and Linda park your brooms in the lot or in the waiting room?"

Georgia gently elbowed me, warning, "Savannah,"

Through my beaming smile I mumbled, "She started it."

"And I'll finish it, if need be," was the abrupt reply. "We didn't come to argue, we came to support Grace."

I seethed but kept my mouth shut. Evidently feeling reckless, Teresa upped the stakes, "So I'm s'pposin' your daddy hasn't drunk your family's fortune away yet?"

My smile evaporated, "Georgia,"

Her hand gripped my elbow to the point her nails began digging in. She whispered a gem of wisdom from Mama, "We're in public. We don't argue in public." Then she cautioned me about the baby. Babies don't fare well in jail and neither do their mamas, she said. And, I thought, we were standing in the middle of a shark tank. Yeah, my sister and I were real Mensa material.

A gentle patting on my back snapped me around to face Linda who'd crept up behind us. "It's okay, honey," she said. "It's hard to grow up with an alcoholic father. You girls and Seth did mighty good for all your misfortunes."

"Public," Georgia repeated uneasily. She remembered the fiasco at Mama's funeral and Daddy and Seth were not currently around to help pry my hands off Linda's throat.

Teresa shifted her sights to my sister, "Georgia, where's that big ol' strappin' man you married, anyway?"

I could tell the question knifed Georgia in the heart. Her divorce from Matthew – or his from *her* – classified as old news and Teresa knew it. It destroyed my sister to lose him. She loved Matthew deeply and he dumped her for a nurse who'd tended to his battle injuries. If I ever saw him again, Major Carlisle U.S.M.C. would sport more than a little shrapnel wound.

I glanced at Georgia who stumbled for an answer since she expected Matthew to be tucked in everyone's File 13. She should have realized our cousins thrived off File 13.

"He's in the military, right?" Linda asked. She waited a beat then suddenly, "Oh, *now* I remember. You split up 'cause of his whoring around."

One look at Georgia's horrified expression lit my temper, "Linda, find the emergency brake on your yap before you get hurt. Georgia is engaged to Ennis's brother Dane and I doubt you're invited to the wedding."

The beginnings of tears glistened in my sister's eyes as she nudged me forward, "Let's go before this escalates."

Good idea. We started toward the nurse's kiosk when Teresa couldn't resist one last shot, "Savannah, why aren't you out there finding that brute that murdered that precious little girl? Raped her and cut her throat. You're supposed to be protecting our city from those beasts."

I'd seen the article in the paper that morning. Nine year-old Cherise Aldridge was found on the east side of town, raped and murdered. The parents filed a missing person's report a week earlier and we'd all been on the lookout for her since. There were no leads that I'd heard, no evidence to go on. Bad as the Davenport case was, I was *really* glad the Aldridge case wasn't mine.

Linda chimed in, "This city is swirlin' the drain when our police won't even catch a killer. But what do we expect when they hire an alcoholic?"

Before giving me a chance to react, Georgia towed me alongside her, "Let's go, Savannah."

Clearly my sister sensed that another *public* warning would fall on deaf ears. She stood three inches shorter than me, weighed less and somehow still managed to physically haul me away from those obnoxious villains.

I fought to free my now tingling arm but my sister possessed the squeezing power of an alligator. *Good God, Georgia,* "The least you could do is allow me to refute that," I cringed and slung at my arm, "without maiming me."

"Silence is the source of great strength," she said.

"Wonderful. A pearl of wisdom from who? Yoda?"

"Lao Tzu."

Like I knew who Loud Zoo was. "Whatever. Believe me, my foot has *plenty* of strength, especially going up some idiot's behind. The little girl wasn't found in our precinct," I glanced over my shoulder at Linda, "so how could I be assigned to her case? And they didn't hire an alcoholic, you hateful –" A sharp pain shot up and down my arm as Georgia's nails sank into the skin. I glared at her, "*Let go of me, Georgia, before I hurt you.*"

My sister sighed and reluctantly released me, "God, you're so much like Daddy."

I rankled at the comparison, "There's no need to insult me. They fired at us first."

"I'm talking about your temper. You have his temper and that's not good."

"At least I don't hit people when I get pissed off."

Georgia nodded, "You're better at curbing it, yes, but you were two shakes away from jumping them and I know it. As appealing as that sounds to you right now, think of Lily. Maybe *she* doesn't want to fight them."

"You know, you can't always use my kid to keep me in line."

"Anger isn't healthy for you or Lily. Remember that." She glanced at me, saw my frown and held her hands up in surrender, "That's all I'm saying."

She was right, of course. Georgia was almost always right and it really annoyed me. It was as if our mother's spirit slipped into her skin. My mother's wisdom rarely aggravated me but there was something about my older sister dispensing the advice that occasionally ruffled my feathers.

What really chafed me – Aunt Katherine's girls and Abby. My hackles rose at the mere mention of Katherine's side of the family. No one but Aunt Emma's daughter Abby managed to get along with them which told me all I needed to know. But me and our older brother Seth – who possessed the same ferocious temper as I had – launched into full scale attack when Linda or Abby lobbed the first volley. That left Georgia to pry us all apart. There was no real graciousness between us most times, especially after our mothers passed on. The Prince side tried to ignore the insults and criticism but as anyone knows, a person can only tolerate so much.

Georgia and I wandered down the hall until coming to a door located across from the nurse's kiosk. Aunt Emma's name was posted beside the door. Georgia reached to push the door open then stopped. I looked at her, questioning her hesitancy. My sister shook her head, "Awful as it sounds, Aunt Emma may not remember us. It's not as if we spent a lot of time together."

She had a point. For the most part, we saw each other at a few holidays. We tried to avoid situations and getting together with Katherine's family always turned into a nightmare. When we all spent time together I noticed Aunt Emma seemed oblivious to the universal verbal abuse Katherine's clan heaped on us. Only Emma's youngest, Grace, tended to be like Georgia. Quiet and most important of all, stable. While Grace's sister Abigail, or Abby, enjoyed the attention from all sides, Grace saw the injustice Katherine and her spawn inflicted on my family and, like the Prince side, she detested it.

Like vultures, Teresa, Linda and Abby preyed on people at their most vulnerable. I discovered that first-hand at the worst time in my life – my mother's funeral. Amazingly, the three sat quietly through the service but once it concluded, they swooped in. They left no heart unbroken, no dry eye among Charlene's children. Seth ordered them to leave with me seconding the motion. But Linda couldn't keep her mouth shut. "Well, honey," she said to me, "look at it this way. Your mama is out of her misery. What with marrying that worthless drunk and you following in his footsteps. Dying was a blessing." I pounced with the precision of a tiger. I managed two good swings on her before Seth, Georgia and Daddy separated us.

I answered Georgia, "If Aunt Emma doesn't remember us, she doesn't. But Grace knows us. Come on, let's do this."

Her courage renewed, Georgia reached to push the door open when a female voice called, "Ladies, I need to see some identification before I let you in."

Confused, Georgia and I turned. A nurse dashed around the kiosk and headed straight for us. My sister glanced at me with a what-the-hell-is-going-on look while retrieving our IDs. The nurse glanced at Georgia's driver's license then my police ID. I wanted to know, "Why are our IDs required?"

The nurse focused on my ID complete with the title *Detective* and back-peddled, "I was informed of an argument earlier between the patient's daughters. They were asked to leave the room. We're asking visitors for identification until one of them returns with power of attorney papers."

Grace involved in a heated argument? Unlikely. She and Georgia shared the same disposition. If they were countries, they'd be Switzerland whereas I was Germany – ready and raring to go to battle. Still, I thought, when someone pushed Georgia pretty hard, she lashed out. Maybe the same thing happened to Grace. Either way, "It shouldn't take Grace long to find the papers."

The nurse shook her head, "I was told Abigail Hawthorne had them."

Whoa. Now that threw me harder than imagining Grace in an argument. Incredulous, I asked Georgia, "Aunt Emma have a stroke or brain fart? Cause that's the only way she'd choose Abby over Grace."

Then I saw Linda and Teresa wandering toward us.

Linda pursed her lips. I sincerely yearned to tell her she looked like a homely old lady when she did that but I managed to refrain. I was tired of Georgia thumping on me.

Linda motioned, "You girls go on in. Aunt Emma would love to see you."

I slipped my ID back in my jacket, "In a minute. We're trying to figure out this power of attorney shocker. What do you know about it?"

Teresa volunteered, "Only that Abby went home to find the documents."

This was getting ridiculous. "Oh, come on," I nearly laughed. "There's no way Aunt Emma trusts Abby over Grace. If anyone's got those papers, it's Grace."

"Then why didn't Grace say she had them?"

I didn't know the answer but I knew my aunt well enough to realize she did not want the Wayward One in charge of her at any point. "Grace has been nothing but good to her mother all her life. Now Abby, on the other hand —" Pain registered right at my funny bone. Georgia nudged me hard enough to hurt and rouse my temper. I rounded on her, "Stop thumpin' on me."

"Stop acting like a child and I will."

I put my cousins on notice, "Whatever transpired in that room today, I guarantee Abby started it. And with or without power of attorney, Grace will see her mother. Once we find Grace, we're escorting her in there. The first one giving us trouble will be face to face with my husband and he's a very tall, *strappin'* man who'll kick you outta here so far and fast they'll arrest you for speeding in Valdosta. Now where is Grace?"

Linda drew back as if I threatened to hit her. Timidly, she pointed downward, "She's downstairs in the lobby."

I grabbed Georgia by the arm, "Let's go." We stalked down the hall toward the elevator. We got halfway when an idea hit me, "Hold on a sec." I retrieved my cell phone from my belt and flipped it open.

"What are you doing?" Georgia asked.

"Every dog has a few fleas, right?" I dialed Ennis's number and waited. "I need you to run this name through the computer. Linda Madigan, Douglas County —"

Georgia seized the phone, thoroughly scandalized by my actions, "Savannah Charlene..." She lifted it to her ear, instructing, "Ennis, don't listen to her, she's gone mad..." She slapped at my reaching hand, punctuating the action with a firm look. Then her eyes widened, "Really?" Suddenly engrossed now, she turned to me, whispering, "Linda's got outstanding tickets from two years ago. Six of them for running red lights."

A wicked smile crossed my lips, "Run Abby and Teresa too. God only knows what they've done." I reached for the phone to tell Ennis but Georgia continued talking, "Thanks, Ennis. She won't be needing anything else." She hung up to my supreme displeasure *then* handed it back to me.

All I could manage was, "Spoilsport." Still, the nasty meeting with the cousins lingered in my mind, gnawing and fraying my nerves, not to mention my anger. Five steps down the hallway and I stopped again.

"What now?" Georgia sighed.

"Georgia, I'm an officer of the law. I have a responsibility to uphold it." This time I meant business. I admitted to wanting revenge but letting six outstanding tickets slide by me? I'd be an idiot, no matter the name on them.

I dialed Ennis again while fending off my sister's attempt to confiscate my phone, "Me again. I need copies of those tickets. Every one of 'em, even if they're classified as antiques by now. Yeah, I'm still at Grady. Fourth floor. But Ennis, call me before you get here. I'll meet you out front. Do *not* come up here alone."

4

Being three years her junior, I'd always admired Grace for several reasons. Her determination, her movie star beauty and fluid, elegant movements. She'd taken ballet and performed on stage as a youngster and possessed a real talent but when hers and Abby's father passed away, Grace stopped taking dance in her late teens and focused on caring for their mother full time. Meanwhile, Abby left home to pursue her own happiness which meant fast men with loose wallets. That dogged pursuit resulted in a rushed marriage, an abusive relationship and a quickie divorce with no payoff except a busted nose, two black eyes and numerous trips to the ER. The outcome of Abby's second marriage ended up sending the guy to the psych ward for a year then he announced he'd turned gay. Abby's third nuptial turned out three kids and yet another divorce but at least Lee, her last ex, stayed semi-sane. At the rate Abby racked up ex-husbands, they'd pile up faster than the national debt.

Georgia and I searched the lobby for our cousin. It didn't take long to find her. Grace sat by herself in the sparsely populated room, her face buried in her hands. Her long, pretty blond hair draped her face, concealing the misery from passersby. If someone looked hard enough though, they saw her shoulders shudder as she cried.

I scouted around for her kids but came up short on locating anyone resembling offspring. Grace had Michael who played football for Georgia Tech and Katie who was still in high school. I hadn't seen either in ages but I did remember both children being fiercely protective of their mama like all good children were. They grew incredibly close after Grace's husband mastered the art of philandering when the kids were still in junior high. She discovered his indiscretions, filed for divorce and their children sided with her. A true steel magnolia, Grace supplemented her ex's meager child support with any employment she could find until landing a clerk job at the General Administration Department. The woman epitomized strength so seeing her in such emotional shambles shocked me.

Grace's despondency spurred me and Georgia to quicken our pace toward her. I called Grace's name, hoping a friendly voice might help slow her tears.

Our cousin's reaction came slowly. She sniffed back tears, her head gradually lifted from her hands. Warily she glanced over her shoulder. I knew why. She feared it was the cousins or her sister. Upon seeing us approach, Grace's wary frown melted into another round of uncontrollable tears. Georgia reached her first and wrapped her in an embrace. I plopped beside our cousin and took over the hug after Georgia pulled away.

Grace spoke first, her words barely understandable through the sobbing, "Thank you both for coming. I don't know what to do. I'm falling apart when Mama needs me the most."

Georgia looked at me for help. I mentally drew back. What the hell did she expect *me* to say? I wasn't the warm and cuddly one in a crisis. I was the bouncer. Trouble? I'll mow over the rabble-rouser while letting Georgia console the onlookers. I shrugged like *whaddya want me to do?*

Realizing I was virtually useless in that department, Georgia's expression evolved into one I'd seen a million times. The empathizing motherly one, "Grace, honey, calm down. Savannah and I are here to help you."

Grace looked at us. Her cheeks flushed beet red, her eyes were red and swollen from constant crying. I remembered the look from experience. The evening after Mama's funeral, both me and Georgia sported the devastated appearance. Abby, Linda and Teresa left their mark on the Prince family and now Grace stood in their crosshairs.

I said the only thing I hoped might help, "Soon as you feel up to it, we'll go see your mama." But instead of ebbing the waterfall of tears, the statement produced a violent shudder of emotion as Grace broke into a renewed bout of crying. *See*, I stared tight-lipped at Georgia, *I open my mouth and make people cry.*

I silently appealed to my sister, the perennial peacemaker, for help. Grace verged on hysterical and we needed to stop the runaway emotion if possible. Before having a chance to, Grace launched into a hypersonic chatter that stunned us both, "I don't know what happened. Abby started yelling at me, saying terrible things and the nurse kicked us both out. I – I didn't raise my voice or argue with Abby because I was in shock at what she was saying. Why did they kick *me* out?"

"Gracie," I tried to soothe her, "sweetheart, you gotta calm down.

Georgia and I will take you in to see your mother."

Georgia nudged me with a *don't make promises you can't keep* frown. I glanced at my badge then back at her. Just let 'em try to keep a cop out of the room, my expression said.

Grace held tighter to me and grabbed Georgia's hand as if we buoyed her from drowning in sorrow. "Why is this happening? Why is Abby doing this to me?" She cried. "What did I do to her?"

Georgia stroked her long blond mane, and shifted her vision to me. My face, due to Grace's noose-like hold, began to ripen to a dark red hue and blood pounded in my cheeks and ears. Neither of us could honestly answer why Abby loved tormenting people. "You didn't do anything," Georgia and I said in unison.

Georgia glanced at me, "I'll be right back. I'm getting her some water and more tissues."

And grab a crowbar to pry me loose, I nearly said. Grace's python-like embrace thankfully lightened once Georgia left. Damn, I thought. For such a slender, petite woman, Grace had a serious grip.

To her credit, Georgia wasn't gone long, "Here you are, honey. Drink this." She extended a paper cup and Grace finally released me and took it in her trembling hands.

Grace stared out the window, finally calm enough to speak clearly, "I remember what they did to you at Aunt Charlene's funeral. They said the most awful things." Her reddened eyes lifted to mine, "I didn't blame you for attacking them. In fact, I was hoping you could beat the meanness out of them."

The corners of my mouth rose slightly, "Well, I gave it my best shot."

As if attempting to ground herself before broaching her own problems, Grace continued, "How old were you then? I forgot."

"Nineteen. I was at the police academy at the time."

Georgia leaned in, "And I tried telling her that an assault charge wouldn't look too good with the instructors."

Grace managed an infinitesimal smile, "Suppose that would encumber your law enforcement career somewhat." She turned to Georgia, "How are you and your husband, what was his name again? Matthew?"

Most people would've never noticed Georgia's minuscule flinch but I did. Lately references to Matthew subsided from hysterical crying to that tiny wince I saw. That's why I was so glad Dane stepped in as Georgia's friend – then of course their relationship blossomed into a matrimonial one. Georgia planned a late summer wedding and used her spare time lining out details for their nuptials.

Unlike Linda, Teresa or Abby, Grace didn't intend to hurt Georgia with the question and my sister knew it, "Matthew and I divorced a while back but I'm engaged to Ennis's brother Dane now."

It took a moment for Grace to process the fact Dane was my husband's brother. Then recognition dawned, "Oh, Georgia, I'm so happy for you." After a second, her smile waned to confusion, "Wait. So two sisters are marrying two brothers? What do they call that relationship?"

"Complicated," I chuckled. My answer inspired Grace's smile to return. I realized how lovely she'd grown over the years and how much lovelier when she smiled. Like Georgia, the Culberson genes had not skipped Grace in that respect.

"And Seth and your father?" Grace asked. "How are they?"

"Mean as ever," I said only to receive another swat from Georgia, this one on the knee. My brow lowered, "Keep doing that and you'll walk home." I directed the next statement to Grace, "She's trying to beat me to death today."

Georgia's vision narrowed, "Only because you won't behave. You have the baby to think about. Stress isn't good for her."

"She's right, Savannah," Grace added quietly. "The baby's more important than all this drama."

I yielded to my cousin's comment. Grace was upset enough without me adding my two cents. I nodded, "I'll try to do better. In the meantime, you straighten your face and we'll go see your mama."

"But they won't allow me in. You two can see her but not me. Even if I tried, Linda and Teresa are there, watching the door."

To reinforce my point, I removed my badge and held it for her to see, "That's where this comes in handy. This is an all-access pass."

Grace worried with the wadded tissue in her hand, "Y'all are awfully sweet to protect me. You don't have to. It'll inflame Linda and Teresa all over again."

So what, I thought. "They're always inflamed at us, Gracie. At least this time when I jump into the fray, my job has provided more experience dealing with psychos. Handcuffs usually help."

A brief smile brightened Grace's features but faded quickly, "What confuses me is Abby. I know she's gullible but," she paused to wipe more tears, "I didn't think she could be as mean as they are."

Grace tried to see the best in everyone, bless her heart, but one thing was sure to always break the quixotic heart. Reality. It surprised me it took that long for Grace to discover her sister's true nature – or at least *admit* to it.

The more I thought about Abby's betrayal, the angrier I grew. Georgia's cautionary glance stopped me from speaking. Instead, Georgia answered, "I think Abby is very impressionable –"

"Georgia," she interrupted, "I appreciate your attempt to salve my feelings but right now," her voice grew stronger by the second, "*my* sister is treating *them* like her sisters and treating me like crap."

"Wanna do something about it?" I offered.

Grace's shoulders fell as she sighed, "Desperately."

Georgia and I stood, both held our hands out for her. She grabbed each one and once on her feet, Grace straightened her face as best she could. Georgia must have seen the determination in my eyes because she lifted a brow in question. I winked while addressing Grace, "They'll never know what hit 'em."

5

When Georgia, Grace and I stepped off the elevator, I saw Ennis standing in the midst of Hell. Hell, in this case, was the middle of my extended, outrageous family and Ennis looked ready to go down for the count. Did he suffer from selective deafness? Had he not heard my stern warning *not* to show up without calling me? Cops never entered a dangerous situation without backup and my family held Guiness Records for menacing and harassment. By his expression, he now understood the reason behind my emphatic warning.

Ennis scratched his head then began rubbing his temple while Linda, Teresa and Abby flapped their tongues about how handsome he was and *where on earth did Savannah find such a tantalizing morsel.* Their tone suggested the state of Georgia managed to breed only men named Bubba, Booger and Frog that wandered out of the hills during moonshine season with a Mason jar in one hand and shotgun in the other. Truth was we did occasionally cultivate nice looking male specimens. Ennis just happened to come from Texas where they grow them in bulk.

Ennis gave his right temple a solid massage, "I asked where Savannah is. Do ya know or not?"

"Ennis!" I called, trying to keep my voice at a reasonable level. A thump on my shoulder indicated I'd failed. I slanted Georgia a do-that-again-and-lose-an appendage glower, "I'm saving him from the vultures. Do you mind?"

Before she could answer, I hot-footed it toward him as panic set in. Ennis would lose his temper then his mind if I didn't intercept him quick. He'd never met these people before and plunging him headfirst into the fray was not only dangerous but cruel. They didn't play nice, nor did they try.

I hurried toward him, waving at him, hoping to catch his eye. It didn't work. Ennis's vision frantically darted from Linda to Teresa then Abby (who surprisingly showed up) like a trapped animal about to be ripped apart for supper.

"Ennis," I called again, keeping my voice under the nurse's radar. Finally he glanced up and relief slacked his shoulders.

"Thank God," he sighed. Once within touching distance, he wrapped his arms around me in a grateful hug, "I thought I'd taken a wrong turn and landed in the middle of the netherworld."

The feel of his embrace inspired a smile, "I'm actually afraid you have. Meet Mama's side of my twisted family tree."

He nearly swallowed his tongue, "Your mother's side? But I figured the worst nuts were – "

"On the Prince side? Nope, the Culbersons have their own unique spin on crazy."

He glanced back at them, "But... But those people need *medication*. Tranquilizers or something."

"They have 'em. Multiple prescriptions, in fact."

Ennis was struck speechless. I looped my arm around his waist in a sympathetic move, "That's why I didn't invite them to our wedding. Well, I invited Grace but Texas was too far for her to travel."

"Thanks for not inviting the others. My family woulda wondered about inbreeding if they'd met those dragons." He still wore the look of a shell-shocked man who'd been shot at and missed and shit at and hit. What war had he stepped into, his expression seemed to ask. My neurotic family war, I would tell him later, and it was best to dive for cover and pretend he didn't know them.

His brow dove between his eyes, "Wait a minute. Is that Linda the same Linda that asked if you had a will?"

Uh-oh. Shell-shocked metamorphosed to homicidal. I tightened my hold on his waist, "Yes, but we're not here to put her in ICU today. Let's just try to escape with what hide we have left. Believe me, she and Abby can bring blood."

As though the names triggered a memory, he reached into his suit pocket, "Here are the outstanding tickets. I assume they belong to one of... those?"

I removed them from the envelope and scoured them visually, "Yeah, the short stumpy one with the bob and tight jeans."

"No offense but that's the shiftiest critter I've seen next to a sidewinder."

"And just as deadly if you're not careful." I returned the violations to the envelope with elaborate ceremony.

Ennis gave me a cautionary look, "What exactly are you planning to do? If that old girl's as mean as I think, pissin' in her Post Toasties ain't the wisest move. And you just said we're taking our hides home."

Sure thing. Yeah. Right after I present these gems to their rightful owner, "These are directly from officers in the Atlanta Police Department, right? We work for the APD and she owes this money. She can pay it or go to jail."

Ennis peeked over his shoulder at the buzzing swarm supposedly related to me. None of the three women had stopped for a breath in minutes as they clucked about Ennis and me. Before I knew it, my teeth clenched so hard my jaw ached. This was exactly why I used an answering machine and voicemail – to avoid assholes and headaches.

Ennis, bless his heart, blocked my view of them while bracing me, "I don't know the story behind this feud but I heard enough to learn they hold a serious grudge against your part of the family." He clamped his hands on my shoulders. He must have sensed my intention of bolting toward them so he reinforced, "Stay put and listen. They're spurrin' you, sugar, and you're lettin' 'em. We got more important events in our life than kickin' at mules that kick back."

I noticed he added a little glance to my swelled belly to reinforce his guilt trip. Nice move, Ennis. Really nice. And of course, "You're right. And thanks for not slapping me upside the head or generally thumping on me. I'm getting annoyed with that."

At first he looked confused then it dawned on him – Georgia. "So," began his uneasy question, "these are the people cooking for us Saturday night?"

Holy crap. I'd forgotten all about the cooking contest they'd invited us to called Family Throwdown. The show where family members challenged each other to cook a specific meal and the winner got bragging rights and a sum of money. Firstly, I should have RSVP'd "Not no, but *hell* no" on the elegantly filigreed card inviting "Join Us For Good Eats!" In this case the show should have rewritten the invite to say "Join Us For Ptomaine Poisoning!" because Linda and Teresa's collective culinary I.Q. leveled out at zero. As children, they thought French Fries were actually grown in France and shipped to the United States. Okay, they were pretty young at the time and of course do-gooder Georgia corrected their mistaken notion, thus destroying a perfectly good delusion I was willing to laugh at for a lifetime.

Secondly, regarding the RSVP, I should have been accused of child abuse for even marking yes on that card. No mother in her right mind would have done that if they'd known what probably awaited them.

Thirdly, Georgia wasn't an angel in the situation. I held her as culpable as myself. I'd called to tell her I was busy that day and what did my older sister do? What my older sister did best – she guilted me into going. "I'm going and so is Seth," she said. I thought about reminding her that neither her nor our brother was pregnant so back off. But I hadn't. "Yes," I answered my husband's question, "these are the lovely people who will prepare our last supper."

He cringed, "Can they cook at all?"

"I already told you they mastered burning water ages ago."

He shook his head in disbelief, "I'll bring the Tums. Hey, did you see your aunt?"

I tried leaning past him to see if the rabble inched toward us but Ennis blocked my view. Had he understood the depth of their subversive behavior, he'd have stepped aside to let me recon the area. I finally sighed, "No, we've been busy finding Grace and directing traffic." I pointed at the group behind him, "They tried preventing her from seeing her own mama but Georgia and I are fixing that."

Ennis shook his head. I assumed frustration set in – like it had with my parents after time. Finally he looked Heavenward as if praying for advice. "You can't keep fighting everyone's battles. You're carrying a baby and God willing the baby will be healthy and have a more sedate personality than you."

"God willing," I agreed because raising a kid as unruly as I'd been would kill me. "Ennis, I know I'm carrying precious cargo. I'm not stupid but I can't let those vultures pick apart the only decent cousin I have on Mama's side."

"I hear there's safety in numbers. How about I tag along?"

I lifted to my toes and kissed him, "Lily and I would love to have you. Just be careful of Georgia. One wrong word and she'll pop you harder than Muhammad Ali."

6

After Ennis and I finished eating supper, my full belly emboldened me to dial my sister. My intent: talk sense into her. Going to the contest flagrantly dared our cousins to poison us. I'd suffered innumerable indignities during pregnancy so why risk death because some idiot couldn't cook? Might as well play in traffic, I'd tell Georgia.

But, as usual, my sister bludgeoned me with the fact, "We're not reneging on our promise."

I'd learned one thing over the years. Unless a person possessed considerable blackmail material *or* a considerably large mallet, bullying an older sibling was impossible. Or maybe it was just my sister. She used a variety of tools to wield her power over me, a woman in her early thirties but still treated like a five year-old. Georgia used a firm, commanding voice. She harassed me with her vast vocabulary, articulating words that she knew were over my pay grade. She exercised her body language which lately was too reminiscent of our mother's with a pointing finger or the parental hands-on-hips stance. But her most preferred tool of wielding power over the sibling six years her junior? Guilt. Absolute, chaste guilt. The woman must have boxed it, kept it nice, shiny and clean then removed it when she felt the necessity to bash me with it.

"After the way they treated us today? Especially after they ambushed Grace? You're still going to that…" I, unlike my sister, had no burgeoning vocabulary to club her with. "That joke?"

"We RSVP'd that we'd be there, Savannah. It's rude to bow out of a commitment."

There it was again. Guilt. "*They* are the rude ones, Georgia. C'mon. You saw how they treated Grace. How can you go to that cooking contest in good conscience knowing Aunt Emma's in the hospital and Abby's on the loose and out for Grace? Just because Teresa and Linda will be gone doesn't mean Abby won't jump on her."

"Savannah, Grace grew up with Abby. She's able to deal with her. When the three are together, that's when everything goes to hell. We'll attend the contest because we committed to go then we can drop by the hospital if we need to."

My sister was hopeless. When a little guilt failed to work, her strategy was *heap more on*. My mouth opened to argue but she cut me off, "Do you really think the hospital staff will refuse Grace after your stunt today? You made quite an impression."

"They deserved it. Lemme talk to Ennis about this contest thing. Maybe he's more reasonable." I looked at my husband who looked anything but reasonable. He dried a plate a bit too vigorously then snapped the damp dish towel at my thigh mouthing *we're going*. Sure, I thought, side with my stubborn sister. Oh well, I told Georgia, "See you Saturday night. Hey, maybe they'll let us share a hospital room afterward." We said our goodbyes and when I turned to Ennis, he offered an apologetic shrug that I quickly countered, "Don't even start with me. You saw those women. Do you want to consume their food?"

"Not particularly but we did RSVP that we'd show."

"What are you two? Clones? I'm the only rebel in the family. Plus I was thinking of Grace but everyone seems hellbent on heading over to the Dark Side. We're traitors, Ennis. Mindless, *beholden* traitors."

I felt bad for backstabbing Grace since she was the only good and decent female cousin I had. And Ennis should have too. Grace instantly fell in love with him. She'd blushed when I introduced them. Her slender hand trembled slightly when Ennis kissed it. I knew the feeling, alright. Seemed like any time Ennis touched me, it made me tremble in a good way. He'd seemed rather impressed by Grace as well, mentioning what a genuine lady she was. He wasn't as impressed by Abby. What a surprise. She managed to run off family, friends, strangers and husbands and in the seventh grade, even her violin teacher. He left town after giving her three lessons. No one ever heard from him again. All her life she'd used her looks, blonde hair and long legs to get her way. But my husband was immune to her bullshit.

Abby was as nice as she *could* be which didn't mean much. She pretended to smile when she shook Ennis's hand but I sensed a high degree of animosity toward me for bringing Ennis into the family fray. After all, I did kinda threaten them with my big strappin' Texan if they started anymore trouble.

True to his word, Ennis lingered around the door, ensuring Grace some peace while visiting her mother. Even when Linda tried to insinuate herself in the room he and I blocked the way while he reminded

Linda who Emma's daughters were. It was only fair, he'd added, for Grace to have quality time with her ailing mother who'd suffered a heart attack. I told Ennis having a kid like Abby would give anyone a heart attack. Then, right on cue, Georgia elbowed me again.

O O O

Morning dawned through the window, the sun's soft glow intensified to a powerful laser-like intensity as it streamed through the curtains. The glare on the wall forced me to ease the covers back with the intent of getting up before going blind. That's when a heavy, hairy leg swung over mine, trapping me. "Where do you think you're going?" a sleepy Ennis asked. He swept my hair aside and his warm lips pressed beneath my ear, his voice a mere whisper, "You're staying put."

"You're getting really bossy lately." I meant it too. So far I had little say in anything the last twelve hours and I wasn't taking kindly to it. Between my sister and husband, my decisions lacked one important facet. My input.

Ennis kissed my ear then my shoulder, "Turn over," then added a "please" to the end.

Now that was more like it. I turned in his embrace then felt his leg imprison me again, pulling me directly against him. Oh, this would be fun, I mused. As fun as parallel parking the Titanic in a duck pond. That leg move usually indicated he wanted to romp. Sex was a nice idea but horribly complex lately. So I hoped he devised a clever method of positioning the important parts.

His warm fingers curled my hair behind my ear. His expression read something other than let's-get-it-on and that worried me. Ennis always wanted sex. "What's wrong, babe?" I asked.

He propped on one elbow, "I don't mean to be bossy. I wanted to hold you, be close to you."

I smiled, "Only one way to get closer and you'll need a crane for that." My joke landed flat. Something really bothered him and I needed to coax the problem out. I leaned in to kiss him, "My carefree Libra is pensive this morning. Wish I knew why."

He hesitated a moment then, "It's those people. I don't like them. Grace is a sweet lady but the others... I can't stand them."

His vision dropped from mine when he spoke. His fingers spread across my back to nudge me closer. Whatever bothered him about my cousins went deeper than usual. He normally didn't brood and usually didn't mind sharing. It *was* my family, after all. The nuts, the squirrels, every one of them, but he obviously didn't want to insult me by exposing his true feelings about them. I thought his loyalty was more than touching – at times it was downright frightening. "You already know how I feel about them," I said, trying to ease his concern. "So what happened?"

"I don't like the way they talk. They're hateful and horrible."

So they said something about me and he doesn't want to tell me what it was... "What did they say about us? Or was it me they tarred and feathered?"

Ennis shook his head, silently telling me that, no, he wasn't divulging a word. I gently prodded, "Come on. Believe me, I've heard it all."

He pursed his lips, closed his eyes as if debating with himself. After a few moments he settled on clamming up so I took a wild guess, "They brought up my drinking, didn't they?"

A loud sigh filled the room. His eyes popped opened as his official verbal boycott abruptly ended, "You haven't had a drink in ages and they talk like you throw back a bottle every day. It took every ounce of self control not to strangle them."

"I've tried that but there's always someone around to pull me off before I succeed."

Ennis didn't smile. Instead I saw anger rising in his expression. A little flame of rage flickered behind his brown eyes. I'd hoped humor might break his dark mood but it hadn't. My attempt seemed to inflame him instead, as if I'd dismissed his feelings.

I drew my hand along his stubbled jaw, brought his vision to mine, "Babe, I understand your anger. I still have it. Why do you think I avoid them? Because they bring up the past and wallow in it. Then they drag me into it and we all get muddy. The people I love know I don't drink anymore, that's all I care about."

"It's the point that they're spreadin' rumors. Hateful lies. What if Lily hears these lies later? What if they plant them in her brain? I don't put anything past them."

"Good. Then we don't have to worry so much. If you never underestimate the Culbersons, you're halfway prepared. Ennis, I don't intend for Lily to ever meet them, much less spend unsupervised time with them. I'm not having this baby so they can poison her against me."

I leaned in for another kiss, "Stop worrying. They'll keep yapping about my drinking and I'll keep throwing monkey wrenches into their plans. That's the way it's been for years."

My explanation irritated him. I realized how I sounded. *Don't worry about the crazy people in the family. They're just harmless nuts.* But I also knew my child would rarely encounter them because I would make sure they hardly saw her. Abby and Linda were anything but harmless. They rarely thought through their absurd antics before leaping into them. With them, it was wise to think two to three moves ahead like playing chess. Teresa used a more cerebral approach before whacking people over the head. She tended to analyze the outcome before randomly lighting the fuse. Either way, only foolhardy souls turned their backs on a tried and true Culberson.

After a frustrated sigh, Ennis groaned, "Savannah –"

"What?" I groaned back.

"I know they're your family but I've seen rattlesnakes that weren't that vicious. I don't want them to drive you screwy too."

"Honey," I assured, "I survived Jeffrey Holland. Twice. These birds are nothing compared to him."

He went quiet again. He loathed hearing Jeffrey's name. The man who'd tried – and nearly succeeded – in killing me and Georgia now resided in prison for a good long while. But Ennis still bristled at the mention of him. "I want you to be careful," he warned. "They're dangerous. Maybe not like Holland but they're dangerous."

Ennis's hand brushed my swollen belly. The warmth and motion of his palm must have roused Lily because I felt her nudge against it.

"Hey," Ennis brightened. "She's awake."

Finally. A change in subject. "Indeed. Daddy's got the magic touch."

He seemed enchanted with the movements beneath his hand. For a long moment he stared at my stomach as if he could actually see our little girl playing footsy with him. The smile on his face was priceless. Moments later, Lily settled down and Ennis lifted his vision to mine, "She's gonna look like you. I can feel it. She already kicks like you do."

"Never gonna let me live that down, are you?" I joked. "One lunatic ex-partner tries to heave me over the side of a building and I kick *you* thinking it's *him*. Hmmph."

7

I sat at my desk, perusing the Davenport case file. Ramos dropped it off the day before, all too happy to rid himself of the albatross case. Since the body's discovery, the media coverage exploded, leaving my phone ringing incessantly. I bribed the desk sergeant with the last of Georgia's Apple Cobblestone Cookies to reroute the calls to anyone but me. My baby, my family and now my new assignment tested my sanity's limitation. Between the TV and radio coverage, I figured every witness and possibly the killer absconded to foreign countries or deserted islands.

I was in the middle of deciphering Metcalf's henscratch when a deep gravely voice barked, "You're Prince, right?"

Without looking up, I pointed to the nameplate on my desk, "According to that, yes."

"Yeah, I remember you now. Always the smartass. Just never pegged you for a thief. What kinda juice you got, stealing my case from under me? You screwing your captain?"

The pleasure of Darren Metcalf's presence equaled the joy of a root canal. I removed my reading glasses, rose from my chair. Metcalf was still a butterball whose suit coat strained against the buttons. His comb-over sustained minor wind damage but he didn't seem to notice or care. His naturally sour expression worsened the angrier he grew and the second he zeroed in on my pregnant belly, his mouth opened to heave another volley of insults.

I cut him off, "Metcalf, if you bothered to talk to your captain, you'd realize that he transferred the case to our precinct. You know, that bothersome *jurisdiction* issue and all. So ease up."

He wobbled in my office, put his hands to hips, "You ain't stealin' my case."

"No, I *ain't*. My captain – who I'm unequivocally not screwing – dropped it in my lap like a steaming turd."

I could imagine his childhood report cards. *Doesn't play well with others* or *Hide the scissors.* I pointed to my thankfully quiet phone, "Call your boss or talk to mine about custody of the case."

I could almost see Metcalf deflate. His shoulders nearly slumped in defeat. Nearly. He scowled but not at me. He aimed it at the folder on my desk, sighing, "Ah, crap. I knew that body would show up at the wrong time. Shaping up to be a good one too. You mind if I sit down a minute? I ain't feelin' too swell."

I motioned to the chair facing my desk, "You okay? Ramos said you'd been feeling ill."

He waved it off, "Yeah, yeah. I'm fine. Just need a vacation. Guess I can take one now."

I slid my glasses back on, turned my attention to the folder on my desk, "We all need time off now and again."

"Looks like you're about to get maternity leave. Sure you wanna tackle this case right now?"

Without bowing up, I used his phrasing, "I'm fine. Besides Rutherford can take over if need be." And there won't be a need, I wanted to say.

Metcalf spied a bowl of cookies on my desk. He stared at my homemade goodies - and stared - and stared. I wasn't stupid enough to set out Georgia's luscious creations. I used those only in emergencies such as buying quiet time instead of admitting myself to the nuthouse. Georgia's were off limits but my own baking, sure, go ahead. Take one.

I offered the bowl and he thanked me while digging out two. Munching on one he answered, "People I talked to said Davenport was a bastard to work for. Overtime without pay, late paychecks, made the chefs and waiters wash dishes, shit like that." He lifted a brow and popped another cookie in his mouth, "These are pretty good. Where'd you get 'em?"

I smiled demurely, "Yours Truly made them."

He stopped chewing. His whole expression changed, making me worry he'd spew like Vesuvius. Instead he squinted as if trying to detect a fib, "You?"

I nodded, waiting for a reaction similar to kids who heard they just consumed broccoli. I mean, cops didn't bake. Cops didn't cook. But then cops didn't normally get pregnant either.

Metcalf resumed chewing, "You did a good job. Can I have another?"

I pushed the bowl toward him, "Help yourself." Another perusal of the papers in my hand revealed emails between Bob and a number of individuals. A brief scan detailed that Mr. Davenport either didn't have the experience to run a restaurant or he just plain screwed up. "A lot of these are employee complaints about not getting paid. He referred them to a Troy Quinn. Who's that?"

Big 'ol burly Darren Metcalf sat back, appraised my request then patted his stomach, "If I can swipe two more of those cookies, I'll tell ya."

Finding that information was a matter of a few minutes work but considering Metcalf's rare decent mood, I smiled my most charming smile then nodded toward the bowl, "Swipe away, Detective."

I waited for him to dig out what he wanted then he proceeded, "Troy Quinn is Davenport's son-in-law and resident bank. From what I can tell, after Quinn arrived people started getting paid and business picked up. He and Davenport's wife Jessica were my two main suspects. Davenport and his wife were on the outs and he and Quinn were seen arguing days before he went missing. Quinn said he and Davenport were drinking at the restaurant after it closed, got drunk and Bob called his wife Jessica to try and patch things up. Also said Bob got all enraged after the call and huffed out of the restaurant."

"Say where he was headed?"

"Quinn said he grumbled about 'that bitch' and headed out to go see her."

Hmm… "Did Quinn give you any ideas about what Davenport planned on doing once he got home?"

"Nah, but according to Quinn, Davenport was one hundred proof by the time he left."

"Do you believe Quinn?"

"I don't believe a word he says and you'd be smart not to either."

"How's baby today?" a woman asked from the doorway.

"Kicking like a kangaroo," I waved my new colleague into my office, introduced her to Metcalf. Christine Clark and her partner Alex Nesbitt transferred from a precinct up north. She and I were the only female detectives in the station and we got along pretty well despite the fact she latched on to me in a Girl Power sort of way. I understood her determination to be taken seriously. At first glance, she didn't fit the detective label. She was twenty-five, model gorgeous and tall with jet black eyes and hair to match. The latter draped in waves nearly to the middle of her back when not tied in a ponytail. Her slight frame and narrow hips fell short of convincing the guys of her capabilities. To me it conveyed a woman who probably relied on karate or judo for her strength and I'd bet money she qualified as an expert marksman and could outshoot any badge stupid enough to challenge her.

She and Metcalf shook hands. I noticed Metcalf scowled at the Carolina Panthers mug in her hand. "What's with the pussy mug?" he asked.

Christine bowed up. Upon her arrival, she schooled us on three things. One, her name was Christine. Not Chris, Chrissie or babe. Two, always knock before entering her office. Three, leave her Carolina Panthers mug alone. Do not damage, destroy, hide or blaspheme it. She neglected to state the repercussions but her expression left no question of the offender's fate.

I quickly shook my head, a silent plea for her to retract her claws, "Metcalf, not everyone in Atlanta is a Falcons fan. My partner likes the Cowboys."

"That's even worse." He rose from his seat, "I gotta go. If you need any pointers on the case, you know where to find me."

He ambled out, grumbling about the Panthers mug and staring at Christine as if she dropped from outer space.

She snorted, "Like you'd need pointers from an ass. You get any decent leads on the Davenport case from him?"

"Not much. Stuff in the folders is about all."

She reached in the cookie bowl, frowned as she grabbed the last two, "Surprised he left two. You're making more of these, right?"

I nodded, told her to take them. She threw one in her mouth, "Baby still active?"

Again I nodded and she laid her hand on my stomach. Lily obliged her by tapping against her palm. It tickled Christine. "That is so cool. Makes me think about having kids but I've already got my hands full with the job."

No shit, I wanted to say. Pregnancy was a challenge anyway but being a full time cop too? It was like juggling chainsaws blindfolded sometimes. "So what are you and Nesbitt working on?"

She rolled her eyes, "Boss has us working a cold case to keep us busy. Nesbitt's still yakking about his vacation house in Hilton Head. I mean, what bank did he rob to afford that? Now he's thinking about a new car. I'm telling you, Savannah, this guy doesn't need this job, he just comes to work to get away from wifey."

I'd had the same feelings. Nesbitt's bragging exhausted me. I couldn't imagine being his partner. He was good for the intimidation factor though. He stood six feet tall, was built like a brick shithouse with a natural expression of a hungry lion. His intense pale blue eyes made it hard to look at him, as though he saw right through me. If he instilled that degree of unease in me, I pitied any suspect they interrogated. But that was as far as his influence went, in my opinion. Once he opened his mouth, it was all about him.

Christine consumed the second cookie then winked, "If you need any help on your case, come get me. I'm bored out of my skull and sincerely thinking about taking up knitting to keep busy."

8

An ominous cloud of doom swept over me when Ennis and I pulled into the Family Throwdown's parking lot. After a laborious effort, I hoisted myself out of the car and stared balefully at the building with knowledge my cousins – possibly the worst cooks in the universe – planned to serve us supper. On TV, no less. The only saving grace: the show aired Sunday evening after the local news and weather. That gave us a week to succomb to whatever pathogen my relatives unwittingly laced into the food. If we died, chances were decent the show would decide against airing the segment.

"Stop biting your lip," Ennis said, taking my hand.

I glanced at Ennis then realized I'd been chewing my bottom lip. Anxiety. Dread. E. coli. Listeria. Salmonella. Botulism. The list went on and so did Ennis, "Stop thinking about Hepatitis and all that stuff."

Oh, I'd forgotten about Hepatitis. Yay. *Another* worry. But to ease his concern I shrugged, "Sorry. Just nervous." I tightened my hold on his hand a bit, and he reciprocated in kind. The warm, gentle strength in his hold diminished my unease until we stood at the entrance of the revamped restaurant.

The recession killed numerous businesses downtown, leaving

empty shells of once thriving establishments. Family Throwdown's building once housed an Italian joint that received good reviews in the papers but also had expensive prices. The owners closed up shop and left everything as is – even the chairs and tables – which meant the Throwdown team had very little expense regarding furniture and cooking equipment.

Or employees. A clean cut college kid flanked the door, trés debonair in his black tuxedo. "Good evening," he greeted with a toothy grin. "You folks have your invitation?"

Unfortunately yes, I wanted to say then berated myself for lacking the shrewdness to rip up the invite. No invite, no entry.

Ennis removed the invitation from his jacket and handed it over. The young man thanked us, took the card and replaced it with two ballots, "Y'all have a nice time."

"Question," I blurted to my husband's surprise. "Have you got EMTs on standby in case of choking, poisoning, heart attacks and such?"

"Savannah," Ennis whispered. "We'll be fine." He waved my question off, "She's nervous is all."

"Terrified is more like it," I corrected as we stepped inside. I took a moment to look the ballot over. It had three columns, the first listed flavor, texture, visual appeal and overall taste. The second and third left room for the victims to mark their choice "A" or "B" before keeling over from food poisoning. Personally, I wanted to know, "Where's C?"

Ennis looked at his ballot, "What?"

"There's A and B. Where's C?"

"What would that stand for?"

"None of the above."

While Ennis shook his head, I silently grumbled over the show's concept. Family Throwdown's motto was "Settle your family feud in the kitchen!" Number one, I didn't see either Teresa or Linda cooking themselves anywhere except into an ambulance ride to the burn unit. And number two, I felt the show made light of one of law enforcement's worst nightmare: domestic disputes. Any cop could explain how festive and whimsical they were not. No one slapped each other with spatulas or beat each other with spoons. Family feuds were usually settled in kitchens with sharp knives.

The show retained the previous restaurant's rich décor of earthtones which classed up the show in some way. The brick walls, dark hardwood tables and chairs gave the image of Old Italy, the picture completed with grapevines twined through ceiling beams above diners.

Looking around, the place wasn't as full as I expected. It appeared at least some people had the presence of mind to mark "no" on the invitation. One might anticipate seeing other family members for such an event. Besides Charlene's side, no one from the Culberson side showed. Just Mama's kids. The other folks I assumed were friends or relatives by marriage. There were few smiles and plenty of clock watching. Almost everyone dressed casually as had we. "Help me look for the warden," I told Ennis over the noisy din of conversation.

"Come on, Georgia didn't twist our arms."

"Speak for yourself, Rutherford. She's not your sister." I scanned the small crowd and finally located Georgia and Dane. They stood with Seth and his family at a table close to the kitchen partition. I didn't know how smart separating the cooks from the crowd was, simply because I thought we should be allowed to see the origin of our demise.

Georgia glanced up and I waved. She, in turn, waved us over to their table. I breathed a sigh of relief. Friendly faces among so many strangers. At least we'd go down together…

"Everyone's health insurance paid up?" I asked, skillfully dodging Georgia's prodding elbow.

Georgia followed it with an obligatory scold. Dane and Leah looked shocked at my comment but Seth actually laughed. Sometimes I really liked my brother. He appreciated my sense of humor more lately than ever.

"Let's all sit together," my sister said, probably trying to change the subject. "Dane, you and Seth pull another table over to ours. No sense in everyone being scattered hither and yon."

While the men scooted the tables together, I whispered to Georgia, "Who in their right mind would agree to something like this? A cooking contest? Not me. Not ever."

"It would be stressful but I think it would be fun."

My expression questioned her sanity. I mean, my sister considered vacuuming fun so naturally she'd think sweating over a hot stove - on TV - might be entertaining.

"Ladies and gentleman," a man announced, causing every head to turn toward the front of the room. He looked like a cheesy game show host in slicked back hair and a suit that saw its heyday in the seventies. He smiled, waved his hand over the crowd, "If y'all will take a seat, we'll proceed with the contest."

"Oh boy," I enthused under my breath. "Can't wait."

Lindsey, my young niece, took a seat beside me and giggled, "Aunt Vanna said she can't wait."

Seth shook out his napkin, "You're lucky that's all Aunt Vanna said."

Georgia took up residence across from me probably to keep me respectable. Guessing from her expression, that was exactly why she sat there so I fired a friendly warning across the table, "Kick me and you'll limp home. You wrangled me into this and I'll say what I want."

Ennis patted my hand. He did this to calm me down without speaking. My husband was under some illusion that Georgia was a downright pleasure to grow up with. She hadn't been entirely awful, just entirely bossy like older sisters tended to be. The goal, I'm guessing, was to guide the younger sibling through the intricacies of life, avoiding social potholes and such. Our lives at home were giant unavoidable potholes more akin to a giant black abyss and my sister saved me from plenty of those. But I wasn't born stupid and with age came wisdom. I didn't step in front of bullets on the job. I didn't heave gasoline on fires. Usually I knew to come in from the rain. My sister, bless her heart, just didn't realize this and Ennis refused to see the dictator in her.

But I smiled at him anyway, letting him know I appreciated his attempt to keep the peace. That smile vanished upon sight of the plate a waiter sat in front of me. Flashes of my first trimester percolated at the back of my mind. Racing for the bathroom and heaving. Besides peeing, that *was* my first trimester.

I swallowed hard, "Anyone else seeing what I'm seeing?" A plate of stuff only desperate, starving hogs might snark down?

"Savannah, please," Georgia bemoaned, her vision riveted to the fare before her.

Was that disgust I saw curling her ever-so-proper upper lip? I cupped my hand around my ear, "Georgia, listen. Hear anyone digging in? Me either."

My family fell quiet as if listening for sounds of hearty consumption around us. There was utter silence.

"What's this stuff supposed to be?" Dane asked.

Ennis eyed it suspiciously then poked at it with his fork, "Pasta? Rice maybe?"

I pushed the plate away, "We should have left someone home to carry on the family name." I expected Georgia to sear me with one of her motherly "behave yourself" looks but she appeared too stunned to move.

Lindsey leaned closer, whispering, "We don't have to eat it, do we?"

Her younger brother Dylan backed away from his plate. 'Nuff said, I thought. When kids were afraid of it, leave it alone.

"I strongly advise against eating or getting too close to it." I, in turn, leaned to Ennis's ear, "Any woman who's had a first trimester recognizes this and it's not a happy memory. Stay away from it unless you enjoy vacationing in a hospital."

His crinkled brow deepened when he looked from the food to me. Not in a judging way. More like a *no shit* way. I identified the first dish as Linda's handiwork. The woman couldn't cook if her life depended on it.

I scanned the table for anyone willing to taste the plate of whatever-the-hell-that-was. The men sat their forks down. Leah and Georgia stared at it, pausing momentarily then both swallowed hard. Then they sat *their* forks down. Uh-huh, I thought. The repulsive gruel trumped good ol' fashioned Southern manners.

I searched for the guy roaming the room with a TV camera on his shoulder. He was across the room filming some poor unfortunate who dared consume Linda's dish. I leaned forward, whispering, "Let's see what Teresa has to offer. Hers might look less lethal."

Leah, a trauma nurse at Grady, stared warily at the plate, "I hate to be rude but landing in my own emergency room with food poisoning isn't my idea of a good weekend."

The show's host wound his way to our table with the camera guy in tow, "Have you sampled the first dish?"

We all nodded in unison. What liars we were. But the important part was we were *convincing* liars. The host continued, "How would you describe the taste and texture?"

I opened my mouth to answer and saw Georgia slant me a warning glance. I was on local television. In my business, lying got me by pretty well. I wasn't about to alienate the city of Atlanta with my wit so I pasted on a smile and replied, "Creamy."

The host seemed less than impressed, "Does that pertain to the taste or texture?"

"Take your pick. Incidentally, do you happen to know the name of this creation?" Because it certainly wasn't anything I'd seen on a plate before.

My question took him aback. His mouth twitched. His eyes widened as if I'd asked him the precise distance to Pluto. Then, "I believe this is the polenta."

I acknowledged his answer with a nod. This was no polenta I'd ever seen. Polenta was made from cornmeal. Linda's dish was a sickly white and the lumps added to its general visual repulsiveness.

The cameraman and host moved on to another table – he probably feared another question from me – and I heard Dane ask Georgia the definition of polenta. Ever the diplomatic one, my sister replied, "It's not this."

A waiter placed a second plate beside the first. This was Teresa's contribution. The room collectively bent and smelled the food before venturing to lift a fork. This one looked decent and smelled pleasant – not great but better than the first dish. I supposed Teresa meant to make vegetable soup but the weak, watery color and small celery and carrot chunks reminded me of a scene out of The Exorcist.

Seth stared narrow-eyed at the dishes before him, "Who's idea was it to come here today?"

Finally, a question I wanted to answer, "That would be Georgia." My sister seared me with a heated glare. Oh, *now* all the talk of fulfilling commitments sounded corny to her. *Now* she didn't want to take that *responsibility* she hammered me with the other night.

Seth harrumphed, threw his napkin over his plates to hide the food. No one ate a bite but followed my brother's lead.

"What do we do?" Ennis asked. "Neither one deserves to win in my opinion."

The table fell quiet. We all looked to each other for answers. No one had them. So I suggested, "Close your eyes and mark a winner. Let fate sort it out."

o   o   o

Once they tallied the votes, Teresa won by twenty. We all applauded and smiled like good little soldiers then got up to leave. That's when a new nightmare began. "So, how'd y'all like our dishes?"

The question came from Linda. I refrained from speaking as did a few others. Georgia braved into it, "Interesting. I've never seen anything like them."

No, but I've flushed a few things that did. I grunted as Georgia elbowed me, evidently sensing every word in my mind. I really wanted to chime in with my two cents but I'd been trying restraint lately, for my child's sake.

Ennis's hold on my hand tightened as a silent plea for me to stay silent. Anyone who knew me realized the difficulty in my battle against stating the brutal honest truth. *Your dish was so ugly it didn't deserve to be prison food.*

"You're as purple as a grape, Savannah," Teresa mentioned. "Is there something you want to say?"

Well, since you asked... Ennis's hand gripped my hand in a viselike grasp so I shook my head. According to my hubby, I was taking the silent Swiss road. That meant no confrontations.

A man wearing a dark blue suit approached us, eagerly shook our hands. His age: mid-twenties. Hair: black and hippie length. He also had a wily grin that said *lawyer.* But after introductions, I discovered he was the producer of Family Throwdown. And the director. And, and, and... Andrew Abbott was his name and it was such a pleasure to meet us.

"Mrs. Rutherford," Mr. Abbott called in an almost sugary sweet fashion.

Since Georgia and Dane had yet to exchange vows, I took a wild guess he addressed me. When I acknowledged him, he continued, "Linda and Teresa tell me you're a police detective and your sister is an author. The show would love to host a contest between you two and Linda and Teresa." With his hands he framed an imaginary marquee, "Cousins versus cousins."

I dropped the words like bricks, "No, thank you." Thankfully Georgia also appeared less than enthusiastic so I continued, "I'm in the middle of a case right now and Georgia's behind on her book." Okay, so I fibbed about the book but who the hell would ever find out?

"So," Teresa shrewdly arched a brow, "you're refusing. It figures."

Linda leaned to her sister, mumbling, "She knows who'd win, that's why."

Georgia bristled, "Yes, that's why we thought we'd save you the humiliation of losing."

"Whoa there, ladies," Andrew stepped between them. "We could get down and dirty or settle this in a civilized competition." He addressed me and Georgia respectively, "Mrs. Rutherford, Ms. Prince, the entire show takes only an afternoon to tape. We provide the food, the work area, everything you need to produce your meal. If you're willing to sacrifice one afternoon, it will be worth it. The winners can receive up to twelve thousand dollars."

I nearly swallowed my tongue. *Twelve thousand dollars?* It didn't matter if the twelve grand was split handily down the middle, it was still cash Ennis and I could use. But still, cooking on TV and having the whole city watch? Sheesh. It was a high school drama on steroids and I hated high school.

"Nevermind, Andrew," Teresa waved us off. "They're too chicken. They know we're better cooks."

Georgia broke into laughter, "Since when? We'll all be lucky not to get ulcers from that slop you served today."

Linda's eyes popped wide, "Slop?"

Andrew took advantage of the squabbling, "Speaking of chicken, how about fried chicken as the challenge? Side order of biscuits and whatever you like? Sound good?"

"Sounds great," Georgia's chin lifted, her words bold, final, "We'll be there, won't we, Savannah?"

What the hell. We *accepted* the challenge? No, I told myself, Georgia accepted it and I, once again, got hoodwinked. I referred to my spouse for answers but he looked as shell-shocked as I was. My sister gifted me with an expectant shrug as if to say *well, are you with me or not?* "What about your book?" I lamely inquired.

"I can catch up quick enough," she said then turned to Teresa. "Get ready to be booted as champion. The Prince sisters will kick your sorry a—"

"Georgia," I clapped my hands over Lindsey's ears, reminding, "little pitchers…" My niece just giggled but my sister took cooking deadly serious. No one impugned or questioned her ability in the kitchen.

"So, Mrs. Rutherford, are you in?" Andrew's eyes sparkled with such zeal I wondered if he needed a drug test. "We've never had a well known author or a police officer on the show."

Oh, why the hell not? "Just one thing, Mr. Abbott. During filming, let's refer to me as Savannah or Detective Prince, shall we?" Because the department would have *my* ass if my marriage to my partner became public. I tried phrasing it for a producer's ears, "Let's give that civil servant angle all the punch we can."

9

My mother was an excellent cook. She never developed a pretentious attitude about her talent, she just prepared delicious, filling meals for her family. My aunt Katherine, on the other hand, was one of those snooty types that labeled herself a "self-taught chef" which meant she read Julia Child's cookbook one too many times.

At Thanksgiving and Christmas, Aunt Katherine always brought the prettiest dishes. Pretty, not tasty. Mama made the majority of the meal, the turkey, dressing and sweet potatoes without marshmallows "because it was a sacrilege to add them".

At suppertime, the family swarmed the layout of food. My mother, bless her heart, always tried Aunt Katherine's dishes. She also made my father try them. It was the only time of year my father and I shared a very closely held secret. He'd take a small bite of Katherine's food, screw his face up tighter than a pig's tail then excuse himself. He'd return to the table minutes later minus the elaborately prepared dish and in its place sat two huge spoonfuls of Mama's potatoes. Daddy would catch my eye and wink. It wasn't so much a private joke as it was survival. No one knew what was in Aunt Katherine's creations and it was safer not to poke around in them, either physically or figuratively.

Daddy had a point. Once the fluster and bluster of Christmas (or Thanksgiving) supper passed, Mama's bowls and dishes looked like a pack of wolves converged on them. Aunt Katherine's sat perfectly placed in its vessel, still pretty but basically untouched.

The moral of the story: no matter how gorgeous the food looked, if it wasn't yummy and visually appealing, it was left to petrify. Linda and Teresa boasted that they'd learned from their mother. In that case, Georgia and I could have won with one hand tied behind our backs – and blindfolded.

"What can go wrong?"

Ennis's question derailed my train of thought. I wished my husband understood these people. He grew up on a ranch outside Vega, Texas, a small community around a thousand people or so. In a town that small there's a kinship among the residents. They come together when disaster strikes. A farmer has a heart attack, the others pitch in to help run the farm. Ranchers help each other round up their herds before a blizzard sweeps in with bitter winds and blinding snow.

This was Atlanta, Georgia. The New York of the South. The Atlanta Metro area housed over five million people. That included the over eighty suburbs of the city, including Dunwoody where Ennis and I called home. Our little ol' suburb claimed forty-seven thousand of those five million residents. In the midst of such a crowded populace, there was bound to be some meanness and some of it was named Culberson. Oh, the names changed by marriage but they were Culbersons all the same. Katherine's brood perfected the art and Emma's child Abby joined the chorus.

My sweet small-town, overly trusting husband hadn't yet learned the wicked ways of the Culbersons but he would and I feared that cooking contest would be the biggest lesson of all. "What could go wrong?" I repeated as if he'd announced he'd bought a condo on Mars. "Ennis, my darling, you are so sweet yet so oblivious of the evils of my family. Most of them look pretty on the outside but, like belladonna, they're dangerous if you get too cozy with them."

What could go wrong, he asked. Sheesh. Everyone has witnessed it in some way or another. During a football game an announcer inevitably declares, "He's kicked five hundred consecutive field goals without a miss. This is a *chip shot*." Or perhaps during a gathering with friends, "Your cakes rise so tall and beautiful – they *never* fall." And what happens? Murphy's Law, that's what. The chip shot goes wide right or the cake falls into a miserable heap the thickness of slate. *What can go wrong?* Those four words were the kiss of death.

It took a few moments for a palatable response to form, "Please don't jinx us, Ennis. Normally, Georgia and I could cook circles around those two big mouths but one statement like that and we'll crash and burn."

He wrapped his arms around me, pecked a kiss to my lips, "You worry far too much but I'll try not to jinx you."

Jinxing wasn't my only issue with people. Overt planning was. All my life I felt convinced my sister was a military general in a previous life. She planned everything to the nth degree, even laundry day, her meals, her route around the city when she shopped. If Eisenhower had had Georgia Prince along with George Patton, the Nazis would have surrendered in a week.

Along with our family drama and my murder case, I received calls from Georgia about the contest. The latest one consisted of which fried chicken recipe we'd go with. We decided on Mama's recipe along with traditional cole slaw, my biscuits and Georgia's savory corn.

Once the tediously detailed phone call ended, my head spun faster than Linda Blair's in the Exorcist. My sister was a born leader when it came to cooking – or any other aspect of life. A take-charge, bulldozing Rita Hayworth clone. Give the woman a whole chicken and she could cut it apart – de-bone it if necessary – coat it, fry it, and serve it in record time *with* a smile and *without* breaking a sweat. I took my time but if speed was required, I could keep pace with her – with the sweat and minus the smile.

I trembled to think what details, exactly, needed refining. The show shouldered most of them. They supplied the food, seasonings, plates and silverware as well as a spacious kitchen in which to prepare the meal. We only had to supply the energy, the guests and the ratings, the last Andrew assured would be higher than ever. With bestselling author Georgia Prince at the stove and not the computer, the episode promised stellar ratings. Plus, he added as a postscript, with a cop who actually cooked, it was sure to be a hit.

I had other ideas. I figured he not only took advantage of Georgia's popularity but the fact our run-in with serial killers Jeffrey Holland and Cole Jordan still stood fresh in everyone's minds. Nothing like two survivors of torture killers to drive up ratings.

"…spicy, are you?"

I blinked my way out of the skeptical mood I'd developed – Georgia always said I never turned off the "cop" in me. By his expression, Ennis awaited an answer to whatever question he'd posed. "What?" I asked.

"You're making your mama's chicken, right? That stuff'll clear people's sinuses *and* their kitchen drains if you go by the recipe."

I rolled my eyes, "Ennis, I *remove* some spice for your serving and *add* spice to the recipe for mine. I make two separate recipes. Mama's wasn't fiery like mine."

That eased his frown lines. He broke into an relaxed grin and kissed my cheek, "Then my gorgeous wife is a shoo-in. Otherwise people might vote for Linda's just because you torched their taste buds."

That was my husband. The supportive, loving male I exchanged marriage vows with. The vows saying *for better or worse, in sickness and in health* and so on. Ennis Rutherford was a sexy, thoughtful hunk of man. But he also suffered hoof in mouth disease on occasion. It wasn't wise, I nearly told him, to call his pregnant wife beautiful than basically accuse her of culinary arson.

10

Ennis and I trailed the long busy hospital halls. I'd hoped to see Grace and Aunt Emma during our lunch hour. We tried to visit during the hours Teresa, Linda and Abby might be out flying their brooms and harassing other poor unsuspecting folks. At least I could hope.

We continued our trek to Aunt Emma's room, passing by the crowded nurses station and stepping aside for beds being wheeled down the hall. This day no one stopped us or demanded to see IDs. Just as I began to relax, fate reminded me how obnoxious it could be.

"Savannah," a woman's voice called. "Savannah Prince."

Oh boy. A new voice who knew my name. That could not be good. Wincing, I turned to see a girl in her mid-teens rushing toward us. Glancing at Ennis, I plainly saw one thought roll through his mind – *oh no, it's another one*. Problem was, I wasn't completely sure myself.

"Thank God you're here," the girl breathed. "Are you still with the police?"

"Yes, and I apologize for this question but who exactly are you?"

The girl, still trying to catch her breath, allowed a hint of a smile to surface, "Kate Howard," she said, as though the name should ring a bell.

It did. "Little Katie? Good Heavens, you've grown." I drew Grace's daughter into a hug, "Last time I saw you, you were what, ten, eleven years old? Look at you now. Practically a debutante." In those few years, Grace's little girl blossomed from cute to gorgeous with features favoring her mama. After introducing Ennis and Katie I watched my husband's shoulders relax, the tension melt from his expression.

Katie took my hand with a firm grip. Yep, like mother like daughter. Tightest grip this side of a miser with his money. "I need your help," she begged. "Michael's losing it. Linda kept pokin' at him and Abby and Teresa jumped in the fray. He's threatenin' to tear them apart."

My heart sank while Katie proceeded to drag me to the scene of the insanity. Michael, Grace's oldest child, possessed a temper similar to mine. The boy never exhibited signs of violence, just storms of anger regarding Abby. Throughout the years, Abby picked at Grace's kids the way she needled her own sister – with relentless, sometimes outright hateful expertise. I understood Michael's anger. One could only tolerate so much hate directed at their loved ones without fighting back. In those instances, as divine as committing murder sounded, it tended to destroy everyone's lives, not help them. Now if I could only convey that to Michael...

"I'm hoping you can stop him," Katie added. "He's trying to protect Mama's character and they've circled like piranha."

We rushed down the hall past Aunt Emma's room toward the waiting room. The instant we stepped in I stopped, stunned at the man standing in the room. If I thought Katie changed over the past few years,

Michael redefined the term. Instead of the wiry fourteen year-old I remembered, he grew into a massive frame of solid bone and muscle poured into a blue t-shirt and jeans. Instead of a linebacker for Georgia Tech, Michael Howard belonged on the Atlanta Falcons team with his sheer powerhouse size. Standing about my height, his shoulders spanned wider than Ennis's and his arms blossomed into tree trunks of defined muscle. Muscle currently bunched as tight as his fists. And *I* was supposed to stop *him* from attacking anyone? I felt like a Christian thrown into the arena to defend myself against the lions and everyone remembers how well that went.

"Mikey," Katie called, "Savannah's here. Maybe you'll listen to her."

He never moved. Michael rooted himself to one spot cornering the huddling trio.

I hated family confrontations. Domestic problems were the worst. The best part though – Michael liked me when he was younger. The worst part – five years passed and people changed during that amount of time. Maybe Michael's feelings toward me leaned in a different direction, especially since his mother and I hadn't regularly kept in touch.

I stepped beside him, lightly touched his arm that tensed upon contact. "Michael, do me a favor and back down. They're not worth it."

"They're attacking my mama." His voice rang of a full-grown, don't-screw-with-me man, not a young teenager able to be called down by his elders. His enraged, flushed expression boldly met my calm one, "*No one* attacks my mama."

My blood ran cold from his stare. I forced myself to retain solid eye contact and not look away. I replied, "They attack everyone, not just Grace."

"How would you know? You're never around them. You're never around *period*."

Now that was a low blow. His statement was true but I wasn't there to argue about my absence in his life. I was there to *try* to stop a killing. I stepped in front of him, returning the favor of looking him square in the eyes, "You don't know anything about my life, what I've seen and experienced with them. They trounced all over my mama when she was alive and wouldn't let her rest in her own grave after she died. The day of her funeral they made accusations and insinuations that made a circus out of the most painful moment in my life. They wreaked havoc with my family to the point I stood in the same position you are right now – ready to snap their necks. I understand your anger toward them but you are in a public place and if you hurt them, there will be witnesses which means I'm obligated to arrest you. That's something I couldn't stomach. You're a good boy and always have been. Back down and walk off."

"That's right, honey," Linda agreed. "Just go on home."

Michael strutted against me. Lily protested the sudden bump and my expression warned of significant repercussions if the boy dared make that move again. I told Linda, "Shut up or I'll turn him loose on you." I felt the muscles solidify to rocks as his anger regrouped full force. His heated vision shot past me to the three huddled in the corner. Wrapping a hand in his shirt, I redirected his vision to mine with my other, "Think of Grace. She's worried about her mother and if you get arrested, she'll be worried about you too. Doesn't your mama have enough on her plate?"

"She's right," Katie said from somewhere behind him.

I saw Ennis ready to brace Michael if forced to. My whole family was a trial by fire. Poor unsuspecting people like Ennis married into the chaos only to reel when hell broke loose. After meeting the Culberson side, I fully expected him to file divorce papers and run back to Texas like his feet were on fire. "Michael," I continued, "you and Katie come with me and we'll go see Georgia. She'll serve us something nice, refreshing and fattening."

He stabbed a long, meaty finger at the trio, "I'm not done with them. You should have heard what they said about Mama."

I wrapped both hands in his t-shirt, seizing it hard enough to sacrifice a few chest hairs for good measure, "Are you hearing me, young man? *Leave 'em alone.*" With that phrasing, for some reason, I reminded myself of my mother.

"Someone needs to teach them all a lesson."

"It won't be you." I felt his muscles stir beneath my fists. Again they all amassed like a pack of leopards ready to pounce. Holding him back failed big time and Ennis seemed to sense it. He stepped behind Mike as I vowed, "I'm not letting Grace's son end up in the pokey." I dropped each word with the weight of a boulder, "Think about your mama."

"Mikey," his sister tried again. "Mama needs you. We both do."

My hands shook from the pressure of battling his strength. The boy regularly lifted weights and could probably bench press ten of me at once. Hurling me aside would have been child's play for him. I wasn't sure how long he intended to bully me physically but I wanted to end the scene quickly, before Ennis really did step in.

Michael appeared just as determined to push the limits, both verbally and physically, "Someone oughta kill 'em, do the world a favor."

A collective gasp rose behind me, followed by the horrified voices of the cousins. *We should go to the police,* they whispered. Then, *What good would it do* – she's *the police.*

Michael's temper overrode his common sense again and pushed against me again which inflamed Ennis. He took Mikey by the arm, "Let's go or I'll book you on assaulting a police officer, no matter who your mama is."

While Ennis escorted Michael out, I turned to the trio huddling in a corner, "If I hear of a complaint being filed against that boy, I'll make it my life's mission to drown you in violations. You'll not only need a lawyer but a loan and a deep sea diving suit to survive it."

O   O   O

On the way to Georgia's house, I noticed how Grace's kids had grown. Michael, once a willowy boy, now fit the role of his linebacker position for the Georgia Tech Yellow Jackets. His dark hair matched his eyes and his silent, brooding nature. Katie, though, favored her mother. Long blond hair to her waist, a trim petite frame and a smile destined to break a thousand hearts before the girl finally found Mr. Right. As a youngster, she'd been outgoing, vibrant and happy. She hadn't changed a bit.

Guilt settled in for not visiting them more often. Five years was a long time for adults but a lifetime to kids. I couldn't imagine how Grace's kids truly felt about me now. They'd heard about my cancer and read about Jeffrey Holland but *everyone* heard about Jeffrey and the two victims that got away – Georgia and me.

To Katie's credit, she acted as though not a week passed without seeing me. The bubbly personality and brilliant smile I remembered brightened her face when she pressed her hand on my tummy and felt Lily kick against her palm. And Michael, despite his meltdown at the hospital, still presented an inner strength reminding me of Ennis. Like every good Southern boy, Michael adored his mother and protected her with a vengeance.

The trip to Georgia's took longer than I expected. At first I blamed afternoon traffic clogging the streets. Then I realized it was Michael's griping that extended the agony of it. His grousing put women to shame. Katie told him to hush but his sister held no clout in that respect. Younger siblings never did.

We finally arrived at Georgia's and I prayed my sister was home. I dreaded another ride with Mikey's fussing. With a headache tapping at my forehead, I sent one last prayer to God. If Georgia wasn't home, strike me temporarily deaf or Mikey temporarily mute, I didn't care which. Either way, I should have realized Georgia was in full "chef" mode by now and prying her from the kitchen required a crowbar and possibly a threat to drop out of the competition.

The door opened and a rich, chocolatey aroma caressed my

senses. God not only answered my prayer but rewarded my enduring patience with a luscious snack. The tantalizing smell of brownies coaxed loud hunger pains from my stomach. My sister stood, decked out in full cooking regalia. Jeans, a pretty purple pullover and a pink floral apron tied around her waist. You never knew when company may drop by, she always said, so always dress accordingly. I would have bet a hundred bucks she prepared for any company except *us*.

Our brood filed into her house and I tracked the source of the chocolate to the oven. Brownies. Not just any brownies but my all-time favorite Black N' Whites. Before filching one, I explained the situation to Georgia, finishing, "Okay, lecture him."

Georgia frowned, "I beg your pardon?"

What, did she think I was kidding? I pointed directly at Mikey who'd suddenly found our conversation a bit humorous. I, however, didn't, "Lecture the boy. You know, like you did me when I –" the words stopped cold. I came within a gnat's eyelash of admitting to jumping the trio at my mother's funeral so I hastily rephrased, "When I got this angry at them."

"You mean when you tried to kill them?" she so eloquently enunciated.

Katie and Mikey turned to me, their mouths dropping open. Well, so much for saving my meager dignity… The blood rushed to my cheeks. My whole face felt ablaze with embarrassment. "Yes, Ms. Discreet, when I tried to kill them. Would you explain to Mikey that murder isn't a good idea because he's certainly not listening to the police detectives."

This was my sister's specialty. She refined lecturing to a fine art.
She specialized in guilt and if that failed, she shamed a person into
submission. Mikey stood no chance.

Georgia's vision shifted from me to Mikey, determination steeling
her backbone. Oh yes, I recognized this stance. In a matter of minutes,
Michael Howard would be begging for mercy – mostly for Georgia to
shut up but she perfected the art of ignoring such pleas. When the
victim lay sufficiently drained of fight, only then did she relent.

My sister wiped her hands on a dishtowel, removed her apron
and handed the latter to me, "I've got some Black N' Whites in the oven.
Five more minutes then you can finish them."

I took my sister literally. I'd finish them alright. Evidently my
voracious smile indicated that fact since she wagged her finger at me, "No
eating them. They're for the church."

"The church? I'm your sister. Your pregnant sister. I don't rate
a little nibble?" I could tell my spiel grated on her and I sighed, "Okay.
I'll get the spread and finish them out." The spread consisted of cream
cheese, butter, vanilla, confectioner's sugar and walnuts. That created the
White in Black N' White brownies. The Black layer had chocolate,
brown sugar, vanilla, walnuts and the usual eggs, flour, baking powder
and such. That sat on top of a rich base including flour, sugar, baking
powder, coconut, oats, butter and a splash of milk and salt. Anyone
lucky enough to taste one predictably wanted more. Clearly only the
Southern Baptists rated higher than Baby Sister. Sheesh.

As if hearing my silent lamenting, Georgia pointed to the corner
counter, "Bring those over for us. They're still warm. And Savannah,

don't eat too many or you'll get sick."

I was knocked up and hungry. Was there such a thing as overeating? Still, horsing down half the food was rude so I'd behave. I could almost taste the heavenly chocolate delicacy. I tied the apron around my waist, sure of two things. One, Georgia's lectures took *for-freaking-ever* and two, that pan of Black N' Whites was destined for a short lifespan.

O   O   O

Black N' Whites without milk was like Peanut Butter without Jelly. Rudolph without a red nose. A car without wheels. It just didn't look, sound or work right. I not only owed my sister three Black N' Whites and a half quart of milk by the end of Georgia's lecture, I owed the Baptists a healthy contribution for swiping her portion of Sunday's bake sale. We were raised Southern Baptist. As a kid I learned to say my prayers, read the Bible and go to Sunday School when Daddy's binge didn't leave him passed out on the couch holding his scotch bottle in one hand and an empty glass in the other. Mama mostly took us kids to church. Daddy wasn't inclined to religion except for using God's name in a particularly unflattering way.

I helped Georgia finish her brownies and she decided to pack up and head back to the hospital with us, probably to help pry Mikey off the terrible trio. She spent a good hour talking to him, calming him down and explaining the basic theory of survival: Don't tangle with strange, unpredictable animals.

While Ennis parked the car, I reminded Mikey, "Remember, you're not here to spar with anyone, you're here to support your mama and grandmother." I wasn't sure when or why Michael developed the anger problem but his rivaled mine and it scared the bejeesus out of me since he possessed the muscle to back his temper. I merely hoped the cousins cleared out since we'd left.

We rode the elevator to the appropriate floor and the moment the door slid open, the old anxiety set in. They were nearby. I could feel it. It was like war and I considered the cousins snipers waiting to pick us off one by one. The only thing keeping me halfway composed was Ennis. He'd held my hand since we exited the car. My grip about amputated his fingers so before I accidentally injured him, he settled for an arm around my waist.

We all marched down the quiet hall until familiar voices in the waiting room slowed our progress. Linda and Abby.

"Savannah's husband is a slice off the ol' beefcake, ain't he?" Linda asked.

"M-hmm. She's gonna have a hard time keeping him only in *her* bed," Abby added. "Not that she's ugly but the poor thing sure didn't inherit the Culberson beauty."

Ennis slid his hands from my waist to my shoulders. He rubbed gently, whispered we should leave and find Grace. Not before I heard these heifers out, I'd explain. Not a moment before.

"No, Georgia got the looks. She's Aunt Charlene dead out and she still got divorced. Now that fella was a hottie too."

"Goes to show you've got to have personality to keep a man. All she does is write those books."

"It's hard to keep a man satisfied while you're banging a keyboard instead of him," Linda said. "But at least Georgia's got her looks to land another man. Savannah'll have to quit that job to keep – what's his name again? Dennis, Danny–"

"Ennis, I believe," Abby answered.

Linda continued, "That's right. She'll have to quit that job to keep Ennis in the sack. It's good she's knocked up now so she can lock him in."

Ennis's hands constricted on my shoulders, a silent plea to remain calm. He knew me. I was boiling and about to blow. His fingertips bore down slightly harder as though my every thought transferred to him.

"Think he knows about her drinkin'?" Linda asked.

My husband fortified his grasp on me.

"Doubt it," Abby sounded sure of herself. "What woman's gonna admit they crawl in the bottle like their daddy?"

"'Member when Aunt Charlene was sick and dyin'? 'Member how Savannah'd come to the hospital drunk? Such a shame. Broke Aunt Charlene's heart."

"Let's go, babe," Ennis urged. "You're close to killin' 'em yourself. I can feel it."

"Savannah's just like her daddy," Abby declared.

"M-hmm," Linda added matter-of-factly. "Bad seed."

Ennis was right. At that point all I focused on was wringing their sorry necks. Airing dirty laundry in public was their specialty. They thrived on humiliation and Abby just heaped more on, "I'm surprised the police department hired her with that temper."

"And it gets worse if she drinks, you remember. That boy she married is in for true heartache."

Michael leaned to my ear, "I guess you *do* know about them."

"I'm a veteran of this war," I replied in a deceptively calm tone. I squirmed away from Ennis to enter the waiting room. Both women turned, their eyes rounded like deer in the headlights. I volleyed a glare between them, "By all means, don't stop on my account. I'm sure there are plenty of utter lies you haven't spewed yet."

Georgia stepped beside me, presenting a united front. The frown she leveled on them gave *me* an icy shiver. Pinning them with the glare, Georgia crooked her finger at me, "Let's go, Savannah. We don't want fleas."

Ennis wrapped a hand around my elbow, "You people are worse than snakes. And for the record, you're wrong about everything too."

The strength he used allowed no argument as he tugged me along. Once outside the waiting room, I stood face to face with Michael who cocked an eyebrow, "Don't say something you'll regret."

"Mikey," I replied, "sometimes regret is overrated."

I stomped from the waiting room, my mood darkening to the old days of silent brooding. Mama hated when I opened my mouth to confront the cousins' lies and half-truths. I spent my teenage years holding my tongue. Mama's reprimands caused me to withdraw and brood. I wasn't allowed to speak out and call them on their lies. Over the years I'd learned murder fell under a couple of definitions. Physical and emotional. Family squabbles caused a different emotional pain from

any other. It drove deeper, bled more, and never healed. In the waiting
room I held my tongue like Mama wanted. Why? Because I tried to
present a good role model to Grace's kids. Yay me.

Lord, I really wanted out of there. I wanted to go home, to work,
to be anywhere but Grady Hospital with those two witches. A sudden
flurry of movement broke my commiserating as I watched Katie and
Mike rush to their mother who'd stepped from Aunt Emma's room.

The three meandered back to us with Grace embracing us one by
one, "Thank you for taking care of my kids. I know Mike can be a
handful sometimes, especially around Abby and Linda."

A handful? More like a *truck* full – of dynamite. The boy
needed warning labels. But then again the same could have been said
about me in my younger years.

Georgia took care of the niceties while I still stewed over the evil
ones. Nothing changed over the years, nothing except we were older.

My phone cranked up with its familiar tune. Thank God Elvis
saved the day. I didn't care who it was, I'd use it as an excuse to am-
scray. "A Little Less Conversation" played again and I raced to answer
it. It was Mathis, "That Ramos guy from Zone 3 dropped off another
file for ya."

"Really?" I glanced at my watch. "Tell him we'll be right there."

"What? I said he dropped off a file. He ain't here –"

"He hasn't been waiting long, has he?" I looked to Ennis and
whispered *we gotta go.*

John's crabby side surfaced, "Prince, have you lost your marbles?"

"Yep, and we'll pick those up on the way to the station if we find them. Thanks, Mathis." Then I broke the eleventh commandment. I hung up on Mathis. I'd hear about it later, I was sure. Mathis took snubbing like a cat took to bathing but right now he floundered in confusion. I placed my phone back on my belt and turned to Ennis, "We gotta go." Then I tried to save my sister, "You need a ride back home? We'll drop you off and head to the station."

11

When we arrived at the station, Ennis and I noticed the new file on the Bob Davenport case on my desk. In thickness, it compared to an encyclopedia and we all knew how interesting those were. I barely opened it when Josh Hunter leaned in the door, "Bad news. Darren Metcalf had a heart attack. He's in surgery right now."

Ennis and I looked at each other. Wasn't it just the other day my husband alluded to heart attacks in the same breath as Darren Metcalf? Indeed, Mr. Rutherford's expression said. It also conveyed shock that his off-the-cuff remark actually came true.

I shook a finger at him, "Never, never, never utter the phrase *heart attack* with my name attached – that or anything else medically unpleasant or deadly. I'm having a baby. That's traumatic enough so I don't need any additional complications."

Josh did a double-take, "What?"

I explained how Ennis mentioned he hoped Metcalf didn't suffer a heart attack when we interviewed his witnesses for our case. "Look what happened and we haven't even touched the witnesses yet."

Josh rubbed his forehead, "It's gonna be another Tylenol day, I can tell. You two belong in the circus. I'll let you know his condition when he's out of surgery." He about-faced and headed to his office, probably to indulge in that painkiller he mentioned.

I read through the missing person file Ramos dropped off. Metcalf was nothing if not thorough about interviewing people. Page after page of family interviews then he talked to Davenport's mailman, lawn guy and plumber. I skipped those and headed directly for Troy Quinn's account, "When Metcalf interviewed Troy Quinn about Bob's disappearance, Quinn said he and Bob went out for dinner, got drunk, then went back to Bob's restaurant Blackstone shortly before it closed. Bob tried calling his wife several times but she refused to talk to him. Quinn and other employees witnessed Bob's attempts to contact her. Quinn said last time he saw Bob was about 2:00 a.m. on the 5th. Bob was still drunk and upset then stormed from the restaurant, supposedly heading back home on foot.

"Then the owner of a diner close to Bob's restaurant told Metcalf that a call came in just before midnight on the 4th. It was from Blackstone. The caller, later revealed as Troy Quinn, ordered four cheeseburgers to go but he never picked up the order. The owner said he got another call from Quinn at 2:00 a.m. saying he wouldn't be picking up the order because "he had a problem" but would settle up later.

"On the 18th, the Journal-Constitution ran the missing person article about Bob Davenport and shortly after, Metcalf got an anonymous call saying they'd heard a disturbance at Blackstone about 2:00 a.m. on the 5th and saw Davenport crawling out the front door on his hands and knees. The caller said Troy Quinn pulled him back in and 'things got quiet'. The caller continued that sometime between 3:00 and 3:30 a.m.,

Quinn pulled the restaurant's white van to the front entrance then went inside."

"Who the hell is this witness?" Ennis asked.

I scanned down a little further, "Metcalf and Ramos tracked him down to the apartments across the street. Witness's name is Frank Russo but when they approached him, Russo became belligerent and refused to cooperate."

"He's scared and probably had help getting that way."

"Watching that scene would scare anyone. That was basically in full view of anyone along that street and only one phone call reporting this incident."

"What was he doing up at that hour anyway?"

Further down the page it stated, "Russo said he'd been working on his computer and had the window up because it was warm that night."

"Seriously? Warm? The man's got hormone issues as bad as you."

Lily shoved a foot against my stomach, thankfully not beneath my ribs. I rubbed at the little appendage, "Your daughter says shut up. Ennis, we had a week of unseasonably warm weather around that time, remember? I saw people wearing shorts at the park."

"If you say it was warm, it was warm. I don't need both women in my life trying to strangle me in my sleep. Did Metcalf pry any other details from Russo?"

"Not much. Just that about 2:00 a.m. he heard crashing sounds coming from Blackstone, saw Davenport crawl out twice and Quinn pull him back inside both times. Ah, here it is. Russo didn't call until the 18th, he said, because he'd heard that Quinn was involved with organized crime."

"Organized crime?"

"Just telling you what the report says." I perused the remainder of the file, "Quinn had the carpets cleaned around the time Davenport's daughter reported him missing. Six days later, the 14th, Quinn had new carpets installed."

"That's hinky."

"I got something hinkier. The guy that installed the new carpet said when he got there, the old stuff was already pulled out. Cops found it in the alley and forensics tested it the next day but discovered a 4 x 12 foot section missing."

"Hey," another voice entered the conversation.

I recognized our colleague John Mathis not just by voice but by his sentiment. He sounded miffed. I looked up from the file while he stomped into the office, his narrow gaze aimed at me. "That baby discombobulate your brain or what?" he asked. "'Cause you never hung up on me before."

"Sorry, John. I was in a bad place – literally – and your phone call saved me and Ennis." I reached in my drawer for the trusty bowl of cookies. "Cookie?" I offered.

He gave it a sideways glance, "You bribing me?"

"Absolutely. Anything to keep you from murdering the pregnant lady behind the desk. Baby is making her miserable enough."

He removed one macadamia nut chocolate chip cookie. They

seemed to soothe Darren Metcalf's soul so I hedged my bet about Mathis. My round detective friend lifted it to his nose for a cursory whiff.

"I didn't put anything weird in it," I assured. Mathis hated anything foreign regarding food. He barely accepted pickles on a hamburger.

He sniffed it again, "It looks funny but it smells great. What are those white things?"

"Macadamia nuts. They're from Hawaii."

He bit into the cookie guardedly then lifted a brow. "Very good," he said, evidently impressed. "Nearly as good as your sister's, which, by the way, I'm empty on those chocolate chippers she made last week."

"I'll be sure to tell her."

Mathis stuffed the whole cookie in his mouth and after swallowing, drew the back of his hand across his mouth, "I take that back. They are as good as your sister's."

I reached the bowl out again, "Then by all means, have another. Maybe that'll make up for me hanging up on you."

Mathis was fat, he was grumpy and exactly the kind of cop no one wanted to have questioning them. He tended to push too hard, say the wrong things at precisely the most inappropriate times and I guessed he had more enemies than friends. He toned it down around me, probably because I'd been there for years and we'd formed a pretty good friendship.

"I'm considering it." He extended his hand palm up, "One for the road, Betty Crocker. For good measure."

John's smile appeared promising so I handed him the bowl. Anything to keep him from holding a grudge. Once he left the office, I continued reading the report to Ennis, "Metcalf and Ramos re-interviewed Quinn about the discrepancies in his original statement. When confronted with Russo's witness statement, Quinn explained that Davenport was drunk and kept falling down and he helped him to his feet a few times. He also amended his times by saying he'd last seen Davenport around *1:00 a.m.* but no later than *1:30 a.m.* when Bob left the restaurant. Quinn said he left about fifteen minutes later, locked the doors, set the alarm and went home."

"Did Davenport's daughter verify he came home at that time?"

I sorted through the family interviews to find the daughter's account, "Said she couldn't remember what time he got home because he was always late. She did confirm only Quinn and her daddy had alarm codes to the place."

I searched out the alarm company name, "I want to call ASAP Security and check out Quinn's story about the alarm."

I found the number and called. With a lot of persuading, the representative told me that the alarm had been switched on at 12:14 a.m. on the 5th, turned off 14 minutes later then turned back on at 3:59 a.m. It remained set until just after 11:00 a.m. the next morning.

My call ended about the time a forensics tech dropped off his own contribution to the case, "Here are the phone records from Troy Quinn and Blackstone Restaurant."

I thanked him and turned to Quinn's phone bill first. Two calls were placed from the restaurant phone at 3:34 a.m. and another ten minutes later. Quinn said he left the restaurant at 1:45 a.m. and headed home. He couldn't be two places at once so either he was lying or someone else was in the restaurant at 3:30. When I saw who the calls went to, I realized it was likely the former. Both calls went to Quinn's brother in Charleston. According to Metcalf, Quinn denied making the calls then abruptly ended the interview. Two days later, Metcalf got a call from Quinn's lawyer saying there would be no further contact with his client.

I looked at Ennis who replied, "Sounds to me like Metcalf had his murderer."

"But proving it is the problem. It's not illegal to call his brother, even from a business phone in the middle of the night. If we can't put Quinn with murdering Davenport and finding the missing carpet and a murder weapon, it's gonna be a challenge. Griffin is still performing whatever kind of autopsy can be done on body parts." Eating glass sounded more appealing than being in the same room with our medical examiner. He insisted on dwelling on the macabre side of life with morbid jokes or pranks. Worst of all, he loved re-enacting crimes which, in this case, I'd have unequivocally passed on.

My phone rang. I pretended not to hear it. Ennis smirked, "Afraid to answer your phone?"

"Terrified. Whoever it is will survive despite Savannah screening her calls."

When the call transferred to voicemail, I started back with the report, trying to make sense of the case. Quinn didn't try very hard to hide the fact he probably killed Bob Davenport. Instead he changed his story and times, making me think he enjoyed screwing with Metcalf and Ramos.

The phone rang again and I punched the off button. Savannah was out of business, off the radar, and out of town as far as phone calls went. I did my time in hell that morning with my crazy family. Somehow I didn't expect the Georgia Lottery called to announce I'd won a million bucks.

"They're not gonna give up, you know."

My husband's observation drew a sigh from me. He could really be a wet blanket sometimes. I wanted a quiet, peaceful day – at least what remained of it. Only way to have it was pretending my service conked out. I was not above doing it. The "off" button got a lot of use on busy days. "Why would Troy Quinn not give a crap if anyone knew he killed Davenport?"

Ennis adopted a twangy Irish accent, "He's an Irish mobster, ain't you heard? Mob connections. Concrete shoes, sleeping with the fishes…"

"That's the Italian rabble and you sound like a conflicted Texas Irishman." Just as I finished, the phone on my desk rang. I stared balefully at it but reluctantly picked up.

"What's wrong with your phone?" Georgia wanted to know. "And don't tell me your service is out. You ignored my calls, didn't you?"

"If you must know, yes, but in my defense, I didn't look at Caller ID so technically I didn't ignore *your* calls, I merely ignored my ringing phone."

Georgia's sigh rivaled mine earlier. I smiled at Ennis who shook his head. I could nearly see my sister rolling her eyes skyward, asking the Lord for help. Then she bulled into the reason for calling, "Can you take an hour off? Seth and I will pick you up at the station."

From her tone I assumed all hell broke loose, "What's happened?"

"We need police intervention at the hospital. It's that ridiculous power of attorney argument again."

"I thought Aunt Emma was going to be okay."

"She is but you know Abby. She's stirring the pot to hurt Grace. She's insisting she has the papers but can't produce them. Katie told me Grace has the power of attorney and she'd go home to find them but Michael stormed out before we could stop him. No one can find him."

Oh geez. My head fell into my hand. Lily tapped against my belly, perhaps as a gentle warning not to go ballistic. I'd really hate to be my kid. My temper weakened since meeting Ennis but I still scared half my family when I blew my top. I trembled to think about Lily's disposition in future years. I prayed she inherited her father's easygoing nature. A prayer I prayed every night because our daughter was destined for Taurus-hood, one of the most stubborn zodiacs in the clan. "What the hell am *I* supposed to do? Unless someone strapped a GPS to the kid, I can't find him."

Ennis leaned forward in his seat, a deep trench furrowing his brow. Yes, I wanted to say, it's my family again.

Georgia huffed, "Well, do ya think you could come to the hospital and help us prevent bloodshed? The nurses have already threatened to call the police because of the raised voices."

Sure, I'll just tell the city not to go killin' each other in the meantime, I nearly replied. "You gonna beg Josh Hunter for time off on my behalf? 'Cause he ain't in a great mood today."

"I read your mind. I already called…"

About that time Hunter leaned into my office, "Georgia get hold of you?"

I pointed to the phone. He nodded, hitched his thumb behind him, "Go save your family. If anything comes back on the Davenport case, I'll let you know."

My sister had a knack for persuasion that astounded me. She could sell a truckload of sand to a sheik in the desert. No wonder her closet brimmed with beautiful sweaters and dresses when we were kids. She sweet-talked Mama and Daddy into anything. Now she had my boss wrapped around her little finger.

I thanked Josh then tended to my sister who, in the meantime, managed to maintain a steady, rambling one-sided conversation. "Georgia, please," I begged. "Cease and desist. I'm on my way."

12

Seth and Georgia picked us up at the station and filled us in on the calamity befalling Grace in our absence. Abby and Linda huddled together until broaching the power of attorney subject to Katie and Michael – in front of the nurses. Michael, of course, reacted by pushing and shoving and hurling threats. That left little Katie to pry herself between her powerhouse brother and the two nitwits inciting him. When she failed, she ran to her mother who explained *she* possessed power of attorney. By the time Katie raced to the elevator, her brother was gone, leaving Abby and Linda pale and cowering from whatever he'd done or said. Now Grady Memorial deemed Michael persona non grata because he caught a case of the Culberson Crazies and lost it in public.

"Thanks for coming, sis," Seth met my gaze in the rearview mirror as he drove. "You and Ennis both."

I nodded. At least one of my siblings exercised their manners. Georgia rode shotgun and offered a half-hearted thanks. Her tone annoyed me, "Georgia, Ennis and I are working the Bob Davenport murder. As thrilling as it is to interact with the family idiots, the departmental pressure to solve this case is immense. If we don't show some progress, it's our asses on the line."

Seth frowned at me in the mirror, "Murder? Last I heard he was still missing."

With that expression, my brother favored Daddy way too much at times. With age, his facial features and moodiness mirrored our father. Both developed the skill of conveying their feelings without uttering a single word and right now, Seth waffled between surprise and concern.

Seth watched TV as often as astronauts landed on the moon these days. He stayed out of touch simply because he wrapped most of his life around his self defense studio. Admirable, I thought, but an occasional brush with current events never hurt anyone.

The body at Lake Acworth hit the news days ago so I simply replied, "They found Davenport hacked to bits at Lake Acworth the other day."

Georgia groaned. She detested gory details. I usually never troubled her with them but that day I'd do just about anything to pay back her sanctimonious phone call.

My brother pulled into Grady's parking lot, "I thought two guys were working his missing person case. How'd you end up with it?"

"One of the detectives suffered a heart attack so they're a man down." I didn't go into particulars about jurisdiction, evidence and oh, those pesky gory details, probably due to Ennis's grasp constricting on my hand. He always wanted peace and quiet. For that he probably realized he married into the wrong family.

Georgia groaned again. That stepped on my last nerve, "What's wrong, Georgia?"

"Nothing except that job of yours," she spoke bitterly. "I've always hated that job. You've been shot, Ennis has been shot, God only knows how many scrapes you've escaped that you haven't told us about, and then there's that bastard in Norcross Prison who's after you. Now you're into a case involving the Irish mob and one of the original detectives has already fallen from a heart attack. It's all just too much for me right now." She turned in her seat to make eye contact. She looked so much like Mama I blinked to ensure my mind hadn't played a trick. Even her lecture sounded like our mother, "You're pregnant, Savannah. Something's gotta give. I'd hope it's the job, not your baby or your life."

Seth wheeled the Tahoe around a row of cars, still searching for a parking place. I saw him glance at me in the mirror then return to watching the road. He knew I hated people pouncing on my choice of occupation. Literally hated it. Fact was, even if I wanted to retire I couldn't. Not with the bills we had, the mortgage and now the baby. Jeffrey Holland – or "the bastard in Norcross" – vowed to kill me and take his time doing it. I bore scars from our previous meetings and my shoulder and back suddenly decided to remind me of them. I'd stayed awake nights debating over finding another job. Ennis and I discussed it at length numerous times. My sister's sermon ran through my mind, word by word until it stumbled on, "Irish mob? What makes you think the mob is involved?"

Georgia sighed loudly, crossed her arms and looked directly at our brother as if to say *she's hopeless.* Seth answered, "There've been rumors about Blackstone restaurant being a front for the Irish mob."

"I think it's *blarney,*" I half-joked.

He shrugged one shoulder, "Just telling you what we've heard."

"*Did you hear anything I said a minute ago?*" Georgia snapped.

Oh, for God's sake, "Yes, Mama, every word. Now tell me how to change jobs and still maintain our mortgage and raise a child. Don't forget to tell me what job I need that I'll love *and* be successful at."

"Being a mother," she shot back.

Seth kept searching for an empty parking place and inserted his two cents before my temper exploded, "You're damn fine at cooking, like Mama and Georgia."

Ennis agreed, "You are."

I looked to him like *who invited you into this fray?* My expression failed to intimidate him as he followed up with, "Everyone loves your cookies. They love anything you make."

"See?" Georgia defended herself. "I'm not crazy. You have options, Savannah. Take some time to explore them."

I leaned forward to address her, "You think I've spent the last eight months just puking, eating and peeing? I have explored them."

"Explore them again," she demanded.

The urgent desire to blurt *butt out of my life* dangled precariously on my tongue when Ennis pulled me back, took my hand with a pleading half-smile, "We can reexamine them."

That did it, "Stop drinking the Kool-Aid, Ennis. I don't need to fend off my siblings and you. We'll talk about it later."

Seth slowed the car to pull into a parking place. In the near distance, I saw Michael and Katie standing beside a row of cars. They stood with another person that looked unfortunately like Abby. As usual, the meeting appeared explosive. Great, I thought. Here we go again.

Michael drew back his fist and Katie attempted to stop him. The girl's guts outweighed her smarts if she thought that hulk might listen to reason. I unlatched my seatbelt, hopped out of the Tahoe and headed toward the confrontation – all at the protests of my family.

"Michael Howard, don't you dare!" I shouted while I weaved between parked cars.

Michael's non-reaction told me his anger ramped to rage. Katie wheeled at the sound of my voice. She pleaded with me to hurry. Pregnant women only moved so fast, I wanted to say, so gimme some time.

Seth jogged up beside me, "Back off, sis. You're not in any condition to fight with him."

"I'm past fighting, Seth." I reached back for my handcuffs, "This time the little shit's gonna listen to me or go to jail." I intended to once and for all, explain to Michael that parts of our family fell short of one important facet. Class. No amount of threatening or fighting would change it, just back away and let them implode on themselves. Because for all the crap they dealt, eventually their tricks caught up with them.

And if he didn't leave peacefully and stop acting immature, I'd cuff him and stuff him in the back of Georgia's Tahoe to cool down for the evening.

"I'll kill you," I heard Michael swear to Abby. "And when I'm finished with you, I'll send Teresa and Linda to Hell too."

This time I grabbed his elbow. His reaction surprised me. He slung my hand away, nearly knocking me off balance. That settled it. I stood in front of him, dangling the handcuffs in his face, "If you don't stop, you're headed for lock-up and make no mistake – I *will* haul you away this time.   If you insist on heaping more stress onto your mama, step past me now and commence beating the tar outta her sister.   But remember, you do that and you'll shame your mama and her good name."   Guilt usually worked with decent Southern boys.   Hell, I'd seen it work thousands of times on Seth.   Even Leah and Georgia succeeded in guilting him into things, not just Mama.

"Savannah's right," Abby's voice trembled.   "You'll go to jail. You want that?"

I tossed a threat at her, "I'll take you too, just for your big mouth and being a nuisance to me."   I saved my sternest expression for Grace's boy, "How many breaks do you think you get in life, Michael?   I gave you one the other day.   Your last one.   Do you understand *that?*"

His arm shot straight out, pointing at the bane of his existence, "She's trying to steal power of attorney from my mama."

"No one'll steal it," Seth spoke from behind me.   It scared me half to death.   He'd used that tone no one argued with, not even me. "Grace already has it.   She's keeping it.   That's final.   Stop being a damned idiot."

If only, I thought, but that concept appeared to be in the realm of unicorns.   Pure, unadulterated fantasy.

Fortunately Michael seemed to listen – a little – to my brother. Of course with *that* voice, even the dead heard him in the hereafter.   So I tried my hand again, "Does Grace have the papers with her?"

Katie, still wide-eyed and panicked, rummaged her purse, "They're right here."   She handed them to me like they were on fire,

"The lawyer said it's all there."

I glanced over them as if I had a clue what I was reading. Seth knew the truth. I was dumb as a post when it came to legalities but to calm Michael down, I had to make it appear believable. "Looks right to me. Let's get a copy to the hospital staff. Will that be sufficient, Michael?"

His blue eyes blazed at Abby, as if daring her to refute my statement. She stepped back instead. He finally made eye contact with me, "Fine. But I want everyone to know who's really in charge of Grandma's care." Then he stabbed a finger at Abby, "And it ain't her."

13

A deep, dreamless sleep descended over me that night. I welcomed the absence of hassling relatives, pressure of solving murders and general chaos of real life. Not long ago, I dreaded nighttime but now I longed for it every day, to return to the unconscious revelry of slumber.

I was in the middle of said reveling when an elbow jabbed me in the ribs. "Savannah, the phone's ringing and I can't reach it... *Wake up.*"

My husband nudged my hip this time, and when my eyes blinked open, I found him halfway atop me, reaching toward the nightstand. "I'm awake now," I mumbled. "You can get off me until you've got other ideas more fun than answering a phone."

I glanced at the clock, noticed the time and lost my humor. 2:00 in the morning. Nothing good happened at 2:00 in the morning. Realizing that, I decided the answering machine should hear the bad news first. I told Ennis, "We bought the stupid machine so it might as well earn its keep." Whether destiny played a part, I wasn't sure, but the message was quite clear as was the voice, "Savannah, it's Linda. I know you're there and I should hang up now but Teresa *made* me call since you're *family.*"

Anger fired my temper. So much for the respite from unscrewed relatives. Linda said "family" like she'd spit out a piece of rotted meat. Ennis rose to one elbow, "What the hell's her problem?"

"Drama, Ennis. The Culbersons thrive on it." I grabbed the receiver, "What is it, Linda? It's too early in the morning to harass people, even for dragons like you."

The silence on the other end was priceless. Linda tipped her hand, consequently losing her bet that I wouldn't pick up. "Um, uh..." Linda stuttered then turned instantly weepy, "Abby's dead. She was murdered."

Normally such news triggered utter shock or disbelief. It depended on who the deceased was and their overall character in life. Not many tears were shed over Jeffrey Dahmer, Ted Bundy, cockroaches, ticks or fleas, I figured. And with Abby's disposition, she rated somewhere in the middle.

Still, despite my personal feelings, she was family and had been murdered. I swung my legs over the side of the bed, rubbed my eyes to clear them and sharpen my focus, "Where'd it happen?"

"Gosh, Savannah, your emotion is so moving."

"Hey, *you* called *me* so answer my question or go away. Where is she and are the police there yet?"

The tears and sentiment magically disappeared from Linda's once trembling voice, "At her house. Someone shot her, if that matters to you." The line went dead and I sat, a thousand thoughts flooding my mind. My first thought was of Michael. He wouldn't... Would he? The kid's explosive temper teetered on violence and his mouth proved a calamity all on its own. That afternoon replayed in my mind, his blatant disregard of my authority and his bold promise to murder Abby…

Well, I lamented, so much for sleep. I slung a robe around my shoulders and headed for the kitchen. Ennis asked, "What happened and where are you going?"

He'd soon regret asking those questions, "Abby's dead. According to the grapevine, she was shot. I have to call Michael."

With that, Ennis rolled out of bed and followed me to the kitchen, "You think he did it?"

"If it walks like a duck and quacks like a duck, it sure ain't a horse." I lugged the thick, heavy phone book from a drawer, thumbed through its mountain of pages for Michael Howard. To my surprise – and ultimate frustration – there were four but only one was listed at the Georgia Tech campus. I dialed and waited, praying the little shit answered his phone good and drowsy-like because if he didn't, my suspicions would blossom into bigger, uglier doubts about the boy.

The phone rang three, four then five times. On the sixth ring I nearly hung up when a male voice answered with a sluggish, drawn out, "Hullo…"

"Michael?"

"Nah, Mike's not here," the slurred voice replied. "Who's this? I'll scrawl a message."

"His cousin Savannah. Has he been home at all tonight?"

"Nah," the voice yawned. "Said he was going out to kill rats. Who're you again?"

"Savannah Prince, his cousin. I'm also a detective with the

Atlanta Police. Tell him to call me when he gets in. It's important."

"Will do, Hannah. Bye."

I stood, staring at the phone. Michael's fate rested with a plastered college kid barely able to string three coherent words together. But a few of those slurred words struck me hard. Out killing rats? What the hell did that mean? The routine figure of speech now formed a more ominous tone. Did he mean out boozing and partying or out ventilating Aunt Abby into the afterlife?

"He's not there, huh?" Ennis asked.

With great ceremony, I dropped the phone into the cradle, "Nope. Out killing rats, according to his roomie who sounded one hundred proof." I turned to him, hoping, *needing* reassurance my gut feeling was wrong, "You don't think Michael would... I mean he was so angry... But murder?"

"Don't jump to conclusions. Maybe he's out with a girl."

Or his new best friends Smith & Wesson. I headed to the closet for a change of clothes. Ennis tailed me, his tone incredulous, "You'll never find him in this city. You don't know his habits or his haunts."

I grabbed the first shirt I came across, pulled it on, "Too bad he's not a Prince. I'd look in the bars first. But a Culberson? Maybe the zoo. Is there a full moon tonight?"

Ennis's vision swept me from head to toe then shook his head, "You're staying put."

My brow sank at the assessment. Okay, middle of the night. My hair needed combing, I knew that. I looked two steps from utter shit but I had to find Michael before the cops did. "Because I compared my weird family to wild animals or werewolves?"

Ennis pointed to my breasts – or I thought he had, however his expression lacked the usual lustful overture. He cleared my confusion by saying, "No, because of what you're wearing."

I tilted my frown southward. In my frantic haste, I'd managed to locate the only Dallas Cowboys sweatshirt within two feet of my wardrobe. I gasped in mock horror, "My God, it's sacrilege." I started to shrug out of it as if it were ablaze – except for one thing, "It's wonderfully comfortable though."

"Wear it at your own risk. Just don't blame me when you come back dripping with rotten tomatoes."

I thought about that one a moment. "You're right. Grab something more appropriate for me." Ennis and I had a running squabble over who played better – or worse – Dallas or Atlanta. This last year the Cowboys pounded the Falcons into dust. Twice. I nearly had a stroke both times.

I kept thinking how snug and warm his sweatshirt was – and so roomy for my rapidly expanding belly. God, I hated leaving my nice cozy house. Ennis protested me leaving without him but Grace needed help. Her mother remained hospitalized and now her sister was dead. If I didn't know where to search for Michael, I should at least go to Grace.

I headed for my purse on the dresser when a paralyzing pain in my stomach stopped me cold and stole my breath. Lily pointed out her displeasure of our late night by crippling me. She pushed harder against me, causing the pain to escalate and envelope my entire consciousness. After a sick whimper, I rubbed at the protruding foot while considering spewing a fountain of profanities not heard since my days as a single woman.

In a flash Ennis was by my side, his arm around my waist, baby-stepping me back to the bed, "You can't get out like this, babe. The detectives on scene won't tell you anything anyway."

I nodded in agreement, winced the tears from my eyes, feeling them roll down my cheeks. Holding a hand to my stomach, I continued rubbing the little foot but it locked itself into place, not budging.

"Can you lie down?" Ennis asked.

I shook my head, "Not now," my words came in shallow hitches. "Give me a few minutes."

It took twenty.

O O O

By 3:40 that morning I had a new goal for the day. Flush the phone down the toilet. That or back over it with Ennis's Dodge. Anything to evict the noisy creature from my house so I could rest. The thing began jangling again at exactly 3:40, only minutes after I fell into a fitful sleep. Getting Lily back to sleep proved harder than Chinese arithmetic. My muscles still ached from her earlier ambushing and any attempt to move might incite a riot with my unborn daughter so I chose the kinder, gentler choice. Ignore the damn phone.

Despite my decision it kept on ringing. "What the hell is going on with this person?" Ennis said, his voice sleepy and hoarse.

I wanted sleep, not to mention peace. To get it, I'd answer one last phone call then rip the cord from the wall. I answered with a tone as rough as my edges lately, "Yeah?"

"Savannah, it's me."

Considering the time and my lack of patience, the name "Me" just wasn't cutting it. "Me who?"

"I'm sorry for calling at this time. It's Grace."

It didn't sound like Grace. The person at the other end of the conversation sounded teary-eyed and frightened, "I wasn't sure if you'd heard." She sniffed back more tears, "Abby's been murdered."

I flopped back to the bed. Crap. I should have fought through Lily's tantrum and resulting pain and gone to see Grace like I originally planned. My cousin clung to the edge of her control and was slipping fast. I had to lie, at least a little, to salve my own guilt, "Someone called but they mumbled a lot on the message." Sure Linda would swear she called and spoke to me but I'd just deny it. That was how a person played verbal tennis with a Culberson. Truthfully, a courtesy call from Linda or Teresa would sound rather far-fetched anyway, considering how they felt about me. "When did this happen?" I asked. I already knew but let Grace inform me anyway. She gave me the details of what she knew and what she didn't. Afterward she paused. When she spoke again, her fragile thread of restraint snapped, "The police arrested Michael. They think he murdered her."

Ennis rose onto one elbow, rubbed the sleep from his eyes, "What's going on?"

"Michael's in jail. The cops think he killed Abby."

"You already knew about Abb –"

I quickly slapped a hand over his mouth and shook my head in a don't-you-dare-say-another-word glare.

He lifted a brow in response, removed my hand with a delicate touch. I recognized his expression warning me about lying but what choice did I have? My baby physically crippled me when her beauty sleep got interrupted. Let's see how glamorous he walked hunched over gorilla-like with a five pound sack of taters in *his* belly.

"Savannah, he couldn't have killed her," Grace continued. "He's got a bad temper but he'd never murder anyone."

I'd heard those very words from every human related to a murder suspect. I'd heard them so often I learned to do a mental eye roll and assure the family that we'd not hastily arrest their loved one. I couldn't say the same for Michael Howard. Every threat the kid uttered returned to my weary mind. He'd not only threatened to slap the snot out of both Linda and Teresa but Abby as well. The coup de grace occurred in the parking lot that afternoon, "I'll kill you," he'd sworn to Abby. "And when I'm finished with you, I'll send Teresa and Linda to Hell too."

I sat up on the side of the bed, said goodbye to any remaining sleep that night. "For shit's sake, I warned that kid about his temper. He slung enough threats at her, of course the cops'll look at him first."

"Savannah, please help him. He didn't do it."

By this time, Ennis maneuvered beside me, his hairy legs hanging over the bed's edge, resting his elbows on his knees. In a few months we'd look just like this, two bleary-eyed parents trying to make sense of the moment's insanity, only it would revolve around our own infant, not Grace's overgrown one.

Ennis leaned in to listen as I asked, "Grace, are you sure? Michael was pretty angry this afternoon." I regretted having to ask but Michael's state of mind hadn't been warm and cuddly lately. It even unnerved me, mostly because I carried a child. Any other time, I'd have leapt into the fray and been more proactive with the boy. He actually reminded me of myself with his short, fiery temper. That thought brought back memories of Seth and Daddy pulling me off Linda at Mama's funeral. I'd been aiming to kill the trio at the time too. As I struggled for freedom, I'd *vowed* to kill all three.

Realizing the question basically rendered Grace mute, I tried to soften the impact, "Grace, I'm sorry but I have to ask. Do you know where he was tonight?"

After a long pause, Grace admitted, "No. He wasn't at the dorm when I called earlier to tell him about Abby. Savannah, I know he's innocent. Michael may have a big mouth but he'd never actually kill someone."

There's a mother's hope, I thought. The hope her child's mouth did verbal damage instead of his hands resorting to physical harm. The desperation in Grace's voice tugged at my heart. I'd soon be a mother and I'd suffer the worries, travails and ulcers all mothers developed when raising a child. "What do you want me to do?" I asked.

"I need a good lawyer. Do you know one?"

If the time hadn't been two hours past insane, I might have laughed. Sure, I knew sharks that bounced the guiltiest cold-blooded murderer from the clutches of the death penalty – or just a day in jail. Every cop knew about those lawyers. I hated them beyond normal reason but I also kept note of their names – like every cop – in case certain circumstances arose. This would be one of them, "I'll find him a good one but Grace, no matter who it is, it's gonna cost."

"I know. Just find a good lawyer for him and I'll work out the finances as best I can."

14

My mothering hormones must have kicked in because I felt the urge to visit Michael. After Grace's call, I couldn't sleep which thoroughly aggravated me because it was Saturday, one of the only days I had off work. After a grand total of three hours of sleep, I was walking past the desk sergeant's kiosk, headed for lockup. I was not happy.

I felt sure my image with my colleagues would nosedive once they caught sight of me. Before leaving the house I attempted combing my hair that magically turned as tangled as my life. I fought my hair until it capitulated and draped down my back in an orderly manner. There was no time for makeup so I gave my face a quick washing then threw on some jeans and a splotchy reddish-pink sweatshirt that at one time had been dark red until Ennis accidentally washed it with bleach. The latter I debated over before leaving the house but it felt comfortable and less controversial than Ennis's Cowboys shirt.

As expected, when I passed by a few whispers arose and I heard my name planted in the middle of them. It figured, I fumed, making my way toward the sergeant's desk. Michael not only screwed up, he conveniently screwed up in my precinct. The number of detectives totaled five, two of them being Ennis and myself. Three other gold shields stood in line to lead the case against my cousin, including the two newbies, Alex Nesbitt and Christine Clark. I did not know them as well as I knew John Mathis. I wanted a friend on his case, not some newcomer bucking for a commendation.

The desk sergeant leaned across the desk, a languid smile easing across his features, "Never seen you with your hair down like that. Looks real nice." I noticed his eyes roamed to the funky colored sweatshirt stretched across my bulging belly. Yes, it felt rather *snug* as Georgia might have said. If Sergeant Bailey thought it looked tight, he should have been in my shoes – literally. His smile virtually faded, "Rough night?"

"That's an understatement. You've got a Michael Howard in lockup. I need to see him."

The sergeant hitched his thumb down the hall, "You know the way. Be careful though. That guy'll go wacko on ya."

No shit, I thought but reconsidered verbalizing the tidbit. Look in a dictionary under *raging maniac* and Michael's furious mug likely would be there.

I walked off with a mumbled thanks. Following the semi-quiet hallway, I passed the captain's office, then mine and Ennis's. The trek down the stairs gave me pause. What would I say to Michael? I'd learned the hard way about promising anything to people. Ditto on telling them not to worry and that things would work out. Woe be unto the foolish cop who did that. The second the verdict is *guilty*, the wrath of God engulfed the detective – in the form of the convict's family. Best I planned to do was tell the kid to keep quiet and listen to his lawyer.

Then I wondered if everyone knew we were cousins. To further the paranoia, I ventured into the horror of every cop in the zone knowing Abby was my first cousin and Michael my second cousin, one the victim of a murder and the other accused of committing it. *Damn*, I lamented again. *People will think we're hayseeds fresh out of Bumpkin County...*

I stopped by the gate officer's desk and asked for Michael's cell to be opened. Charlie Sullivan, a uniform cop for two years and blessed with pleasant features and thick crop of coffee brown hair, blatantly stared wide-eyed at my belly. His vision slowly lifted to mine, "Considering your condition, I'd rather you speak through a locked door, Detective. That kid gave us a helluva fight. I don't want you or your baby hurt."

Charlie had good intentions. He reminded me of Ennis. A good Southern boy who respected women and protected them. Unfortunately this situation demanded a face to face meeting. Mr. Michael Howard needed a serious wake-up call. Maybe the cold, dull, musty ambience of jail walls might inspire him to finally listen. "Thank you, Charlie, but I want to speak with him in the cell. Just don't go far, if you don't mind."

"No problem at all, Detective. You just let me know if he gives you problems or even looks at you wrong. My Taser needs some exercise and that boy fits the bill."

I started down the narrow hallway, a solid wall of gray concrete to my left, a row of jail cells on my right. After passing a few occupied units, I saw Michael standing, his face pressed against the bars to view his new visitor. "I thought that was your voice," he said. "I'm glad you're here."

That makes one of us. My hands went to my hips, "You know, you're becoming the poster child for why I wouldn't have kids for the longest." I patted my belly, "But I've signed the eighteen year contract now so I'll be praying that my kid actually listens to me, unlike you did."

"If it's any consolation, I didn't kill the bitch."

Charlie winced at the comment, his hand hesitating midway through unlocking the door. He looked at me, unease written in his features, "Rutherford's gonna kill me if I let you in there."

"Rutherford will answer to me if he jumps on you." I nodded for him to open the door.

He sighed, shook his head, twisted the key in the lock until it snapped open. I turned my attention to Michael, "As for you, young man, just keep that winning attitude and you'll wow the judge." It dawned on me why Daddy's temper grew shorter with every child my parents conceived. Kids drove people nuts – not nuts enough to beat them like Daddy but nuts enough to lay down their sanity and call it quits.

Taking a seat next to him on the small squeaky cot, I grimaced at the lumpy surface beneath my butt. I tiredly blew out a breath then stretched my back, "Better get used to these prison issue Serta Not-So-Perfect Sleepers, kid. Hope you don't have back problems."

He frowned, "Did you come to help or taunt me?"

"I came to help but that's what I've *been* trying to do. I told you to mind your mouth in front of those women, Mikey. You blurt out you'll kill them then one ends up dead. That's not just coincidence, that's plain spooky. But you kept threatening her, that's why the police have no choice but look at you closer."

Michael's hands fisted on his knees, his voice dropping to a lower, hostile growl, "I told you I didn't kill her."

I watched his hands. The boy I remembered as a polite, gentle youngster developed into an angry man, ready to dole out his brand of justice on anyone within reach. I needed to tread carefully, "I heard you. And for what it's worth I believe you. The problem is getting everyone else to."

"I wasn't near Abby's house, I was at Piedmont Park."

"At that time of night? What for and can anyone corroborate your story?"

Michael leaned back against the brick wall and for the first time, my claustrophobia kicked in. The jail cell was just this side of a shoebox. Between that and his temper, I began regretting the visit altogether and I scooted closer to the door. Michael gave me a quizzical look, "You afraid of me?"

Yep. "Nope," I replied diplomatically then whispered, "I'm claustrophobic. Don't tell anyone."

He rolled his eyes, "I got bigger problems than to gossip. I went to the park for some peace from that damn phone. It kept clanging away and I couldn't stand it. As for corroboration, the folks that hang out at that hour don't exactly get along with police so I don't think you'll get any help there."

I sighed. It figured that he'd not only get accused but not have a decent alibi to back him up. One thing about the Culberson clan: when they screwed up, they went for blue ribbon perfection. "Who's your lawyer, do you know?"

"They're sending a public defender, Keith somebody."

I heaved a groan. This day really started off peachy. Keith
Wilson was a lawyer in name only. I'd seen him at his best and his worst
and couldn't tell a difference. "Don't say a word to him. I've got a
lawyer for you, one that will actually defend you." And he wasn't exactly
thrilled with a four a.m. phone call from a cop who'd splintered one of
his biggest defense cases last year – but just barely. He knew how to
phrase questions, discredit people, sling mud and accusations and all but
shred the prosecution's witnesses. No matter our past, I knew the man
was good and managed to finagle a decent price from him on Grace's
behalf.

"How much is he gonna cost 'cause I'm sure I'm fired from my
job after this."

"Your job is the last thing you should care about right now.
Grace is meeting with your lawyer right now so keep your lip zipped
around Keith Wilson."

"They can't prove I killed her so why do I need a lawyer?"

"Because if you have the right one he can protect you. Right now
the detectives will question you, try to prove your alibi. You'll make bail
since there's no real evidence but believe me, you need a lawyer."
Because I knew how some cops worked. They did *anything* to clear a
case. If Clark or Nesbitt caught the case, I didn't trust them as far as I
could throw 'em.

A man appeared at the cell door, dressed in khaki Dockers and a
powder blue dress shirt. He reminded me of a vacuum salesman. All

except the smug grin curving his thin lips, "Mr. Howard? I'm Keith Wilson and I'll be your attorney." His vision shifted to me then my swollen belly then back up again, "Who are you?"

"I'm Michael's cousin and he's already got a lawyer. Sorry you rolled out of bed for nothing." I shooed him with my hand, "You can go now." I pushed to my feet, wobbling a bit when I stood. Michael's large hand softly encircled my arm to steady me. His current demeanor reminded me of Ennis, gentle with me, ferocious with others. When Mr. Wilson neglected to leave, I verbally helped him along, "What part of *he doesn't need you* don't you understand?"

The blunt question caught him short and the smug features melted like a snow cone in an Atlanta summer, "But I've been appointed to represent him."

I nearly laughed. Him represent one of my relatives? Granted, if that relative had been Abby or Linda, I'd have stepped aside and happily let him in. But this was Grace's child. In my heart I felt Michael was innocent. It's always easy for cops to point fingers at the obvious suspect – especially when the cops have help being pointed in that direction. Linda and Teresa worked overtime at it and Michael's name and face became synonymous with being a killer thanks to them.

I turned so Wilson saw the badge clipped to my jeans pocket. His vision fell straight there and he swallowed. I repeated, "Thanks for your time, Counselor, but as I said, Michael already has an attorney." I stood stock still, waiting for Wilson to back off. He didn't. "Sullivan," I called to the guard.

A moment passed when Charlie approached, nudged past Mr.

Wilson and unlocked the cell. In the process of stepping around the gate, I reminded Michael, "Remember what I said, Mikey. Don't say a word because I got you a good attorney."

"But *I* am a good attorney," Keith whined at my back.

I strode off, my words echoing in the hallway, "That, sir, is a matter of opinion."

15

The next morning, my eyes gritty and swollen, my patience bottomed out and my back ached. Ennis begged me to stay home and get some meaningful sleep but I knew the truth. Sleep was a mere luxury until Abby's killer was found. Besides I might as well adapt to the 'no sleep' policy since I was a month away from delivering Lily. In a few years I could entertain the indulgence of a full quiet night in bed. Till then, not a chance.

Thanks to all the hubbub, my right eyelid developed a relentless twitch that refused to stop no matter how hard I rubbed it. It set in with ferocious tenacity, leaving me to pray no one noticing the annoying quiver.

The medical examiner left a note listing Davenport's cause of death as two gunshots to the head. His postscript was more than discouraging. It stated that submersion in the lake skewed Davenport's time of death, making it practically impossible to nail down to a useable timeframe. Water compromised the rate of decomposition one way or the other, cold water preserved, warm water hastened a body's demise. It didn't matter anyway, I thought. Whether being submerged in cold or warm water, being minced into chunks was the biggest hurdle in that regard. Oh well, I shrugged, setting the note aside. We pretty much knew who killed Bob Davenport. We just needed evidence and that was harder to come by than peace these days.

"I saw your commercial last night," John Mathis poked his head in my office and chuckled. "Nearly choked on my pastrami."

I looked up from my desk, certain that my colleague suffered a disconnect between his ears. My eye didn't believe him, however, and commenced twitching at a faster rate. I tried ignoring it, telling Mathis, "I never made a commercial."

John smoothed a hand down his brown suit coat that sported more wrinkles than a Shar-Pei. His tie lay askew on his round chest and he hadn't shaved that morning. The only official looking part of the man: a legal pad tucked beneath his arm. He peered over his glasses at me and suddenly I felt scrutinized, like he prepared to interrogate me.

"It's for your cooking contest. They showed you and your sister and two other broads they said were your competitors. You're cooking against your cousins?"

The tic kicked into overdrive, fluttering faster than hummingbird wings. A commercial advertising our contest. Wonderful. As if I needed anymore publicity this year. I tried to act casual, "More like showing 'em how it's done." I removed my glasses, "So is it a decent portrayal of me and Georgia?"

Mathis gave me a sideways glance, "Yeah, but the photos of your cousins? Something went awry in the gene pool. They ain't got the looks you two do. Georgia's picture looks great – I think the show used a publicity photo for her."

Naturally. So she'd look more absurdly fantastic than usual. That was no exaggeration. My sister rivaled beauty queens – she was the spitting image of not only our mother but of Rita Hayworth. Yeah. *That* beautiful. My eye double-timed its tempo, forcing me to give it the what-for with my thumb.

Feh, I thought. Who cared? Only the cooking mattered, right? I maintained the theory until Mathis slammed me with, "Your photo was from the Holland sentencing."

I gave up on my eye. When he mentioned Jeffrey Holland, I figured I was destined to frenetically wink all my life. While Georgia wowed the public with her picture, mine would mortify them. By Jeffrey's sentencing, my external wounds had healed but I still suffered emotionally. I figured I resembled the walking dead on the commercial. But, "At least it wasn't a naked baby picture."

"Hey, kid. You look good on TV. Don't worry about it."

There were rare times Mathis possessed a heart beneath his greased-spotted dress shirt. His ties suffered the most over the years since they caught the majority of his hamburger mishaps. Sometimes a slacker, other times a bother and boorish ninety-nine percent of the time, Mathis still cared about me and that meant a lot. When he took a moment to smooth over my hurt feelings with kind words, John's true nature shined.

"Hey, what's wrong with your eye?" he asked.

And sometimes I wanted to kill him... "A nervous tic. Is it any wonder with my family the way it is?"

John stared at my eye a moment longer then shook his head, "I've decided they're either really hated or really misunderstood." Mathis had a way with words. He almost never softened them, electing instead to hammer people with the pure unvarnished truth.

I didn't take offense to the remark, probably because I'd never heard my crazy family described so diplomatically. "Probably both. Some families breed for lawyers or doctors. Ours specialized on breeding drunks and nuts for the most part."

"Mama's or daddy's side?"

Chagrin took over, "Both. Why, do you have something new you can share with the outcast?" I was grateful Josh Hunter assigned the case to Mathis. He'd be fair and thorough, unlike Nesbitt who'd slack or Clark who only seemed interested in carving another notch in her belt.

Mathis peered over his Ben Franklin specs, "I've checked with Abby's neighbors and they put her two shakes away from the mental ward."

"If she'd ended up there, I would have superglued the door shut. Problem solved."

A smile crossed his face, "I can see why your cousins love you so much." He referred to his notes, "The plumber, hairdresser and yard guy ain't sayin' nothin' flattering. The guy at her auto repair shop said, and I quote, 'If the bitch ever called again, I was gonna offer to melt the car down with her in it'. And her neighbors said she kept hosing down their kids when they got in her yard. Even got a motion sensor sprinkler to spray 'em down."

Ah, dearest Abby. Mean enough to sour milk with one look. "See, Mathis? It's not *me*. These people drive others to think bad thoughts. That's why the confessionals and shrinks are so busy. My family keeps them in business."

"Yeah, but that motion sensor – it ain't a bad idea."

I frowned. I'd pistol whip anyone who watered down my kid but I'd also expect my kids to stay off the neighbor's lawn too. "So with that surplus of suspects, you still think Michael killed her?"

"From what I've heard, I wouldn't have minded taking a whack at her myself. Professionally, I have to look harder at him because he threatened to kill her."

I rolled my eyes. People had the tendency to threaten when pushed to their limits. Linda, Teresa and Abby dabbled in harassment the way Leonardo da Vinci tinkered with painting and inventing. They excelled in their medium so successfully I wondered how they survived this long in life without someone taking a swing with a baseball bat. "Mathis, I threatened to kill them all at my mother's funeral." I watched his brow sink but continued anyway, "I tried to follow through on it too and don't," I shook my finger at him, "give me that squinty thing you're doing right now."

I didn't want him labeling me as a suspect along with Michael. It'd been years since the fiasco at Mama's funeral and that was a long time to nurse a grudge without acting on it, I'd say, *then* remind him patience wasn't my biggest virtue.

"Squinty thing?" was all he said.

I defended my statement, "That scrutinizing look you get when you're squeezing perps for information. Don't use that on me. I've got one of my own and I don't want to duel with you."

He shrugged, "Hey, I gotta cover all angles on this case. You just confessed to your own threats of physical harm toward your cousin…"

"Yeah, that took place approximately *many years ago*."

"Your tic is worse." The corners of his mouth kicked up, telling me he was enjoying our bantering. "I could take that as a guilty conscience, you know, or even a confession."

I rubbed my eye again, "John, my life is harassing enough without you adding to my grief."

"Seriously though," he continued, "did Abby suffer from obsessive compulsive disorder?"

Abby suffered from a lot but OCD wasn't exactly the term I would use. Unbalanced, Unhinged, Dingy and Whacko came to mind, not OCD – at least as far as I knew. My silence answered his question and he proceeded, "What's with all the rabbits in her house? Everywhere you look there are bunnies. On shelves, tables, even the floor."

I raised a hand in a stop gesture. Abby was nutty but I hadn't realized she developed a rabbit fetish. Just what the family needed. A bunny aficionado.   Collecting   was   one   thing   but,   "Bunnies everywhere?"

Mathis chuckled at my reaction, "So it's not all in the family. Yeah, rabbits all over the house. I was grateful they weren't real. She had shelves and shelves of 'em. Looked like a Stephen King novel, all those damn little bunnies staring at me."

Without delving too far into my cousin's weirdness, I asked, "Mathis, where was she shot?"

"A .38 slug in the heart."

"You mean she had a heart?"

He ignored me, "The moron who killed her used a pillow as a suppressor. A feather pillow."

"I'll bet it looked like a flock of geese exploded in the room." I hoped Georgia Tech taught better physics than that. Michael seemed intelligent enough to realize that shooting a pillow also resulted in a blizzard of feathers.

"It was messy, yeah." Mathis peered over his glasses at me again, "A witness described a large broad-shouldered figure running from the house after the shot."

"And did the witness identify Michael as the shooter?"

"Nope. Your cousins volunteered him as a suspect. And they mentioned you. Apparently you both rate very high on their love list." He tried that irritating squinty thing again, "Hey, you sure you didn't slip in the house and drill her in a moment of anger? Being knocked up throws the hormones off, you know."

I did a double-take, "Really? You're still suggesting I killed Abby? What's worse, you're suggesting that I'm a large, broad-shouldered figure that could actually *run* from a house after shooting someone."

Mathis merely shrugged, "You do carry a .38."

"I'm also carrying a baby that launches her foot in my ribs when she's upset. Don't you think the sound of a gun discharging might upset her? Geez, John, you've seen me during those moments. I look like I need an exorcism." I pulled my .38 from its holster, sat it on the desk, "But be my guest and test this gun."

Mathis lifted his hands in defeat, "Stop chewing on me. I can't help you got tangled in this case. Besides, I already figured you didn't do it 'cause you wouldn't leave a body."

I flashed a satisfied smile, "*There's* the Mathis I remember. You do know me after all."

He removed the legal pad from under his arm and tossed it onto my desk. It landed with a slap. "Here's what you can do for me. Draw me your family tree. That way, I can try to guess who my next victim or suspect might be."

Disgusted, I replied, "You're not funny."

"I'm not laughing either." His finger tapped the legal pad, "Get busy."

Ennis strolled in, ignored Mathis and his comment, and let a languid grin spread across his lips. Immediately I drew back, "That smile means one of two things." I pointed to my belly, "And one of 'em got me in this shape."

"And frankly, I'm too young to hear this." Mathis stepped to the door, telling me, "If I have any questions for you, I'll be back."

Ennis waited for him to leave then spilled the reason for his joy, "I was hanging out at the sergeant's desk and saw a commercial on TV."

My head dropped into my hand with a resigned sigh, "This is turning into a disaster. I'll be the laughing stock of the department by day's end."

He leaned across the desk, "The uniforms are taking bets on the competition. They ain't betting *against* you, if you catch my drift."

Oh? "Do tell." Most of the uniforms avoided me at crimes scenes. They recoiled when I called their names. My temper and attitude preceded me through the years, even with rookie officers. The only exception: when I brought food to share.   They knew I could cook and bake.   They'd all tasted Georgia's fare at one point or another.   For the uniform officers to toss money into the ring meant they had tremendous faith in mine and Georgia's abilities.   Maybe this whole cooking contest *would* work out…

Ennis's chest broadened with what appeared to be pride, "There's five hundred dollars in the pot already and that's just this shift.   Wait till the nightshift shows up."

"And they're betting on me and Georgia to win?"

He nodded, "That's what the sergeant said.   They're taking bets on *how much* money you win."

"If they knew the depth of Teresa and Linda's culinary ignorance, they'd pool their 401k plans into it also."   Okay, so I bragged.   Georgia and I could win that contest blindfolded.   It wasn't like they regularly interacted with chicken except to buy takeout.

Ennis reached in his suit coat, retrieved a few slips of paper that he handed over, "These guys want invites to the competition.   For them and their wives."

Wow.   Requests.   Glancing through the names I noticed even the sergeant wanted an invitation.   Of course the competition would be aired over local TV and chances were good each person would find a camera aimed at them.   As alluring as that sounded, it lost its appeal when some clod with a camera the size of a bazooka points it three inches away from your nose demanding a critique of the food.   I spared my ego the notion these cops just wanted TV time and that they *really* wanted to support me and Georgia.

I tucked the list of names in an upper desk drawer, "I'll get the list to Andrew and his staff later today. We can't forget Clark and Nesbitt either." In the meantime, "How about we go to Blackstone and poke around? There might be something Metcalf or Ramos missed."

Ennis wrinkled his nose. He considered it for a several seconds then, "Forensics went over the place. What did *they* miss?"

I rose from my seat which took far more effort than it should have, "We won't know until we get there."

My darling hubby rolled his eyes with a mild curse. He'd spent the last half hour around "the guys", talking about wagers and bragging about how his wife and sister-in-law would win without even trying. Ennis never presented himself as a braggart but throw me in the mix and he strutted. I thought he was nuts. No one bragged on me. Ever. I drove my parents and siblings crazy with my antics and rebellions. I drank my friends under the table in my younger years. Most of my boyfriends were losers and my partners treated me like a whining four year-old. So Ennis's crowing flattered me but it also grated me to a degree because I wasn't used to it.

"C'mon, cowboy," I called with a wink. "Let's check out the restaurant then you can hang with the fellas again later."

16

Against Ennis's wishes, we drove to Blackstone Restaurant for our own search of the place. Snapshots and drawings only gave the two dimensional aspect, I told him, and we needed to see for ourselves what Metcalf and Ramos wrote about in their investigation. Sometimes what made sense to one person didn't gee and haw with another. One of the most important lessons of being a detective: never completely trust another detective's investigation.

We pulled into the parking lot of the old red brick building. The architecture and arched windows flanking the heavy wooden door gave it a quaint appearance, like an old Irish pub. Located in a historic part of town that fell into some disrepair in the seventies and eighties, Blackstone, along with other area businesses, was cherry picked in the early nineties for revitalization. According to city records, a rich entrepreneur bought the place and opened Virtue & Vice, a restaurant/bar. It stayed in business until Bob Davenport bought it many years later and renamed it Blackstone. Despite his money problems, Davenport kept the restaurant squeaky clean according to health department records – until he brought his brand new son-in-law into the picture. The health department stayed mighty busy after that, yet the business remained open and thrived. Those two points clashed with me and I sought to discover why.

A young, fresh-faced officer stood sentry at the front doorway crisscrossed with yellow tape. A person can always tell a rookie by their assignments. Besides desk duty or writing tickets, security is the dullest job in our occupation. Officer Reynolds leaned against the brick wall next to the door, hands in pockets and looking quite bored and a bit sleepy.

I heaved myself from the detective's car and shut the door. Reynolds snapped to attention and hurriedly donned his cap.

"Afternoon, detectives," he nodded at the sight of our shields.

"Afternoon. Keeping this place nice and tight?" I asked.

He blushed, "Yes, ma'am. No one gets past me."

Ennis and I slipped on latex gloves, a little smile crossing my lips. Oh, I remembered the first year on the job. Eager to please but not brown-nose. Determined to change the world, make it a better place. Oh yeah, I thought with a mental eye roll. Rookies really needed a reality check and by year's end they usually got one.

We ducked beneath the tape and Ennis inserted the key to unlock the door. The door swung open to a large dim room with a bar along one wall, the shelves well stocked with various liquors. The main room held several heavy dark wooden tables and chairs to match. I gave Davenport credit. Inside and outside, the place had the ambiance of a typical Irish pub. It also had a musty smell mixed with the slight chemical odor of new carpet. Then an unexpected odor drifted to me – the hint of pipe tobacco. The smell hung heavier than it should have. I whispered to Ennis, "Someone's been in here today."

He sniffed the air and nodded. A thin veil of smoke shrouded the room, clearly visible in the muted light filtering through the curtains. I leaned closer, pointing to the cloudy interior, "I think they're still here."

I leaned out the front door, whispering, "Did you let anyone in today?"

Reynolds shook his head, "No ma'am. I was informed only you and Detective Rutherford were allowed inside."

Newsflash, Rookie. Me and Detective Rutherford weren't the only people in the place. Ennis and I simultaneously turned toward the empty room, reaching for our guns. Crime scene tape blocked off the front and back entrances so no one except police had authorization to be inside the building. How had someone breached the place if it was constantly being guarded by our trusty, bored rookies?

Ennis kept nudging me behind him. It annoyed me but I understood why. One nutcase with a gun and a jerky trigger finger and our daughter might get hit. I dutifully stepped back while he continued forward.

A noise at the rear of the restaurant alerted us that the kitchen was the place to concentrate on. I scouted our surroundings while Ennis forged on. Movement from the corner of my vision trained my gun straight ahead. The mystery person in the kitchen didn't seem to care that he or she had broken the law. The figure moved again, this time giving me a better view of him. A fit, trim redheaded male in his mid-twenties dressed in Dockers and Kelly green polo shirt moved about the small room as if the place was open for business. Between his teeth he held a pipe that appeared old and hand-carved, like an heirloom.

When he turned and caught sight of our guns, a smile brightened his impish face. Leaving the pipe clamped between his teeth, he raised his hands in surrender. A smile curled his mouth and a thick Irish brogue emerged, "Ah, me fair lass. 'Tis just me, no worries."

Yeah, as if that might loosen the grip on my .38. "Who the hell is *me*?" I demanded.

He slowly extended his hand, "Troy Quinn, of course. Such a lovely sight you are and a pleasure it is to meet you. Well, except for the peashooter, that is. That's a disappointing drawback."

The guy sounded like the Lucky Charms leprechaun with a crazy accent. *That* became *dat* and *sight* emerged *soight*. If my heart hadn't been bouncing against my ribs in sheer panic, I might have found the humor. Troy Quinn, Bob Davenport's son-in-law and Metcalf's primary suspect stood smack in the middle of a potential crime scene. And he smiled about it.

"Keep those hands up," Ennis warned. "Or you're liable to discover that peashooter's trigger is mighty touchy."

Quinn's hand lifted again, "Sorry, friend. No harm meant."

"How the hell did you get in here anyway?" Ennis barked, tightening the grip on his gun.

Quinn laughed, looked to me, "Well, he's as rough as a bear's arse, isn't he? I used me key to get in. It's in me pocket here. Fancy me to get it for ya?"

I answered the question, "I fancy you to keep your hands where I can see them. If you noticed, there's crime scene tape blocking the doorways of the restaurant. That means keep out for everyone except the police. Why are you here, Mr. Quinn?"

"It's my business, don'tcha see, lass? I *should* and *will* be here."

The last of his statement fell like boulders. A challenge to the police. I hated people like this. The ones who called me nice names while believing they were smarter than me.

"It's Bob Davenport's business," I corrected, "and you're trespassing."

Mr. Charms ignored every word I spoke. Quinn took his pipe in hand, "Ah, but where are me manners? Have a seat while pointing yer guns. Be more comfortable, 'specially for you, Mother." The unexpected term of endearment sounded like Mudder, not Mother. Oh boy, were we going to have fun interpreting Mr. Quinn, I thought.

Ennis stepped forward to search him for weapons. I kept a solid grip on my .38. Quinn was a bold bastard, sneaking into the restaurant through the back door. It made me wonder how long he'd been holed up in there and what he'd been doing.

Quinn jerked with surprise when Ennis's hand brushed up then down one pants leg then the other. "Listen, friend," said the thick Irish brogue, "there's a particular etiquette yer overlookin' if ya touch me there and I'm not of that persuasion in the first place."

He'd evidently meant it as a joke but we hadn't laughed. He shrugged at our lack of humor, "So're ya here to roust me from me establishment again? 'Cause a man's gotta make a livin' and that yella tape 'cross the door doesn't inspire appetites."

"That tape means stay out, even for you," Ennis searched Quinn's pockets to find a fat wallet and set of keys. He placed both on the table then reached back for his handcuffs.

A flame of Quinn's temper flared. "Now, now, Officer. Let's be reasonable," he said despite his expression implying otherwise. "I've done nothin' wrong. It's that fekkin' fat cop's allegations that have ya jaded. No surprise the heinous eejit dropped of a blessed heart attack. A blight on yer police force, he is."

I tried not to notice the way he pronounced *force* as *farce*. I nearly smiled but for the way his right eye twitched. For an instant a cold shudder raked down my back. That one simple gesture remedied any fallacies that Troy Quinn was simply a big-mouthed punk. This man was cunning and definitely dangerous, no matter how cutesy he acted.

Ennis grabbed his hand only for Quinn to sling it away, "*May the curse of Mary Malone and her nine blind illegitimate children chase that cop so far over the hills of Damnation that the Lord himself can't find him with a telescope.* I'm tellin' ya, he's spreadin' poison. Now *you*," he pointed directly at me. "You surprise me, lass. I thought of the lot of ya cops, you'd be less apt to believe frivolous accusations from the boys in blue."

Not that it mattered but, "What is that supposed to mean?"

"The female gender and yer colored brethren have had struggles with yer job and they were all due to assumptions and allegations from fat white men carrying that same badge. I expect you've had yer share of verbal abuse over the years. The term cold-hearted dyke, perhaps –"

Ennis bowed up, grabbed Quinn's wrist in a brutal grasp, and locked a cuff around it, "Watch your mouth, Quinn. There ain't no witnesses to the beating I'll give you if you don't."

"It's a fer instance, friend. Get a grip on yer panties. My point is that gack's got the lot of you spreadin' his poison. What did ya say yer name was, lass?"

I spoke evenly, making sure to precisely articulate my name so he'd never forget, "Detective Savannah Prince."

There was less venom in his words, "Ah, yes. Prince. An' I expect yer lineage is from across the pond. Sounds either English or French."

My better judgment kicked in and I kept quiet. He led up to something and I doubted I'd like it. I really loathed the way he pronounced the word *either* with a long *I*, like a hoity-toity snob putting down the blue collar crowd.

That was until the corner of his mouth lifted, "So which is it? Are you the seed, breed and spawn of a French or English whore?"

...And my better judgment immediately vacated the building. No one insulted me then leapfrogged to my family. Protocol dictated I grab my gun and aerate the bastard like Swiss cheese but my fists itched to pound the grin off the smug Irishman's face. I bulled toward him with fists doubled to show him just how effectively this Heinz 57 English and French mix could kick his ass.

But Ennis used physical leverage to make his point. One solid shove bent Quinn over, his forehead striking the solid wooden table with a sick thud. My husband, his hand still holding Quinn by one handcuff, pressed the man's face against the tabletop until Quinn cringed. "I warned you," Ennis growled. "One more word from your sleazy mouth– "

"There's no need for violence," Quinn remained still, not moving a muscle. "I wanted to show her how it felt to have lies spoken 'bout ya."

Ennis didn't buy it, "I said keep your mouth shut." Then he shot a searing glare my way, "Are you nuts? Trying to fight him in your condition?"

Okay, so old habits died hard but I'd bet a hundred bucks he'd jump Quinn if the bastard insulted Mama Rutherford that way. Why should I have acted any different about my mama?

Quinn winked, "Got a drop of Irish blood in ya, lass? Ya scrap like ya do."

No one in their right mind taunted a cop – two cops, actually. Before I spouted what came to mind, I clenched my teeth to trap the words. I'd underestimated Troy Quinn. He not only mastered the art of wise-ass but was unquestionably more dangerous than I imagined.

Ennis finished handcuffing Quinn and we both escorted him outside to the uniform officer. Reynolds' jaw dropped at the sight. My once good humor with him vanished, "Wouldn't kill you to do a sweep once in a while. This guy's been coming and going in there for God knows how long."

"How the hell did he get in?" Reynolds asked.

I stated the obvious, "There *is* a back door and he had a key." The latter I dangled between my thumb and forefinger. I plopped it into Reynold's palm just as his chagrin deepened to a third degree blush.

The rookie profusely apologized but movement diverted my

attention across the street. Two men in khakis and dark blue jackets stood with arms crossed, watching the scene unfold. They, like Quinn, displayed an arrogant tilt of their chins and a piercing stare. Both appeared to be in their late twenties, lean and muscled. Both focused on me and Ennis, their gazes so intense I nearly turned away. Neither of them looked particularly happy. After a few seconds, five more men joined them, these appearing less refined than Blue Jackets. My first impression – they were knuckle-cracking thugs.

"Ennis," I cut my vision to the scene across the way.

"I see 'em." Without leaving my side, he addressed the agitated assembly, "Unless you're aimin' to share a cell with this fella, you'd best move along."

Long, uneasy moments passed. They stood their ground, challenging us since they considerably outnumbered us and I had a distinct disadvantage being pregnant. Another ten excruciating seconds ticked away. My hand eased back to my holster. I wasn't sure what transpired in the last few minutes but I'd shoot first and ask questions later if need be. Blue Jackets turned to the group who subsequently dispersed, each man headed his own way. But the Blue Jackets stayed behind, still watching. Best to move things along, I thought. I looked at Reynold's who resumed apologizing. I leaned closer to him so Quinn didn't hear, "Be more careful from now on or you'll be saying *sorry* to mine and Detective Rutherford's families. I want my kid to grow up knowing me, not knowing *about* me. Take Mr. Quinn to jail and book him for trespassing and log that magic key into evidence."

"Yes, ma'am. Right away."

Reynolds gathered up Quinn, took him to the cruiser parked next to our Ford. I turned to Ennis, took a deep breath, "Now that was unnerving. Felt like West Side Story."

"Or the Godfather," he added.

"You'll regret this, lassie!" Quinn shouted from the cruiser. "Yer jumpin' from the bucket into the fire!"

"It's frying pan into the fire!" I yelled back then mumbled, "You moron." I motioned for us to go back inside. Quinn's arrogance confused me. He wore handcuffs, was read his rights and carted off to jail yet it didn't overly disturb him.

Ennis and I headed back in but I refused to holster my .38. No telling what other surprises awaited us inside. This time when we walked in, I looked past the furniture to the stained glass lamps hung throughout, casting a soft glow in the room. That combined with dark wood paneled walls gave it a slightly creepy, dungeon-like atmosphere. No cheap furniture or booze, nothing to reflect Bob Davenport's once scarlet red credit rating. Everything ventured downhill financially until good ol' Troy Quinn stepped in. He turned it into a profitable, popular hangout even with a rotten health department record.

I headed to the kitchen that had seen better days. Grease buildup on exhaust hoods and stove spelled impending kitchen fire. The floor seemed slightly more acceptable, save for the gaps between the stove, fryer and fridge that collected sticky black gunk an inch thick. This place was a nightmare which explained why the health department spent reams of paper slamming the place with infractions.

"*Don't touch anything*," Ennis warned behind me. "There's

probably rats in here. Rattle something and it'll turn into a horror movie."

I shuddered, "Thank you for that image. Until then, I hadn't thought of rats, mice and roaches the size of Chevys."

Ahead of me was a closed door. It was, quite possibly, the cleanest item in the kitchen. The gold doorknob shone bright in the dim room like it was frequently used. But the cabinet to my right caught my attention. The storage area usually used for hand towels and such items had a wide door about knee level that stood cracked open. I reached toward the door only have *I said don't touch anything* hissed in my ear. Ennis followed up with, "Remember the horror movie I mentioned? That's the door to hell right there."

I frowned back at him, "Well, someone's gotta open it. There might be important evidence in there."

He returned the frown, reached in his pocket for a hanky and shook it out, "Yeah. Evidence of vermin. I'll remind you of your words when I'm taking the rabies shots. Move."

I stepped away to let him closer. He covered his hand with the hanky, reached forward then hesitated. After a deep breath, he yanked the door open and clambered backward, waiting for the mass exodus of rodents. It didn't happen. Instead, we both stood staring at a brand new shiny butcher's saw.

Feeling braver now, Ennis bent down with his flashlight and shined the beam across the saw's teeth, "Looks like blood."

Uh, well, "It *is* used in a restaurant." When his brow sank, I rephrased, "But we'll get forensics to check it for human blood, I totally agree." Metcalf's report didn't include a reference to a band saw in the evidence. I hoped the Mighty Quinn snuck in and deposited this jewel of evidence thinking we were finished with our search. Or likely he just didn't care. Either way, we'd get forensics to check it out.

To Ennis's disgust, I turned to the mysterious closed door.

"Always pushing your luck, aren't you? You know that door on Let's Make a Deal? The one with the smelly jackass and a wagon full of turds? The booby prize? That's exactly what this door is. We pass the threshold of that door and some idiot will walk in and slam it behind us. We need Mathis here to stand watch."

"We don't have Mathis. Mathis is too busy unwinding my twisted family tree to find out who killed Abby. I estimate half the county should be suspects but hey, who am I? Just a relative."

"Good afternoon, detectives!"

I jumped like someone shot me which systematically caused Lily to seize up. She kicked straight out, missed my liver and hit a rib causing a lasting, reverberating pain akin to a baseball bat slamming into a metal pole. I cradled my side and cringed, "That better be God at the door 'cause He's the only one I won't maim for yelling at me."

Ennis tended to me, leaving only after I assured him I wasn't having a heart attack. "It's not God," he called, dragging in another uniform officer. This guy, like Reynolds, was fresh from the academy with his crisp, new uniform on. "It's another rookie."

The young officer looked about twenty-one, stood my height with hardly a pound on him, his short sandy blonde hair combed straight up Bart Simpson style.

I forced a smile once the kid realized his mistake of yelling at us. "For the record," I stated mildly, "yelling usually causes knee-jerk reactions from other cops. Be glad my baby occupied my hands or I'd have instinctively drawn down on you."

"Sorry 'bout that. Reynolds radioed that he needed a replacement so here I am. Officer Curtis McNeal at your service."

"Great," I said minus the enthusiasm he probably expected. "Do us a favor. Stand guard at this door and don't let it close on us. If it *should* close, you'll find out how crazy a hormonal, pregnant woman can get."

He positioned himself by the door and Ennis squeezed in front of me, "I'll go first. You shoot the first rat that tries to climb my leg." He opened the door to a yawning black hole. A dank odor wafted past. *Horror movie hell. Thanks, Ennis. Just the image I needed.*

Flicking on his flashlight again, Ennis swept the beam through the darkness. The creaky old stairs lead to rows of wine racks and cases of beer lined up like soldiers in formation.

The basement presented a slightly better impression than the kitchen in that at least the liquor only showed dust, not a thick layer of grease. We descended a few steps when my hand brushed a switch. I flipped it on which triggered a riotous swearing streak from Ennis. He wheeled to me, his hand pressed to his heart, "God sakes, woman. Just shoot me or shove me down the stairs next time. That scared me."

"Sorry," I flipped the switch, cloaking the room in inky blackness again. "Guess I'll just let you fall down the stairs then."

Ennis turned the lights back on. He turned to me, deadpanning,

"Funny. Hilarious. But can you shoot a rat?"

"I shot Cole Jordan, didn't I?" We descended the stairs slowly until reaching the bottom stair.

Ennis removed a wine bottle from a nearby rack, blew a cloud of dust off and read the label, "Petrus Pomerol, 1998. Is this a good wine?"

"Wouldn't know," I replied, still searching for critters with hairless tails. "My specialty was Jack Daniels, any year." Once I gave up the hunt, I turned my attention past the stacks of beer cases to the wooden wine racks stuffed with old dust-covered bottles. It amazed me how people hoarded those things. Buy a wine then mothball it for twenty or thirty years. When I bought, it was to consume immediately.

A scuffle of feet drew my attention away from my task. Ennis stepped back to let a gray mouse skitter by, "Great. He'll tell his whole family they have company and greet us en masse."

I armed myself with a nearby broom but that impressed him even less, "What're you gonna do? Clean the place up?"

Leaning down, I saw the mouse huddling in the corner, "I'm getting him out of our way since you harbor such animosity against mice."

The mouse made a run for the wine rack against the back wall and I took a swing at him. The broom's bristles nailed Mickey across the butt and after a brief high-pitched squeak, he darted along the wall and behind a case of imported beer.

I gave the wine rack another hefty whack for good measure – in case Mickey's relatives hung out there too. My action sent the heavy rack backwards an inch or two against the wall. I cringed, waiting for the resulting crash of shattering wines bottles on concrete. Thankfully the only sound was an echoing thud as wood met wall. But the noise hadn't sounded right.

"What was that?" Ennis asked.

I didn't know, I said, so we turned our attention to the back wall now. I nudged the wine rack against the wall once more. The same hollow echo filled the room. Stepping a few feet to the side of the rack, I rapped on the concrete wall. It sounded solid unlike the wall behind the rack. Ennis pushed then pulled the rack slightly, testing it. With a little muscle, the rack moved.

He pushed it along the wall and into the corner. The wine rack concealed a well constructed concrete façade. Only a close discerning eye would have spied the fine seam where the façade met real concrete and the wine rack was built to clearly hide it. That explained how Metcalf, Ramos and the forensics team missed it.

Ennis unfolded his pocket knife, lodged it in the well-worn edge at the bottom of the façade. He pried it loose, shoved it behind the wine rack. We stood in mute shock at what it revealed. We stared into a pitch black cavernous hole in the wall that resembled a gigantic mouse hole. The opening had been crudely carved into the stone basement wall.

Ennis gave the opening a cursory glance, "I have a feeling we're not in Kansas anymore."

"And I figure *this* is your door to hell right here." I retrieved my flashlight, switched it on, shining it into the darkness. It revealed a long, arch shaped tunnel that went on farther than my flashlight beam. This couldn't be good. Secret, hidden areas never improved a cop's day, and exploring them practically guaranteed a disastrous day.

"I'm not sure I want to go in there," Ennis stated flatly.

Spelunking that hole wasn't the highlight of my day either, considering the whole tunnel measured about my current width. My claustrophobia reminded me of the misery I'd suffer if I stepped foot into that cave. My heart already raced and my lungs squeezed tight in my chest at the prospect of heading inside it.

Old, flat cut stones reinforced the arch-shaped tunnel, giving it an ancient drab gray hue when I shined my flashlight into it. It looked medieval. It looked small and it looked perfect for hiding secrets.

"You can't go three feet in there without going nuts," Ennis said incredulously. "You'll have to stay here."

Thanks for that *nuts* comment, I wanted to say but he was right. I could do it but I'd pay dearly. "Well, you aren't going alone. God knows what's at the end of this thing, if anything at all." I glanced at my .38, "Let's just avoid using these unless we enjoy being deaf."

Ennis shook his head in disbelief at the tunnel, "I swore this trip was a waste of time. I won't question your sixth sense again."

With both flashlights blazing, we ducked under the tunnel's low ceiling and stepped into the dank, musty smell. Ennis first, me second – as he directed.

We headed further into the bowels of the passageway, my heart slammed against my ribs and the sweat seeped to the surface. My gut implored me to back out but I refused to leave Ennis. The tunnel traveled straight ahead for several feet then abruptly turned right. One glance behind me threw me into total darkness and unease. We hadn't even told the uniform we'd found this place or that we were exploring the newly discovered depths. Images of being locked inside the tiny channel mushroomed fear into near panic. We might die down here, I thought. *Our daughter* might die.

My flashlight beam swept across something odd. I stopped, taking Ennis by the wrist, "What is that?" I shined the light at the wall near the floor, highlighting a stripe of brownish red measuring around six inches wide. It smeared the wall along the pathway from where we stood toward the uncharted area ahead.

Ennis hunkered down for a closer look. "Might be blood. Let's have forensics check. Let's follow it."

Yes, let's, I thought with profound sarcasm. Let's follow the red brick road to our *own* demise.

Ennis straightened a little, "I think I see an opening ahead of us."

Thank God. A ray of hope. I needed it because my breathing grew ragged, panic replaced decent judgment and common sense. The walls appeared to close in, creating an impossible obstacle to overcome. I really needed out fast or I *would* go nuts, as Ennis so eloquently stated.

We ventured further while I employed Seth's breath control strategy to calm down. Deep breath, hold, count to ten, then slowly release the breath then repeat. It failed miserably. The sheen of sweat doubled into droplets that rolled down my forehead and started down my back. I was losing the entire battle. "Ennis," I gasped, stopping short of asking for help.

He turned, saw my panic and put his arms around me to comfort me, "We're just about out, sugar. Close your eyes, take deep breaths."

I followed his instructions, allowing his embrace to wrap me in his strength, his effortless calm. My heart rioted in my chest while his continued a slow, steady rhythm. My shaking body clung to him, grateful he was there and ashamed I'd let him down. So much for being his dependable backup.

A soft cloth bathed the sweat from my brow and face. Ennis always brought two handkerchiefs, his "blowin' rag" and one for other emergencies. This constituted as a full out, five alarm emergency to me but his embrace and soft words eased the wild rampant terror. I wasn't sure how long we stood there, me trembling in his arms on the verge of tears *and* fainting but eventually the tide of panic retreated to a manageable degree.

Ennis stroked my cheek, "I admire you for coming in here but I hate that you're suffering."

I nodded, held his hand, as tears trembled in my eyes. I really wanted out of that cave. Sensing my thoughts, Ennis squeezed my hand, led me forward, "It opens up down here, I think. Maybe you can settle down then."

It did open up into an underground room about as large as three prison cells and just as quaint. Narrow makeshift shelves lined one wall. A few folding chairs, lined together, faced the room's front where another makeshift entrance/exit stood. Great. Another damn tunnel. My day just kept getting brighter however, since entering the somewhat larger room, my claustrophobia leveled out to barely tolerable which helped.

What the hell had we stumbled on, I wondered, finally able to think straighter. I thought of the Underground Railroad but the building's age nixed that idea. Blackstone was once a family home in the early nineteen hundreds. Over the years the city grew around the once residential area, forcing families to other parts to gain peace and quiet from traffic and business. Blackstone's history as a restaurant began in the sixties then the last few years evolved to what it was now.

So what was the tunnel for anyway? It had been around for many decades according to the sight of it. The only other answer that came to mind: a bootlegger tunnel. During prohibition, some Southerners brewed moonshine and bootlegged the hooch to keep their families fed. I'd read about such tunnels but not in Atlanta. The room we currently stood in looked like an ideal place to store illegal alcohol, at least to me. Problem was I felt convinced Troy Quinn used it for something far more sinister, otherwise why not have those chairs upstairs?

The more I stared at the room, the more it looked like a staging area for performances.

A sparkle of light on the floor caught my attention. Glancing down, I saw a gold earring glinting against my flashlight beam. Donning a latex glove, I picked up the delicate jewelry. "Ennis, look at this." He eased around the chairs to meet me. The earring was made for a triple pierced ear. Three miniature hearts connected with a dainty gold chain dangling between them – except the chain had been broken. I tilted the earring and noticed what looked like blood on the back, "It was yanked out."

Ennis reached in his suit jacket for a small evidence bag, handed it to me, "Maybe forensics can match the DNA. We could use a break on this case."

I dropped the earring in, sealed the bag and pocketed it, "Did you find anything?"

He shook his head and I motioned for us to go, "Then let's get out of here." I braced myself to enter the tunnel at the back. This one was entirely more rudimentary and slightly smaller. If claustrophobia killed, I was dying by degrees. I really needed a hug. I needed Ennis's reassuring embrace but I also needed to protect my husband in the crazy Alice in Wonderland nightmare. I kept my flashlight pointed ahead along with my weapon, though neither of them were very steady. The phobia crept back slowly and I struggled to control it. Ennis needed me, not a heap of crazy on his hands.

Evidently, Ennis saw the trembling .38 in my hands and heard my shallow, ragged gasps for air, "Put your gun away and hold on to me."

"No," I squeezed the word from my shrinking lungs.

"Savannah, do it. I don't need you accidentally shooting me." Then his voice softened, "Let me handle this. Put your gun away."

I did, making sure my free hand remained on his back. As we traversed further into the black abyss, the tunnel veered to the left then straight ahead. I'd lost track of Blackstone's location above us but I guessed we headed East in the direction of another block of old homes/businesses. "How much further?" I asked, battling the total raving insanity rising inside.

"It ends up ahead from what I see. We'll have to climb."

"I don't care. I'll *claw* my way out if need be." We went another twenty feet or so until meeting a stone wall with an old ladder built into it. Black iron rungs jutted from the rough stones. Two things went through my mind. One, I prayed the rungs held a woman the size of Shamu and two, I prayed the wooden door above us accommodated a woman my size.

Ennis clamped his flashlight between his teeth and climbed the ladder. One good heave on the door and it creaked open. He ascended far enough to poke his head into our destination and inspected it for bad guys and probably rodents. Evidently he didn't see either one because he descended again, "Go on up. I'll help you."

"Gonna put your shoulder into it, huh?" I goaded.

"Just making sure you don't fall," he diplomatically replied.

I climbed the medieval ladder carefully, wishing I had three hands, two for the ladder and one for my gun in case someone surprised us. I found my way up the ladder and into the new area which turned out to be a small room like a closet. I'd never get fresh air again, I bemoaned. Everything was small and musty and driving my claustrophobia off the charts.

Ennis climbed in behind me, his front brushing my back for lack of space. He opened the closet's door and we entered another room, this one somewhat larger. Finally a spark of hope. It resembled an old garage or shed with stacks of dusty boxes lining the walls left and right of us. A rake, shovel, hoe and other yard tools leaned against a far corner. We'd gone underground at Blackstone and popped up in someone's shed.

Ennis and I made our way through another door ahead that opened into a house. A house in need of serious care. A thick layer of dust caked kitchen counters and furniture. The placed smelled closed up for centuries. I wondered aloud about who'd lived here. Ennis replied,

"We'll check on that as soon as we get back. Be interesting to find out because that tunnel's been used a lot lately and this place hadn't been lived in for years."

17

When we returned to the station, we handed over the earring to forensics. We let Quinn cool his heels in his cell while forensics collected blood samples from the tunnel. By late afternoon, we knew two things. One, Quinn owned the musty old house and two, the blood in the tunnel matched Bob Davenport, at least in type. We'd wait for DNA to prove it was actually Davenport but we had plenty to discuss with Quinn without it.

Ennis had a uniform take Troy Quinn to an interview room and as we headed to the room, we heard Quinn boisterously singing an old Irish song, "For you were all I had, Mary, my blessing and my pride, And I've nothing left to care for now since my poor Mary died..."

I looked at Ennis who blew out a breath, shook his head, "You'd think by now I'd be used to weirdos after meeting your family but singing when he's chin high in shit?"

"And often in those grand old woods I'll sit and shut my eyes," Quinn proceeded with his song, "And my heart will wander back again to the place where Mary lies..."

My patience with the bold Irishman wore thin. Whatever his intentions were by singing, all it did was make my head hurt. I opened the interview room door, putting an abrupt stop to the musical interlude. Quinn sat, leaned back in his chair, handcuffed hands in his lap, his feet kicked onto the table. The man certainly made himself at home. He flashed a pleasant smile at me, "Ya feelin' alright, Mother? Ya look pale."

I laid my notes and evidence folder on the table and forced a smile, "You're a regular Lothario with that charm, Quinn."

Ennis followed me in. His expression warning Troy Quinn against any remarks considered inflammatory. Quinn ignored him, instead he focused on me, "An' what brings the lovely lass to see me?"

I eased into the uncomfortable metal chair across from him, "My partner and I finished searching Blackstone."

"While you were there did ya find that wayward sock I lost a while back? Been after it for months."

My smile belied my inner loathing for this man, "No socks. Instead we found an interesting feature of your wine cellar. There's a tunnel that pops up into a garage on the next block. It's also got a room with several chairs set up for some kind of show or meeting. What kind of meetings do you hold in that room, Mr. Quinn, and what is that tunnel used for?"

Troy Quinn's expression darkened. He never expected his tunnel to be discovered and now he was angry. He leaned forward now, his eyes narrowing, "I don't know what yer talking about, Mother. And if I were you, I'd tread lightly with future inquiries."

Funny how he used the term *Mother* to intimidate and threaten me. As funny as Darren Metcalf's heart attack. "We also found blood in that passageway," I pushed. "Blood matching Bob Davenport. How do you explain that?"

A long uneasy pause ensued. Normally that meant the suspect weighed his options by gauging our expressions and words for signs of bluffing or lying. Quinn did none of that. His steady gaze shifted to Ennis, "Maybe you'll listen for her. We Irish have a saying. *Don't be breaking yer shin on a stool that's not in yer way.*"

Ennis bowed up, "Explain how Davenport's blood ended up in that tunnel. We've got witness accounts of yelling, of you arguing with Davenport the night he disappeared. You suddenly replaced the restaurant's carpet after that argument. Now we find blood in that tunnel. We also found this down there too." He opened the folder containing a picture of the earring, "What are you using that tunnel for, Quinn?"

"Are ya farcing me to call ma lawyer? Ya have no evidence I committed a crime so I'm free to go, yeah?"

"No. We arrested you for trespassing, remember?" I leaned closer, "Listen, that tunnel pops up on a property recently purchased by you. The previous owners mysteriously died in a car accident two years ago then you snap the property up. That's not a coincidence."

Quinn casually bent forward to meet my gaze. "I suppose a more American expression is in order, so you'll both understand. I can't make me sentiments clearer except to say…"

Troy Quinn cut loose with a true American phrase alright. A two word phrase beginning with an *F* and ending with *You.* Ennis shot from his chair, his fists white-knuckled with rage. I scrambled to restrain my husband while putting Quinn on notice, "We'll find out what you're up to and when we do, we'll put you *under* the jail."

A knocking on the one-way mirror intensified to a solid pounding. That signaled my boss either having apoplexy or a stroke.

Quinn shook his head, "Now, now, Mother. Yer lettin' yer hormones have their way with ya. You've got Babaí to nurse later." He whispered, "Ya wouldn't want anythin' happening to ya or the little one."

Now *my* fist bunched as I leaned forward, "You really don't want to threaten my baby, Quinn."

Ennis took the precaution of grabbing my throwing arm before I cut loose with a right hook on Lucky. "Let's go, Savannah," my hubby urged, gently wrestling me from the room. The second I stepped out of the room, Josh Hunter leveled me with the frown from Hell.

Ennis slammed the interview room door shut as Josh clamped his hands to his hips, "You're a crazy woman. Certifiable. You provoke this guy into threatening you and Lily?" He rubbed his forehead, "You really need to consider another career once you have kids. You're endangering your unborn child when you poke sticks at Quinn. He basically said so."

Yes, he had. And it enraged me. All my life I fought aggressors. My father, my uncle, people in the department, the mayor, Jeffrey and Cole... I'd spent my life swinging either physically or verbally. I'd fallen into my old habits by prodding Quinn. Now I just prayed I hadn't let my mouth write a check my ass couldn't cash...

18

If dealing with Quinn wasn't bad enough, my husband refused to let me sleep. Between his snoring and tossing and turning, it took three hours for me to drift off. Then, at three fifteen in the morning, he nudged me awake, "There's someone banging on our door. I'm gonna see who it is."

"I'll go too," I replied half-heartedly. I figured my nutty relatives stood outside, pounding on the door with new demands or problems. Ennis didn't deserve facing the crazy alone, I thought.

By the time I sat up in bed and swiveled out, the phone began ringing. I rubbed my eyes, "Good and decent people are in bed," I told the phone as if it could comprehend my aggravation. I scooped up the phone and answered it, mumbling a sluggish greeting.

"Your car is on fire!" a panicked male voice yelled in my ear. "I called the fire department but you gotta get out of the house before it goes up too!"

"Huh?" was all that came to my weary, sleep-leaden mind. Someone was telling me my car was aflame and for some reason the information hadn't reached the panic button in my brain.

"*Fire!*" the person screamed in my ear. "*Get out!*"

The words and inflection not only pushed the panic button, it shoved it all the way to China. "Ennis, get my robe. There's a fire." I glanced at the caller's name – Edward Collins, our next door neighbor.

Ennis threw my robe around my shoulders and I slid my arms through and shouldered the phone while I secured the robe at my waist. "We're on our way, Edward. Thank you."

Ennis shrugged on his robe over his pajamas like I had. We gathered our badges, guns and I grabbed my purse just in case the place was already ablaze.

He grabbed my arm and tugged me along – as if I couldn't race out the door myself, I thought. "That's who's been pounding on our door," he said.

My husband, the master of understatement. We neared the front door and I began smelling the caustic fumes of a car fire. The thin veil of smoke hanging in the living room triggered a coughing spell and I prayed the fire department arrived before the house caught fire. We'd not lived there a year and if it burned to the ground, it would end me.

We passed by the coat rack and I grabbed my wool coat and Ennis's overcoat. If we were braving the chill outside, we'd do it bundled up because we had enough problems already without suffering hypothermia.

I watched him press his palms against the front door, checking for heat. He glanced back at me, "You ready?"

No, I was quite sure I was *not* ready for what awaited us on the other side of that door. Edward prepared me the best he could but once Ennis flung open the door, the sight paralyzed us. Nothing prepared us for what we were witnessing. My blood sank to my toes and dizziness swept in at the sight. Ennis sensed my unsteadiness and put his arm around me.

The smell of burning rubber, metal and fabric filled the neighborhood in a thick, acrid, billowing fog. My Camaro was alive with fire. Flames danced along the hood and roof while others stretched like eager yellow and orange fingers from beneath the wheel wells.

Shattering glass forced us back a step, the sound punctuating the once silent morning as heat and flame punched its way out of the windshield and side windows. The light from the fire illuminated half the block and the fierce heat emanating only emboldened the blaze threatening our large oak and the Collins' magnolia tree. The whole surreal scene resembled a bad dream. I heard myself cry, "My car. My beautiful car."

At first I thought I'd imagined it but Ennis's tightening embrace confirmed the words had indeed fallen from my trembling lips. Flames engulfed my magnificent, loyal Camaro, leaving it groaning as if pleading for help.

Edward Collins rushed over from next door still dressed in his suit and overcoat, "I called the fire department as soon as I drove up. Are you guys okay?"

I'd never be okay. I realized the Camaro was only a car. A means to travel from Point A to Point B but she'd been a sturdy beast, and endured a lot in her long life. It broke my heart to see the calamity before me. My Chevy was gone.

Sirens neared while Edward herded me toward his house, "Katherine's waiting for you inside. If the car blows, you don't want yourself or the baby hurt."

The baby. For the brief time I watched my personal bonfire, I'd completely forgotten about Lily. Edward was right. Lily's safety was paramount but my body rooted itself as I stared at the carnage in tearful disbelief. The gravity of the scene began to register, gradually splintering my meager control. Not only were we minus a reliable vehicle, with one small wind shift our house would join the blaze. Ennis already bounded off the porch for the water hose in hopes of protecting our home.

Edward continued nudging me toward his house but I couldn't leave my husband or my home. A flash of Troy Quinn's smile slithered into my mind. *You'll regret this, lassie! Yer jumpin' from the bucket into the fire!* Without outright threatening me, he'd basically told me to expect a blaze of some sort. I only prayed he meant for the car to go up in flames and not me and Ennis.

Sirens and revolving red and blue lights heralded the arrival of the cavalry. Cop cars and fire trucks rounded the corner, the latter's engines rumbling to an stop while men filed off en masse. The patrol units cut the sirens and set up barriers for traffic. Firefighters shouldered hoses up the driveway. Ennis switched off the garden hose and joined me on the porch. By then tears began falling down my cheeks.

A fog of water blasted from the two fire hoses, producing a sickening hiss and crackling when it met flame and hot metal.

"It'll be okay, babe," Ennis slid his arms around me. "I know you loved the car but we'll get another one. I promise it'll be okay."

O O O

Thirty minutes later, I still stood on the porch, staring at the burned-out shell of my precious, trusty Camaro. Wisps of smoke still trailed from the frame, filling the air with an acrid stench of what I deemed vehicular homicide. Only one or two places revealed its former shiny red glory. The rest succumbed to the fire, the body ashen and mottled with shades of scorched gray. The fire reduced the seats to metal skeletons and springs, the tires melted, leaving only the rims. The steering wheel jutted from the melted dash, a warped memory of the many hours I'd steadied the red beast with my hands or just the occasional knee.

Tears welled again as my next door neighbor Katherine Collins stepped from her prime vantage point of her front porch. Like Ennis and I, Katherine and Edward were in their early thirties. Katherine, however, rivaled Martha Stewart on perfection. Even at three-thirty in the a.m. she looked the epitome of Vogue with her slim figure cloaked in a pink silk robe beneath her cream colored fleece car coat.

She headed straight for me, placed a hand on my shoulder, "Are you alright, dear?"

Just dandy, I wanted to say. All we needed: marshmallows, weenies and a log to sit on while we cranked up a rousing rendition of Hot Time in the Old Town Tonight. My neighbor never approved of my car, simply because it was a ninety-nine model and not fresh from the showroom. Her past comments grated me since I considered the vehicle part of my family. I'd maintained it, washed it, had it repaired, babied it and loved it. The Camaro saw me through plenty of scrapes and travails. It didn't deserve to die that way. No faithful companion did.

"It's a good thing," Mrs. Collins continued, "Ennis had his truck in the garage or it would have been in flames too."

Oh goody. An optimist. My perky, persistently hopeful sister said shit like that and it drove me nuts. She'd say something unintentional that agitated me and I'd barely bite my tongue to keep the peace. With my neighbor, I had to play it cool so I just nodded.

Katherine looked to Ennis who verbally agreed with her. She turned the conversation toward him, "Do the firemen know how it started? I've never heard of Camaros just bursting into flames, even the older ones."

My jaw clenched so hard it ached. One more remark about my car's age and I'd turn that big ol' fire hose on Katherine. Always the diplomat, Ennis told her no. It was a lie of course. The firefighters said the car had been doused in accelerant and torched but neither of us wanted to alarm the neighbors. No need to confess I was the target of a crazy Irishman.

"It was older but seemed to run well," my neighbor added.

My vision strayed to the fire hose laying in our front yard. It invited me to pick it up and drench her with a powerful, cold wake-up call. Cops didn't drive BMWs or Jaguars. We simply couldn't afford what Katherine deemed acceptable.

Did she think my car, overwrought from old age and being driven daily, had rolled into the driveway one last time, heaved a final labored breath and decided to turn itself to toast in a brutal yet spectacular display of vehicular suicide? "I took care of the car, Katherine," I dropped the words like stones. "It was a ninety-nine but I kept it maintained."

She patted my shoulder again then used a placating tone, "Naturally you did, dear."

Ennis pointed to the street, "That looks like Georgia's Tahoe pulling up."

That brought me out of my staring stupor. I turned to the street and sure enough, Georgia piled out along with Seth. They both ran up the driveway like the devil chased them.

"Did you call them?" Ennis asked.

Between chatting with nosy neighbors and being front page news on the block, I found time to call my sister. If I thought my car's demise had been a flaming spectacle, it paled in comparison to my siblings' reaction if I failed to call them. "Thought I'd better," was all I said.

Georgia had thrown a coat over her fluffy rose colored robe and matching pajamas. That was my sister. Color coordinated in both calm and chaos. Seth, on the other hand, never looked like he went to bed. He still wore jeans and a sweater beneath his black leather jacket festooned with the army Ranger insignia. Once at a dead run, both siblings abruptly stopped, their jaws dropping upon sight of my smoking, skeletal car.

Disbelief crossed Seth's expression while wide-eyed horror twisted Georgia's beautiful features. Her head slowly swiveled from the car to me. Her gaze slid from mine to my belly, the message loud and clear. *Yes, Georgia, I know. I'm in danger and so is Lily but I'm a little too freaked right now for a lecture.*

She bounded up the stairs, her arms wrapping tight around me,

"Are you okay?"

I embraced her hard, my shaking voice finally admitted, "No." My voice broke over as Seth joined the group hug. I danced on the precipice of total collapse for an hour. With my siblings' comforting hugs and words of support, I lost the battle with tears. They fell in earnest for a minute or two until I shored up my courage to speak. "I'm just glad Ennis and I *and* the house were spared." I hadn't the heart to voice all my insecurities, especially in front of Katherine and Edward Collins. Truth was, it horrified me to imagine what Quinn's lackeys might have done if my Camaro had been garaged like Ennis's Ram. The Irish S.O.B. wanted his point made and if it took burning our house down with us inside, they would have done it.

Georgia squeezed me harder, "You and Ennis pack a bag and stay with me and Dane."

My legs were tingling and so were my toes. Bones in my back snapped into place from the pressure. My sister hugged like a boa constrictor and my brother wasn't helping one little bit. His strength squished the three of us together like a giant Prince sandwich. "Uh-uh," Seth shook his head, finally releasing us. He put hands to hips, "You're staying with me, sis." He turned to Ennis, "We'll pack your bags and Georgia'll drop us at my place."

Ennis bowed up slightly at the order. Ever since Jeffrey Holland got hold of Georgia and me, the two barely acknowledged each other in a civil manner. Seth blamed Ennis for not contacting him at the time even though Ennis was busy trying to find us. I understood both sides of the argument but my brother held grudges tighter and longer than Georgia's hugs.

"We'll be okay," I said, trying to give Georgia a verbal cue to let go which she ignored. "We don't need to bunk with anyone." I'd hoped to ease the strain on my husband's face. It failed. He'd stay with Georgia and Dane in a heartbeat, but not Seth.

Now Georgia let go. She held me at arm's length, her expression suggesting I'd lost my mind, "Have you lost your mind? The Irish mob just gave you a warning. They torched your car. I'm not having you, Ennis and Lily go up in flames as well. *Pack your bags.*"

Ennis entered the conversation, "Thanks for the offer, Georgia. We'll be ready in a few minutes." He about-faced into the house and left me alone to bear the backlash of Georgia's comment.

"The Irish mob?" Edward Collins asked.

Great. More complications. I expected the questions would start right about...

"What does she mean Irish mob?" Katherine looked to me.

"It's nothing," I tried to assure. "It was probably our cousins."

"Your cousins?" Katherine drew back as if the meanness jumped like fleas. "You have cousins that would burn your car?"

I shrugged, nonchalant, "Doesn't everyone?" Then I faced my siblings, "Listen, whoever did this has made their point. They torched the car, not the house. Ennis and I should be safe now." Unless the car's fire was intended to spread to the house and poof, no more police detectives but I dispensed with voicing that remark.

"Unless the fire was supposed to spread to the house," Seth said, seemingly reading my mind. "Either way, you'd be safer at my place than here. No offense to Georgia or Dane but I have training and friends that they don't."

"You also have small children," Georgia reminded. "Do you want the Irish mob messing with your family?"

Seth's jaw set, "They already have by nearly cooking our sister and Ennis."

I opened my mouth to protest when my brother lifted his hand in a "stop" gesture, "Don't, Van. For once, don't argue. I want you and Ennis safe *and* I want to protect my niece."

Perfect. The old fashioned guilt trip. Georgia usually honed her skills to a deadly precision. Seemed like my brother developed the knack too, only he threw in a facial expression that could only be described as quarrel-proof. Now I needed to further ruin Ennis's evening by explaining we were bunking at Seth's that night, not Georgia's. Lucky me.

19

Ennis took the news better than I expected. Unfortunately, my brother's tyrannical attitude reared up in the car with accusations toward Ennis that he'd failed yet again to keep me safe. This was a reference to Jeffrey Holland abducting me and that accusation ran its course the first day I heard it. I advised Seth to shut up or we'd bunk with Georgia and thanks to my sister's accompanying glare at him, he clammed up but his silence only warned of further mayhem later.

After we'd greeted Leah and the kids, Ennis and I decided to retire for what remained of the night. We all hugged – with the exception of Seth who reluctantly eased his hand out to Ennis and gave it a stern shake. Ennis and I started up the stairs when I heard Leah tear into my brother about treating Ennis like a flea-bitten dog, "Stop blaming Ennis. He's no more responsible for Jeffrey Holland or what happened tonight than you are. Lately, Savannah's maturity exceeds yours and she's a decade younger, for God's sake. My advice is shape up or be prepared to lose your sister because you're attacking her husband and no woman tolerates that."

I slowed my ascent to hear Seth's reply. He grumbled an intelligible response that inflamed Leah further, "Really? R.J. attacks him all the time and how often does she visit your father?" After a pause, she finished, "*Now* you understand."

I loved Leah. It took patience and tolerance to put up with Seth Prince and Leah overflowed with both. Standing about Georgia's height, she kept herself trim as a willow and her golden brown hair cut shoulder length. Her outward beauty was a reflection of the lovely woman inside. She defined the epitome of patience, fairness and common sense. Since marrying my brother, her job as wife extended into mother of two children and referee among us Prince siblings. Years ago, Seth and I butted heads over everything but since the Holland incident, he'd eased up on me and transferred his hard-hitting manner to Ennis. Seth was not an easy man to love but he was loyal to the bone. If his family ran into trouble, he was there. If only his mouth could shift from *overdrive* to *neutral*, I thought, we could all get along.

Ennis and I couldn't sleep a wink. We wrestled the bed and the covers until we got up exhausted and groggy but grateful to be alive. We tip-toed past the kid's rooms then Seth and Leah's bedroom then downstairs to the kitchen. We needed time to talk, to sort out what to do. Plus I really needed a cup of coffee.

Halfway down the stairs, the sultry smell of bacon frying and the warm, buttery sweet aroma of pancakes filled the air. Leah was already cooking breakfast before six o'clock. The woman amazed me with her energy. Ennis and I stumbled around two steps short of comatose and her kitchen smelled deliciously alive with a full array of breakfast fare.

We stepped in the kitchen and offered our best 'good morning' considering our traumatic night. Leah turned from the stove, her expression softening, "Y'all didn't get any sleep. I'm so sorry about Seth. I had a talk with him last night. I think he'll behave somewhat better today."

Ennis nodded acknowledgment. I yawned and thanked her. She'd done plenty of balancing acts between Seth and me and Seth and Georgia. I felt truly grateful for my sister-in-law. Her wisdom far surpassed her age of forty-one years.

Leah nodded to the kitchen table, "Sit. I'll get your coffee."

Two steaming cups appeared in a flash, Ennis's black, mine with a touch of cream and sugar. The moment the rich, luscious brew flowed past my tongue, I groaned my gratitude to Leah.

She flitted around the kitchen, tending the stove, coffee pot and her bleary-eyed guests. My guilt kicked in, knowing she had herself and her family to feed besides us so I offered to help with the meal. She politely refused, "You and Ennis need to rest after last night."

Leah sat two brimming plates in front of me and Ennis. The sight and smell inspired a moan from me and a grumble from my belly. Three Frisbee sized pancakes graced each plate with yellow trails of butter sliding down the golden fluffy flapjacks. On our saucers: an equal number of bacon slices fried to crispy glory. I nearly cried at the idea of savoring the meal after such an awful night.

Leah chuckled, "Someone's hungry. Here's the syrup." She sat the carafe between us. Ennis nodded to me, "Women and children first."

I drizzled the syrup over the pancakes, covering them in a warm, sweet brown blanket. I snatched up my fork and dug in just as Seth stepped in the kitchen smelling of Old Spice and soap. He wore jeans and maroon polo shirt.

He leaned down, kissed my cheek, "Good to see you have a hearty appetite."

"I'm starving," I replied, shoving the forkful of food in my mouth.

My brother then offered an astonishing gesture. He extended his hand to Ennis which suspended all other activity in the kitchen. Leah removed the skillet from the heat and I stopped eating in mid-chew. We both watched guardedly to see what transpired between the two.

"Ennis," Seth began, "I apologize for my behavior the last several months. I realize you did the best you could last night and with Holland." He temporarily shifted his vision to me, "Last thing I want is to alienate my sister or you because of my big mouth. Forgive me?"

Ennis glanced at me then at slid his hand into Seth's offered one, "Forgiven."

They shook hands and Seth kissed me again, "I'll be a better brother to you, sis, and a first-rate uncle to Lily."

A smile brightened Leah's face. She replaced the skillet back on the burner and added more bacon strips. For some reason, the frantic sizzling triggered a flashback of flames consuming my Camaro. The inferno came so dangerously close to the house, I shuddered that Troy Quinn's objective was entirely more sinister than intimidation. I feared he wanted us dead.

Seth kissed his wife, then swiped a plate of pancakes. He smothered them with maple syrup then dug into them with a hunger usually reserved for teenage boys. "Guess you'll need another car," he said, chewing his way through the statement.

"Seth Prince, your mama raised you better," Leah scolded then winked at me. "Chewin' and talkin' don't mix."

"Yeah, yeah," he complained. "I've got a friend who runs a used car dealership. He's honest for the most part but if he knows you're my sister, he won't screw you. You want to go this morning?"

I saw Leah's eyes cut to me then Ennis who appeared less than pleased by the offer. "Honey," she urged, "give them time to breathe. They haven't had a chance to discuss anything yet." She patted my shoulder, "I'm just glad you and Ennis are safe."

I considered my sister-in-law more of a sister. She gently guided without pushing. Georgia could have taken a lesson.

Seth bulled onward, "You want another Camaro? A ninety-nine'll be difficult to locate but my guy might be able to. You might consider an upgrade."

Leah brought over her own plate and sat across from me while quietly advising Seth to back off.

Meanwhile, my husband just stared at me. For the last hour I'd seen the concern in his eyes. The same concern I'd seen when Jeffrey Holland and Cole Jordan came after me. We needed to discuss safety issues, not cars, Ennis's expression said. If Seth pushed any harder, Guinness could chalk up their truce as the shortest in history.

My quandary was this: both men's agendas were important. I needed a car and we needed safety. I also remembered my brother's impatience and his blistering temper so I addressed his topic first, "I need something that will easily accommodate an infant seat without breaking my back at the same time. I think that leaves a Camaro out."

Seth's eyes brightened. I suspected why his eyes brightened too, "I don't mean a minivan, either. I'm not *that* domesticated. A four-door is as far as I go."

Seth nodded, returned to his breakfast, "I'll call him today, see what he's got." That was my brother. All business, all the time. Solving problems, fixing things.

I noticed Leah kept a sharp eye to Ennis while she ate. His tolerance of the car conversation came to a head during that time. He'd stopped eating – in fact, he hadn't moved a muscle during my brief exchange with Seth. Until now, "How do we pay for this car? We've got house payments, medical bills, insurance, and don't forget the baby's coming shortly." In other words, *shut up, Savannah.*

Leah slowly chewed a bite of pancake, swallowed uneasily then sat back, dabbing her mouth with a napkin. She heard the stress in his tone, the clipped delivery of his words. Most of all, she focused on the fork fisted in his hand.

"If we get another car, what happens if they torch it too?" Ennis continued, seemingly oblivious to the extra ears in the room. "Or if they torch it with you inside or they set the house on fire –"

"Ennis, hush up," I snapped then purposefully calmed down. "It's not the time to discuss that."

"When's a good time? When I'm choosing your casket? Seems kinda late."

That did it. His flagrant disregard of my not-so-subtle hint incensed me but I held my temper for Seth and Leah's sakes, "We are guests in this house. Seth and Leah have given us a bed to sleep in, their love and support and Leah got up early to prepare this delicious breakfast for us all. The least you and I can do is suspend the murder talk for now, don't you think?"

Apparently not... "It's a legitimate question," he argued. "What are we going to do? How will we protect our child from scumbags like Quinn that we encounter every day?

Leah motioned to Seth, "Let's give them time to talk."

"No," I countered gently. "Leah, I apologize for this. You and Seth have been very generous and gracious with us and we repay you by acting out. Ennis," I leveled a warning glare, "there are children in this house and if they walk in on this conversation, I swear I won't speak to you all day."

Ennis sat back with an angered sigh. Oh, he'd cool off soon enough. But I wouldn't. For a few brief minutes, I'd delighted in my home-cooked breakfast and relaxed while chatting with my brother. That was until Ennis brought the whole ugly Troy Quinn situation back to the forefront again.

My brother, bless his heart, tried to mend fences, "Hey guys, I'll ask around about the car but don't feel pressure to buy. Take your time."

I kept my vision trained on Ennis, "Thank you, Seth. Remember, four doors, no minivan."

O O O

Ennis Rutherford was a sweet man with a heart of gold and a charm that wooed a woman to her knees. But he also possessed a devil of a temper. His aggravation started small but when it blossomed to full fledged anger, most people headed for the hills. I didn't. I stood toe to toe, dug in and stood my ground. It positively drove Ennis nuts. Even good men possessed a bit of chauvinism at times, the need to "take care" of the woman, and the desire to protect. And for that, the little lady's role remained simple. Stand back and let him take over.

Ennis Rutherford was a thoughtful, well-intentioned man but he married the wrong woman if he considered me a typical Southern Belle. I never stood back or gave in.

The scene in Seth's kitchen ended promptly after I voiced my ultimatum. Ennis backed down but swore we'd talk about it later.

Seth drove us home in his F-150. It was a squeeze for two grown men and one very pregnant lady but we managed. He turned the corner onto our street and eased down the street. I saw the carnage half a block away. The hulking black mass sitting in our driveway. The firefighters departed hours ago but their efforts still soaked the front lawn into a soggy mess.

My brother pulled in behind the remains of my car. For the longest, we all sat, staring at it. The heartbreaking image sprung tears to my eyes but I forcibly shored up my resolve, heaved a sigh and climbed out of the truck. Quinn waged war with the wrong woman. He'd discover that later but for now I turned my back on the calamity and thanked Seth for his hospitality.

While Ennis piled out, Seth leaned out the driver's window and kissed my cheek, whispering, "I'll find you a car, sis. Don't worry about money right now. Just stay safe."

I kissed him back, "Thanks, big brother."

He backed out of the driveway, and before driving off, honked his horn twice and waved. I waved him goodbye then I turned to Ennis with a distinctly darker tone, "What the hell is wrong with you?"

"You need to retire from the department. That," he pointed to the scorched Camaro skeleton, "is what our child will grow up with. The uncertainty of her mama coming home alive, the fear of losing you. Do you want that?"

"Of course not but I don't usually provoke the Irish mob."

"It's not only about the Irish mob. It's about Jeffrey Holland –"

"Shut up."

"And Cole Jordan –"

"*I said shut up.*"

"And Terence LeVeau."

The mention of my ex-partner who tried to kill me was the crowning glory. I wheeled to face Ennis, my heart pounding in my chest, my face throbbing with anger, "I don't understand why you're doing this but you're really pissing me off. I have a mess in our driveway that requires attention unless you enjoy being the main attraction of the neighborhood. After that, I have to find transportation to work. Once I get past this sorry case we're working, I'll talk to you about my profession and my future. But right now," my voice broke over, "I have to salvage what precious little might be left in that car." I stomped away, wiping a stray tear.

The old car and I traveled many miles for many years. Back and forth to Augusta for various reasons and it knew the Atlanta streets as well as I did. It helped me move from an apartment to my little house then to the new house with Ennis. It carried me and Georgia wherever we went, it drove Lindsey to the doctor, me to work and now it was toast. My longtime friend was gone.

The stench of burned rubber and upholstery hung heavy as I leaned to the open door and glanced inside where I'd spent so much of my life. My watery vision rose to the gaping hole where the windshield once was, where the rearview mirror once hung. My gaze dropped downward, looking specifically for one item. Through the bits of glass and warped plastic, I thought I spied it.

I reached in then gasped when a hand grabbed my arm, pulled me back. "What are you doing?" Ennis asked.

"I'm trying to find something dear to me." I reached back in, pushed aside pieces of debris and finally located it. I backed out of the car and rubbed at the four inch piece of handcrafted metal, not caring that black soot covered my hands. I rubbed and rubbed until a sliver of its once former luster shown through.

Ennis's voice softened, "Your angel. It survived the fire."

Indeed. The silver angel dangled on my rearview mirror for years in honor of my mother. The ornament traveled with me for so long it became second nature to get in and not even notice the beautiful symbolic keepsake. I'd obsessed over it for the last several hours, praying it survived and it had. The wings still outstretched and the angelic upturned face smiled skyward, even after its baptism of fire. A true phoenix. And I fully intended to show Troy Quinn that despite his unspeakable act, I was a phoenix too.

20

The moment I stepped into the station, the place went stone quiet. No one spoke but instead chose to nod my presence as I walked by. I guessed the grapevine stayed ablaze much like my car had that night. What did one say to a person targeted by the mob, I wondered. Probably *see ya, wouldn't want to be ya.*

With the boss at a doctor's appointment, I decided to zero in on a few details of the Davenport case so I could update him when he returned. I called forensics for a report on our evidence from Blackstone. They found blood on the butcher's saw but none of it was human. I referred back to Metcalf's notes on the Davenport case. An employee remembered an old beat up butcher's saw that Quinn used and kept in the restaurant. It went missing after Davenport's disappearance.

I called forensics, "Are there any markings or names on that saw we found?"

The tech paused then, "There's a large H on the handle, the left side of the letter curves like a comma. Mean anything to you?"

It sure did, "That's my first good news today. Thanks." I dialed a local business, Horizon Cutlery. Georgia bought her chef knives there because they sold hand-crafted steel knives.

The manager at Horizon wasn't too helpful until I mentioned a murder investigation. Then he remembered records indicating he'd sold a brand new butcher's saw to Blackstone Restaurant on the 5th, one day after the raucous fight between Davenport and Quinn.

The manager went on to say he remembered thanking Quinn for buying the new saw because the store no longer manufactured custom blades needed for the old one.

"You still got the particulars of that custom order? The length of blade, number of teeth and such?" I asked.

"I'll do you one better. I have the design for that blade on the computer. I'll fax you a copy."

Finally, the day began picking up hope. The Mighty Quinn had some 'splainin' to do. The new saw, the new carpet, the giant rat hole with Davenport's blood in it and the funky little cave with the mysterious bloodied earring. The DNA on the latter would take a while so I decided to wrap up what I had and talk to Troy. All I had to do was locate him. If he used his gray matter correctly, he was in Belize right about now, but guys with Quinn's arrogance hung around to watch the fallout of their evil deeds.

I called Charlie Sullivan in lockup to find out who bailed Troy and what time he left. Expecting a name and time, I was stunned to hear, "He's still here. Never even asked for a phone call."

"That's ridiculous. He was booked on trespassing, not murder, at least not yet. People like him have bail in an hour. He should have been home playing with matches by five."

"Dunno, Detective. I only know since they brought him in, he's sat back there singing some Irish ditty to the point I'm coming unhinged."

"Then bring him to the interview room for me. Maybe I can change his tune."

O   O   O

I stood outside the interview room door, listening to Quinn sing. Charlie's complaint had merit. If I heard the song over and over all night, I'd be loony too. Something about a dirty old town. While being serenaded, I debated on whether to mention my car. I battled my conscience until Quinn sang another verse of his song:

> I heard a siren from the docks
>
> Saw a train set the night on fire
>
> Smelled the spring in the smoky wind
>
> Dirty old town, dirty old town.

Well, maybe I'd leave the car conversation for last – if I mentioned it at all. I felt Quinn pecking at me with the song, as though he sensed my presence outside the door. I'd proceed with business only and wing it from there.

I opened the door and stepped in. Our eyes met and I swore I detected surprise in his expression. A shiver raked my spine. He expected someone else which meant the fire was probably intended to kill. It also cleared my confusion as to why he hung around the jailhouse when freedom was one simple phone call away. No one enjoyed the food, the lack of privacy or the loud neighbors in the cell next door. No one wanted to be in jail except someone who needed a solid alibi for a murder taking place at the same time.

"Mother," his tone sounded less than thrilled to see me. "'Tis quite a surprise seeing you this morning."

"I could say the same about you. Why are you still here?"

Quinn regrouped his poise, leaned back, stretched and smiled at me. He appeared relaxed for a man who spent the night in a loud, uncomfortable cell, "I couldn't sleep last night, could you?"

I ignored his silly question, "Bail is cheap for trespassing and I know your wife or friends could have and should have bailed you last night. Why didn't you call someone?"

The brief glimmer in his green eyes told me the inquiry caught him short but again he quickly recovered, "Didn't see the reason to wake the world to me plight. It's just an American jail, after all. Seen worse in Ireland." He winked, "You get real meals 'ere, lassie. Decent meals that, as you Southern folk say, stick to yer ribs."

Maybe the American prison might change his mind about the cushy surroundings. "So glad you approve," I sank down into the metal chair, grateful for the relief on my back. "Let's get you caught up on today's developments. Yesterday we found a brand new butcher's saw that mysteriously appeared after the first search of the place. Where is the old saw, Mr. Quinn?"

"Ah, the old one broke. Shame, really. Pearfectly balanced too."

I'll just bet it broke, I wanted to say, especially when you hacked your father-in-law into chunks. "How did you dispose of the old saw and where?"

"Threw it in the trash outside the restaurant. No sense keeping a broken saw."

"But you'd been ordering custom blades up until Davenport disappeared." I pulled the faxed diagram and information from Horizon Cutlery, showed it to him, "That custom blade's teeth can be matched to the hack job on Davenport's body. I'd bet money it matches *pearfectly*."

"Would ya bet yer life?" he inquired out of the blue. "Ya know, lassie, ya not only have a tongue that could clip a hedge but ya remind me of that git Metcalf. So stupid he'd stare at a carton of orange juice for thirty minutes because it says *concentrate* on the label. Or perhaps, he's the product of an English whore like you are."

The door to the interview room swung open as I pushed from my seat. Josh Hunter and my husband stood in the doorway, arms crossed, neither looking particularly happy with me.

"Finally, yer knight has arrived, Mother," Quinn said. "Saved from the evil Irishman, at least for now."

Strong fingers closed around my elbow, gripping to the point of pain. Ennis physically towed me from the room but not before Quinn had the last word, "May you be a load for four before year's end."

The quip ignited Josh's temper as he warned the Irishman, "Zip it, Quinn, or I'll book you on threatening a police officer."

Ennis and I jumped as Hunter slammed the interview room door. Maybe I was naturally dense but Lucky's wisecrack failed to ring my bell like Josh's. Ennis explained in a grim tone, "Remember the casket I mentioned this morning? *That's* the load for four and with Quinn, one word and it'll happen."

According to Quinn's initial reaction, the load for four was scheduled for last night. I kept that to myself though. No need to give my husband more fuel for his personal campaign of heaving me from the job.

Hunter took over where Ennis left off by escorting me down the hall by my arm, "Before you dismiss Quinn as a blowhard, here's the news on Metcalf. His heart attack was brought on by something he ate."

I rolled my eyes. Well, *yeah...* "Have you seen Metcalf lately? It's not exactly a newsflash," said the woman who scarfed down half a dozen donuts by herself not more than a week earlier. Now I felt stupid for saying a word.

Annoyance crossed his face as he leaned to my ear, "Someone put digoxin in his food. Screwed up his heart rhythm and nearly killed him."

Ennis shot me a penetrating look, "Don't make me choose your casket, Savannah. Do the right thing and retire." He had a possessive desperation in his voice. I realized he loved me and wanted me and Lily safe. I did too. But retiring seemed cowardly at this point. Leave just because of a crazy leprechaun? No way. Exasperated at Ennis's nagging, I replied, "I told you we'd talk later." To change the subject, I turned to Josh, "Speaking of general health issues, how'd your doctor's appointment go?"

He kind of sneered, "Thanks to this tranquil working atmosphere, he put me on migraine meds. At this rate I'll be on Valium before Christmas."

21

May you be a load for four before year's end. Quinn's ominous words kept me awake until three-thirty. My mind refused to rest, my nerves ramping my paranoia to the brink. I sniffed the air for smoke, listened for any noise outside. When I eventually drifted off, scenes arose of Troy Quinn laughing over my grave then spitting a curse regarding Mary Malone and her nine blind illegitimate children chasing me over the hills of Damnation. Whoever Mary Malone was, she and her kids could leave me the hell alone and the same went for Quinn but I doubted he'd be so easy to convince.

At five-thirty, the alarm jangled me awake with a start. I bolted upright in bed, fearing it was the smoke alarm, not the alarm clock. My heart raced, my skin glistened with sweat and I felt fairly sure I looked like shit.

Ennis rolled out of bed, caught sight of me and not-so-tactfully confirmed my suspicions, "You look awful."

I rubbed my eyes, grumbling, "Thanks, Mr. Sauve. Lemme guess. You were voted *Most Likely to Sleep Alone After Marriage.*"

He winced, realizing his error, "Sorry. You look exhausted, that's all. What kept you up?"

I brushed a hand through my hair, bringing order to it. "Oh, the thought of burning alive in my own home, or perhaps expiring from a delightful drive-by shooting through our bedroom window."

I watched him round the bed in only his pajama bottoms, jealous of his bright and shiny alert attitude and wishing I had the energy to get frisky with him again. Between all the general maliciousness lately and the pregnancy, my sex drive abandoned ship. Without meaning to, Ennis combined sexy and sweet with his trim, muscular form and the stubborn cowlick standing at attention at the back of his head. My own personal centerfold and my hormones chose now to vacate the premises. Great.

Ennis extended his hand to help me up. I grasped it and one tug brought me effortlessly to my feet. In another month this chivalrous act would likely produce a hernia if he tried it so I enjoyed the gallant effort while it lasted.

He drew me close, pressed his lips to mine then gifted me with a gem of Rutherford wisdom, "If you stay away from Quinn, he has no reason to bother you."

Yes, Master Yoda, but, "How, pray tell, do I investigate Davenport's murder without interacting with Quinn?"

"You ask the boss to reassign you and that prevents the interaction. Problem solved."

I bristled, "I'm not a quitter."

He kissed me again, apparently in an attempt to ease my frustration, "I know that but your talent can be used to solve another case. Let Nesbitt and Clark take this one."

No matter his wording, it reeked of quitting. I refused to talk about it. Instead, I'd take my shower, eat, and let Ennis chauffer me to the station in his massive Dodge Ram. Then I'd continue work on the Davenport case. So there.

After a gentle slap on my bottom, Ennis winked, "You grab the paper and I'll shower. I'll get the bathroom nice and warm for you."

"That's a really rotten way of saying *I'm using all the hot water,*" I teased while slipping into my fluffy pink robe. I headed to the front door but before opening it, I peeked out the front window. Nope, no gunmen, cannons or flamethrowers. Hopefully I'd escape the snipers and poison arrows too. I'd dash the ten yards for the newspaper and retreat inside, safe and sound.

My eyes cut to my service weapon on the entry table along with Ennis's. It couldn't hurt adding insurance from Smith & Wesson. I pocketed the revolver, making certain it remained hidden from sight from any unexpected neighbors wandering outside at that hour.

I took a deep breath, opened the door and bounded outside. One step out and my toe jammed against something, causing me to stumble forward, frantically fumbling for a handhold. In those brief seconds, my brain registered the fact I tripped over a box and the box was now open. My hands clamped around a porch post to stop my descent. My initial fear: bomb. I'd considered other, more bizarre ways to die but overlooked the good old traditional bomb. It was small, got the job done and made quite an impression with witnesses. My immediate panic waned, however, when the box revealed its contents. No bomb but an equally deadly alternative. Four gray snakes, each one five feet long with a black diamond pattern down the back, slithered across the porch. A couple of the daring bastards headed straight for me. I clambered over the railing, straddling it for more support. I never proposed to be a snake aficionado but anything long and scaly with a forked tongue *and* a diamond pattern down its back screamed *death* to me.

"*Ennis!*" I yelled, not caring if I roused the whole state from a sound sleep. The world needed to know that the neighborhood had an infestation of, "*Snakes!*"

I reached in my pocket for the gun and aimed with trembling hand. I fired off three rounds, one after another, and luckily each bullet found its target. Three down, one to go.

The front door crashed open and Ennis stood, a bath towel wrapped around his naked waist. He didn't even seem to notice the cold air whipping past him – but he *did* do a doubletake at the sight of me clinging to the post like a chubby koala in a eucalyptus tree. "What the hell?" he asked.

I jabbed my gun at the lone snake slithering across the porch, "Snakes. Stay back." I aimed again and shot. The snake twitched then flopped back, lifeless. Now I felt safe about removing myself from my own personal perch.

By that time the neighbors meandered out, some stood in their yards or their porches, seeking the source of the fracas and noise. But not the Collins family. No, Katherine and Edward stood at the property line, surveying the commotion from a safe distance. "Everything alright?" Edward inquired.

Just peachy, stupid, I groused inwardly. *Thought I'd get some impromptu target practice to liven up my morning.* People like this gave me hives. "Snakes," I said with curled lip. "I hate snakes and there were four of 'em in that box. I tripped over it and they slithered out after me, the venomous monsters." I ended my explanation with a visible shiver.

Ennis looked at Edward and Katherine then at my gun, whispering, "Maybe if you put *the gun away* they'd come closer."

Well, I had to think about that one. Did I really want the Cleavers analyzing our newest, current horror? Did I enjoy hearing the obvious, that fires and snakes were deadly and dangerous? No, not really. So I kept the .38 at my side and cautioned our neighbors, "I think I got 'em all but I'm not sure."

Katherine kept her distance at that statement – however she did sweep her vision up and down my husband's physique. That tweaked my temper. I turned to Ennis, shooting my own little arrow, "Perhaps if you *clothed yourself* Katherine would stop ogling your nekkid body."

Ennis glanced down at himself. He still kept a death grip on the bath towel around his waist. He looked up at Katherine who smiled and blushed ever-so-slightly.

"Ennis," I prodded. "Now please."

He nodded sheepishly at Katherine then skittered into the house. Edward stepped onto the porch, took a brief glance at the dead snakes and proceeded to annihilate my snake identifying skills, "These aren't venomous."

"Any snake is venomous to me," I defended. "They don't belong anywhere near me and that's why I don't talk to half my extended family."

Eddie didn't find that funny. Instead he studied the carcasses of the beasts I slayed, "They're Gray Rat Snakes. They grow up to eight feet long, they eat rodents, lizards, and even birds. They're usually found in the southern part of the state though."

"Well, today they were on my porch. Are you a serpentologist or something?"

Edward chuckled, "I'm a novice herpetologist, yes."

"Herpetologist sounds like you study diseases, not snakes."

Ennis stepped out in jeans and a dark blue sweatshirt. Katherine wandered closer, "How did this happen? First your car, now these snakes? What's going on, Savannah?"

I'd chew off my own tongue before admitting the Irish mob sent me a box of snakes. "Y'know, Katherine, I'm not really sure. Obviously, UPS mistook our address for the zoo's."

Everyone looked at me like I'd lost my mind. I shrugged, "What? You think I ordered these miserable creatures?"

"We're working a difficult case right now," Ennis said. "But if it's causing this, it's time for us to be reassigned."

Despite the fact he was fully clothed, Katherine's vision seemed to settle at my husband's chest. The salacious way her vision swept across his broad shoulders then headed southward inspired thoughts of slapping her so hard she turned inside out. Yes, Ennis sported a nice thick sprinkling of dark hair that spanned the width of his chest then dove straight for his nether region. A region meant for my eyes only.

Playing it cool, I merely nudged him, "Then we'd best get to work so we can talk to the boss about this."

Oblivious to his wife's wandering eyes, Edward stood up with a friendly smile, "I'll take care of the snakes for you. Save you the trouble."

"Thanks, Edward." I winked, "If you're really good at this, I'll introduce you to my extended family and you can take care of those vipers too."

22

I skittered past Josh Hunter's desk upon arriving to work. I had business with The Mighty Quinn and my forthcoming conversation required privacy. I planned to put the unscrupulous weasel on notice, that his attempts on my life were over.

I marched down the stairs to lock-up. Always the gentleman, Charlie Sullivan rose to his feet with a smile. A smile that disintegrated once he observed my murderous expression. We'd worked together long enough he'd seen my white-hot temper before so he merely stepped back, nodded.

I nodded back, on my way to Troy Quinn's cell. Halfway there, I heard Charlie's phone ring. After a few *yes sirs*, he called out, "Detective, the captain wants to see you."

"Not now, Charlie," I replied in a don't-screw-with-me tone.

"But Detective, he's insistent. He wants to see you, *right now*, he says."

Poor Charlie. Stuck in the middle again. Between my cousins, my boss and me, he'd need a vacation by week's end. I stopped at Quinn's cell to see the red-headed jerk casually sitting on the narrow bed, his back propped against the wall. He still hummed that Dirty Old

Town song from our earlier meeting. Our vision met and he rose to face me.

"Nice try, Quinn," I ground the words between my teeth. "*Real* nice try but it didn't work and it won't. First your toadies light my car on fire then they put snakes on my doorstep?" I pulled my .38 from its holster, popped open the fully loaded cylinder and made a show of spinning it, "Guess what? I didn't use all my bullets on the snakes. I've got plenty left."

Quinn drew back in mock horror, "Was that a threat, Mother? In yer condition that's not very wise."

I dropped the words like stones, "Tell your flunkies to back off and leave me alone or I'll exercise my .38 on a few choice people."

"Detective Prince," my boss's voice boomed throughout the room, "come with me."

I refused to break eye contact with Quinn. My anger boiled over until I'd basically threatened him. If my boss heard, he would have my head on a platter which wouldn't exactly be new but after the last two days, I felt justified with my actions.

"Your boss is calling, Mother."

I stared straight at Quinn, hoping he understood the depth of my outrage and gravity of my warning. And another thing. *Stop calling me Mother.* Those words fought for freedom but Josh Hunter cut me off before I spoke, "*Detective, if you value your employment status, get your ass over here now.*"

I popped the cylinder back into place and holstered my gun before turning to face Josh Hunter. He met me halfway, far enough to remove me from Quinn's visual range but not his hearing. "Savannah, you're off the Davenport case."

"What?" Now my rage transferred to Josh. He put me in this jackpot, I would remind, so he should at least let me finish my job – whether or not Quinn still drew breath. "You've got to be kidding. We're still waiting on evid–"

"I need you working another investigation. I'm reassigning the Davenport case to other detectives."

"You gave me and Rutherford this case. What's so important you're booting us from this one?"

"You and Rutherford are needed elsewhere. Come with me and I'll show you the file."

My gun hand itched to finish Quinn. My irritation with him and the whole surreal week surpassed insanity. My boss kicked me to the curb on the Davenport case for whatever idiotic reason. My life changed so much the last year with Jeffrey Holland then moving and getting pregnant – now my job, the one stable and infallible facet in my life, slipped through my fingers. I had no control over anything, I decided. My existence relied on others making decisions for me and I absolutely, unequivocally, hated it.

I headed toward the stairs when Troy Quinn pushed his luck. "Sorry, Mother," he called from his cell. "'Twas fun while it lasted."

I heard the smile in his voice and I stopped, my body stiffening with the sincere desire to yank my gun and show Quinn my definition of fun. My boss had other ideas and put a firm hand to my shoulder, "Keep walking, Savannah. Keep walking and keep quiet."

Hunter ensured I kept moving. I climbed the stairs slowly, still debating over that one bullet I'd saved special just for Quinn. Josh trailed me up the stairs, verbally nudging me, "Faster if you can. The more space between you and him, the better."

"Let's see you carry a sack of taters in your stomach and climb these things. I'm not a kangaroo." Okay, I felt bitchy because my week, like my car, went up in flames – and there was no end in sight.

At the top of the stairs, I felt the burn in my legs and Lily made sure I understood her point of view by lodging her foot somewhere near my spleen. I continued on to Josh's office, rubbing at the tiny foot paining me. Once inside, Hunter offered me a seat. Evidently Lily approved because she recoiled her appendage and settled down. I sighed with relief, "This kid is killing me by degrees."

He massaged his temple, "Wait till she's a teenager."

"Why did you boot us from the case? It's not like we're stagnant on it. We've got leads."

"I know that. So does Quinn. Why do you think you're suffering all this grief? Your car? The snakes? To back him off, I'm taking you both off the case."

"So Quinn gets his way again. Nice for him."

"Hey," he snapped. "Michelle's all over me about this. She and Georgia still give me grief over not tossing you from the Holland case early on." He rubbed his temple vigorously, "I'm saving myself a stroke here, okay? Between my wife and your sister, my migraine meds don't even work and I'm losing my mind trying to choose suitable names for the baby. The last thing I need is the trifecta of you, your baby and

Rutherford being murdered by that crazy leprechaun."

I couldn't exactly argue with that. The snakes about finished me off. I dreaded to think what Quinn's people might do next. Before something more serious occurred, I'd listen to the boss and back down. "So who gets the booby prize now?"

"Nesbitt and Clark. And for future reference, remember I am your superior officer. When I say *see me*, that means immediately. A little respect would be nice."

I nodded, ashamed that I let Quinn push my buttons again. No matter how I griped, I felt a significant sense of relief shedding Troy Quinn and his homicidal gang. I'd drop Christine a few hints on surviving the jerk, primarily to stock up on snake antivenin and rent a garage for her car. I asked Josh, "And the case I'm relegated to is…"

Exasperation shadowed his features, "You're not *relegated* to anything. I need you at Grady to see the girl they found at the lake. She's still not conscious but I want pictures of her and any other evidence they collected on her. I'm hoping we can match her picture to any missing kids around here, like the last girl."

"I'm your first choice for interacting with young kids?" I pointed to my gut, "Because I'm pregnant?"

"No, you're good with kids but I don't think the girl is conscious yet. Just see what you can glean either from the evidence or the hospital staff. We're taking a beating in the press on this. We've got to find the asshole killing these girls."

O O O

Okay, so I didn't feel relegated. I felt screwed. I went from target of a homicidal Irishman to spotlight in the city's other biggest law enforcement fiasco. Little girls being raped, beaten and slaughtered. This time the killer botched his effort and the girl survived.

I spent the ride to Grady shoring up my courage to face this girl, to prepare for the brutality I'd see. Truth was, facing a victimized child rated next to lowest on a cop's list. The very lowest and most unbearable: a deceased child. Violence should never involve children and when it did, cops found it near impossible to cope. And people wondered why law enforcement rated high for alcoholism and suicide…

I flashed my badge at the officer guarding the girl's door. The second I stepped in the room, tears welled in my eyes. She was no older than seven, her golden hair draped the pillow, her angelic face marred with bruises and a bandage spanned her throat from ear to ear. The killer cut her throat as he'd done to all the other girls. Another bandage concealed another laceration, this one slicing her left cheek.

I approached the bed and felt my heart painfully squeeze in my chest. My mind plunged into dark places, ones that berated me for bringing a child into a world that abused darling little girls and left them dead or clinging to life with a breathing tube and IVs. I pressed a gentle hand to my belly with an apology to my unborn daughter – and a promise. For her safety, I'd honestly consider my future with the department.

I touched the girl's foot through the blankets, hoping the feeling might rouse her or change the rhythmic beeping of the heart monitor. It didn't. I cleared my throat of emotion, dabbed my tears and softly introduced myself, telling her why I was there and that she was safe now.

I saw no movement except her chest rising and falling in time with the ventilator. I took my phone in hand as an uncomfortable feeling overwhelmed me. The feeling I was invading this girl's privacy and that I was no better than the beast that attacked her.

Unfortunately, I had a job to do. That required taking her picture for identification purposes and photos of her injuries for evidence. And the pictures I took that day would be the first step in finding the monster who loved killing girls. I pointed the camera at her battered, swollen face and after snapping a few pictures, I uttered another apology. My job was rarely fun but that day it was excruciating.

"Who are you?" a voice asked.

I jumped like someone screamed in my ear. Turning, I introduced myself, showed my badge to the stern-faced nurse who then relaxed and went about her business checking monitors and IVs. "She's still unconscious," she said. "Has been since they brought her in but she's strong. She's a fighter, you can tell."

Anyone who survived having their throat cut, yeah, they were tough – and damn lucky. "Did they do a rape kit?" I asked.

She nodded, "Sent it with a coupla officers that morning. I heard she was raped repeatedly."

I winced, put a hand to my belly. The nurse's vision dropped to my stomach, "When are you due?"

Next month, I replied. She gave a sympathetic smile, "Difficult job to have when you're pregnant. More so on days like this."

I nodded to her, afraid to voice my actual thoughts because they'd get me suspended at best and fired at worst.

The hospital gown covered the girl's torso to her thighs. I eased the sheet to her waist, mortified at the numerous deep purple bruises. A sickness rumbled low in my gut. I silently cursed Josh Hunter for assigning me this case. I'd lose my lunch and my mind before shift's end.

Images assailed my already emotional brain. Those of the girl's screams, her little fists flailing to beat her attacker while his powerful blows sank into her flesh. Then finally the coup de grâce. A knife drawing across her throat, digging in, slicing until silence and blackness descended on her. She never knew why the man took her, why he raped her, and why he wanted to kill her.

"Detective, are you okay?"

I shook free of the unspeakable visions and nodded, "Hard to see this, much less catch the S.O.B. without killing him on sight." Well. So much for discretion. My knack for savoir-faire rated as high as Georgia's ability to mind her own business. I only hoped the nurse understood my bluntness.

"If you find him, call me. I'll hold him down for you," she offered. She checked the girl's vitals and recorded them, "We found something on her after the police took her clothes. I'll get it for you."

I waited for her leave the room and return with the item. The sound of the ventilator grated on me. I'd heard those things too often in my life and just when I decided to step out, the nurse rounded a corner holding a plastic bag. "It's part of a piece of jewelry."

Without opening the bag, I tilted it, examining the little gold heart inside. I'd seen this heart before, I thought. Just the other day. Pulling out my phone, I scrolled through the photos from our trip to Blackstone. We'd found an earring in that tiny stifling room in the tunnel. Suddenly the sickness in my gut churned. Josh thought he got me off the Troy Quinn rollercoaster by reassigning me. Little did he know. I dialed my boss, "I'm throwing my saddle back on the Quinn case."

"No, you're not because my wife and your sister will kill me and my burial plan isn't paid up."

"Doctors found evidence pointing to this girl being in the tunnel beneath Blackstone."

Josh cursed. "What evidence?" he asked.

"Looks like part of an earring that matches the one Ennis and I found in the tunnel." I heard my boss sigh and say God's name "the naughty way" as my niece said.

Finally Josh Hunter mumbled, "I hope I survive the wrath of the female population in my life." Then he whispered, "Don't breathe a word of this to anyone, Savannah. I don't want Quinn finding out you're anywhere near this case. I'm scared of him and you should be too."

Did he think I was stupid? Only two people weren't scared of Troy Quinn. One, Quinn's mother and two, an absolute fool, and frankly I wasn't too sure about his mother. She may have been fertilizing the roses back home – from underneath. I put nothing past Quinn, not even killing his own mother.

23

"I hear you want my evidence." The accusation came from Christine Clark who stood in my doorway, arms crossed and none too happy with my request. Great way to polish off the day, I bemoaned to myself. With another argument.

I prayed our child developed a lighter side than this particular Christine because *I* began to develop the same paranoia Josh Hunter had associating baby names with certain people. Please Lord, I prayed, let Lily Christine inherit her daddy's laid-back, even tempered manner. "Just want to borrow it, that's all," I assured the willowy raven-haired beauty.

"Why?"

Before I answered, she advanced into the room the way predator stalked prey. The woman's possessive nature regarding evidence verged on fanaticism. Detectives protected their cases but she needed a rabies shot.

Leaning back in my chair, my expression reflected the fact she might bully the men but I was tougher than a pine knot about investigating a case. Few people bullied me and the ones who did usually possessed power to end either my career or my life. She possessed neither one.

I lifted the plastic bag from the hospital, "This earring matches the one Ennis and I found at Blackstone. I was hoping to get a jeweler to identify it and track down my victim's name."

She chuckled. Actually laughed. I declined to join her show of joviality, choosing instead to entertain thoughts of tying her lovely tresses in a giant knot and shoving the whole thing in her mouth to shut her up. "They are probably mass produced in China," she said, "and sold in a thousand stores here."

Hmm. Maybe loop the hair around her neck for good measure then tie the knot and shove it in. I shook loose of the vicious fantasy and tapped the evidence bag, "I looked at this little heart and it's engraved and not with *Made in China*. Without bionic vision I can't make it out but it looks vaguely like 'ATL' and a weird symbol next to it. Now, may I borrow the earring from your case?" I put extra emphasis on *your* to ensure Christine I didn't intend to wrestle that minefield Davenport case from her.

Her stance changed. Instead of the brazen, challenging posture, her shoulders relaxed and thankfully so did her expression. Sighing, she apologized, "I'm coming across all wrong. You and I have been pretty good friends and I really don't intend to alienate you. I'm sensitive lately because Nesbitt treats me like a sidekick and questions every damn thing I do."

"I remember those days." When I got the promotion, all the detectives were older, part of the boy's club. To them the mid-twenties interloper was only good for fetching coffee or answering phones. Except Mathis. He'd been the only detective to call down the chauvinistic remarks and treat me like an equal. Oh, yes, I sure did remember. "Just settle down and keep doing your job. Nesbitt will eventually realize he underestimated you."

"Thanks, Savannah," she said with a sincerity I hadn't expected. "God, I really dread your maternity leave. I'll be the only chick around these parts."

"Ennis will be here and you can count on him to be a gentleman."

She sidled up to my desk, glanced around for listening ears then whispered, "Yeah, how *did* you score such a hunk?"

I wasn't sure she knew Ennis and I were married so I shrugged, "The boss assigned us as partners. Luck of the draw, I guess."

"Luck of the Irish, you mean."

I winced. If she only knew what my luck with the Irish had been. Fires, snakes… I fully expected a battalion of machine guns to open fire on our house, blasting away until only splinters and two dead detectives remained. Luck of the Irish. Feh.

Christine tilted her head with a smile, "C'mon, let's go get the evidence. You mind if I ride along, just to enjoy the outdoors? This place is a museum."

Despite her earlier apology, I still sensed the request to ride along meant to keep her eyes on her evidence. As if she couldn't track down the pregnant cop wagging around an orphaned earring. I reached in my desk for my .38, shoved the gun in my holster, "As Ennis says, 'Saddle up.'"

24

Like most jewelry stores in Atlanta, I'd never been inside Harvey's Jewelry. The same could not be said of my husband. He'd bought my engagement and wedding rings at that establishment and had them designed and created by the proprietor himself. Mr. Harvey sounded like a nice fellow and since he helped Ennis, I hoped he could help me.

When Christine and I walked in, the place was quiet, save for the old school jingling bell announcing our entry. A young couple hunched over a display case of rings, their faces aglow with the same cheery, love-struck adoration Dane and Georgia exhibited.

Each case sparkled with rings, necklaces, bracelets and earrings. Blood red garnet necklaces, yellow topaz, lime-colored peridot bracelets and shimmering diamond rings abounded which inspired thoughts of Georgia. A crowbar nor stick of dynamite could have extricated my sister from this place if she saw all the glitter and gleam.

I noticed two security cameras, one at the front of the store, the other at the back, giving the owner full view of his store. A saleslady tended to the happy couple and before the door closed behind us, a middle-aged fellow with a paunch, graying temples and friendly face emerged from the back room.

"Welcome, ladies," he greeted. "Brook Harvey at your service. What can I do for you?"

In unison, we plucked our badges from our belts, displayed them and introduced ourselves. I reached in my jacket for the small plastic bags holding the earrings. "Is there any way you can tell us if these were made locally?"

A patronizing half-smile crossed Mr. Harvey's plump cheeks as he gave the bags a fleeting look, "They were probably internet buys."

The bell over the door jingled again, indicating another customer entered the store. I glanced over my shoulder at two men in their early twenties, dressed in jeans and blue polo shirts. They meandered in, feigning interest in the diamond necklace display and I felt the hairs bristle on the back of my neck. I'd seen these guys before and not in a good way. Outside Blackstone when we arrested Quinn.

Returning to my conversation, I extended the bag containing the single tiny heart, "I saw an engraving on that one. Could you at least look at it, see if you can make something out?"

He began another protest until his vision strayed to my wedding ring. He smiled, "I remember that ring." Harvey equipped himself with an eyeglass and took my hand in his. He studied the ring for a mere two seconds, "Oh yes, remember it well." He let go then dropped the eyeglass into his palm. "Your husband, a nervous guy about six two, had a Texas accent. He's a cop too, right?"

Oh crap. I never expected him to possess an elephant's memory. At least he hadn't spouted Ennis by name or I'd need to perform serious damage control with Christine later.

Then, as my Irish luck continued its copious generosity, Mr. Harvey verbally accessed his memory, "Rutger, Russo... No, wait. Rutherford. That's it. He spent hours instructing me on how he wanted your ring to look. Oh, he loves you, alright. Any man spends that kind of time and money, he loves his lady."

While I blushed, Christine turned to me with chagrin. No, evidently she hadn't known of our marriage but did now and that meant trouble. I could only ask that she keep quiet about our relationship and I'd pray she kept her word.

I checked on the two guys across the aisle. They waved off the saleslady's offer for help, choosing instead to stand, hands in pockets, still casually staring at the displays.

With renewed interest, Harvey extended his hand, "Lemme see that earring again."

I handed it to him and he removed it from the bag. Eyeglass back in place, he angled the tiny piece back and forth between his fingers.

One more glance behind us and I made eye contact with one of the men. A painful shiver crawled down my spine. An unmistakable bulge beneath his jacket told me he carried a weapon. If Quinn told the guys to follow me, that bothered me but if he told them to shoot me full of holes, I needed a backup plan and fast.

Before turning back to the display case, the guy narrowed his eyes at me. Now that wasn't comforting at all. "Mr. Harvey, could we talk in private?" I nodded in the direction of the back room.

Both Harvey and Christine appeared surprised by the unusual request. The no-nonsense tone of my voice alerted Clark to a problem.

The owner picked up on it and waved us into a smaller back room where his office resided. Christine and I rounded the display cabinets, followed him into a smaller room equipped with the TV monitors connected to the store's security cameras. I motioned to Christine, "Keep an eye on those two at the necklaces. Let me know if they make a move toward us."

"What's the problem, Detective?" Harvey wanted to know.

"There's no problem yet," I replied, grabbing the phone from my belt. "And I'm making sure there won't be." I dialed Ennis. While I waited, I pointed to the earring again, "Could you go ahead and take another look at that right quick?"

In the meantime the happy couple left the store and the sales lady made a second offer to help Quinn's cohorts. Again they refused.

Ennis answered on the second ring, "Hey, how's the jewelry store panning out?"

"Still panning. Do me a favor. Have any nearby units swing by and park right outside the jewelry store. Just tell them it's for security detail and to stay there until Clark and I leave."

Alarm threaded his voice, "What's wrong?"

I stared at the video monitor, watched the two guys failing in their attempt to look innocuous since they kept a keen eye on the closed office door. "Those two guys outside Blackstone. They're here and one's carrying. I need the uniforms to scare 'em off."

"Gotcha. They'll be there in a minute. Be careful, babe." He hung up and I prayed those cops had rockets strapped to their asses because the two guys were getting antsy the longer we stayed out of sight.

"I'll be damned," Harvey said.

I wheeled to him as he sat the eyeglass aside and put pen to paper, "It *is* a designer signature. This is what it looks like." He sketched out a capital "J" then a backwards "3" to the right of it. Beside that was the "ATL" I saw.

"Whose design is this?" I asked.

"His name is Robert Johann the Third. That's the reason for the J and the 3. And the ATL is obvious."

I shot an impatient glance at the security monitor then back to Harvey, "Where do I find him?"

Harvey rounded his desk, opened a thick black binder. Flipping through the pages with names and contact information, he stopped on one and wrote down the address next to Johann's design. "This is a special order so he should have records on who bought it." Now he took an interest in the images on the monitor too. "Is there anything else?"

I shook my head, thanked him for his help, finishing, "We'll be going as soon as we clean out your store of the riff raff."

Christine shifted from the monitor to me, "So what are we waiting for?"

"The cavalry."

Two minutes later, the cavalry arrived in a much grander scale than I expected or asked for. Three patrol units, lights blazing and sirens blaring, screeched to a halt beside the curb. Six burly cops piled out and headed straight for the jewelry store entrance, hands on their weapons.

"Holy Mother Mary." Christine said, jaw agape at the scene unfolding on the security monitor. She looked at me, "Did you call Jesus too?"

"Oh, He heard from me too. Let's go while the gettin's good." I turned back to Mr. Harvey who also stared dumbfounded at the sudden influx of law enforcement. I thanked him again for his help and Christine and I sauntered from the office, both our hands tucked inside our blazers, ready to draw if necessary. Quinn's goons stood stone still while we made our way to the exit but made solid eye contact with me as we passed.

"What aren't you telling me?" Christine demanded in a whisper.

Oh, only the fact she got a whopper case oozing with Irish thugs who loved to scare and/or kill the investigating detectives. Other than that, everything was dandy. "I'll explain when we get outside."

All six cops trooped inside, two of them stood by the door, held it open for us while the others nailed Quinn's men with piercing glares. Once outside, I witnessed the clusters of people gathering across the street and nearby street corners. When cop cars screeched to a halt in full regalia of flashing lights and blasting sirens, it tended to draw attention – attention I hadn't asked for. I stopped the oldest uniform officer, "Exactly what did Rutherford tell you?"

"To beat it over here because two detectives were in danger." His vision flicked to my belly then back to my eyes, "Now I can see why he was adamant."

But a parade of cop cars? "I asked for safe passage, not the Normandy Invasion."

The guy was old and gray enough and been on the job so long, he didn't give a crap about a woman cop's complaints, "You needed it since you're keeping unintentional company with two of Troy Quinn's punks."

Christine glared at me, "And you didn't tell me?"

"Calm down, alright? I said I'd explain and it's not like I expected to be followed here."

The older cop, Officer Turner, leaned closer to us, his dark eyes volleying between us, "Those two are his lieutenants. The ones who do the dirty work. That's why," he pointed to my belly, "you'd better be careful out here, Detective." Then he addressed us together, "Both of you women."

Christine bowed up, "Women? Why specifically us?"

Unlike me, Christine let the hostility fly instead of concealing the outright resentment. For Detective Clark, *no one*, not even a seasoned uniform cop would bring gender into the job without suffering a few claw marks. Some of us, after a few years, learned to fling the chip off our shoulder and listen to the older, wiser cops.

Turner's expression questioned Christine's sanity, "You do know their reputation regarding women, right? Those two bums have records for sexual assault and no offense but you two aren't exactly Mutt Weekly material. You're both on Quinn's radar for whatever reason and if he perceives you as a threat, he'll deal with you. There's no respect for women, kids, nothing. Anything goes."

"You got names for the lieutenants?" I tried dragging the tension down between the two. Christine looked ready to pounce – at both Turner and myself. Him for his "chauvinistic ways" and me for holding out on her.

"Sean O'Leary and Kevin Hughes. The short one is O'Leary. The red-headed one is Hughes."

I glanced at the door as Quinn's buddies exited without even glancing in our direction. Turner watched them stroll down the sidewalk, "Hughes has red hair and Hughes means fire in Irish. Funny, ain't it?"

Yeah, I nearly said. As funny as a flaming Camaro.

25

Megan Bowen. The girl in the hospital finally had a name. Ennis tracked down the jeweler Robert Johann and the special order Megan's mother placed for the earrings. Ennis took the job of informing her parents which I was grateful for. Facing Megan was hard enough but seeing the anguish on her parent's faces would finish me off.

Ennis returned to the stationhouse, leaving the Bowens to go see their daughter. I'd left instructions at the hospital for two uniform cops to stand guard outside Megan's room. I'd informed them no one besides cops and hospital staff were allowed in so I had to call and alert them to the parents' arrival.

Afterward, Ennis and I had just enough time to attend Abby's funeral. Not surprisingly very few people attended. Of course Charlene's side made a showing. Seth and Leah, Georgia and Dane and me and Ennis all sat together. We noticed Grace and Katie sitting in the back and that angered me all over again at Teresa and Linda. We decided to sit with Grace and her daughter in the unofficial Black Sheep Section of the church. I felt bad for Grace. The cousins treated her terrible. Teresa and Linda squeezed Abby's only sister out of one occasion family should pull together. Meanwhile they hovered around

Abby's ex-husband Lee, his kids and Lee's new wife Alicia.

During the service, I heard only three people shed tears. Grace, Katie and Abby's middle son Tony. Hearing the glowing accolades lavished on Abby soured my stomach. Anyone who actually met her had the smarts and common decency to dislike her but preachers and priests could make anyone sound saintly. I wrote down the preacher's name because eventually I'd require someone with his gift for creative lying and he was, hands down, the best I'd heard.

Before leaving we offered our condolences to Lee and his boys Willie Dean, Tony and Carter. Lee invited us to the house since they had enough food to "feed the Confederate Army." Ennis, bless his heart, accepted the invitation without consulting me and when Seth heard the gaffe, he snapped around to glower at my well-meaning hubby.

So we all piled in our respective cars and headed out to Buckhead and the rich man's world. "I screwed up, didn't I?" Ennis asked while we waited at a red light.

"Oh, maybe a little," I replied. "We don't usually socialize with my family for good reason. Mostly we fight. No matter how nice we try to be, it never works."

On a general scale of flubs, Custer's last stand, Napoleon's invading Russia and Three Mile Island ranked among some of the grandest blunders in history. Next were New Coke, the Ford Pinto and Hair in a Can. Ennis's goof was a result of his Southern manners – which always got people in trouble whether they meant to or not. Accepting an invitation to the grieving family's house was the proper thing to do. Much as it irked me, I couldn't be completely irate with him. It proved he was a gentleman.

Unfortunately, my brother didn't agree. In the rearview mirror, I spied Seth fuming behind us. To him, Ennis might as well have captained the Titanic. Located somewhere behind my livid brother and his wife were Georgia and Dane though I couldn't readily see them. What really grabbed my attention was Seth's new car. A Dodge Charger. Such a sweet looking thing. Metallic blue with a fierce sounding engine. Lucky guy.

The light turned green and Ennis started through the intersection. Movement behind us caught my attention. Seth hung a right instead of following us. I sighed. So the mutiny began. Ennis and I would be the only ones showing up at Lee's house. I'd hoped my brother and sister loved me more than to abandon me to the wolves, especially since I was carrying their niece.

"We don't have to go," Ennis frowned at the rearview mirror. "Seth just deserted us and I can't find Dane and Georgia anywhere."

I reached for the steering wheel since his truck veered into the other lane, "Ennis, watch the road. I'll keep track of who jumps ship."

He shook his head, "Your family breeds a special kind of crazy."

"And that alone should forewarn you not to seriously piss me off. My psycho gene may be dormant now but later? Who knows?"

Ennis and I approached the gated entrance on Andrews Drive. The two massive iron gates stood open and Ennis slowly pulled into the long driveway, "This is where Abby lived?"

Lee occupied what equated to three of our homes. What's more, his driveway looked around a football field away, flanked by a lush green lawn and colorful flower gardens.   The long driveway ended at a humongous Tudor style mansion.   Yes, this was where Abby resided before Lee came to his senses. I replied, "Before her divorce, yes. It has five or six bedrooms and like eight bathrooms. Not quite Duke Shelton's neighborhood but still enough to make you nervous." My reference to the eccentric millionaire broke Ennis's trancelike stare at the house. Shelton owned twelve thousand square feet of mansion and many acres of surrounding land. Lee and Abby lived in a micro version of it.

We parked then exited the car, trying to figure out whether we should even enter the quarrelsome den of extended family.

To make things worse, Lee and Alicia were basically newlyweds so "family" fell into a touchy gray area. The two tied the knot a year earlier to Abby's protests and in my opinion, Alicia was no step up from Abby. She bullied Lee who tended to be on the soft-spoken side anyway. She stood about to my chin, weighed probably two hundred fifty pounds, and knew precisely how to throw it around to get her way. And judging from the scowl clouding her harsh features at the funeral, she was as joyful to host Abby's family as we were to be there.

A wave of unease roiled through me when Georgia and Dane failed to show. Georgia practically twisted my arm for a promise to meet at Lee's after the funeral. Well, here I was so where was she? Ennis and I stood in front of this massive house discussing our plans.

I opted for waiting on Georgia. I wasn't diving into the deep end without my sister. She started this and I wasn't a damn guinea pig *or* sacrificial lamb. Ennis and I hemmed and hawed outside, stared at our watches then at the road until Lee caught us loitering in his driveway.

Always the gentleman, he invited us in and I felt as lucky as a Christian led into the Colosseum.

We followed him inside and the first thing that hit me wasn't a baseball bat as I'd feared but a concoction of perfumes that instantly made me sneeze. All eyes turned to us as I attempted to gracefully blow my nose into Ennis's offered hanky. Staring at us were men and women dressed in Versace and Oscar De La Renta. Between that and all the expensive furniture and glassware surrounding us, I felt one step above beggar. Ennis and I just came from work. Black maternity pantsuit for me, blue suit without tie for Ennis. Awkward.

Lee led us to a pristine white sofa where three young men sat. I barely recognized Abby and Lee's kids. The oldest, Willie Dean, hauntingly favored his mother, most notably his thin-lipped smile. At Lee's behest, the boy rose and gave me a hug. An obligatory stiff hug. "Savannah, long time, no see," he said.

Not long enough, I wanted to say. Besides looking like Abby, he also acted like her too. Still, I responded with a smile and offered my condolences. I introduced Ennis to the boys. None of them acknowledged him, the closest being fifteen year-old Carter, the youngest, who launched from his seat with a, "Yeah, whatever."

I watched the tubby dishwater blonde, his expression taut and derisive, stick his nose in the air and stomp off. This was why idiots shouldn't breed, I thought. Then I thanked God Georgia hadn't arrived yet or she'd have popped me for thinking it. When Abby married Lee, I wondered if she'd dragged him to the alter drunk. No man in his sober mind would have exchanged vows with a woman like her, I kept saying.

And I kept getting hit upside the head for it too.

Abby doted on Carter more than the others. Spoiled him with anything he wanted – or might want. Not long ago he'd declared his life's dream to become a doctor. Well, his attitude sure suited the profession I said at the time, and since then it certainly hadn't changed.

Lee apologized for his youngest son's actions. I waved it off, "Like he said. Whatever."

He pointed to the teen remaining on the sofa, "You remember Tony. He's quite the young man now. Tony, remember Mama's cousin Savannah?"

Tony was actually the middle child. At seventeen, he looked nothing like Abby or Lee. Tall with black hair to his shoulders and skinny as a nail. The boy glanced up at me. His brow sank, "Mama didn't like you."

Ennis tensed beside me. I touched his hand, a sign to calm down. Tony was born with a mental disability. My theory, though not popular, held merit. Abby and monogamy never mixed – and despite her taunting me about my failings with booze, she'd had her heyday with it too. Booze and adultery didn't mix well and over the years I'd suspected and eventually heard Tony was the result of Abby's overindulgence in too many men and the victim of her copious amounts of alcohol while pregnant.

Lee swallowed hard at his son's candor. He stammered a moment, trying to apologize but again I waved it off while gently addressing Tony, "I know she didn't like me, Tony –"

"But I do," the boy sprang from his seat and wrapped me in an embrace reminiscent of a Rutherford hug on steroids.

"Son, don't hurt Savannah," Lee cautioned, after seeing my cheeks and ears ripen. "She's carrying a baby so lighten up."

The boy immediately released me as though his father scolded him. I tried to ease his feelings by complimenting him but he looked away, shifting his weight from one foot then the other. The praise made him apprehensive for some reason and he quickly changed the subject, "Leesha said Mikey killed Mama."

"That's not been proven yet," I replied.

Most of the room fell silent. Alicia, busy in the kitchen, stopped cold at my words. She stared daggers at me while Lee frowned, "But he's in jail."

I shrugged, "I don't know the details because it's not my case. In my opinion, knowing Mikey, I don't believe he did it."

By this time, Alicia wandered into the living room. A little bit linebacker, a whole lot Bridezilla. Oh, she was pretty enough with her golden tresses, piercing blue eyes and a face that invited men to buy drinks for her at a bar. But her personality ranked one degree short of a Manson groupie on PCP.

Alicia brandished a long chef knife that she pointed at me, "The cops have the description of the killer. It fits Mike. Nurses said he threatened to kill her. It's an open and shut case. Why are you defending him?"

Now *this* was weird. The new wife wanting justice for the ex and at any cost, even if a potentially innocent boy went to prison. I studied Alicia for a moment, "We can't arrest him without evidence."

She wielded the knife in a more accusatory way, "But he was arrested for the murder!"

The whole room fell stone quiet. All eyes turned to me and Ennis as earlier. We weren't exactly received with flowers and smiles but my upcoming comments might have us booted out for good, "No. As it turned out, he was *questioned* about it but some unpaid speeding tickets landed him in jail overnight." Okay, so I sorta stretched the truth. He did have unpaid tickets and they had secured his place for the overnight stay. That gave the investigating detectives a chance to question him about the murder too.

My answer only incited her, "You surprise me. Abigail hated you almost as much as she hated me. Why aren't you dancing in the streets that she's dead?"

Well, how peachy. Right in front of the kids. "Because, Alicia, she has family who loves her. Whether or not she liked me doesn't matter anymore."

She spun on her heel, mumbling something unintelligible as she tramped into the kitchen. Did I not tell my sister that coming here was a bad idea? Yes, I did. I told her we'd be as welcome as leprosy and she still insisted on exercising those damn Southern manners.

"I loved Mama," said Tony, tears rolling down his cheeks.

I gave him a gentle hug, "I know you did, honey. She loved you too."

"Bullshit," Alicia lashed out from the kitchen. "She hated that idiot —"

"Alicia, hush. Just hush." I cut my vision to Tony to emphasize my meaning. The kid already felt out of place in life so why was Alicia so cruel to him? He loved his mother, mean as she was, and I assumed Abby loved him in her own way. And why hadn't Lee defended the boy? Was everyone against this kid except me?

Lee's wife stepped toward me, her face darkening to maroon. Lee whipped a finger toward the kitchen, "You were busy in there, Leesh. Go."

"Savannah," Ennis tapped his watch, "we need to head back to work."

It was a lie because our shift was over but I saw the uneasiness clouding my husband's features. He wanted out now by any means possible, even fibbing.

Lee shook his head, "I'm sorry about all this, guys. I – I don't understand why everyone's acting this way."

"Grief," I said in an attempt to salve Lee's wounds. The man was embarrassed by his family's actions. No need to rub his nose in it. I began extending my condolences once more when Tony asked, "When did Mama die again?"

The question caught us all off guard. Lee cleared his throat, "She died Wednesday, son. Why?"

A spark of recognition lit Tony's eyes, "Oh yeah. The night Carter an' me stayed out late and drove across town. Long ways away from church. I should have gone to church."

"Shut up, retard," Carter snapped. He followed up with a scoff, "You went to church, remember?"

Tony shrank back, "Did not. You wouldn't take me. Didn't

have time, you said. We stayed out past my bedtime cause you wanted to go 'cross town."

Carter's voice held a thread of violence. "I was meeting friends that night, remember, dummy? I only brought you along 'cause Daddy told me to."

Tony's head bowed, "I didn't want to go. I missed church. I always go to church Wednesday night. Got home late. Too late. I was really late for bed."

"Why couldn't Alisha or Willie Dean take you to church?" I asked this softly and with plenty of diplomacy.

Lee sighed, answered on their behalf, "Alisha was at Kroger. Willie Dean had a late shift at Home Depot."

"And I got stuck with him all night," Carter finished. "Why are you asking questions anyway?" He hitched his thumb at Ennis, "Didn't he say you were leaving?"

Lee used a sharper tongue this time when calling his son down. I mentally rolled my eyes. Had I spoken to a guest in that tone, Daddy would have literally backhanded me in front of the guest – and I'd have deserved it.

Personally, I had enough sass from this arrogant little shit. I'd suffered the demise of my beloved Camaro and survived a plague of snakes. I refused to let some boorish little smartass sink his teeth into me, "You still dreaming of becoming a doctor?"

"That's no dream. It's reality," he boasted. "I can attend any Ivy League school I choose. I'm a self-made man."

I cocked a brow, "How wonderful. That relieves the Almighty of a great responsibility." Mama always said arrogance and rudeness were the training wheels on the bicycle of life – for weak people who couldn't keep their balance without them. Before me stood a prime example.

Carter closed in on me. Ennis stepped between us as a precaution. Carter's bravado melted faster than a snowball in summer. Oh, at first he tried standing his ground for his ego's sake but he eventually waved us off, "Go back to writing parking tickets and taking bribes."

Even with a smile, my reply flew hot off my tongue, "First thing I do is run your license and registration for infractions, kiddo." Before I started World War III, I bid farewell to Tony and Lee. The second my feet hit the porch, I took a deep, cleansing breath then reached for my phone to call Mathis. I alerted him to investigate Lee's family until the whole bunch resembled Swiss cheese. Something wasn't right about them but honestly there never was. Our reception, though, felt icier than normal, like they'd closed ranks around themselves. I wanted to know why.

We were halfway to the car and I glanced at my watch again. Where the hell were Georgia and Seth? Late to the hanging, as usual. Of course, it technically qualified as a fileting if Alicia made good on her threat with the knife.

We headed to Ennis's truck when a deep-throated engine rumbled up behind the Ram. It was that spiffy blue Charger with Seth behind the wheel and Leah riding shotgun. He polished the dash a bit with hand and adjusted the rearview mirror. How sweet. My brother tinkered with his new car while we got tarred and feathered. Perfect.

Only then did I see Georgia and Dane pull in behind him. Georgia got out of the car holding a casserole dish. I shook my head. That was my sister. Always bringing the food. One step inside that house and she'd figure out how appreciated her efforts were when they used the casserole as a cannonball and her as a target.

"You're late," I hurled the indictment at Georgia who instantly drew back. While I had her back on her heels, I added, "They're as friendly as vipers in there and personally, I've had enough of snakes."

Dane gulped, "'Fraid it's my fault, Peach. I hit every light wrong then got lost."

"And I rounded them up," Seth said.

Remind me to get lost next time my sister bullies me into something stupid, I nearly blurted to Ennis.

My vision never wavered from my sister, "Enter at your own risk. Your prized Southern manners'll take a beatin' like mine did. Hell, Alicia's brandishing a foot long knife to drive home her point, pardon the pun."

Georgia's eyes widened. She looked to Ennis for verification which he provided, "It's pretty tense in there, especially if you have a badge."

Seth joined the conversation, "Georgia, if they'll pile on a pregnant woman, I hate to see what happens to us. I think we should go home."

Her vision dropped to the foil covered casserole in her hands. I harrumphed, "Wasted effort if you take that inside. It's best to turn around, go home, and we'll eat that ourselves."

She mulled over the idea as Dane winked at me, "It did smell mighty tasty while it baked."

"Then after we eat," I hinted, "Seth can take us for a spin in his new car."

"It's not mine," Seth said, dangling the keys at me. "It's a loaner for you. Try it out, see if it fits."

My pulse quickened. My pupils dilated. An actual smile curved my lips. That childlike joy of Christmas morning wound through me until my toes tingled. I wanted to drive that car the second I saw it. It had everything. An engine. Four wheels. Four doors. Best of all – it wasn't a cinder.

Ennis sighed beside me. I figured he saw monthly payments and higher insurance rates but I saw freedom from riding in a Dodge Ram that rode as smooth as a wild mustang. Before accepting the keys I asked, "Exactly who is loaning the car to me?"

My brother explained, "The friend of mine I mentioned. The one who owns the car lot. He got the Charger yesterday. It's used but in really good condition and drives like a beauty."

Now I took the keys. Ennis could pout in private. I needed my own wheels, loaner or not. And what a sharp looking ride she was.

26

The shadowy figure skulked across the top of the screen, paused momentarily, looked back then disappeared between Abby's house and her neighbor's. The figure wore a dark blue or black hoodie and long shorts. He or she looked heavyset, Caucasian, and a rough judgment of height put that person around five eight.

While Ennis and I attended Abby's funeral, Mathis scrounged her neighborhood for witnesses and clues. The neighbor across the street offered the security footage from his front porch camera. He'd seen the black blob lurking across the screen when he finally reviewed his tapes. For some reason Mathis asked me to watch the video for ID purposes. I had no formal experience in identifying black fuzzy blobs, I said, but what the hell I'd give it a shot. After catching a glimpse of the blob, I wondered if Mathis lost his mind. Not only did the individual walk hunkered over, he or she never turned completely toward the camera. The futility of the exercise annoyed me but not as much as Mathis' earlier accusation that, "You thought *that* was *me?*"

Mathis ignored my indignation. He merely shrugged, "I was working with witness descriptions, Prince. You're about that height and you're not exactly trim anymore thanks to Rutherford's energetic swimmers. How do I know what you do at night? Or what you wear while you do it?"

I thrust a finger at the monitor, "John Mathis, how the hell could you suggest *that* was me? I may be the size of a battleship but I've *never* worn a hoodie in my entire life."

"Yeah, but you don't dress like this," he pointed to my pantsuit, "every hour of the day, right? Again, that person is white, around your height, heavy in the middle and never really turns to the camera..."

Oh, this was insane. "My shoulders aren't that broad," I defended. "You could land a cargo plane on those things." Then I pointed to my belly, "This is a baby," then to the monitor, "that is fat. If I tried to move that stealthily, Lily would grab my gall bladder and swing it like a dead cat until I crumpled on the lawn."

He smirked, telling me he'd purposefully – and successfully – yanked my chain. "Yeah, your kid's more like you than you think," he said then pulled a photograph from his suit jacket. "Maybe this'll brighten your day. Coroner placed your cousin's death around 9:30 to 10:00 that night, right? While you were paying your respects yesterday, a girl came in with this."

He handed me the photo. It was from a digital camera. The focal point: a woman with her bulldog. She kneeled down, allowing the dog to slurp her cheek. The effect of the park lights against the scene created a subdued glow around the two like a heavenly aura. I didn't get his meaning, "How's this supposed to brighten my day?"

"Look behind the woman to her left. Who does that look like to you?"

Mathis indicated an area in the semi-background, just yards from the charming scene of lady and pup's special moment. The man observing the touching sight was Michael Howard. He'd told me that he spent all night at Piedmont Park. This verified he was there at some point that night. The photo rekindled a spark of hope, "What time was this taken?"

Mathis reached back in his jacket. Normally I'd complain about his theatrics but I wanted Mikey to be innocent. Grace raised her kids right. Regardless of Mikey's temper, I kept his good old Southern upbringing in mind. He might have wanted to kill Aunt Abby but disgracing his mother's name and her utter disappointment prevented him from following through. Before handing me another photo, Mathis explained, "The photo you're holding is enlarged from the original. The photographer keeps the time and date on each picture for records. Then she hides it somehow for publishing purposes. Here's the time and date."

I grabbed the photo, checked the time and date stamp. The date: the night Abby died. The time: 9:40. John's mouth curled into a proud grin while he offered me two other photos with Mikey in the background. These stamped 9:46 and 9:58. I resisted the urge to throw my arms around him and kiss my colleague, "John, this is excellent news. I can't wait to tell Gracie."

Pride broadened his chest, "Be sure to tell her who cleared her kid. Detective John Mathis and I *do* accept thanks in the form of food, but only if her abilities measure up to yours or Georgia's."

"As I recall, they do."

"Then pass that along. And tell her the kid's either got an angel on his shoulder or a stalker. Either way, he ended up in this woman's pictures during the time your cousin met St. Peter so the boy can breathe easy again."

I patted his shoulder, "Thanks, John. You still coming to the contest tomorrow? You'll get some good eats there, at least from our side of the family."

"You still going through with that? Even after your cousin got knocked off?"

It was a cruel reality but, "We signed a contract and their lawyers don't care who died. Georgia contacted the producer, told him what had happened with Abby but he's holding us to the agreement."

"Don't seem right, does it?"

"No, it doesn't," I sighed.

"Hey, I gotta ask. Does your family – not you per se – but does your family inbreed?"

I'd never heard John Mathis use the term *per se*. I did a doubletake at the phrase even falling from his lips. Plus, my stomach churned at the mere suggestion of my lineage trailing back to brothers and sisters and fathers and daughters participating in such depravity. To know I descended from French dancers on Mama's side and a band of wild moonshiners on Daddy's disturbed me enough. "Mathis, why the hell are you asking that?"

"Because I met Abby's kids. Two of 'em are sociopaths and the other," his finger circled his temple, "ain't all there. I mean, I'm not accusing your whole family of being from Kentucky, but that branch is pretty cockeyed."

Why did I suddenly feel defensive again? I mean, Mathis was painfully correct. Abby's kids *were* blockheads – with the exception of Tony. "John, I agree that Willie Dean and Carter are loosely woven but Tony's problem is Abby drank while she was pregnant. Fetal alcohol syndrome, at least that's the story."

My colleague peered over his glasses, "Did she drink her way through the distillery?"

"Mathis," I warned. "Tony's a good kid. He's a little slow but he's sweet."

"Well, the other two ain't. We'll be seein' more of those shits later, I'm sure of it. That youngest kid cozied up to step-mama so close he coulda crawled into her skin. You got some cracked nuts for kin, Prince. Cracked like the Liberty Bell. At least Lee's alibi checks out. At work until late. As for the spawn, the oldest, Willie Dean – and where they found *that* name is a mystery best left unsolved – clocked out at Home Depot at 10:23. Middle kid, no alibi except little brother Carter who swears the two were with his friends. I've yet to track those down because I doubt Carter's likable enough to have friends. Step-mom Alicia said she was at Kroger but the three nearest stores ain't got security video of her in their stores or parking lots. I've called the other stores for their security footage. If she don't show up on any of those, I'm taking aim on her because Abby kept nagging Lee for more money for the youngest sociopath. Alicia admitted to confronting Abby about being a 'greedy bitch' and said they got into a screaming match."

"Oh, I bet there was more action than that."

"Me too so I'm gonna put pressure on her, see if I can dig out the real details. Phone records show calls to Abby's phone from," he flipped through a folder, slid his finger down the page, "Lee, Alicia and the youngest turd Carter. All within thirty minutes before Abby's death. Wonder what all the fuss was that night."

God only knew. Family could make mountains out of molehills and mine could freeze water to ice with one glance. Give 'em a gun or knife and they'd ravage a group of good and decent people quicker than a plague of locusts could strip a farmer's field.

"Well, I'm headed out to talk to step-mama again. Any words of advice?"

"Just one. Duck."

27

"The Cooking Network bought the rights to our episode," Georgia bubbled with joy. Me? I sighed while my sister raved on about the joys of nationwide television "or even worldwide viewers seeing us".

My lack of enthusiasm on the phone failed to dampen hers, "I spent all morning on Facebook and Twitter. People *want* to see us, Savannah. They want airdates and times. This is great!"

Yeah. Great. My sister, the social butterfly, got her fans all hyped about our cooking show. All that meant was more people would see my burgeoning belly, my short temper and my contempt for Linda and Teresa. What I hated most? I had to behave myself. I never wanted to participate in the contest anyway, I nearly reminded her. Now we had both red and blue states weighing in – and agreeing – on one collective subject. Food. My sister's excitement overrode her common sense at times. Her passion for cooking steamrolled the simple matter of privacy and she plastered the whole damn mess on the internet. Sheesh. "And I assume you accommodated them with all the details."

"Of course," she gushed then decided to hint, "and they wanted to know if you have Facebook and Twitter accounts."

"Tell them why should I when I have you?"

"Savannah, what's wrong? Think of this as an opportunity to explore new horizons. Other doors may open for us after this show. Besides, Lily needs a mother with a stable job, not one where she's worrying if Mama will come home at all. Cooking is enjoyable and you might actually have fun."

"First of all, Lily needs *a stable mother*, not one pining for the job she quit under duress. Second, I love to cook, just not in front of millions of people. I'm not Julia Child and what kind of opportunity is this exactly? Are you going to quit writing if the show is a hit?" Gotcha, sis, I thought. Take that.

"No," she answered too quickly for my taste. "Because writing isn't hazardous to my health and I can fit it in my schedule. This is an incredible chance for us to work together. We've always worked well as a team."

Well, that was true. Ever since we were old enough to crack eggs into a bowl, we'd helped Mama with meals. The older we got, we managed to whip out a large, tasty meal to feed our family. I understood her logic but I had retirement pay to think about. It didn't make sense to retire from the department at my age. I gently reminded, "Let's get through this contest first before we start changing my life plans. But tell your tweets, twits, tweeps or whatever not to judge our whole lineage by the two idiots we're competing with."

I'd just hung up with Georgia when my phone rang again. I assumed it was her again, "I'm not apologizing for calling them idiots so forget it."

"Still making friends I see," the deep, gravelly male voice

chuckled.

My brain, expecting Georgia's thick drawl to shoot back a reprimand, screeched to a halt instead. "Riley, is that you?"

"Nah, it's your Aunt Pearl. Don't you love my new voice?" He allowed no time for any crass or witty response, "Hey, spare a minute for your old partner?"

I had no *seconds* to spare, much less actual minutes but for Riley, I'd drop practically anything. He'd bailed me out of trouble so many times I lost count. He didn't though. The man possessed the memory of an elephant – and had the belly to match. Now he supervised undercover operations instead of babysitting rookies. "Sure," I said. "Come on over–"

"I'm at our old haunt. Can you beat it over right now?"

Funny how he never mentioned O'Malley's Bar by name. He chose his words carefully and instead of coming to a police station, he insisted we meet in private. I wondered if it related to his job since undercover cops shied from police stations when on assignment. There was a reason for this meeting and his manner of requesting it. When Riley's cautious side emerged, it made me uneasy, "I'm on my way."

O   O   O

Opening the door to O'Malley's immediately threw me into the past. Memories returned of tossing back Jack Daniels with my partner, feeling the stinging warmth slide down my throat, coat my stomach to begin working on all my day's demons, helping them fade away. Back then I yearned for end of shift so I could trudge into this place, soak my troubles in the clear amber liquid then go home and pass out.

The place looked, smelled and sounded the same. The dim lighting and smoky air mixed with both loud and quiet conversations at the tables and bar. Of the various liquors I smelled, I pinpointed Jack in an instant. Experts said smell was the most powerful sense. One whiff transported a person to either good times or bad. It took me back to walking into O'Malley's and ordering my Jack. My mouth began to water for it and I pushed the memory and desire away, telling myself I was different now. Older, more mature and certainly happier than before.

I spied Riley at the bar. He was hard to miss. He was big, loud and gruff, and Irish through and through. He frequently quoted his mother's Irish gems of wisdom, good luck followed the man like a shadow and drinking meant never getting drunk. I envied the man in my drinking days. We'd drink, I'd sway and he'd laugh as he steadily moseyed out of the bar.

Riley personified the definition of cop. No nonsense, by-the-book unless he deemed otherwise, and a man no one tangled with. He started as my training officer then later my first partner and I drove him nuts. He nicknamed me PITA for Pain In The Ass, a moniker that persisted on occasion, but we still cared for each other. I respected him and loved him like an older brother – an older brother fifteen years my senior. And I was still his PITA.

"Oopsa-daisy," Murphy chuckled as I approached the bar, shrugged from my suit jacket, slung it over my arm. That gave him front row seat viewing of my eight month condition. He pointed to my stomach while addressing the bartender, "Lookee there, Joe. This is what happens when you leave rookies without chaperones."

"Nice to see you too, Murph," I slid onto the barstool next to him.

He waved off my tone, "I'm surprised Rutherford ain't walking sideways for doing that to ya. I remember the days when you swore you'd never have kids."

"People change." In front of me I saw my old nemesis. A small glass of Jack sat, waiting for me to partake of a sip for old time's sake. There were times the craving reared up, mostly under extreme stress. I supposed once a person fought the battle, they always fought it, no matter what, no matter when.

I nudged the Jack toward Murphy and ordered a club soda. Riley downed the whiskey, "Sorry about that. Wouldn't have ordered it if I'd known. So I guess you and Rutherford are married for keeps if you took that step. Cause you might have been reckless as a rookie, but I damn well know you ain't reckless as a woman."

A thin, older gentleman, Bartender Joe perfected the passive expression of a man who'd heard too much bullshit in his life. He flat didn't care, his face said as he sat the club soda down then went about his business. I watched the bubbles dance to the surface and I smiled. Back when, I never would have accepted such a "ridiculous" drink. People change, I'd told Riley. Over the years, I changed more than I ever thought possible. "We're here to stay, Murph," I said. "We've hit some really rough patches and our marriage still survived."

Murphy looked away, stared at his drink instead, "Yeah, I heard what happened with that Holland bastard. At least he's out of your hair and rotting behind bars. I'm glad you and Rutherford are happy, kid. You finally found someone you can trust. He's a good guy. Better than that dirtbag you were with years ago."

Ah, yes. Toby Jackson, dirtbag extraordinaire and Satan's other minion besides Jeffrey Holland. Toby dealt his own version of hell and had I bothered to stay sober, I'd have dumped him much sooner.

To avoid prickly subjects like men who tried to hurt or kill me, I asked if he received the invite to the cooking contest the next day.

Murphy nodded, "I'll be there. Didn't realize you cooked." He stopped, looked straight at me, "You *can* cook, right? I'm not going home with Ebola or tape worms, am I?"

"Not from our food. Can't speak for my cousins."

He tapped the empty glass on the bar, a sign for a refill. Joe obliged as Murphy chuckled, "You *have* changed, kid. Married, knocked up, you cook and avoid whiskey. Miracles do happen."

Riley wasn't a man to call a meeting for no reason. If he said 'hi' before getting down to business, a person called themselves lucky so it surprised me that he indulged in any pleasantries. His blatant hesitance set me on edge, "Murph, why did you want to see me?"

"Wow, look who's reverted back to her impatient nature. Can't your old partner just invite you down here for a drink and chat?"

"No, not you. You're straightforward and blunt. Always have been."

Joe passed by and Riley announced with pride, "She knows me,

Joe. She knows me too well."

Joe didn't respond with words or expression. He chose instead to glance at me then pour another drink for Riley without prompting. Joe's silence was a change from the bartender I remembered. The guy serving me drinks back then joked and regaled his customers with funny stories. Joe was stone quiet which made me feel even more out of place.

Riley's voice lowered to a near whisper, "Word is you're on Troy Quinn's radar. That's hazardous, especially in your condition."

"I'm not working the case anymore, Murph. Hunter reassigned me to the Jane Doe in the hospital."

My answer neglected to ease the worry lines on his face. He toyed with the glass of whiskey then took another swallow, "I'm tellin' ya be careful, kid. If ya never listened before, listen now. There ain't no cure for death."

I caught the fact he cautioned me but after telling him my new assignment, I expected it to ease his concern but it hadn't. And how had he heard about Quinn's vendetta anyway? A knot of fear formed in my gut. Riley knew something and I hoped he volunteered it before my phone beckoned me back to work.

"I heard about your car and the snakes," he continued. "I realize you have a granite skull but take my advice and lay low. Take a vacation. Take lost time. Get out of town for a while until things blow over. Your kid's more important than this punk."

"Where did you hear about all this?" I realized the man's sixth sense verged on spooky but a chill raked my spine until I shivered. Information moved freely in the department at times but for Murphy to know those details, the department had a hole the size of Dallas.

He tapped his glass again, signaling for a refill. Joe dutifully poured another drink and respectfully backed off. Riley waited then asked, "You remember John Hawkins, the beat cop from way back?"

Who could forget? Internal Affairs proved Hawkins was on the payroll of a gang leader in the city. He abused his authority in various and creative ways like taking payoffs and intimidating and strong-arming people for handsome sums of money. After Internal Affairs crucified him on the job, they finished him off in the press until he ate his gun one Friday after boozing it up at a nearby bar. "I remember him," I said, wondering where the conversation led.

"You got one in your midst. A Hawkins."

Now my fear darkened to anger. "Who?" I demanded. I hated being terse with my friend but I also hated to think *my* sixth sense screwed me over too. I lost my confidence when I misjudged Cole Jordan a while back. I just about choked on fury to think I'd overlooked another Judas in our midst.

"Think about it, kid," Riley deadpanned. "Who's new in your precinct?"

I resented his tone, "You mean uniforms or detectives? We all coexist in that building."

"This ain't no uni, Prince. That's my point. There's a pipeline of info leading straight to Quinn and it comes from a gold shield."

That meant either Nesbitt or Clark. Perfect. But which one? Nesbitt and I rarely interacted but Clark warmed up to me lately – particularly after being assigned the case. Asking questions, prodding for clues or information I might have.   "How do you know this?" I asked Riley.

"Uniforms in Zone 3 overheard a couple of scumbags talkin' about you and Quinn.   Scumbags working *for* Quinn.   The uniforms wanted you warned that you're in danger.   So take your husband and kid and get the hell out of town before Quinn and his cop crony take matters into their own hands."   He lifted the glass and gulped the whole drink. "Y'know, Prince, when we met you were a real pain in my ass.   Then you went and grew on me.   Don't make me have to attend your funeral.   It'd ruin my week."   Riley scooped his coat over his arm, tossed money on the bar then clapped me on the shoulder, "Watch your back, kid.   There are people out to get you.   Again."

28

Riley's warning haunted me through the night. Mentioning it to Ennis meant another battle over my retiring so I chose to wait on telling him. With the contest the next day, I needed rest and I failed to get it. I compared Nesbitt and Clark, their personalities, their actions and words. Nesbitt treated the job the way plenty of cops did. A means for a paycheck and benefits. He loved spending that money on things most cops found either ostentatious or just plain useless or overrated. Boats, Tybee Island house rentals, private schools for the kids and spa days for the wife. Clark wanted respect and fast recognition. She adopted the bullying trait female cops tended to develop when striving for them. She drove a semi-new car, lived in an apartment and had a Pomeranian. Not so much a big spender. Whoever was Quinn's mole either was flaunting their payoffs from the Irishman or stashing the cash to look modest. And personally I grew weary of trying to figure it all out so I closed my eyes, hoping for a *modest* four hours sleep.

O O O

Food verged on a religion in the South, its holy trinity being sugar, butter and salt. Every dish a Southerner prepared required at least one of those ingredients, otherwise it was labeled *just plain wrong* or, in other words, *Yankee.*

We prayed over food, used it to please palates in times of celebration and comfort folks in times of mourning. The Southern way defined hospitality because no one dared arrive at a pot luck supper or family reunion empty-handed simply because it was *just plain wrong.* And every self-respecting Southern woman stewed and sweated over the stove and/or oven to personally prepare said dish since offering purchased edibles ranked as low as a snake's belly in a wagon rut.

Below the Mason-Dixon line, food wasn't an art-form, it was our heritage. It involved recipes handed down for generations, secret ingredients, and the sacred moment when mothers turned their kitchens over to their daughters. The ceremony, however brief or informal, was a significant and meaningful rite between the two women.

Food was love in the South so it made perfect sense that a TV show capitalized on it. What didn't make sense: Teresa's bright yellow dress. She probably chose the outfit to appear cheery. It made me think of a canary. Linda dressed for comfort in a turquoise t-shirt and her usual Wranglers. At least my eyes didn't hurt when I looked at her. Georgia's attire reflected confidence and comfort. A pine green pullover with snug fitting jeans. She looked magnificent. Me? I went with a Monday morning go-to-work black pantsuit/ violet blouse ensemble that I prayed slimmed my formidable girth on television.

The four of us arrived at the restaurant at 8:00 that morning. The crew arrived two hours before us, setting up cameras, stocking the pantry and fridge. Andrew gave us a brief summary of the day's schedule. We'd spend an hour being interviewed for clips they'd edit into the cooking segments. We'd get an in-depth tour of the kitchen so we'd feel more comfortable when the contest's timer began. Then he handed us a schedule for the afternoon. We had a couple of hours to prepare our chickens and give them time to marinate if we chose to do so. Guests arrived at 5:00 to be served at 5:30.

Split into two distinct cooking areas, the kitchen sparkled with spotless cabinets, stainless steel fridges, stoves and ovens. The show allowed us to bring our own cutlery which pleased Georgia since she prized her knives. She bought me an identical set years ago. They stayed packed away when I was single since I rarely cooked meals. Now I could handle the knives nearly as proficiently as Georgia.

Our formal kitchen tour ended on a casual note from Andrew, "They'll be filming while you work. Just act natural, pretend the cameras aren't there."

Say what? Pretend not to see the guy holding an object the size of a bazooka aimed *directly at me*? Sure. "Just ignore the elephant in the room."

My sarcasm spurred Georgia to frown, "You've been on TV before. What's the problem?"

"I'm usually in the background while someone else takes the heat."

"Pretend we're helping Mama." Her frown lines deepened, "And for heaven's sake, *smile*. With that expression and a knife in your hand you'll look like a serial killer."

Well, I thought, if it kept the cameraman away...

Georgia claimed our side of the kitchen by setting her knife case on a cabinet. She unzipped the canvas case, suggesting, "Why don't I cut up the chicken and you can start the buttermilk brine and spice rub?"

I set my knife case aside, "You're faster at cutting chicken anyway."

Older sisters tended to take over. At least mine did. She commandeered everything from church suppers to my life. In reality, the contest belonged to her anyway. She accepted the challenge and I was there to help. So I stepped back and opted to take orders. To a point.

Across the room I saw Linda and Teresa with their bin of chickens and a utensil comparable to a paring knife. Oh, this'll be good, I mused. Georgia skillfully wielding a blade barely short of a samurai sword and there was Linda using a frog sticker. Our cousins were a sitcom in the making.

A cameraman caught me staring at Linda and headed that way. While he busied himself with the cousins, I gathered ingredients for the spice rub. First I grabbed the garlic and onion powder, cradled them in the crook of my arm and added thyme and marjoram. I stuffed the cayenne in there too then added the salt and pepper.

The camera guy kept filming Linda, still entranced by her adeptness at gashing poultry to bits with the equivalent of a pen knife. I couldn't resist. Walking by her, I stopped to observe her frantic hacking then asked, "*What* are you doing to that poor bird?"

"Cuttin' it apart for fryin'. What's it look like?" she shot back.

A scene out of Friday the 13th, that's what. I had the decency to keep that tidbit to myself.

I marched back to Georgia's station to see her *cuttin'* our chickens apart. Her knife moved with smooth, quick precision. The wings and thighs came apart with flawless ease. That's more than I could say for my cousin's wild butchering. "You make that look a lot less terrifying than Linda," I told Georgia.

She continued working without looking up, "What do you mean?"

I leaned to her ear, "She's slashing those birds to pieces. Looks like a horror film back there." I turned, surprised to see that the cameraman somehow crept behind me, ambushing me in my moment of uncomplimentary honesty. I defended my statement, "Well, it does."

Georgia smirked but, unlike me, exercised good judgment by not speaking. I tried to develop the knack of diplomacy for my child's sake since no kid wants Oscar the Grouch for their PTA representative. The last minute reminded me I needed to try harder.

"Did you get the onion and garlic powder?" Georgia asked for some ridiculous reason. Had I exhibited signs of confusion or ineptness? I made Mama's chicken thousands of times. I remembered what Mama used and basically in what amounts. I pushed my aggravation aside, "Yes, I got 'em."

"Thyme? Marjoram?"

"Y'know," now the aggravation clawed to the surface, "the walls have ears. Why don't you announce the recipe over the PA system? The astronauts at the space station didn't quite hear you."

Georgia swiveled to face me. Her mouth quirked with humor,

"You're honestly concerned they'll copy our recipe? Even if they try, how many times have you seen Teresa or Linda produce an edible meal? Especially one that could win money?"

"Teresa won the last one."

"Against Linda. Not much competition there, agreed?"

My sister's penchant for being right usually chafed me – until that moment. "Yes, I got the thyme and marjoram," I answered. "And I'm going after the other ingredient now." No need tempting fate by actually naming the hot sauce, just in case the cousins overheard. So off to the spice cabinet I went. Mama was a fire bug. She loved hot food and somehow the love of it transferred to me. Normally when I prepared the chicken, I made two separate batches, one for Ennis and one for me. Ennis liked his food mild with less cayenne and I preferred mine wild like Mama.

I stopped by the fridge for the buttermilk. When I opened the door, a welcome blast of cool air wafted across my warm face. In the midst of all my running I'd begun to sweat which wrecked the refined, graceful image I aimed for. Covertly wiping my brow, I lamented how pregnant women had enough stress growing a sweet healthy baby. This pregnant woman, I groused, should have slapped Teresa when she insulted our mother's culinary abilities, walked away and called it a day. But thanks to my trusty, honor-bound sister, I got strong-armed – and, of course, *guilted* – into the competition and now I sweated heavier than a linebacker in the Super Bowl.

I grabbed the buttermilk from the fridge and noticed Teresa hawking me. Now what could she possibly be doing – except what I warned Georgia about. Spying. If we were playing the espionage game, I'd play too. Hey, all was fair in love and food and I wanted to win. Plus, no one said I couldn't mislead the competition...

I tucked the buttermilk under my arm with hopes she didn't see it. Then I scouted the rest of the fridge. Ensuring Teresa saw every move, I grabbed the sour cream, a stick of butter and package of cream cheese and headed back to my station.

Setting the buttermilk aside, I saw Georgia glance at my extra parcels. A half-second passed with she did a doubletake, her jaw dropping in disbelief.

"Calm down," I assured in a whisper. "It's for Teresa's benefit."

My sister teetered on the verge of a genuine conniption so I explained, "She's nosing around – no, she's *cheating* – so I decided to mislead her on our ingredients."

Once the words digested and she realized I hadn't lost my faculties, Georgia's shoulders relaxed and her face split into a grin, "Where'd you learn that?"

"On those cooking shows, of course. I've watched just enough to learn their devious ways. Gosh, I can't wait to see what her and Linda fry up for supper."

Unbeknownst to me, the cameraman lurked behind us, catching the whole shrewd plan on video. I rolled my eyes. After seeing that segment, the public would never trust a cop again. I wasn't mean or vicious or an evil genius. Hell, I wasn't even a straight "B" student in school. As a kid, I thought Solomon had seven hundred wives and three hundred porcupines. But I was a child. Even now Teresa still thought a migration was a bad headache and last I heard, Linda believed the Berlin Wall was built because Germany was competing with China. I wasn't stupid and I wasn't entirely smart but I *was* clever when I suspected someone tried to steal something precious like my Mama's fried chicken recipe.

Georgia and I tossed a casual glance over our shoulders to see both sisters hovering around the fridge. Linda held the cream cheese and Teresa the sour cream. She studied the small carton as if ruminating on how we used the stuff. Their lack of knowledge surprised but mostly entertained me. For two people claiming their mother taught them the finer points of cooking, they sure acted like doofs. They trekked back to their station with the items and I chuckled, "She forgot the butter. It won't turn out right without it."

"Savannah," Georgia scolded under her breath.

"What? If they're silly enough to copy us then why shouldn't I protect Mama's recipe?"

I swore I saw a glint of pride in my sister's expression. She arched one brow, agreeing I was right. My sister said I was right? I immediately checked around for flying pigs.

Slipping on a pair of latex gloves – the only thing about this ordeal besides the cameras that felt like my usual job, I began measuring out the dry spices. I started with the thyme and marjoram then moved to the onion and garlic powder. Salt and pepper and... Wait. We hadn't discussed the amount of cayenne pepper, "Should I make it mild or wild?"

"Try for in between. We don't want to light them on fire but we want some bite to the coating."

Nothing helped like vague answers so I used my judgment, praying I didn't send anyone to the hospital or us to the Hall of Shame. Then I robbed Georgia of her chicken parts and systematically coated the pieces in the mix. We'd need one hour to marinate the chicken in the mixture. For better zest, they needed every minute to steep in the spice rub. Mama's chicken came out with incredible flavor and a dark, crispy skin. When those diners crunched through it into the juicy, tender meat, the heat of the spices would warm their palates. The more they chewed, the more subtle heat set in – not enough to singe their tongue but just enough to turn a Southerner's cheeks pink with delight.

Georgia glanced at the clock, "I'll get busy with the mashed potatoes, you work on the corn. By that time we can start the biscuits."

"Aye, aye, captain." I poured the buttermilk into a bowl, stirred in the hot sauce then transferred everything to the fridge.

With Georgia busying herself with the potatoes, I headed for the amply supplied vegetable bins provided by the show. For the savory corn, I needed to shave corn off the cob, chop chili peppers, onion and cilantro for seasoning. I chose a very mild pepper since our chicken was the star of the show. The corn would have its own personality without stealing the main course's thunder.

After shaving corn and chopping onion and peppers, I moved to the cilantro, added a couple of eggs, some flour and vegetable oil and salt and pepper. Before I mixed everything, Georgia magically appeared at my shoulder, "How's it going?"

Her sudden hovering came as no surprise. When time got tight, she ensured we maintained the schedule. Holidays, church bake sales, everything required timing for her. "Fine," I said. "Just about finished with the first batch."

That seemed to calm her down. Anyone who knew Georgia knew she took three things deadly serious. Marriage, writing and cooking. If my life depended on an answer to one of those subjects, Georgia was my "phone a friend" to bail me out. She approved of my effort and despite my seemingly cavalier attitude, I valued that approval.

So I proceeded mixing everything and left the whole mess until time to cook. The savory corn tasted better freshly fried and hot.

Soon the kitchen filled with the aroma of a Southern family reunion – fried chicken, corn, potatoes and biscuits. Linda and Teresa managed a nice potato dish that smelled pretty good and that annoyed me to no end. All our food looked a hell of a lot better than *we* did – well, with the exception of Georgia who could survive a tornado, flood, six family holidays and nuclear Armageddon and still look April Fresh. That also annoyed me. Linda, Teresa and I wiped our brows, braced our aching backs and grumbled our discontent but did so in the nosy cameraman's absence.

A couple of hours later, the diners were seated and ready to eat, I rushed around the kitchen, grabbing plates and filling them while Georgia fried the last of the chicken. In my haste, I fought to avoid colliding with Linda and Teresa who did their own relay race to and from the stacks of plates.

I peeked at their culinary endeavor. My heart sank. I experienced a feeling I never expected to have regarding those two. Fear.

Heading over to Georgia, I whispered, "Theirs doesn't look or smell half bad. What happened? I thought they'd fry dirt or something."

Unflustered, Georgia took over plating the mashed potatoes and corn, "You say it all the time. Never underestimate your opponent. Put the biscuit next to the chicken otherwise it'll get mushy from the corn and potatoes."

How the hell did my sister keep her cool under these conditions? My God, my head hurt, my stomach was a giant clenched fist and Lily's patience dwindled fast. And to think we might lose to my cousins? The possibility crushed me. How could I face my colleagues, not to mention my husband *and* the mirror after losing to them?

"How y'all doin'?" Teresa sounded far less lively and pretentious than earlier that day.

"Peachy," I smiled in case a camera lurked nearby. "And you?"

She dragged her arm across her forehead and sighed, "Exhausted. I swear I feel a migration comin' on."

Georgia chuckled and I fought off my own laugh because the cameraman caught Teresa's grand faux pas on film. He advanced on me and Georgia as we worked, the lens lingering uncomfortably close over our shoulders and zeroing in on the flurry of activity on the plates. Behind him, Andy swooped into the kitchen, "Ladies, time to get these plates out. These folks are hungry." He stretched the word hungry to the point he sounded like a bona fide, backwoods hillbilly.

A slew of waiters converged on us, half at my plating area, the other half at Linda's. They carried three plates each and with a flowing gait, marched the food out to the diners.

When the cousin's plates passed by, Georgia appraised their effort. One eyebrow hiked higher as if to say *so what, ours is still better.*

Twenty minutes later all the guests feasted on our fare. A TV hooked up to cameras in the dining room allowed us private viewing of our soon-to-be judges. The feeds switched from area to area, giving us views of every group and their reactions to the meals. I saw Ennis and Dane, Seth and his family and from work I spied Josh Hunter along with his wife Michelle whose pregnant belly stuck out as far as mine. John Mathis attended as well as Christine Clark, a few uniform officers and the desk sergeant and his wife. Even Riley Murphy, dressed in his Sunday best, kept his promise to come. Georgia and I invited most of the diners but Linda and Teresa had a few loyalists out there too. I recognized a few extended family on the Culberson side – and oddly, I noticed Lee and Alicia and the boys attended the event. Alicia picked at both plates of food. The boys, however, dug into the food with typical teenage zeal.

I watched the desk sergeant and his wife. The gruff middle-aged uniform cop softened in the company of his spouse. Their conversation inspired an easy smile, something I'd never seen much of from him. His wife, a lovely woman in her mid-forties, appeared prim, precise and dressed for a formal occasion, migrated mostly to our plate, not our cousins'. That gave me hope. The best sign of all: Murphy plowing into our chicken dinner and not slowing for anything, not even the pesky cameraman loitering beside him.

Christine Clark sat with Mathis. They took a bite of Linda and Teresa's meal and to my absolute horror, nodded their approval. My lips pursed in indignation. This wasn't the slam dunk I'd hoped.

Now I focused on those two in particular. They moved to our chicken dinner. Mathis showed the first reaction. His brow shot up then uttered a comment to Christine who appeared amused by his remark.

Georgia pointed to Christine, "Oh look. John brought a date. She's pretty. Kinda young for him though. She looks younger than you."

Dear God. Seriously? Christine Clark and John Mathis a couple? Why didn't we just throw a lit match in a gas tank? "That's our newest detective, Christine Clark. Not his date. Unless you enjoy watching the carnage on nature shows, you don't want those two alone together." First day on the job, Christine not only drank all the coffee but complained about the disarray of the coffee room. Anyone assigned to our stationhouse knew John Mathis brewed the coffee and kept his own system regarding the room's chaos. No one with two brain cells to rub together uttered a word if they valued their life. But Christine had. From that point their interactions digressed. Only lately had Mathis and Clark begun to speak civilly to each other.

"They seem to be getting along okay," my gullible sister remarked. "They're conversing without bloodshed."

"Georgia, there are cameras everywhere. They're not going bananas in public, not when their badges are at stake."

She pointed to another couple of people in the background. Two men sitting at a table in the back, "Do you know them?"

I squinted at the screen. The images remained blurred and almost indistinguishable. Almost. My heart leapt in my throat and I swallowed hard, "No, but I certainly recognize them." Quinn's minions

Sean O'Leary and Kevin Hughes. The two guys from the jewelry store sat eating our food meant for invited guests.

I reached to my belt for my cell phone. Georgia saw me and frowned, "Who are you calling? Everyone we know is here."

"I'm calling Ennis. Those two guys are trouble." I started dialing his number only to have the phone swiped from my hand. I looked up to give Georgia a very opinionated piece of my mind but her stormy frown discouraged that. She closed the phone and pocketed it in her jeans, "Savannah, stop being a cop. You're a cook right now. A cook hoping our meal wins the prize money. Or don't you want Lily to have a college fund?"

"Don't lecture me, Georgia. If those two guys get a phone call from their boss, Lily won't have a *mother*, much less a college fund."

With hands on hips, she retired the frown for a motherly glare, "As you said, there are cameras everywhere. If they're trouble, they won't cause it during the meal or voting."

That's what *she* thought. I bridled the urge to remind her of my char-broiled Camaro and the den of snakes Quinn gifted me with. The man didn't give a crap about cameras or innocent victims.

Georgia and I stood, staring each other down. Her daring me to wrestle my phone back and me wishing I could. I wanted, *needed* the phone but according to my sister's expression, I stood a better chance of prying the gold from Fort Knox. Evidently sensing my thoughts, Georgia finished, "Talk to Ennis after Andrew reads the results. Then you can go back to being Supercop."

O   O   O

Andrew gathered and tallied the votes. He assembled the four of us before the crowd in firing squad formation, the cameras pointing at us like rifles, ready to record smiles or tears. Or both.

Teresa and Linda resembled the last roses of summer. I felt weary, my back ached and my nerves frayed at an alarming rate. Georgia remained steadfast, sweat free and gorgeous, of course. She hadn't spent the last thirty minutes staring at everyone's reactions to each bite, or tried lip-reading or judging expressions. Nope, not my sister. She was sure we'd win. I still felt anxious because I smelled the cousin's food and saw people's favorable reaction to it. If we lost this contest, we'd never hear the end of it from Linda and Teresa. I'd never have peace at work but worse, I'd have failed Georgia and Mama.

Had I sabotaged Georgia and along with it ruined her culinary reputation? She cherished her status in the community, not just for her writing but her cooking talents too. If I spiced the chicken too heavily or added too many onions to the corn, I may have just slashed her self-esteem to bits along with my own.

"Ladies and gentlemen, we have our winners," Andrew announced.

I glanced over the crowd. My family, friends and colleagues all stood in judgment of us. Even Quinn's goons had a say in the outcome and that really irritated me.

Andrew dragged out the results longer than a Southern man with a stammer. "The total votes amount to seventy. The meals were labeled simply 'A' and 'B' and our guests were asked to taste each component of the meal and judge each for flavor, texture, visual appeal and overall taste. Our diners were to circle the meal they thought tasted best and looked most appetizing." He fanned out a few three by five cards for all (and the camera) to see, "The results are as follows."

A was ours. If *A* got more votes, I'd pass out with joy. If *B* got more votes, I'd either retire my knives or just throw myself on them hari-kari style. Georgia took my hand and I noticed I'd been holding my breath all through Andrew's dissertation. I gripped my sister's hand, praying I had done our mama proud.

Andrew cleared his throat, "For flavor, our diners voted their favorite meal as meal A, Georgia and Savannah Prince's meal."

I released my pent-up breath. One down, three to go. I tried to remain calm while Andrew revealed more results, "For texture, meal A wins again. Visual appeal was a sweeping victory all around for…" he hesitated and I wanted to mug him for it.

"Meal A. Now for overall taste and satisfaction," he said. "Georgia and Savannah have won three thousand dollars for winning three categories. One more vote would give 'em the whole twelve grand – or, if they lose the final category, they'll take home their three and Linda and Teresa will walk off with nine… thousand… dollars."

… mug him and leave him for the rainstorms to drown and for dogs to pee on. That's what I was thinking. If Andrew kept stalling, I'd lose my mind.

"The winners of Family Throwdown Chicken Dinner are…"

Mug him and leave him. Mug him and leave him….

"Georgia and Savannah Prince!"

Cameras swooped in, recording our collective reactions. Georgia's blissful, beaming smile took center stage while I flirted with total collapse. Linda and Teresa bowed up, ready to dispute the results. Most of the room broke into applause, whistles and cheers. Only a few people refrained including Alicia, Willie Dean and Carter. Tony and Lee, however, joined the crowd's enthusiasm.

Andrew turned to us, "Congratulations, ladies. You've won twelve thousand dollars. What will you do with this bounty of cash?" He thrust the microphone beneath my chin and the room fell quiet.

My tongue went numb and dry. I hadn't planned on a pop quiz. The main objective was survive the day. The audience waited for my answer. My mind struggled to bring forth the answer I'd rehearsed in case we won. One glance at Ennis's proud grin broke my tongue loose, "It's going into the baby's college fund."

Satisfied, Andrew poked the bulbous microphone at Georgia who clearly never got stymied for words, "I'm using my portion for my wedding plans."

The majority of people left after the show wrapped up. I noticed Quinn's men slipped out during the result portion of taping and that ticked me off. If Georgia had let me call Ennis when I wanted, we could have at least hauled them outside and harassed them some, asking why they were there and more importantly where did they get their invitations.

A few stragglers roamed the dining room, including the desk sergeant, Josh Hunter and their wives who asked for the chicken recipe.

Mathis and Christine still hung around along with a couple of uniform cops and surprisingly, Lee, Alicia and the boys who busied themselves consoling Teresa and Linda.

The evening turned sideways when Lee's family approached us, Alicia bulling ahead of them all. The woman thundered across the floor like a freight train ready to flatten any idiot dumb enough to stand in her way, "I wanna know why Michael isn't behind bars. He murdered Abby, we all know it."

Alicia specifically addressed me and to add fuel to the fire, Linda and Teresa faced me with arms folded and lifted brows. The uniforms shifted closer to intervene if necessary.

Without hesitation I volleyed to Alicia, "Is that so? Then how do you explain the videotape of someone else breaking into Abby's house minutes before she was murdered? And let's not forget the photo evidence exonerating Michael of the crime. *He's not guilty*, Alicia. Stop trying to convict an innocent boy."

I heard chuckles among my colleagues. Yes, my extended family – even the ones by marriage – was a basketful of extraordinary nuts from our big ol' gnarled up family tree. A fact I hated since fellow detectives and uniform officers discovered it in such a crude way. "If we're airing dirty laundry, Alicia, where exactly were you when Abby was being offed? I heard she was suing for more child support for Tony and Carter. That would have downsized your vacation plans if she won."

I'd hoped my tone might settle her down or at least shut her up but I'd forgotten how Alicia loved to exercise her mouth. The woman leaned in closer, her voice dropped to a growl, "Carter lives with us. He prefers it that way."

"Because of your charming personality?" That's when my sister closed things down by grasping my arm. She whispered in my ear to shut up. Georgia was older than me by six years. Older and wiser like my personal Yoda just without the green complexion, big ears and wrinkles.

Lee pulled Alicia back, evidently sensing impending danger. Lee was handsome but thick as a plank. He really needed a reality check. Carter moved from Abby's house to his because Daddy had the moola, not because he wanted to bond with Pops. Alicia took offense because I cornered her about Abby's child support intentions. Regardless of where Carter laid his pretty head at night, Abby still retained legal custody. And Tony, well, he just needed someone to love him.

Tony shuffled behind Willie Dean, away from the loud voices. Confrontation scared him, always had. Willie Dean and Carter, however, stood arms crossed, their defiant features daring me to escalate the argument. No doubt their mama painted a colorful picture about my temper over the years. I vowed to eat glass before losing it to the likes of Alicia so I stared back at them with a stony, quiet calm.

Alicia straightened her shoulders, "You people are picking on me and my family for no good reason. That fat cop's been nosin' into our business, talkin' to neighbors and Lee's employees, hell, even the kid's friends –"

"Who you callin' fat?" Mathis rose from his seat a few tables away. "I'm doing my job, lady, and you're making it impossible."

Her eyes narrowed at me, "Savannah, you people better leave us alone. All of us."

My cell phone rang and Georgia basically tossed it to me like it was on fire. She, Ennis and Seth probably feared I'd jump Alicia any second. The thought crossed my mind but so did suspension from the job. Not worth it. Nutjobs never were. "Sorry, Toots. It's not my case. Talk to Detective Mathis right there. You know, the cop you called *fat*." I quickly answered the phone, "Prince." And this better be important, I nearly warned.

"Detective, this is Jamie Moore, a nurse at Grady. Megan Bowen is awake and she refuses to talk to any police officer except 'Savannah' and I'm assuming that's you since your card is with her file."

"I'll be right there." I clicked off to see Lee tugging at Alicia's arm, urging her to leave.
It only heightened her ire, "I'll hire a lawyer. I swear I'll hire one."

"Please do," I replied, placing my phone on my belt. "Hire one and my colleague will look extra hard at you and your family because innocent people don't need lawyers."

29

I stepped inside Megan's room to find her parents flanking her bed. They held her hands, their words soft and sweet to their little girl. The second they saw me, an invisible wall rose between us. Their posture stiffened, their expressions hardened to a sternness daring the interloper to step closer. I'd knocked before entering but the courtesy fell short according to Megan's father who, with arms crossed, stepped between me and the bed.

I displayed my badge and introduced myself. At least they stopped staring daggers at me. I politely requested a few minutes alone with Megan to ask her some questions. Only when Megan okayed the idea did they leave. She looked at me, a raspy whispered *hi* slipped between her lips. I intended to keep the visit brief for her sake. She'd been through enough. Her bruises remained dark, deep. The long bandage across her throat still sent a cold chill down my back. The killer sliced from ear to ear, barely missing the carotid arteries. One more miniscule amount of pressure ensured her death.

I forewarned Megan I needed to ask difficult questions but that her answers would help locate the people who hurt her. "This won't take long, I promise," I pulled a chair closer to her bed, careful to avoid the many tubes and wires. Children felt more comfortable if I wasn't hovering so close while I barraged them with invasive, uncomfortable questions. Adults were a judgment call, depending on their demeanor. Kids required more space and tenderness.

"You were so nice to me when you were here," she struggled to speak, pushing the words in a voiceless whisper. She touched the bandage on her cheek then the one on her throat. The girl seemed older than seven years old. No tears or emotion surfaced in her blue eyes, only a dull gaze, the innocence of childhood extinguished forever by a cruel, perverted monster. She met my vision with a stoic acceptance found with a tired, weathered maturity, "The other detective wasn't nice like you."

Other detective? Someone tried to interview her without my knowledge? That sailed past *wrong*, ran over *rude* and went straight to a breach of etiquette. Other detectives always asked the lead for "the okay" to interview that detective's witness or suspect. It took conscious effort to mask my annoyance at that person. I kept my voice composed, "I'm sorry the other detective upset you, sweetie. Do you remember his or her name?" Because I planned to share a few choice words with the person.

She shook her head, "She was your age, tall with long, wavy hair like Bella Swan only hers was black."

She. Tall with long, black hair. Christine Clark. I'd bet my life on it. But, "Bella Swan?" I inquired like the clueless adult I was.

She halfway smiled, "From the movie Twilight. You know, the vampire movie."

I nodded as if I'd just forgotten. In reality, I knew Twilight as well as I knew Greek or Latin but with the Bella Swan description, I offered a name, "Was her name Christine?"

Megan nodded, resuming the laborious effort to speak, "I remembered your name because we went to Savannah on vacation last year. I like you, you remind me of my mom. You're kind and gentle and your voice is soft like hers."

A blush warmed my cheeks. The mere sound of a mother's voice held the extraordinary ability to instantly calm and comfort. I hoped one day my daughter spoke of me with such love and adoration. It was apparent the Bowens were a tight-knit family. The devotion to each other went both ways and it was that love, no doubt, that pulled Megan through those dark hours with the monster and later from her coma.

Megan continued, "That detective asked the nurses if I was awake yet and if I was going to live. I pretended to be asleep so I wouldn't have to talk."

She sounded almost apologetic as though she committed an unforgivable sin. I patted her hand, winked, "I'd have done the same thing." When I asked about her abductor, she couldn't remember many details except the fact there were two men, not one. I tried a different approach, "Did they drive a car or van? Were they –"

"They weren't from here. Their words sounded different."

Now we were getting somewhere and I figured the best way to get answers was to ask, "Is there a movie or TV show that reminds you of their accent?"

Megan closed her eyes in deep thought. "Lord of the Rings. Frodo and Sam."

Frodo and Sam could easily have been Sean O'Leary and Kevin

Hughes. According to Megan's description, the two fit my suspect list –
as Troy Quinn might say – *pearfectly.*

"Frodo and Sam took us down a long tunnel into a cold little
room and I hate little rooms."

Being claustrophobic, I sympathized with her, "So do I."

In the room, she said, several men sat in chairs, all facing her and
other girls who were brought in. "Those men scared me so I tried to run.
Sam grabbed me," she flinched, "and my earring caught on his shirt and
ripped out. It hurt and bled the whole time I was there."

I covered her hand, gave it a gentle squeeze. Words were empty
shells when a cop dealt with traumatized children. We said kind words,
used gentle voices and assured them we'd work to catch the beast that
hurt them. Nothing we did actually worked but we hoped it helped
somehow. I did my best to comfort Megan when her eyes glistened with
tears, when her voice reduced to a stammering whisper.

Still, she forged on with more strength than I'd ever seen in a
child, "The men in the room started calling out numbers. Fifty, seventy-
five, a hundred. When a man said two hundred and fifty, Frodo told the
man to come get me but another man shouted he got cheated."

An icy chill shivered down my back. Child molesters. Human
traffickers. Scum of the friggin' earth. If genies existed, my first wish:
That Troy Quinn be delivered to the parents of all those poor dead girls.
Second wish: Once the parents finished with him, I got my turn and
third, that we blast his sorry carcass to another galaxy. It took effort to
keep my rage at bay, "You said there were other girls with you. Do you
remember how many?"

"Three. One's name was Tammy, another was Paris like France, and the other girl's name was Cherise."

My stomach churned. Cherise Aldridge, the first girl found dead. And Megan's "buyer" tried to kill her too, for whatever twisted reason. He cut her throat to kill her but thankfully Megan's will to live proved stronger than the evil that imprisoned her. I couldn't bear much more, and I sure couldn't bear to subject Megan to more either. "Sweetie, I've got one or two more questions then you can rest. Frodo told a man to come get you. Could you describe the man?"

She nodded, "I can try."

"Good. Once you're rested a bit, we'll get a sketch artist to work on it. How about Frodo and Sam? Could you identify Frodo and Sam if I brought a bunch of photos?"

She nodded again and I smiled, "That's wonderful. I'll bring the photos tomorrow."

She looked toward the door at her parents who glanced in at us. I'd kept the family apart long enough. I would talk to her again but right now she needed the love of Mama's arms and the security of Daddy's presence. I patted her hand, "You've been very brave, sweetheart, and extremely helpful. Get some rest and I'll see you tomorrow."

30

I went home furious and confused. Furious that Troy Quinn assumed his mole would shield him from me. And I was completely confused about Christine Clark. Hunter assigned her strictly to the Davenport investigation and me to Megan. Even if our cases meshed, she had no right to interview my witness without asking me. Riley Murphy warned me about a spy – either Nesbitt or Clark. With Clark nosing into my business and Nesbitt off on vacation and his general lack of enthusiasm for work, it left little doubt in my mind who answered to Quinn.

A long warm shower helped loosen the tightness from my shoulders and arms. During Megan's interview, I'd tensed up until my forehead pounded in a relentless cacophony of misery. I became a cop to make the world better, to stop monsters who preyed on kids. One year on the job informed me how naïve I'd been. After ten years, you do what you can and hope you helped a few people. I fast approached fifteen years and each day my little girl poked me or moved inside me, it made me wonder if I needed to redirect my focus. Instead of arresting murderers, maybe raising kids proved slightly less hazardous and perhaps more rewarding…

I toweled off and slipped on a pair of panties and PJs. Ennis –

already in bed, his back propped against the headboard – patted the bed, "Ennis has a surprise for his girls."

I piled into bed, sighing at how the mattress and pillow embraced me. I was too tired to cover up so I left the blanket aside. "I hope the surprise includes a foot rub."

Ennis pouted, "Damn. You guessed it." He scooted down and eased my right foot into his lap. His thumbs moved in gentle circles on the sole of my foot. They worked until my eyes began to droop which took about two seconds. His foot rubs coaxed more moans from me at times than his lovemaking. Five minutes with my feet and I'd do whatever the man wanted.

He rubbed a particularly tender spot on my foot, asking, "You given any thought to retiring yet?"

Eh, anything except that. No, I hadn't seriously considered it until tonight after seeing Megan. With Jeffrey and Cole, I survived the pain and brutality monsters doled out but if my child were subjected to such cruelty, I would die. "No, but I haven't forgotten what I said."

Ennis barely masked his disappointment, settling instead for releasing his emotion on my feet. He bore down a bit too hard on one spot and I recoiled, protesting, "Hey, I said I hadn't forgotten."

He glanced up all innocent-like, "I heard. I also know you get all gnarled up in the shoulders and legs lately. I have to use real muscle to get the knots out. Remember?"

Yeah. And I remembered how huffy he got when my stubbornness clashed against his. Retirement had to wait, I'd say, whether he approved or not.

Finally, Ennis eased up on the pressure. I relaxed as the massage began to feel as grand as I remember. "Thanks evah so, kind and gentle suh. You ah my knight'n shinin' ahmah."

Ennis's dark brows sank in mock frustration, "If I'da wanted Georgia, I'da married her. Find my wife or these jammies come off and I ravish you until you find her."

I laughed. I loved teasing Ennis with that deep drawl. Georgia couldn't help that she sounded fresh picked off the plantation. She certainly looked the part of Southern Belle excluding the parasol and billowing taffeta ball gown so why shouldn't she sound like it too?

I slumped against the pillow after a mere ten minutes. I yawned, glad the day went as well as it had. We won money for Lily's college and Megan woke up from the coma. Not a bad day at all.

At nine-thirty, Ennis and I leaned back in bed, the baseball game long over with the Braves miraculously chalking up another win. I'd just slid under the covers when the phone rang. Over the years I grew to highly dislike Alexander Graham Bell. The man had no conscience. What the hell was he thinking trying to connect people with those annoying nerve-wracking contraptions? I mean he put the pony express and the carrier pigeons out of business. Back then people got precious rest between communications. These days a person felt lucky to squeeze out an hour without an interruption.

I reached to the nightstand, glanced at the Caller ID and my gut tightened as I answered the call.

"Detective, this is Jamie Moore at Grady again."

My stomach tightened. The worst case scenario weighed like lead in my brain. Something had happened to Megan. "Is Megan okay?"

"She's fine. She wanted me to call you so she could tell you one more thing."

I heard the nurse hand the phone to Megan and say she'd return shortly. Megan spoke next, "Savannah? I remembered something. The men who drove me to the lake. I want to tell you what they looked like before you bring the photos."

I threw back the covers, nearly burying Ennis in the process, "Sweetheart, you should be resting but I'll take the information if you're ready." After grabbing the pen and paper beside the phone, I urged her to continue.

"One had short red hair and a scar down his left cheek like mine."

My heart squeezed at that description. The poor girl would forever have that reminder of the brutality she suffered. A part of her until her dying day. I struggled to keep the emotion from my voice, "Red hair, scar on his left cheek. You did great, sweetie. I'll be there in the morning with the photos."

"That's not all. The other guy was short and reminded me of Emmet Cullen."

"Emmet Cullen," I wrote. For some reason I had a feeling the name was a movie reference, "What movie is he in?"

"Twilight. It's my favorite movie. You really gotta see it."

"I'll check into it." If for nothing else to see what this Emmet Cullen looked like. My gut said Red and Emmet were Hughes and O'Leary.

When I hung up, I did an internet search on my cell phone for the Twilight movie. Scrolling down the cast list, I stopped on the fellow playing Emmet Cullen. A satisfied smile curved my lips, "Got him." Then I rephrased, "Or at least Quinn's thugs. Megan just described Hughes and O'Leary. They're the ones who took her to the lake and slashed her throat."

He snuggled under the covers. "That's good. She's an observant kid for her age. Now lie down and get some sleep. Lily'll keep you up if you don't put her to bed soon."

Ennis was right. Our daughter despised late nights so I sank beneath the covers, snuggled next to Ennis and reveled in images of slamming the cell door on Quinn's henchmen once and for all. Once they were behind bars, Quinn was next. What a wonderful day tomorrow would be...

Then the phone rang again. Ennis groaned, "No one sleeps in this city anymore."

No shit, I wanted to say. Between the calls for the contest, the case, the kooks in the family and general nuisance calls, the thing rang all the time. I blindly reached for my cell, not bothering to check Caller ID. I sounded weary and probably a little cross but the day sapped me and – as Ennis predicted – Lily began showing her nocturnal side by fidgeting. When I answered, this time the voice on the other end wasn't a nurse or Megan. It was Tony Hawthorne, "Is this Savannah?"

"Yes, Tony, it's me. What can I do for you?"

"Can you give me a ride home? Carter forgot me. I'm at St. Paul Methodist."

St. Paul Methodist, Catholic, Episcopalian – none of them rang a bell with me so I took a stab in the dark and mentioned the church where they held Abby's funeral, "The one on Grant?"

"Yep. Can you come now? It's dark. I don't like dark."

Apparently my baby felt the same way since she lodged a foot in my ribcage. I grimaced then rubbed at the foot while answering, "I'll be there in about twenty minutes. Stay inside the church until I get there."

o o o

I pulled to the curb facing St. Paul's Methodist. At that late hour, few people mingled around the church and surrounding area. Seconds passed when the church's old ornate wooden door opened a crack. Tony peeked around it. I rolled down the window, called him to the car.

The teenager emerged dressed in matching blue shirt and slacks, a black and yellow backpack clutched to his chest. After suspiciously eyeing the stragglers nearby, he dashed to the car as if the devil chased him.

Breathless and flustered, Tony piled inside, slamming the door a bit too hard. He resumed hugging his backpack. I noticed he'd been crying judging by his red, swollen eyes. He sat in silence, staring straight ahead, the street lamps casting a soft glow on his somber features.

I waited a moment before asking if he was okay. He slumped in the seat, his lip quivered with emotion, "They forgot about me again." He sniffled, wiping his nose on his sleeve. "Ever since Mama died thingsa been crazy. Carter's always supposed to pick me up. Every

Wednesday, Saturday and Sunday I got church. He's supposed to be here and he's not."

I reached to comfort him but he recoiled. I'd forgotten that stress intensified his paranoia and withdrawn manner. Small talk lightened his anxiety if I remembered correctly so I eased the car and my mouth into gear, "He's not answering his phone?"

He shook his head. Finally he turned to me, his eyes glittered in the oncoming headlights, "Thanks for the lift. I thoughta you 'cause you got a baby inside. You wouldn't leave your baby at church on a Saturday night."

Well, that was certainly true. And if Lily's siblings left her by herself at night, there'd be hell to pay.

"Pastor Ray called the police for your number. I asked him to." Then he apologized.

Yep, the polite, laid-back old Tony was back. I assured him I didn't mind helping. Lily, on the other hand, did. "What are you doing at church on Saturday night anyway?"

"We got choir practice. Special service tomorrow."

We drove in light traffic for a few minutes. At last he sighed, relaxing his death grip on the backpack, "Wanna see something funny?" He retrieved his phone from his pocket, worked with it a minute then thrust it at me, "Look at this. Don't he look funny?"

I stopped for a red light, taking the opportunity to watch the small screen. The recording was at night and judging from the herky jerky camera movement, I guessed Tony served as cameraman. Sure enough, I heard him laughing on the video.

A figure wearing shorts and a hoodie slipped in and out of visibility like a ghost in the darkness, visible only in the muted street and yard lights. It disappeared into the shadow of a small house. I heard glass breaking and a minute later a distinctive pop registered in the background.

A horn honked behind me and I glanced at the light. It turned green while I watched the video so I asked Tony to pause the video while I pulled into the nearest parking lot. I took the phone in hand, tapped the play button. On the screen, the person lumbered, huffing and puffing toward the car window. That person threw open the car door, climbed inside and shoved the hoodie back. The second he saw Tony recording him, Carter Hawthorne slapped at the phone, "What the hell are you doing, retard?"

The screen blurred and tilted as the two fought for custody of it. Tony ultimately won the battle. For one instant, I saw Tony's fright as he clasped the phone in his shaking hands. All I saw was blackness where his palm covered the camera. But I heard plenty. Carter leveled a chilling warning on his older brother, "You didn't see or hear anything, understand? We never came to Mama's house. If you tell anyone and I mean *anyone*, I'll break your phone then I'll break your neck. Do you understand?"

Beside me Tony retreated from the sound of his brother's voice, "It was funny 'til then. He looked funny dressed that way but he didn't laugh. He got mad at me."

I wondered if Tony realized the danger Carter posed to him now. Dr. Death killed his own mother and hadn't broken a sweat or shown an ounce of remorse. Killing his brother would be child's play. Yep, Mathis was right. We'd be seeing more of Carter in the future however I bet he hadn't expected it this soon...

Stark fear paled Tony's complexion, widened his eyes, "You ain't supposed to know about us being at Mama's house!" He grabbed a fistful of his thick dark hair and commenced yanking on it, "Oh no, Carter's gonna kill me. He's gonna kill me."

I reached across, put a hand to his which he slapped away. "Tony," I said, "stop pulling your hair. Carter won't touch you. I won't let him."

"But you wasn't s'pposed to know. You won't tell anyone, right? You're my friend, right? Leesha and Daddy don't trust you 'cause you're a cop. They say you'll hang Carter if you find out. Now you know everything and now Carter'll kill me, just like he said."

"Calm down, Tony," I assured. "No one will hurt you or kill you, I promise, but my friend needs to see this video."

o   o   o

Carter, like his mama, refused to go down quietly. John Mathis towed the pajama-wearing kid by the elbow, rolling his eyes at the threat of lawyers and lawsuits. The youngster whined and protested about the handcuffs, the officers who arrested him and the ride to the station. Most of all he complained about the "bitch cop who Mama said was white trailer trash".

As the entourage approached *the bitch cop*, Mathis stretched his arm out as a blockade between us, either against my reaction to being labeled a bitch or Carter's reaction to seeing me. I stood motionless, enjoying the spectacle Abby's little angel provided the night shift. That was until Carter spied me. One look at me and Dr. Death uttered many colorful violent threats of bodily injury if he got loose. Nothing I hadn't heard before from killers, thieves and several extended relatives.

I lifted a hand, stopping the uniforms. Mathis groaned an oh-no-not-again groan. I winked at him then addressed Carter. There were two things he should remember, I said. One, this was my job, I got paid for it and I didn't get paid to lose to dimwits like him. Two, if by some miracle, he *did* manage to free himself from those pretty bracelets and come after me, I had a whole mess of people coming to help me. I concluded my comment by pointing to the six officers present. He surveyed each one, the gravity of his situation sinking in. He swallowed hard then backed down.

Mathis hitched his thumb toward my office and ordered me to *go in there and stay.* I waited a minute then did what any self-respecting detective would. I headed for the observation room to hear Carter lie through his teeth. I wondered if he mastered duplicity as well as Abby. Of course with the video evidence, we had enough to hang the little snot by his ankles for the next millennium so not even creative lying could help him – but it sure would entertain *me.*

While waiting, I arranged for Seth to take Tony in the interim. I explained the situation to my brother and told him Tony feared repercussions from Carter – and probably the rest of his family. The whole Hawthorne family probably targeted him for an innocent recording he thought was funny.

With Tony at home with Seth, Christine and I stood in the observation room, staring at the "doctor". Dr. Death, I called him, and got an earful from Georgia who scolded me with *be kind to unkind people because they need it the most.*

"Thank you, Confucius," I replied. Her goody-goody nature finally flew all over me, "You know, Georgia, Carter wasn't arrested for being kind. They slapped cuffs on him because he offed his mama. She found him cheating to get those swell Ivy League grades he bragged about. He's not exactly a pillar of our community."

"Still," Georgia droned on, "he's family. We can love him from a distance."

I rolled my eyes and sighed to Christine's amusement. One word described my sister during those times. Insufferable. She possessed a conscience harder than stone and stockpiled guilt the way compulsive hoarders squirreled away anything not nailed down. If Carter had stolen a can of corn to feed his family, I'd cut him slack but matricide? "Love him from a distance, huh? Yeah, from about twenty miles when he heads to Norcross and shares Jeffrey Holland's zip code." I rubbed my forehead, "Here's my belief. If you step on people in this life, you'll come back as a cockroach."

When I hung up, Christine chuckled, "If you're sisters, how do you keep from killing each other?"

Believe me, "It's a struggle some days." Her question about killing people reminded me of her impromptu visit to Megan's room,

"Did you go see Megan Bowen earlier?"

Christine confessed, "I hope you don't mind. I was concerned about her, considering everything she'd been through. I heard she regained consciousness this evening. How's she doing?"

I tried not to show my irritation. Maybe she honestly was worried about the girl, "Better than before. I hope she recovers physically and emotionally."

In the interview room, Carter suddenly blew his top with Mathis. Thirty minutes in interrogation and he accused Mathis of being *my* puppet to railroad him to which my colleague laughed, "Your ego is as big as your mouth if you think she cares about you that much." He tapped a computer memory card containing a copy of the phone video, "So Mommy caught you cheating on your SATs, GPAs and MRIs, huh?"

Carter's lip curled in disgust, "GPA stands for Grade Point Average and an MRI is a diagnostic test, not a written exam. Stupid cop."

I fought the urge to rush into that room and restrain Mathis. The man reacted to insult the way most people did – only Mathis exercised his right hook on occasion. He was overweight and sometimes lazy but he could also hit that kid so hard Carter would have to unzip his pants to say hi. I didn't want any chance of Dr. Death being released because my colleague lost his temper.

Big John Mathis began to rise from his seat but mid-way through, sat back down. Instead of hurling a fist at the twit, he hurled his own slur, "Had to pay someone to help you out on your SAT? What's the matter, Hooked On Phonics didn't work for you?"

Carter squinted daggers at him, fuming, "I want a lawyer."

Mathis leaned back, staring over his glasses at the boy, "Kid, you're way past a lawyer. That video is the rope, gallows and hangman all in one. Congrats, smartass, you hit the trifecta."

Carter pounded the table with his fist, "It's my halfwit brother. If my father hadn't given that retard a phone –" he stopped midsentence as if realizing what he'd said.

"Your brother is the smartest one of ya. He recorded it all while you an' the rest of your family sat back like nothing ever happened. You're one twisted bunch. Especially you." Mathis scoffed, "Besides not being able to pass high school science without a cheat sheet, you kill your mama 'cause she threatened to tattle on you."

"I never said that."

"You got a short memory, kid. Remember on the recording when you said your mama accused you of – and I quote – being too stupid to pass gas without help? You said it right after calling her a screwy bitch who deserved to die."

I stood there, staring at a young man supposedly related to me. I swiveled to face Christine, "And Ennis wondered why I avoided introducing him to my relatives before we married."

31

Morning dawned with the beauty of early Spring. An orange glow bathed the bedroom in the promise of budding flowers, warmer afternoons, tweeting birds and murderous thugs tossed behind bars. That wondrous image buoyed my mood while I showered and dressed for work.

We rode in Ennis's Ram, or the *mammoth* as I called it. It rode rougher than a wagon full of corn cobs but not even that stood a chance of spoiling my day. On the way to the station, Georgia called me, bubbling with glee, "Savannah, this is *incredible*." I hadn't heard her that giddy since Brian Cavanaugh asked her to the high school prom. "They loved us," she continued. "The people who attended the contest *loved* us! My Twitter and Facebook accounts are alive with comments – and it hasn't been broadcast locally or nationally yet! Can you imagine the feedback when it does?"

Yes, I *could* imagine but no amount of perky sisterly merriment or her Twitter minions stood a chance of spoiling my morning. I added my cheerful two cents, "That's great, Georgia. Hey, maybe Andy'll ask us back for another episode and we can make more money. You think?" A brief pause later, I heard a frown in her tone, "What's wrong?"

"Why would you think something's wrong?"

"You're never this happy, especially about the cooking contest. What's going on?"

"Locking away bad guys today. That always makes me happier than a monkey with a peanut machine. Say, when's the show airing nationally?"

"You're chipper attitude is scaring me but I'll try to adapt. Andrew said it airs here tonight then Cooking Network scheduled it for Wednesday."

"We'll watch it tonight. Let's hope for high ratings." Note to self, I cautioned myself. Remove house phone before crawling into bed tonight. If the show did garner good ratings, I'd need the peace and quiet, because I'd be celebrating the incarceration of a group of child murderers.

My phone rang again. Laying odds that Georgia forgot something, I answered with the same spirited lilt. The caller turned out to be the desk sergeant, "They call you last night?"

Uh-oh. His tone warned of trouble. "No one called. What's happened?"

"The night sergeant left a note here. Says two guys hauled your witness out of the hospital last night."

My heart sank. The good mood, the smiles and jokes all vanished. Now I seethed from mounting rage, "What happened to the uniforms I assigned for protection? Does the note say anything about that?"

"I read it verbatim. Thought I'd follow up when I saw it. Night shift is lazy."

I thanked him and concluded the conversation. Hot rage flowed through me. I personally assigned those two idiots to protect Megan and once I saw them, I *would* get answers from them. They would explain what distracted them or was so damned important that they neglected their assignments because now Megan's life hung in the balance again and this time I figured her luck ran out.

o   o   o

Ennis and I went straight to the hospital. He pulled the Dodge into the entrance only to abruptly stop. Dozens of TV stations and newspaper reporters clogged the entrance, their voices brimming with outrage about Megan's disappearance. A department spokesman took the brunt of questions. Soon that would be me with microphones thrust beneath my chin while being impaled with pointedly sharp words. Problem was, I deserved it. Those cops let me down but I was the detective on record, the one supposedly in control of the investigation. I'd not only lost control, but my only witness to a series of brutal child slayings. When people wanted heads to roll, I'd draw the first trip to the guillotine.

First thing I needed to do was talk to Megan's parents. I dabbed the growing perspiration from my forehead. The temperate morning failed to hold back an attack of anxiety. I hadn't felt this nervous in a long time. I'd face the parents, then Josh Hunter or someone with more brass on their collar then I'd probably be thrown in front of that bloodthirsty mob as a sacrifice.

Ennis whipped the Dodge around a corner, gunned the engine to the back of the facility and parked in the lower forty. The back entrance stood devoid of reporters, thankfully, so we headed toward it. During our trek, Ennis began preaching, "We're just *talking* to the officers guarding Megan. That's all. Keeping our tempers in check, our voices down, and our badges in tact. Just *talking* to them."

Yeah, right. In *his* world maybe. In mine, I owed those two cops a beating. Poor Ennis forgot who he married. When we met, I'd worn my nickname, the Bitch of Zone 2, until it fit like old comfortable jeans. I fielded barbs, sexual harassment, and outright rudeness from not only criminals but fellow detectives. I learned the hard way about the blue wall erected against women in the department. It took a set of brass balls, backbone, and determination to climb it. When a female ascended the wall successfully, they acquired a particularly unflattering name. Bitch. So yes, I became the Bitch of Zone 2. That's why Ennis Rutherford, the naïve Texan, received a sympathy card from the uniform officers a day after being assigned my partner.

Since partnering with Ennis, his easygoing demeanor settled my temper somewhat which inspired a collective sigh of relief among the uniforms. The two I assigned for protection, however, were about to meet the Bitch of Zone 2. They would go home broken and bleeding – metaphorically of course, but they'd soon learn how this bitch rolled when her witness went missing.

Before opening the entrance door, Ennis stepped in front of me, "Savannah, I mean it. We'll get the security video but as for the cops, we are only talking to them, not annihilating them. I know they let you down –"

"They didn't let me down, Ennis. They let Megan down. They let her parents down. But *I'm* the one responsible, don't you understand? Her folks will blame *me*, not those two numbnuts. *Me.*" I dreaded seeing her parents. More than likely they stood right inside that hospital, wanting answers no one had, wondering how their daughter was snatched from under the noses of two Atlanta cops appointed to prevent that from happening. This wasn't merely a personal nightmare, I wanted to tell Ennis, this was soon to become a media nightmare and I stood right in the middle, the target on my back. Naturally, Ennis chose that moment to remind, "You really should retire. This can't be good for you or Lily."

"*Not now, Ennis,*" I squeezed through clenched teeth. I stood in the deepest shit of my career and he wanted to debate my future? "I need to salvage my job before I can consider retiring from it."

I stepped around him, threw open the door and headed toward Megan's room. Again Ennis slowed my progress by grasping my elbow. He asked, "What are you going to say to the deputy chief?"

All the brass assembled for FUBARs this enormous. Not only Josh Hunter but the major, deputy chief and perhaps the chief himself would be present. It made my head hurt to think about it, "Honestly, what *can* I say past *I'm sorry*?" An apology sounded so empty, so ridiculous, considering the situation. I'd look like a fool no matter what I said.

We rounded the last corner where a small crowd of people huddled near Megan's door. Uniform cops stood around jawing while the police chief *and* deputy chief encircled Megan's parents who were as distraught as I expected. Mrs. Bowen sobbed in her husband's embrace while he scowled at anyone with a badge. His voice carried through the hallway, turning heads of nurses, doctors and visitors alike as he demanded answers, demanded every cop search for his little girl. "You should be looking for Megan," he demanded. Mr. Bowen glanced past the deputy chief, his vision locking on me.

If looks could kill, I swallowed uneasily, I'd be dead on the floor. Instinct forced me back a step when he stabbed a finger at me, released his wife then proceeded pushing past the chief. "You," he growled. "*You* said she'd be safe."

The intrinsic impulse to flee mushroomed into full fledged panic. I wanted to run away from this grieving, tortured family. He used my own words like daggers. I'd told them not to worry, that the two officers would protect their little girl. In their minds, I'd lied and without intending to, I guess I had. "Mr. Bowen, I'm sorry. I assigned the two officers –"

"My baby," Mrs. Bowen's weeping escalated. "She's gone. You have to find her." The woman advanced on me, tissues fisted in her hands, tears streaking down her face. "Please, you have to find Megan. We trusted you," she turned to the other officers, "we trusted all of you and now she's gone."

I felt sick. Blood pounded in my temples. My face flushed vivid scarlet, a sheen of moisture surfaced on my forehead. Humiliation merged with rage. I was ashamed to call myself a cop and ashamed I picked two dummies to guard that precious girl.

My mouth opened to utter the most hollow words a person could speak on that occasion – *I'm sorry* – when the chief mercifully interrupted me, "Mrs. Bowen, we're trying to find her. The department's already alerted every officer and state trooper to her abduction. Detective Prince followed procedure, she did the best she could."

Shock and amazement rooted me to the spot. Few things occurred as rarely as a blue moon or four leaf clover. A superior officer defending me counted as one.

Ennis slipped behind me, his hand discreetly on my waist. I must have looked as stunned as I felt. No ranking officer other than Josh Hunter ever stood up for me. Until now. Still, I owed the Bowens an apology and a promise to try and find Megan.

As usual, instead of stemming the river of tears, my words inspired them in tidal waves. Mrs. Bowen sobbed, her tear-rimmed vision dropped to my belly. I wasn't sure but I swore I felt Lily draw back. "She's our only child," the woman struggled to regain control of her grief. "You'll find out. You'll see that your child is your life, your heart and soul." She returned to her husband's arms, "Please find my baby. Find her before it's too late."

"We're trying, ma'am," Ennis said.

Tears trembled on my eyelids. Before I mired down in my own sorrow, I reminded myself that two lazy cops generated this nightmare. I may have assigned them, but they, not me, walked away from their posts. A quick, decisive swipe of my hand brushed away the tears. Seconds later, I raised the steel door rejecting any emotion except anger. I had a couple of incompetent morons to brace. No time for crying – only ass-kicking.

I made my way to Megan's room, sucked in a deep breath to calm myself and barged in. The two idiots stood, propped against the wall. They looked bored. Well, the Bitch of Zone 2 meant to liven their asses with my temper. "What the hell happened?" I shifted my vision between both men. "I assigned you two for security. That meant sit and watch the door. I didn't realize that assignment was too difficult."

The short one in his late-twenties went wide-eyed, "I had to pee. I left him here while I went to pee, Detective."

"Him" was a tall black officer who crossed his arms, lifted his chin in a sign of defiance, "My phone rang and I figured he'd be back before long. I went outside to take the call because of hospital rules."

I stalked to the black officer who stood a liberal seven inches taller than me, "You never leave a post. If your partner is out taking a leak, you wait until he returns before making plans for Friday night."

He bowed up, "My wife called. Her car broke down in Cabbage Town. You and I both know that part of the city. I called a friend to pick her up before she was mugged or killed. I wasn't *planning* anything."

"Sure you weren't conspiring with some skeevy Irishman?"

Ennis pulled at my arm, "He's explained what happened. Let it be."

The officer's eyes narrowed at me, "If you're accusing me of being dirty, you'd better have some proof, *Detective.*"

I bulled on, "I think it's convenient that you both step away at precisely the same time that girl is abducted. Too convenient."

The black officer strutted against me, "Listen up, bitch, you keep wagging your tongue and I'll –"

"Hey," Ennis squeezed between us and braced the cop, "don't touch my partner and keep a civil tongue in *your* head or I'll have a talk with the captain about your attitude."

"*My* attitude?   *She's* outta line accusing me of being a dirty cop and saying I let that kid get snatched."

"God sakes, tone it down. I can hear you in the hall," the voice came from behind me. Josh Hunter. Oh great. The situation circled the drain already. Adding him to the equation certainly threw fuel on the fire. He waved me over, "Before you make too many friends, how about requesting the security tapes from the staff? Those usually come in handy."

Since an impartial judge arrived, I decided to clear up any confusion on the uniform's part, "It's department policy that if two officers are assigned to guard duty, at least *one* officer is present at all times, is that correct, Captain Hunter?"

My boss shot a penetrating glare at me – one that warned of severe repercussions if I furthered the issue. "That is correct, Detective Prince, and the two officers will hear about it. *Your* orders are to get the security tapes so do it now."

o   o   o

Back at the station, I watched one security tape after another, each one revealing what I already knew. I couldn't prove their identities however I felt comfortable betting my life savings that the two men were Hughes and O'Leary. Dressed all in black, ski masks obscuring their faces, I watched them haul Megan out with her kicking and battling them with every ounce of strength she possessed. The images sank like talons into my heart, tearing, curling and squeezing until it ached in my chest. I'd underestimated Troy Quinn's audacity and arrogance. When he wanted something, he got it, no matter what it took, no matter the cost.

Besides the heartache and headache, immense regret weighed on me. Megan trusted me, confided in me. She believed I would keep her safe. All I'd done was planned. Based on Megan's description, I'd *planned* to drag Hughes and O'Leary into the station that morning. I'd *planned*.

Her parents would soon *plan* a funeral assuming we located Megan at all. They'd have to *plan* which mortuary to schedule, *plan* their daughter's last dress to wear, *plan* the time and place for their baby to be buried.

I headed back to my office, the wretched headache digging in for the duration. My body throbbed from rage, my mind exhausted from the tirade, worry and guilt. Easing into my chair, I covered my face and sighed with a prayer for this day to end happier than I expected it to.

A knock on the door interrupted my prayer. Christine Clark flashed a sympathetic smile, "I heard what happened. Anything I can do to help?"

"Unless you're packing Valium and a bazooka, probably not. The first one's for me, the second I'll use to blast Troy Quinn to the moon."

She shrugged an apology, "Would you settle for help finding O'Leary and Hughes?"

I offered her a seat then an exceptionally short list of places where the two hung out. We were screwed, I told myself. Quinn kept his men close, out of sight for the most part. They followed orders, fulfilled his wishes then faded into oblivion until he called again. Ghosts.

That thought barely registered when a real ghost appeared at my door. This ghost polished off my day. First Megan, then her mother, then the idiots uniforms, now I stared directly at my former brother-in-law, Major Matthew Carlisle, United States Marine Corps.

Dressed in his perfectly pressed forest green service uniform, he stood, staring back at me – with what I labeled a hopeful half-smile. He tucked his cap beneath his arm, which drew my attention to the rows of bright colored ribbons and marksmanship badges lining the left side of his wide chest. The dedication and glory of his military service sparkled and gleamed, unlike his dedication to marriage...

Georgia's ex-husband strode proudly the way marines tended to do. I noticed silver oak leaves replaced the gold ones from years earlier. Oh goody, I sneered. The bastard got a promotion to lieutenant colonel. He hadn't changed much. Still tall, broad shouldered, flawless posture and handsome enough to attract interest from the women. When I first met him, he possessed a boyish charm around Georgia, reserving his military face for uniforms only. As far as I knew, he treated Georgia well until he divorced her. I only remember her reverting to a smitten teenager when they married. So goofy happy she practically floated. But I also remembered how devastated she was when the divorce papers arrived...

Matthew slipped into his old charismatic persona with an easy smile. He acted as if nothing happened, "Hello, Savannah. How are you?"

Christine turned in the seat, observed our guest then swung back to me. My murderous scowl described how I felt about the visitor. Before me stood one of my top ten Most Hated Men on The Planet. Oh, he ranked below Jeffrey Holland and Cole Jordan but not by much. "I'm having a bad day, Matthew. And thanks to you, it's much worse now, thanks for asking," I replied, startling Christine with my frankness.

"You look good. I heard you got married but this," he nodded to my belly, "is a real surprise. I remember when you vowed never to have kids."

"Guess what surprised me? When you shafted Georgia with divorce papers." Cheap shot, I knew that, but if anyone deserved it, Matthew Carlisle did. I glanced at Christine who attempted to engross herself in the teensy list I gave her. I supposed introductions were in order, "Christine, meet my former brother-in-law Major Matthew Carlisle. Major, my colleague Detective Christine Clark."

Always one to have the last word, Matthew pointed to the new shiny decorations on his collar, "Actually it's Lieutenant Colonel now."

"Of course it is," I forced a smile. "The lieutenant colonel always maintained a sharp focus on his career. It was his wife he neglected."

His pompous smile melted to a loud, resigned sigh as he addressed Christine, "A pleasure to meet you, Detective."

She looked at him as if he'd farted. Clark may have been a ballbuster on the job but she still had boobs and hormones and loathed a man who wronged a woman. She offered a polite but succinct *how do you do.* She turned to me, "I'll give you some privacy," then lowered her voice, "and a Taser if you want one."

Bring two, I whispered back. Matthew barely waited until she closed the door before he leapt in, "Look, Savannah, I realize I hurt Georgia but the whole world doesn't need to know."

"Oh, but Matthew," I drawled, "the whole world does know, at least folks in these parts do. Now back home in Michigan, you can tell them any ol' thing you want about what happened." I winked, "But down here in Atlanta, we know the truth." I busied my hands with straightening folders on my desk. It seemed safer than retrieving my gun and playing target practice on those nice, shiny commendations sitting so regal on Mr. Lieutenant Colonel's chest. "What the hell are you doing here anyway?"

"It's about Georgia."

"I didn't exactly think it was about me." Dimwit.

"May I sit down?"

"You will not be staying that long. Answer my question and hit the road."

"God, you're still as hard as the day I met you. Listen, I admit I'm not a genius at marriage –"

"Like you are at divorce, obviously."

Frustration set in, "Will you let me finish?"

With elaborate flourish, I waved for him to proceed. His lips pursed at my theatrics but went on, "The war hasn't been easy for me. I got injured and didn't want Georgia to find out. Shrapnel from an IED. Saw blades sliced through my left leg, tearing up my tendons. Doctors weren't sure they could save my leg. I went through months of physical therapy to return to duty."

Old news, I yawned to myself. Just like his little blonde nurse. I leaned back, stretching, "And that's where you found Florence Nightingale?"

For a second, his eyes narrowed at me. Wasn't supposed to mention indiscretions, I supposed. He squared his shoulders, preparing for verbal battle, "She was a mistake."

"A four month mistake." I pretended to think real hard, "Or was it five? Or six? Or –"

"You can really be a haughty bitch when you want to. You're not perfect, either. You forget I was there when you were crawling into a bottle of Jack Daniels every –"

"You'd be wise to shut up right about now," I bristled, rising from my seat. Debating my shortcomings certainly would not endear him to me. Slinging mud never ingratiated a person. "I have my faults but adultery isn't one of them. I haven't stepped out on my spouse and ruined my marriage. That's what *you* did and you can't blame drinking, youth or stupidity. It was all lust."

"I screwed up, I admit it. But things happen –"

"No, they do not, Matthew. Not when you love someone. You cheated on my sister. She remained loyal to you every day you were deployed. Meanwhile, back at the war, you're banging a nurse and let's not forget the gutless way you ended the marriage." I still remembered every stinging, heartbreaking word his chickenshit letter said. The essence of it: *Dear Georgia, see ya, wouldn't wanna be ya.* And to avoid any misunderstanding on Georgia's part, he tucked the divorce papers inside for good measure.

Matthew leaned across my desk until we met eye to eye. With crimson cheeks and a voice growing louder by the minute, Mr. Marine enlightened me, "I didn't divorce Georgia because I stopped loving her. I divorced her because I couldn't deal with my injuries or the recuperation. I lost my way, got depressed, contemplated suicide. Rachel pulled me out of it. Yes, I screwed around on Georgia and I regret it. The affair is over."

I sat down before Lily volunteered her two cents on the situation, "And because of that, so is your marriage. Did you come here to whine or beg forgiveness?"

My words struck a nerve. His nostrils flared, his large hands bunched into fists. This was a new side to Matthew. An easily flared temper. He and I locked horns during my drinking days and on occasion his anger roared to the surface. When it did, it got ugly but a heated argument firing his temper? That never happened – until today.

Matthew thunderously glared at me, his teeth gnashed until his jaw flexed, "I thought you of all people might understand my perspective."

My mouth dropped open in utter disbelief, "I'm sorry, what?" The man needed a CAT scan if he believed I'd *understand* his perspective. Leaving someone in shambles, in tears, unable to function while they dealt with a devastating, life changing blow? Nope, sorry.

Not in that business.

"You see violence every day with this job," he continued. "Hell, you've even been a victim of it. You understand the complexities of recovering from traumatic injuries. You *get* it or so I thought."

"I assume you mean Jeffrey Holland and Cole Jordan."

One thing about marines. They could stare a person down without blinking. For minutes. "I read about what happened to you and Georgia. I tried contacting her but she never returned my calls."

"Can you blame her?"

He fell into the chair Christine vacated minutes earlier. A sigh and a harsh, ugly curse regarding Jesus fell from his lips, "You are one iron-fisted broad. I'm surprised you're married and doubly surprised you let the guy close enough to knock you up. I'm trying to apologize here. I made a mistake divorcing Georgia. I couldn't handle the pressures of active duty and marriage."

"Gee, Matthew, our brother was a Ranger and he managed active duty, a wife and a baby daughter. If you love someone enough, it can be done."

He rubbed his forehead. I prayed I caused the beginnings of a tremendous, incessant headache for the jerk. He looked at me through pained eyes, "I'm not giving up, Savannah. I want my wife back."

Time for a Come to Jesus meeting, I thought, because the blockhead refused to take a hint. "To clarify, she is not your wife. Her name is Georgia Prince. She's no longer Georgia Carlisle. The divorce papers severed that name forever." I rose from my chair, a sign the conversation was over. Something was different about Matthew.

Something dangerous. Too many bullets, IEDs, Rachels and battles hardened the once easygoing, genial fellow Georgia once called *sweetheart.* I didn't want him around my sister. It was best he find another Rachel to warm his bed because Georgia was off the radar, "She's moved on, Matthew. She's found another man, one who loves her and treats her right."

He finally stood, "You can't stop me from seeing her," his brow sank, "and you'd better not try. You remember how I deal with you."

Yes, and it hurt too. He'd manhandled me in the bad old days when I came to their house drunk. Picked me up like a feather and forced me into Georgia's bathroom where my sister stripped me naked and drenched me in a cold shower. Major Carlisle stood outside the door, giving his sister-in-law her marching orders to sober up or stay away. One day when Georgia was gone shopping, I dropped by – sober – only for Matthew to brace me against the living room wall and lecture me that he refused to tolerate a drunk is his house or around his wife. I was a disgrace, a good-for-nothing that never deserved Georgia as a sister. I'd swung back to counter his ridiculous sermon. Yeah, I admitted to him, I was a screw-up but I loved and respected my sister and no jerk in a uniform would tell me different. That's when the he slapped me so hard it made my ears ring. I never told Georgia about it. At that point, he was still her charming knight.

Ennis stepped in the doorway, curious about the visitor with a crew-cut and perfectly pressed uniform. I pointed to my husband, "I'd bet money *he'll* stop you."

Matthew swiveled on one heel to face Ennis. The two measured about the same height and build. Matthew probably outweighed Ennis by ten or twenty pounds but my hubby grew up on a ranch. He'd dealt with plenty of stubborn, testy animals before meeting Mr. Carlisle.

My darling's relaxed features flushed with ire, his hands tightened to fists. He instantly recognized Matthew. Without uttering one word, Ennis put him on notice.

"Meet my husband Ennis Rutherford. His brother is Georgia's fiancé." I leveled a firm, final warning, "Let her go, Matthew. She's done with you and so am I."

Ennis put hands to hips, an advisement for Matthew to vacate the building, then turned to me, "They found a girl's body. They think it's Megan."

Yes, indeed. A crappy day that just got crappier by the second. I grabbed my suit jacket and passed by my former brother-in-law, "I trust you can find your way out – of town."

32

Without intending to, my sister deceived the world. Her readers and anyone who met her assumed they experienced the totality of Georgia Prince. The easy, sparkling smile. The soft voice inclined to laugh at little things. The deep drawl reminiscent of Gone With the Wind. They didn't see the straightforward side of my sister, the fearless steel magnolia hiding beneath the surface. Besides our mother, she was the woman I admired most. Complain though I might, Georgia was my stabilizing force, conscience and my role model. She loved and defended her family with the same passion she helped the underprivileged and served God and the Baptist church. The woman redefined thoughtful and loyal. As a child she withstood our father's countless beatings, emerging from the pain with remarkable happiness and optimism for life. She fought Jeffrey Holland with the mental strength of a true warrior. Inside sweet little Georgia lurked a fierce woman, one who intelligent people never toyed with, used or abused.

Had Matthew Carlisle's head encompassed a brain, he'd have run for the hills because he knew I'd call my sister. Years ago, upon signing her divorce papers, she vowed with lethal calm that if she saw "that man" again, she'd whop him with her best iron skillet. So when she answered her phone in a slightly terse tone, I purposefully ignored Matthew's name, "Forget the iron skillet. Get your .22 and keep it with you."

"What's the penalty for killing vermin in this state?"

"You could be out in thirty years if you're lucky and it's the needle if you're not. Just wing him and call 911."

"What is wrong with him? *He* divorced *me* for that... that *slut!*"

I proceeded to explain his peculiar visit to my office and that only spurred her anger, "What the hell is he bothering you for? He's my ex-husband so he's my problem. Why, that rotten b –"

"Calm down, sis. Keep your gun and Dane nearby at all times. Matthew won't tangle with Dane."

She grew a tad defensive, "He won't tangle with *my .22!* Dane shouldn't have to fight my battles. I'll take care of Mr. Philanderer myself."

The earlier headache returned, tapping at my temple enough I rubbed it, "Georgia, *don't kill him.* Just call the cops." And let them do it.

The conversation went on another five minutes and when we hung up, I wasn't sure if I'd helped or hindered the situation. Once a person stoked Georgia's temper, it took a while to subside. Matthew kindled it, stoked it then tossed gasoline on it. I only prayed Dane exercised sanity with Matthew because my sister verged on homicidal.

During the phone call, Ennis drove us to the crime scene where the girl's body was. He listened in, cringing at precisely the same times I did. When I clicked off, he shrank back, blew out a breath, "Whoa. Where'd *that* temper come from?"

I smiled at his ignorance of Georgia's inner spirit, "It's like my common sense. It's there but you rarely see it. I hope she knows they don't allow weddings in prison, at least not the kind she's planning."

He passed a slower car then hung a right onto a road originally populated with construction trucks. Now patrol units, an ambulance and fire trucks clogged the street beside a new construction site. I looked past the building's freshly poured foundation where workers cordoned off another area in back for more concrete. All the officers congregated in a grassy area near Peachtree Creek, behind those two areas.

Other uniforms marched across the street with crime scene tape in hand, blocking the street from extraneous traffic. According to the information, the body was dumped on the bank of the creek, an area thick with trees on one side, overgrowth of grass and weeds on the other. The body was located on the latter. Seeing the gentle breeze, I grabbed my coat, knowing the scene would be colder than normal with the nearby water.

"Dane'll tear him apart if he shows up again," Ennis said about Matthew.

"That's assuming Dane gets to him first. She's bound and determined to clean house herself. I just hope it doesn't require a jury later."

We pulled up to the crime scene tape and showed our badges. A nearby cop waved us through. Ennis found an unoccupied slot to park in and we got out.

Sure enough, the chill in the air combined with humidity from the creek scraped a shiver down my back. I shook it off, slipped on my jacket and headed to the small crowd of uniforms gathered at the back of the construction site. Passing by bulldozers, earth movers and pallets of lumber, I noticed the unhappy workers cordoned off behind yellow tape. Their progress on the building came to a brutal and abrupt halt with the discovery. When we walked by I saw frowning impatience among them, heard discontented grumbles. What happened to compassion I wondered? A child lay dead mere yards from them. A child that could have easily been theirs. Would they appreciate bystanders staring at their watches or complaining about deadlines if their child had been murdered?

The gathering of uniforms parted Red Sea-like upon our approach. Ennis caught a glimpse of the body first, wheeled to me and ordered, "Go back to the car."

My expression conveyed the degree of bodily harm I'd inflict if he dared repeat that statement – especially where the uniforms could hear. Surprisingly he ignored the hot glare I responded with. "Savannah, I'm not asking." He thrust a finger at our car, "Go back."

Ennis did this on occasion. His chivalrous nature engaged into Hyper Warp Drive, which drove me into Hyper Bitch Drive. I'd been at this job a few years longer than he – and in a substantially more violent city than modest Amarillo, Texas. I'd seen plenty of bodies and no, none were easy to see. None were easy to investigate without developing feelings for the deceased. No one can dig into the intricacies of a person's life without it happening. But kids were different somehow. When a monster preyed on the vulnerable innocence of youth, it drove a detective to new levels of determination to find and arrest the offender.

Ennis overlooked the fact I *needed* to see this girl, to find out what the killer – or killers – did. If those were Megan's remains, I owed it to her and her parents to face this tragedy head-on. No turning back, no shying away, no excuses. That brave girl risked her life to expose Quinn. The least I could do was acknowledge her final sacrifice.

I grabbed my husband's tie, pulling him eye to eye with me, "I'm not a damn coward, Ennis Rutherford. If that's Megan, I have to know because it's not just my duty to put Quinn away, it's an obsession now." I pushed past him, aggravated that the uniforms and ambulance attendants witnessed our drama. I started toward the creek, hoping to leave the conversation behind me as well.

Stepping around the concrete foundation, I shivered when a cool gust blew past. Fatigue set in from the morning's events, Matthew's unforeseen visit and Georgia's vow to plug him with her revolver. Now this. I wanted to go home, go to bed, throw the covers over my head and forget who I was and what I did for a living.

Several feet later, the concrete changed to dirt surrounded by wooden framework waiting for its own inlay of concrete. I kept going until gnats and flies converged in a swarm over the tall weeds and un-mowed grass of Peachtree Creek. The ground angled toward the muddy water, making footing tricky with the slick grass and soft soil beneath my shoes. Uniforms placed evidence markers beside two sets of men's shoeprints. Shoes I knew would match Hughes and O'Leary.

Through the veil of overgrown weeds and wild grass I saw an ashen, naked form sprawled adjacent to the creek. The body, hidden from obvious view, would have been easily seen by workers preparing the concrete forms. Making my way through the waist high forest, I pushed back three foot high giant reeds and trampled the tall weeds taking hold where the giant reeds hadn't yet. A child's feet came into view. By this time, Ennis caught up to me, his tone resigned, "You don't have to do this."

"I do have to," I countered, still forging ahead through the weeds. Then the naked body came into full view. I swallowed hard, trying to prepare myself.

My vision traveled from the feet, up the battered, tortured body to the girl's face. Yes, it was Megan Bowen. My heart went from frantic pounding to a lethargic, painful thudding in my chest. My knees threatened to buckle at the sight of the bluish/purple bruises darkening her eyes and cheeks, the dried blood staining her mouth and trickling from the corners. I fought the urge to turn away, to listen to Ennis and hole up in the car. I clenched my jaw to bear the nausea creeping up my throat. The once bandaged gaping cut across her throat tested my lunch to its limits. A new slash joined it, this one so deep the whiteness of bone peeked out beyond the abyss of black. This time the killer ensured the girl's silence.

Ennis touched my hand for comfort and I realized I'd rolled my hands into fists. The brutality of Quinn's men, the disregard of human life outraged me. Dozens of small bites spotted her entire body, the flesh ripped free in places. Rat bites. Horrifying images crawled into my brain, those of long, needle sharp teeth sinking into her flesh, pulling and tearing, probably while Quinn watched. And likely laughed. The bastard.

I uttered the fieriest curse in my repertoire. It backed two uniforms off and completely stunned Ennis since I never used the profanity. I finished with, "Quinn is a dead man. I'll kill him."

"Settle down," he cut his eyes to the uniforms. "Anyone hears you or your career decision will be made *for* you."

"Afternoon, detectives," Frank Griffin greeted. The medical examiner crunched over dirt and rocks to the wall of weeds.

Neither of us replied. I didn't trust myself to speak without cussing or crying. Without vowing the same demise for Quinn that Georgia alluded for Matthew. I felt sure once Griffin saw the body, his cheery enthusiasm would wane too. He traversed the weeds and grass until standing directly at Megan's side. Indeed, the warmth in his voice hardened to a businesslike, clipped tone, "Very Mafia. Rat bites." He stooped beside the body until all I saw was the top of his head. The overgrowth provided a modest shroud for the girl, a natural curtain hiding the carnage until someone meandered by. "Obviously the carotids were severed... Bruises everywhere... Broken cheekbone... Oh my," Griffin went silent. Only when Ennis urged him to continue did he finish, "It's been ages since I've seen anything this brutal, particularly with a child. Her tongue was cut out."

My lunch soared up my throat and I swallowed repeatedly to control the urge to puke. The blood pooled in my feet, sending a wave of dizziness through my brain. Griffin's words hit me like a fist to the jaw, sending me off balance and swaying into Ennis. My husband steadied me in his secure embrace, asking if I was okay. No, I wasn't okay. Besides the multitude of indignities she'd already suffered, Megan was tortured, murdered and her tongue was cut out. There was no "okay" about any damn thing anymore.

Ennis demanded an answer and I nodded, my hand resting on his arm as a gesture not to let go yet. I planned to stay on my feet and preferably conscious until we retreated to our car. Then all bets were off. Griffin inquired, "Was she a witness?"

I held together the last shreds of my self-control until I could reply to Griffin in an even tone, "She was my witness."

Frank's head rose above the weeds to meet my gaze, "She spill all the beans on someone? Because this is abnormally ruthless."

No shit. "Her testimony would've put them away forever," I said then realized my teeth clenched hard enough to send pain through my jaw and neck. "Forever."

33

That night I drove to the alley between Blackstone and the house behind it. Megan's description of the girls being led down the tunnel told me the men probably accessed the house's back yard through the alley. I parked across the street from the alley so I had full view of the alley, the street in front of the house and, with my rearview mirror, the back parking lot to Blackstone. No one was dragging anymore kids down that hole as long as I was around.

The street lamp nearest the house's back yard had been conveniently shot out, bathing the area in a black curtain. That night, however, the full moon shined bright, illuminating the narrow alley in just enough light I could see if a vehicle parked there.

Quinn's Audi A8 sat in Blackstone's back lot with Hughes and O'Leary's cars parked beside his. We dragged them in for questioning on Megan's kidnapping only for them to offer alibis we neither prove nor disprove. Without solid proof, we had to release them onto the unsuspecting public again.

I checked my phone for messages, expecting Ennis to check in. I decided not to tell him where I'd be, opting instead to say I needed time alone to think, to try and accept what happened that day. It was a lie and he knew it since he kissed me goodbye with a charming "leave Quinn alone" warning. He drove home his point with the observation if Quinn would murder a child, a pregnant cop meant even less to him. I dutifully agreed to leave Troy Quinn alone, but nothing was said about watching him.

At two in the morning Blackstone went dark. A few minutes later Quinn's Audi pulled out of the lot, followed by three other cars, two of which belonged to Hughes and O'Leary. I started the Charger and eased behind O'Leary's brand new red Corvette Stingray, leaving plenty of space between the cars. Hughes and O'Leary lived west of Blackstone and pulled off in that direction. I followed Quinn. He drove under the speed limit the whole way home. If he spotted me, he never indicated it. Calm and cool, that described The Mighty Quinn.

Once he arrived home, I headed for mine. I pulled into the driveway at three, fatigue enveloped me during the ride, draining everything except routine motions – open door, close door, walk to bedroom... I slipped out of my blouse and slacks, crawled into bed beside Ennis and heaved a sigh.

I leaned in to kiss him when his eyes popped open. His brow sank to a frown, his tongue dripped with disgust, "It's three in the morning. You done *thinking* yet?"

"Probably not." I pecked a kiss to his lips and said goodnight.

"Savannah, stay the hell away from Quinn. I know you're up to something and I don't want you hurt or killed."

"I'll be okay. Goodnight, sweetheart. I love you." Okay, I tried to *Georgia* my way out of it. On occasion my sister refined endearments to serve her purpose. It worked like a charm on Mama and Daddy. She beguiled her boyfriends and the majority of the male gender. She tried the sweet talk with me but being the little sister, I developed a limited immunity to it, the way people formed immunity to the flu. My honeyed words to Ennis were not flattery. They were true. I did love him and his protective Texas ways. His demeanor screamed *gentleman* from the day we met. So that night instead of smacking him with "shut up", I chose the diplomatic, or Georgia, route. And I prayed it worked.

Ennis returned the sentiment, adding a soft tap on my behind to reinforce his earlier warning about Quinn. I closed my eyes, drifting to sleep almost immediately.

It felt as if only minutes passed when a hand on my shoulder gently shook me. Soft warm lips pressed to mine with a whispered *wake up, Sleeping Beauty.* Feh. More like Comatose Hag, I groaned. Eager Ennis announced the time being five o'clock and that we'd be late for work if I didn't hurry. My body refused to move. I'd experienced exhaustion before, just not while pregnant. Babies brought a new aspect to the meaning of the term, one that could only be appreciated by anyone who'd carried a child inside them. Muscles ached, bones hurt and the mind softened to irrational mush when a woman supplied energy for two. It was worse when the woman lost sleep and rest. And now my husband insisted I join the human race again. Maybe, I thought, if I stay really still, he'll go away.

Ennis combined another kiss with a stronger voice, "Savannah, wake up. Or else."

Or else, huh? I would have laughed if I'd had the strength. What would he do, hoist me over his shoulder and drag me to the shower? I'd break his back as heavy as I was. If he attempted to separate me from that luxurious, comfortable bed, Lily would kick me so hard *he'd* feel it. I threw the covers over my head, "Lemme lone. I'm tired."

My husband's death wish reared up again when he announced, "You wouldn't be tired if you stayed home at night and left Quinn alone."

Clearly, Ennis's fear of my temper diminished over the years. Gone were concerns of me going postal because he interrupted the sleep I required to maintain my semi-decent mood. I discovered this sudden change when the covers flew back, replacing my nice warm cocoon with a rush of cool air that swept across my body. I gasped, wide awake now, and gifted him with a mild curse for his barbaric ways. I reached for the blanket again only to feel two warm hands and arms snake beneath my shoulders and knees. He left me no choice but grab his pillow and bounce it on his head, "*Lemme alone,* you meanie. I'll get up."

And I did, for whatever good it served. I spent the day bleary, weary and listless. Not to mention aggravated by unsolicited calls from strangers praising mine and Georgia's win on Family Throwdown that aired the previous evening. By the tenth call, I turned the phone off.

Around noon, pain in my abdomen and groin grew to the point it concerned me enough to call the doctor. I'd had Braxton Hicks contractions on and off for weeks but this one felt harder and longer. I wondered if stress might have sped up Lily's arrival. After answering the nurse's questions about the duration and level of pain, she assured me the contractions were still considered Braxton Hicks, and that they were common. To be safe, she scheduled an appointment for the next day with instructions to call if the pains increased in length and intensity.

The baby wasn't happy with our late hours, I supposed. I sat at my desk, gently rubbing my belly and talking softly to her. Common sense said staking out Blackstone every night qualified as impossible but also kinda stupid for one person. I needed help surveying that slimeball Quinn, but who? Either Clark or Nesbitt worked for him and I hadn't completely decided on which one it was.

I busied myself reviewing Megan's autopsy report when Nesbitt leaned in my office to say hi. I'd heard he returned from vacation relaxed, tanned and ready to work. The last one surprised me. Earlier, Nesbitt broke into hives at the idea. Now he wanted to honestly earn a paycheck?

When I glanced up from the report, I drew back a bit. Nesbitt's natural expression could scare children, small dogs and probably bears. The man couldn't help his features but even Lily, without seeing him, recoiled.

He asked, "You considered maternity leave yet? Seems like a good time."

Well, hello to you too. "Why is it a good time, Alex?" *And why have you begun caring about my maternity leave?*

He shrugged, "Dead kids, for one. For another, this case will take longer than a few weeks to solve and you're about to pop."

The more I interacted with him, the more I considered him like doctors and taxes. They were there so you had to deal with them but you didn't have to enjoy it. "Thanks for the advice. I'll take it into consideration."

"Hope so. You have your kid and let us handle Troy Quinn. He'll slip up sooner or later." He winked, "My mother always said *don't dare the devil.*"

Funny. My mama said it too and until then I hadn't considered my actions daring the devil. Mama once said she prayed harder for me than either Seth or Georgia because trouble sought me out whether or not I looked for it. Maybe I should back off, I thought. Maybe Nesbitt had a point.

o o o

Alex Nesbitt had a point alright. Right on top of his head. His impromptu visit to my office sat wrong. In his own way he tried to sound empathetic, I guess, but came off sounding as off-key as a donkey in a choir.

I'd stop watching Quinn when I chose to, not a second sooner. When I made that decision, I'd try to recruit backup but neither Ennis nor Mathis seemed to keen on sitting in a car all night. My hubby spent our whole lunch hour lecturing me on why I should stay away from Quinn. He itemized dozens of painful things Quinn might do to me. For a mild-mannered fella, Ennis Rutherford possessed a creatively scary, rather vicious mind.

None of his ranting took hold, however, and after leaving work, I headed for Blackstone again. Cars packed the front parking area by that time, the streets fell quiet as patrons and residents alike settled in for a spell. The sun already set, casting the same inky darkness over the street.

The cool night air made surveillance more bearable, particularly for a pregnant woman. I lowered the driver window, leaned back and stretched out for a long wait. If Quinn stayed with routine, he rolled up the sidewalks between two and two-fifteen. That gave me a stretch of about five hours to wait – if my bladder held out.

Ten minutes passed when a dark sedan eased behind my Charger. I watched in the rearview mirror as the driver killed the headlights, exited the car then gingerly pushed the door closed. Cloaked in the shadows, the tall, lean figure stood motionless by their car.

Keeping my vision trained on the rearview mirror, I slid my hand to my .38, removed it from the holster then concealed it beside my leg and out of the person's sight. My heart hammered against my ribs. A million scenarios ran through my mind, all of which dear Ennis mentioned in his attempt to scare me away from Blackstone. I reminded myself to thank him – then slap him – for his terroristic ways, if I survived the night.

The individual now sauntered toward me in a slow, almost graceful stride. A woman. Since when did Quinn send women to bump off the cops? Only one answer came to mind and I turned to face Christine Clark, my fingers still tight around my gun. Just in case.

She leaned in the window, "Savannah, what are you doing?"

I noticed her vision locked on the .38 in my hand. Her Glock remained holstered on her hip. She seemed laid-back and casual about our meeting, as if her weapon was the last thing on her mind. I sincerely hoped it was. My grip relaxed on the .38 but not too much,

"Surveillance. I'm not letting that asshole kill another kid."

She bent closer, pointed to the restaurant, "Quinn called in on you. Talked to the boss about police harassment and his right to privacy so Hunter demanded I round you up."

My jaw clenched, "If we don't watch Quinn, he'll kidnap and sell more kids. He'll *kill* them, Christine, the way he killed Megan Bowen. I need to be here."

In the moonlight, I saw Christine's vision drop to my belly, "We haven't known each other that long so I hope this doesn't offend you. Tackling Quinn isn't the healthiest decision for you or the baby."

I bowed up but she gently put a hand to my shoulder, "Remember what he did to your *car*. Be grateful you weren't in it at the time. And the snakes? Savannah, take those as a warning."

I gauged her sincerity. In the shadows of streetlights, Christine Clark's expression appeared genuine but Riley Murphy's caution screamed to the forefront. Quinn had a spy in our station – one not in uniform but a detective. *Who's new in your precinct...*

My phone rang. It was Georgia. Before giving me time to greet her, she fired words at high-speed, her voice quavering, "Can you get here quick? Safely but quickly?"

Icy fear twisted my heart. I'd heard my sister unsettled and apprehensive before. Only two other times in my life had I heard Georgia truly panicked. At that moment, her usual composed nature dissolved into sheer flesh and blood terror. "What's wrong?" I demanded, trying to remain calm despite the fact I felt anything *but* calm.

"Matthew's trying to break in.   He's going crazy outside, screaming and beating on the door."

Christine leaned closer, "What happened?"

"It's Matthew," I said. "Georgia's in trouble."

"I'll follow you. What's the address?"

I told her then returned to Georgia, "Call 911. I'll get uniforms out there as soon as –"

"No. No patrolmen. I just want you and Ennis. Please don't call this in."

I debated her request while cranking Charger's starter. My mind estimated the distance between my location to her house. At best, I faced a five to ten minute trip without traffic. A lifetime in a domestic dispute. Glass shattered in the background. It sounded huge, not small like a glass or plate. An instant later, Georgia screamed and dropped the phone. I called for her but got no response. The line went dead. I didn't give a rat's ass what my sister said, the cavalry was coming. I thumbed 911, identified myself and explained Georgia's situation, ending it with an order for the uniforms to drive as if their mother lived at the address.

Christine was already in her car, headlights blazing, engine revving. I shoved the Charger's gearshift into drive and roared down the quiet street with my colleague close behind. She stayed on my tail the whole way, weaving through traffic and racing through red lights. On a straightaway, I dialed Ennis and told him about Matthew. He left the second we hung up.

Horrific images filled my brain. Matthew's turbulent expression gnawed away at it, his ominous threat to back off – that he would reconcile with Georgia. If he threatened a cop, God knew what he might do to his ex-wife who hated his guts.

Christine and I pulled into Georgia's driveway, cut our engines. Porch lights blazed, neighbors ventured into front yards. Next door, the Millers huddled by their hedge row beside their garage. Robert and Laura Miller, Georgia's neighbors of fifteen years and close friends called to me, telling me Matthew broke in the house and was still inside. They notified 911 when he began shouting and called again when they heard Georgia scream.

Christine and I both withdrew our weapons, eased up to the garage. Georgia's front door sat back from the garage about twenty feet so once we turned that corner, we were in line of sight of her living room and stairway. Twenty excruciating feet to pray Matthew hadn't positioned himself at the entry with a gun or other weapon, waiting for us to arrive. I tried taking the lead from Christine – after all Georgia was my sister, not hers – but she blocked me, whispering, "Not in your condition, lady. Stay behind me."

She peeked around the garage then turned that dreaded corner. No shots rang out, no giant marine charged from the entry. I followed behind my colleague and the glaring porch light drew my attention to the walkway. The concrete glistened like diamonds with thousands of tiny glass shards. The entire glass screen door had been shattered. The noise I heard on the phone. A few steps closer revealed Matthew not only broke that door but splintered the solid wooden door askew on the hinges. My jaw dropped at the sheer power it probably took to crack it apart.

A car screeched to a stop at the curb. The patrol unit cut the emergency lights and two young burly uniforms piled out. A second unit rolled up behind the first. The four met us at the door while I explained the situation and that Georgia was my sister and to, "Protect her and Rutherford's brother at all costs, if you get my drift."

Oh, they got my drift. By their expressions, Matthew Carlisle better have nine lives because he'd be on his last one once we all finished with him. The four uniforms bulled in front of me and Christine, guns drawn. Before entering the house, one shouted *police* loud enough for Canada to hear him.

They entered then split forces, two uniforms headed left toward the dining room and kitchen, the other two climbed the stairs to the bedrooms. Christine and I approached the shattered remnants of the plate glass door, our shoes crunching over shards scattered across the walkway. Following the other cops' lead, I thumbed the screen door's latch only for more bits of glass to shower the concrete. So help me, I vowed stepping over the glass, if Matthew hurt my sister, he'd leave the house in a body bag.

Stepping inside, I called Georgia's name but heard nothing. A chill chased down my back at the deadening silence. Dread followed in its wake. This wasn't good, the cop in me forewarned. Silence never was. I heard only the uniform's voices as they searched the house but no Georgia, no Dane.

The mess inside the house equaled the one outside. Her cherry wood entry table lay in ruins, broken into half a dozen pieces. The antique glassware once sitting atop the elegant table littered the tile floor, smashed to bits. Instinctively I headed toward the kitchen because I knew if Georgia hadn't had time to retrieve her gun, she'd head for the cutlery.

Busted picture frames lay strewn all over the carpet as though swept off her writing desk and stomped. The two bearing the brunt of Matthew's rage: a photo of her and Dane together, the other of Ennis and me. He wrecked and ruined through the house, bent on destroying Georgia's precious memories and her new life without him. If he'd destroyed her photos, furniture and door, God only knew what he'd done to her. "Georgia!" I yelled. "Where are you? Are you alright?"

"Drop the gun!" a patrolman commanded from the dining room. I rushed toward the shouting only to hear a louder, sterner warning, "I said drop the gun now!"

Rounding the corner to the dining room, I saw both uniform cops, guns drawn and aimed not at Matthew as I expected but at my sister. For an instant, my body released the immense anxiety that mounted during the last half hour. My lungs finally drew breath, and my heart ceased the painful, merciless blows against my ribs. Thank God Georgia was alive. But once my brain processed that fact, it quickly assessed the current precarious situation. Yes, she was alive but she was not okay.

In the corner behind the oak dining table sat Georgia, huddled in wide-eyed terror, knees folded to her chin and tears falling from her beautiful green eyes. Her .22 however, remained firmly in hand and pointed across the room. "Guys," I implored, "that's my sister."

"Then your sister needs to ditch the .22 because she don't look too stable in the head," a younger smartass cop declared.

"Holster your weapons," I snapped. God sakes, I grumbled. My sister not stable? What kind of clod was he anyway? I holstered the .38, headed to Georgia's side then realized by her expression what the guy meant. She didn't exactly appear like the calm, mentally anchored big sis I grew up with. She looked terrified beyond reason. "Georgia," I called softly, "are you okay? Did he hurt you?"

She stared across the room with laser-like intensity. She didn't answer me. I tried another approach, "Honey, you're safe so hand me the gun." I gently wrapped my hand around the barrel but found her grip solid, the knuckles blanched white from the pressure. Her finger rested on the trigger, her unblinking vision still fixed across the room.

I followed her line of sight, expecting to see the bloody, bullet-ridden body of her ex-husband. Instead I discovered the Lieutenant Colonel on his side, hog-tied and pulling and straining against ropes restraining his intimidating form. The only blood was a trickle from his nose and corner of his mouth. Otherwise, Matthew Carlisle seemed fine, just angry and bitching behind a makeshift gag that looked suspiciously like Dane's sock with a belt securing it in place.

Normally, I could predict Georgia, her words and actions. That day she posed a true threat to shooting the shit out of her ex-husband. The determined set of her jaw, the focused stare – straight down the .22's sight. To her, the only people in that room were her and the bastard who destroyed their marriage. My dear sister teetered on a precipice of changing her whole life for the worse if I didn't talk her down. So I tried again, careful to watch her trigger finger, "Georgia, there are six cops here. Matthew is restrained, he can't hurt you. Take it easy, hon. Relax and let go of the gun."

The corner of her mouth trembled. Through the haze of terror, she finally heard me so I finished, "Take your finger off the trigger, sweetie. Loosen your grip."

Her bottom lip quavered and she blinked, sending tears down her pale cheeks. I touched her wrist while still battling her grasp on the weapon.

"She gonna give it up?" the smartass asked. I wanted to slap him until his head unscrewed. Traumatized folks required finesse, soothing voices and time. The young cop wanted me to rip the gun from her hand, apparently, and that always ended wrong. He'd eventually learn that unless someone – namely *me* – didn't clobber him first.

"She need an ambulance or something?" another asked.

I kept my voice soft, composed, "Right now she needs to open her hand. Georgia, you're safe. Give me your gun."

At last, her fingers uncurled from the handle, slid away from the trigger. I breathed a sigh of relief once she relinquished the .22. I handed it to Christine, "See if it's been fired." Because I assumed nothing once viewing the chaos of the house. It was then I witnessed something I'd never seen in my life. My sister, the steel-backboned, confident, placid individual, gave into her tears and emotionally collapsed.

I threw my arms around her, held her tight while heaving sobs racked her. Her arms and hands clamped around me as if searching for not only comfort but stability. She stammered through her tears, "He...

just barged in. Broke my door. Screaming... breaking things. Thank you for coming so quick. Thank you..." Her emotion crested again, leaving the rest of her sentence unintelligible. She held tighter to me than ever before, releasing stress, fear and anger through her tears.

Christine placed the .22 on the dining table, "It hasn't been fired." She glared at Matthew, "Course, I couldn't blame her if she had."

The officers laughed as Matthew's muffled voice gave Christine a piece of his mind. He yanked against his bonds but only managed to appear sillier than he already did.

"Your sister's pretty handy with a rope," an older uniform laughed.

Christine nodded, impressed, "She did do a good job."

The truth finally dawned on me, "She didn't tie him up. Ennis's brother did." In fact, "Georgia, where *is* Dane?"

Still burdened by emotion and fear, her words fell short of being understood by anyone present. Now I worried about Dane. Was he alright? Had Matthew hurt him? The cops hadn't found anyone else inside the house so I told the uniforms to search the back yard and contact the neighbors in case they saw him.

"I thought I had another rope –" the sudden voice behind me scared the bejesus out of us all. Dane was alright, thank God, but I heard guns sliding from holsters and uniforms leveling warnings. They didn't know for sure who the new intruder was and one wrong move might prove deadly.

Before I could call off the uniforms, Dane spied me, "Peach? You got here fast."

I glanced back, seeing Dane's hands lifted in surrender at the bevy of weapons pointed at him. "It's Rutherford's brother," I griped. "Put your guns down."

Christine, the only one who hadn't drawn a gun, sounded amazed, "Man, they look a lot alike."

Yes, they did and I expected everyone to recognize the resemblance. Too bad the officers hadn't because thanks to all the drama with guns, I really had to pee and my sister's viselike squeezing wasn't improving those circumstances.

Meanwhile the uniforms shared a chuckle over Dane's nickname for me. The four volleyed the name *Peach* with such amusement, I reminded them that Carlisle's spectacle was far more humorous.

Heavy footfalls pounded through the living room. I waited for the uniforms to exercise their aiming again, knowing this time I could kiss my bladder control goodbye.

"Savannah!" Ennis shouted while searching the house. "Where are you? Are you okay?"

"Dining room and yes, Ennis, I'm fine," I replied, hoping the cops recognized my husband's name.

A second later, Ennis bolted into the room, stopping short of Matthew's bulky form in the floor. My husband appeared as terrified as I had earlier. "Is everyone okay?" he asked, struggling to catch his breath, "What the hell happened?"

He directed the question at his brother who stabbed a finger at Matthew, "That bastard oughta hang for what he did. He not only broke the front door and everything he could find, he came after Georgia but I made him pay – with interest." He stalked toward Matthew, leaned down to meet his gaze, "Didn't I, you son of a bitch?"

Georgia clutched me harder at the mention of Matthew's barbarian stampede. I shushed her, assured her Matthew wouldn't hurt her again. Because I'd drive him to the country and shoot him myself, I nearly finished.

"I want him to leave me alone," she cried, winding down from hysterical sobbing to a steadier, quieter weeping. "Just leave me alone."

"He'll leave you alone," Dane promised, his hand edging closer to the .22 on the table. I reach back, nudged it away and shook my head. We'd had enough gunplay for one night.

Dane scowled at my unspoken admonition. That's when I caught sight of a golf ball sized lump on his jaw, "Matthew do that?"

Dane waved it off, "I've been hit harder by girls. But I bet he remembers how hard *I* hit."

The comment spurred Matthew into a violent squirming fit, shouting behind the gag at Dane. I smiled with wicked satisfaction, "You broke his pretty nose." Then I addressed the Lt. Colonel, "It's swelling, Matthew, and bruising nicely."

Ennis approached Georgia, gave her shoulder a squeeze, "It'll be okay. You settle down and go with Savannah. She'll take you to our place for the night. Dane and I will stay here and safeguard the house."

Georgia separated from the embrace, her control gradually returning. "Thanks for the offer," she swept away tears, "but this is my home, what's left of it. I'll stay here. Just lock him up, out of my life."

"Or," Dane chimed in, "toss him off a pier. He can keep the

rope."

I chose to ignore his outburst because it sounded way too appealing. I focused on my sister instead, "Georgia, let the boys stay here. They can get your door temporarily fixed. You come home with me. As for Mr. Matthew, he's headed for lockup." I polled the group, "We can cuff him and stuff him or we *could* just haul him in trussed-up like a Thanksgiving turkey. In the spirit of Family Throwdown, is A or B the winner? I vote B."

Christine quickly concurred, along with Ennis, Dane and the four uniforms. I winked at Matthew, "What do you know. It's unanimous."

The four uniform cops began dragging Matthew Carlisle through the dining room by his feet. One opted for a public service announcement, "You screw with a cop's family, you screw with us all, right, Detectives?"

"Right," Ennis, Christine and I said in unison.

I helped Georgia to her feet. She grimaced then leaned into me, taking the weight off her left leg. She apologized and straightened her stance but still favored the left side. When I asked what happened, she sheepishly admitted that she tripped when Matthew ran after her. To my trained ear, it sounded rehearsed – too familiar in a domestic situation. Things akin to *I slipped* or *I ran into the glass door...*

I looked at Dane who avoided direct eye contact, whispering, "Sorry, Peach. He pushed her before I could stop him. She hit her hip on the desk. That's when he broke the pictures."

The mahogany writing desk was heavy enough to survive

Dorothy's tornado and stout enough to dent a Buick. If she collided with that behemoth, her hip needed an x-ray. But first, I tended to personal business. I lit out after the Lieutenant Colonel. He hurt my sister so he'd crawl back to Michigan with a couple more bruises – and a few missing parts, if it were up to me.

A hand locked around my arm in a vise. Wow, I thought. Georgia's strength certainly returned in a hurry. After feeling that grasp, I pitied her .22. The grip probably sported a full impression of her hand. I winced, facing her maternal stare. "I can read your mind," she warned, "and all you'll get is suspended for doing it."

"They can't suspend me for *this*," I called to the officers hauling Matthew to the patrol car. I caught up with them, faced Matthew's glare and leveled my revenge, "Listen closely, Lt. Colonel. No one hurts my family or I hurt them with whatever resources I have available. Bright and early tomorrow morning I'll call your superior officer, tell him what you did, back it up with photos and statements and guess what? You can kiss those shiny new silver oak leaves goodbye."

34

The first item on my agenda the following morning: Notify Matthew's superior officer of the goings on at Georgia's house. Thirty seconds into the conversation, an edge developed to the colonel's voice. He countered my argument with his own, saying that divorces are rarely congenial affairs and that *squabbles* were predictable among those couples. He threw on a healthy dose of skepticism that a marine behaved in such a barbaric manner, believing instead that both tempers flared and that I witnessed the results of a *pair* of agitated individuals.

While he jabbered about the drawbacks of divorce, I faxed him the photos of the damage and witness statements. My voice remained impassive when I explained that besides Georgia and Dane, eight neighbors witnessed his tirade and gave statements to Matthew's behavior. Seeing the pictures and reading the witness and police statements, the colonel's attitude did an about-face from denial to contrite. He guaranteed swift and adequate discipline. I hoped he meant it.

Ennis and I stayed with Georgia and Dane since my sister refused to leave her home. I'm convinced somewhere deep in the cosmos, there are other younger siblings trying to help the older ones only to be slugged with the tired, antiquated assumption that young meant incapable. Georgia loved and respected me but in her mind she saw her baby sister still playing hopscotch or serving pretend tea parties. To her, I'd forever be a child, the one needing help, not the one giving it. I prayed someday she realized I had a family now, held a job, and paid bills. I *could* take care of my sister, if she'd just give me a chance.

I left work early for my appointment with the OB\GYN. Because another woman went into labor, his other appointments were delayed two hours. I called Ennis to forewarn of the delay then I watched the sun fade from its bright, angry glare to a softer reddish orange. Evening soon approached and his nurse offered to reschedule for me. I figured I'd wait because the drive from work cost me forty minutes and the idea of doing the whole thing again exasperated me.

At 5:40, I walked out of the clinic to a beautiful sunset. I felt good. The doctor confirmed the Braxton Hicks contractions were no problem. If they grew longer, stronger and closer together, call him, he said, because they weren't Braxton Hicks anymore but the real McCoy.

For all my bluster, giving birth frightened me. Mama struggled for thirteen hours with Seth. Culbersons notoriously suffered long, difficult labors with the first child. Georgia, as usual, gave no issue about greeting the world and slipped out "quicker than greased lightning", Daddy said. I, of course, broke the record with nineteen hours, twenty-six minutes of wrenching contractions, fits of mild cussing (Mama *never* uttered the heavy hitters), and a fainting spell or two. My mother said one look at me and it was all worth it, even the sweating. Daddy looked at me and said, "There's the one to worry about."

I'd carried this baby for nearly nine months. Eaten reasonably healthy, took my vitamins, never missed an appointment and protected her as best I could. Over the months she'd grown, responded to mine and Ennis's voices, our moods, our laughter. She moved, stretched, punched and kicked so hard I sometimes believed a kangaroo, not a baby, resided in there. Without even seeing our little one, we'd both developed a profound bond with her. Pregnancy leaned toward the masochistic side at times and flat-out miserable at others. But each day drew closer to meeting our daughter face to face, finally seeing this lively, adorable creature with her own emotions, mannerisms and character. Each day I looked forward to seeing her yet I dreaded losing the physical connection we shared for many months. But once I held her in my arms, I knew I'd feel the way Mama did. It was all worth it. I just prayed Ennis didn't look our girl and say, "There's the one to worry about."

Before I slid into a melancholy state, I grabbed my phone and headed toward the Charger. I'd call Ennis and update him on the appointment. Rush hour traffic thinned out along Peachtree Dunwoody Road. I just needed to climb in the car, hit the Perimeter – or Interstate 285 – and within a few minutes, Ennis and I could indulge in supper.

Other patients trudged from nearby doctor's offices. Over the years, the area built into a veritable hub of medical offices. Whatever was wrong, walk half a block and there was a specialist to help you. By the looks of everyone, including me, we'd had enough help that day. We just wanted to go home.

While thumbing speed dial for Ennis, I sorted my keys by feel, slid the car key into the lock as more cars passed behind me, leaving for the evening.

A car entered the parking lot, slowed as it neared the Charger and I hurried to unlock the car so the newcomer could pull into the slot beside me. I put my phone call on hold until I got in the car. The driver revved their engine. Their impatience rankled me. They thought *I* was slow? Try a doctor. They made snails look like racehorses.

I heard the car shift into Park. That worried me since I was alone in the parking lot and this person seemed to be rather restless. I began to turn as a sudden pressure registered below my left shoulder blade, directly behind my heart.

"You've become quite a liability, Mother," Troy Quinn declared in a cool, forbidding tone. "I warned ya just like I warned that feckin' fat bastard cop. He didn't listen so I took care of him. Like a gentleman, I tried to be kind with you, considerin' yer condition. I used words, then a little incentive with yer car. I tried snakes to back ya off but ya ignored it all. Now you've gone to nosin' into me business, stakin' out me restaurant so it's time for pest control. Now, hand me yer gun. Use two fingers if ya please. I'd hate to mistake any sudden movements as aggression."

I didn't move. Any move might be misconstrued as a *sudden* one. "You realize the other detectives know what you're doing with those girls. Eventually you'll be brought down, whether it's me or someone else. You're going to terrorize us all?"

I heard his smile, "No one's caught me yet, lass. I keep powerful, influential people around for useful purposes. They protect me because I protect them. So I'll be damned if I let some fertile sow with a badge stop me." He prodded me with his gun, "Yer thearty-eight, if you'll kindly comply."

With the two fingers he demanded, I slipped my .38 from its holster and dangled it at my side. He snatched it from my grasp then helped himself to the handcuffs at my waistband. A bolt of pain shot through me. My daughter chose that moment to stretch her infinitely long legs. Resisting the reflex to rub at her foot took monumental effort. If I moved my hand, Quinn would shoot me and I imagined it would, no doubt, hurt worse than a baby's calisthenics.

"Hands behind you," Quinn ordered.

"C'mon, Quinn," I protested between clenched teeth. The insufferable affliction worsened. My kid must have been three feet long in there – and all arms and legs. I took a risk at rubbing her foot. Speaking in short, pained breaths, I inquired, "Do I look like a flight risk? I'm big as a whale and my kid's got a foot in my lung."

Quinn sounded displeased at my plight, "Fine." He turned me by the shoulder where I faced a .45 caliber Taurus Judge revolver. When Quinn went big, he went all the way. The Judge fired shotshells and most people considered it a short-barreled shotgun. No one screwed with that thing, not even me.

Quinn tossed the cuffs to O'Leary who, like a good, dependable lackey, stood beside his boss. Lackey cuffed my hands in front.

"You'll be comin' with us then." Quinn said. "And believe me, I'm not above shootin' a cop."

As if I doubted it. He jerked me closer, whispered in my ear, "I'm also not above shootin' yer precious little one."

He relieved me of my phone, turned it off then pushed me toward his Audi, "Get in."

With the Judge at my spine, I followed instructions. I climbed in with Quinn beside me. He leaned forward, handing my cell phone to the front seat passenger Kevin Hughes. "Get rid of this and," he followed it with my gun, "we'll deal with this later."

"Where we headed, boss?" Sean O'Leary inquired from the driver's seat.

"The usual spot. I doubt Mother has seen that part of her city." He flipped open his own phone, dialed a number. "Good of ya to pick up, ya plank. Like to explain why yer colleague is still drawin' breath? Ya followed 'er, yeah? Last night you were standin' *right there* and had a gun, yeah? At what point did ya forget yer orders? Since ya lost yer nerve and grew a conscience, I'll do yer job for ya. Meet us at the warehouse or you'll be next."

35

Quinn was wrong. I'd been to that part of town, alright. Thousands of residents drove past it on their way to work, some avoiding it for its overall decline and gang presence. Others considered it the old warehouse district where furniture stores and clothing repositories stored surplus. There were a few businesses that still called the area home but not many. The violence drove most to safer places in the city.

At night no one ventured into this part of town without a gun. Cops hated the area because of gang wars. The inhabitants were nocturnal, patrolling "their" streets day and night and using lethal force to make their point. A few already loomed in dark doorways as we passed, guns in their waistbands, at the ready. Odd thing was, once they saw the Audi cruising down the street, they retreated back into the shadows, seemingly hiding from Quinn's view. If the Irishman intimidated gang members, I realized how drastically I'd misjudged the man.

We crossed over railroad tracks, made a series of lefts and rights all while the wandering thugs headed inside upon sight of the silver Audi. The car drove to the city's outskirts where the Chattahoochee River bordered miles of warehouses. Half a dozen eighteen wheelers lined warehouse parking lots down the street, waiting for the next day's loads.

The time crept well past regular business hours. No one stirred in or around the cluster of massive buildings. No cars, no witnesses. The perfect place for Quinn's activities.

O'Leary shoved the gearshift into Park. He'd pulled into a parking lot with fault-line sized cracks jagging through the asphalt and knee-high weeds growing up through them. Next to the lot: a red brick relic of a warehouse from the nineteen thirties in need of serious maintenance. The only newer aspect of the building was a steel door with a heavy lock.

Quinn stretched as if we'd spent hours on the road, "Betcha don't know what this place used to be."

Well, since he brought it up, "I have no idea."

He turned in the seat. The river's reflection shimmered in his eyes, "A slaughterhouse. They cut pigs apart here. I bought it a couple of years ago, kept all the equipment. Thought of it as me contribution to city history and preservation."

"How civic-minded of you." *And you told me this because...*

He shrugged, "It's more of an eyesore now but it serves its purpose. I'll give ya a tour of the place, free of charge."

"Thanks ever so but I decline the invitation."

The .45's hammer clicked back, the barrel pressed to my belly, "Such a tragedy to lose a child, especially due to a case of rampant stupidity."

I glared back at him, conveying without words how I felt. For some reason he found it funny, "You got balls for an English half-breed. It's unfortunate ya haven't got brains to compliment them." His smile disappeared, "Get out."

Easier said than done for a woman the size of Cleveland. I opened the door to begin the arduous task of extricating myself. If Troy Quinn ever understood the difficulties pregnant women encountered just trying to stand up, he'd have never handcuffed me in the first place. Hughes and O'Leary met me when my feet hit the ground. Displeased with the speed of my exodus, each wrapped a hand around an arm to hoist me out.

Their boss rounded the trunk, began leading me to the side door with the shiny, heavy lock. "It's a shame it's come to this," he said, not sounding one bit apologetic about it. "With yer tenacity, I could have employed ya. You'da been better than that git I hired from yer station."

Once more the mystery mole appeared in conversation. From Quinn's phone conversation, I guessed Clark was the winner. After all, she'd tailed me to Blackstone where she confronted me. I sure didn't see Nesbitt lingering in the alley or doorway, not unless he was a ghost. "That isn't going too well, is it?" I asked Quinn.

Quinn jerked me to face him. The pressure of a gun barrel again pressed into my belly, only harder this time, "Women can't help themselves, can they? Ya wag yer tongue until someone ties it 'round yer neck and ends ya."

Hughes unlocked the door, opened it to let us in. The stench of old blood and rotten flesh permeated the air. I swallowed back the gag reflex but just barely.

O'Leary flipped on the lights, bathing the whole warehouse in a dreary, flickering fluorescent glow. Massive stainless steel machines crowded the room. None of them looked familiar nor could I guess what they did except torture and kill. One resembled an eight foot tall photo booth, only instead of a camera lens, several shower heads protruded from the walls. Quinn hauled me alongside him as another quaint feature of the place came into view. A line of thick, giant hooks hung from the ceiling, each one caked with a coating of dried blood. The blood beneath them on the floor appeared redder and fresher, making me wonder how many people, not animals, were butchered there – and when.

I backpedaled at the grand scale of Quinn's carnage factory, the many ghastly methods of murder packed into one building. I wanted out. I wanted to go home to Ennis, curl against him and mean it when I said *I'll consider retirement.* My baby deserved to live whether I did or not. I was alone, no one knew where I was and so far I saw no way out.

Quinn's grasp tightened on my arm, "Now, now, Mother. We're just gettin' to the good parts." He pointed to the booth with the shower heads, "That's the vapor scalding tunnel. Helps soften up the pig skin before removing 'er hair and splitting 'er open." He pointed to another piece of equipment, a stand alone steel frame that looked like a door frame. Only this door frame had two restraints loosely reminding me of the setup Jeffrey Holland had. Quinn's apparatus differed with an additional chain dangling from the top crossbar and a motorized cylinder mounted above.

He proudly announced, "This is the skinning machine. Tie the bitch up, attach the chain, give 'er a good slice and let the pneumatic drum do the rest. Strips the skin clean off. Works better on four-legged pigs but you'd still fit the bill."

He laughed at his own joke. My expression conveyed my lack of enthusiasm for his idea. He guided me to one specific tool laying on a long metal table. Thick, dark blood congealed in a pool at the far end. He picked up the power tool that resembled the Jaws of Life with two curved scissor blades. "This is what I used on that chatty little bitch. The tongue cutter. And guess who's next?" He nodded to Hughes and O'Leary who closed in on me.

Panic flooded me. Throughout the grotesque tour, I'd searched for a way out, a way to save myself and found none.

Fingers dug into my flesh until meeting bone. They wrestled me toward the table. I flailed, I screamed, I pushed and kicked but the two gained the leverage I so desperately fought for.

Quinn smiled. "I've waited a long time for this, lass," he said, drawing back his fist and launched it into my chin.

Stars exploded before my eyes, my knees buckled. The pain debilitated me, leaving me vulnerable to Hughes and O'Leary who promptly took advantage of my incapacitated state. Hughes hooked an arm beneath my knees, hoisting me onto the table without uttering so much as a groan.

"Police!" a voice shouted. "Quinn, call off your men or I'll shoot."

A voice I expected to hear – but not with those words. Christine Clark leveled her Glock at Troy Quinn, the man I had guessed paid her handsome sums for doing his dirty work. I'd been wrong about Christine. Yet a troublesome question nagged at me. How did she know where I was? Quinn called his mole to meet at the warehouse, no one else.

At the moment I didn't care. Her entrance and subsequent threat diverted the men's attention. That's all I needed. I delivered a hefty cheap shot to O'Leary's groin with my elbow, sending him to the floor.

Before I gifted Hughes with a knee in the nuts, Christine advanced, gun still leveled at Quinn. "You and Hughes on your knees now." She pointed to O'Leary, "And you stay on the ground."

Christine nodded for me to join her. Her vision remained trained right down the gun sight. Right at Troy Quinn who slowly descended to his knees, hands outstretched as if asking forgiveness from God. His expression lacked one facet of his dire situation. Fear. Instead he narrowed his green eyes at her, scoffing, "Well, if it isn't Mother's friend Detective Clark. What is it about women? Can't keep yer noses out of a man's business. You'da been smarter stayin' to yerself, Clark. Now we have two bodies to dispose of."

Christine handed me her Glock while retrieving her handcuffs, "Oh yeah? Good luck with that, asshole." She headed toward him, "Because we're leaving out the front door with you in handcuffs."

I'd been wrong about Christine. In the back of my mind, I second-guessed her loyalties. For days, I worked under the assumption she worked for Quinn. She hadn't.

"No, you're not," a different voice argued from behind me. A voice that once cautioned me not to dare the devil. The mole was Alex Nesbitt.

I glanced behind me. Nesbitt pointed his Glock at me, told me to drop the gun which I decided wasn't currently in my best interest. Christine turned to see her partner aiming his gun at me and her jaw dropped, "Alex? What the hell are you doing?"

He shrugged, "Quinn pays better than the department. Put the cuffs on yourself and back away. Prince, I said *put the gun down now.*"

Taking her time and keeping a careful eye on her partner, Clark locked one wrist in the cuffs then gave me a slight nod. I dropped to one knee and wheeled, squeezing off two shots. Nesbitt fell with a groan, his gun slipping from his grasp. The first shot hit him in the gut, the second in the hip, just inches away from his family jewels. I scooped up his gun, keeping one aimed at him, the other at Quinn.

Troy Quinn yawned his indifference, "Many thanks, Mother. That's one less problem for me. Ya see, Detective Nesbitt was becoming something of a burden. I instructed him to dispense with ya last night outside the restaurant but the soft-hearted eejit told me Clark was hanging around yer car. I told him to shoot ya anyway but he refused. Said when Clark wasn't around, he'd do it. Said it like *he* made the rules. I can't allow that. So Mr. Nesbitt was next on me list but ya saved me the trouble."

Nesbitt wasn't exactly dead. Disabled for quite a few tasks, yes, but not dead.

"Savannah, my gun!" Christine called in a panic.
I turned to see Hughes and O'Leary running toward the back of the warehouse. Christine raced toward me, frantically waving for me to return her Glock. I clicked on the safety and tossed it to her, cautioning, "Safety's on."

She caught it in midair then took off after Hughes and O'Leary, "Stay there and cover Quinn."

I hated leaving her to chase two killers alone. Training dictated I follow for backup however common sense reminded I was a liability as big and slow as I was. Keeping up with her or the men only complicated issues.

Quinn chuckled, "Just you and me, Mother. And the bleedin' halfwit behind ya. Yer friend is loyal but she should realize yer chances of survival are as small as a mouse's diddy."

"You're going to prison, Quinn. If I don't put you there, another detective will."

"A woman's tongue is a thing that never rusts. That's why I sliced out that little witch's tongue." Quinn's hand mimicked a scissor-like motion, "She kept waggin' it like you do yers so I fixed her like I'm gonna fix you."

I shivered at the notion of him using the horrendous tool on the frightened little girl. It literally infuriated me. My finger tightened on the trigger. No one cared if a kidnapper died. Who shed tears over a child predator? They sure never shed tears over a man who delighted in torturing and killing children.

If Christine failed to show soon, Troy Quinn would suddenly develop a third eye. My anger built to scorching proportions. I wanted answers for everything. Davenport. Megan. All the girls he'd killed. "Why'd you kill Davenport?" I asked.

The humor left his features. His narrowed vision expressed the violence churning in his brain, "B'cause the dumb bastard poked his nose into me business. Sound like someone ya know? He discovered how I supported his little girl, how I paid for all her diamonds and furs. I even paid that lazy arse out of debt and he threatened to bring the police into me business." He leaned forward, the move aggressive, threatening, "So I shot him in the head, cut him apart then dumped him in that smelly lake where he belonged. Satisfied, *Mother*?"

Three gunshots rang out, echoing through the warehouse. Silence ensued until a cry from the back of the building raked another shiver down my back. A woman's cry. "Christine?" I called, wrestling with whether to check on her or keep the gun on Quinn.

Quinn's smile widened, "That sounded dreadful."

No reply came from the dark corner where the three disappeared into earlier. "Christine," I tried again, this time louder. "Are you okay?"

Still no answer. Troy shrugged, "You *could* see about 'er. She is yer friend."

"Shut up, Quinn." I eased around him, trying to see into the darkness down the way. I called Christine's name again. This time Hughes limped from the shadows, blood soaking his beige slacks all the way down his left leg. He cringed, "Bloody hell. The bitch shot me."

Quinn shrugged again, "A hazard of the job. You remedied the problem?"

Hughes gnashed his teeth against the pain. He glared at me, assuring, "I did."

I motioned with the gun, "Sit down."

Disbelief crossed his face, "I'll be doin' nothin' of the sort, ya fat sow. Ya don't understand the gravity of yer situation but ya will." Then he summoned O'Leary.

The first person emerging from the darkness was Christine, not O'Leary. My friend's nose dripped blood but it was the way her left arm hung limp beside her that alarmed me most. Her hands were cuffed in front of her like mine and her shoulder and arm didn't quite mesh like they should have. O'Leary shoved her forward and she struggled to stay on her feet. They stopped a few yards from me. His arm braced across her chest pinning the wounded arm in an awkward position. She squirmed against him with a yelp.

He brandished her Glock, jammed the barrel in her temple, "Drop the gun or I'll shoot her. I won't hesitate like that cop did."

"Shoot him," Christine cringed. "He's gonna kill me anyway."

"*Drop the gun, bitch*," the Irishman prodded, pushing harder at the gun.

"*Shoot him, Savannah*," she urged. "If you drop the gun he'll shoot me anyway. Try to save yourself and the baby. *Shoot him now.*"

I wavered between taking a shot and not taking one. Either scenario ended in a bad way. My police training said don't back down, that letting the criminal have their way never ended well. O'Leary's patience ran on rims, his hand shook and his finger put steady pressure on the trigger.

My split-second decision was to shift my aim back to Quinn, "Shoot my friend and I'll empty this clip into your boss."

That surprised him. He hesitated, measuring my words. He didn't know what to do. So he looked at Quinn who sighed with disgust, "It's a trick, ya git. Shoot that bitch," he pointed to me, "then shoot this bitch."

I heard a groan behind me. A brief glance over my shoulder revealed Nesbitt pushing himself to his elbow, his hand reaching toward his ankle where the strap of an ankle holster peeked from beneath his slacks.

"Savannah, look out!" Christine cried.

A muscular arm swung across my vision. Quinn ripped the Glock from my grasp, pointed it at Nesbitt and a blast rang out so loud it made my ears ring. Nesbitt fell one last time, eyes open and blood pouring from a hole in his throat. Quinn turned the gun on me, "One down, two to go. Okay, Mother, let's get you and yer friend to the back room."

The three men herded us together with guns in our backs. I shook my head in disbelief. I really screwed up. Over the weeks, I'd made wrong assumptions, and horrible, disastrous decisions and my baby and my friend would pay along with me. "I'm sorry, Christine. I never meant to involve you in this craziness."

She nudged me with her good shoulder, "You're my friend. Why wouldn't I look out for you?"

We traipsed over the blood stained floor toward the darker, nether region of the warehouse. Our course narrowed to a corridor where smaller rooms – some sort of offices, I guessed – were located. We passed one doorway after another, their metal doors propped open to reveal the cavernous black hole beyond. No windows with faint street light drifting in – just a long hallway of nothing but pitch black and the flickering fluorescent glow behind us. Hughes and O'Leary prodded us along. The hallway grew darker as we walked. Quinn said the back room. What he meant was a cave.

"How's your shoulder?" I asked Christine.

"Hurts like hell but a dislocated shoulder seems to be the least of my worries right now." She leaned closer, "How's the baby holding up?"

I told her Lily had been knocking on my spleen the last couple of minutes but nothing truly painful yet.

For some reason our chit-chat irked Quinn. "Let's go, girls. I have business to return to."

"Hey," Christine barked, "stop being so anxious to kill us. I mean, you do realize she's pregnant, right? Forget the fact you're winning the death penalty for killing Nesbitt and me but killing an expectant mother?"

"I gave 'er ample warnin' to cease and desist. Two chances. That's two more than I give anyone."

Christine shook her head, incensed at his apathy, "You are *so* going to hell."

"Ah, but lass," he sounded amused, "you'll be there long before I."

We approached the fifth and last doorway. A sturdy metal door sat partially closed. Hughes gave it a kick. The door creaked open and stopped with a solid clunk against the wall. This was it. Our last chance to escape if possible. Once we entered that room, God only knew what awaited us.

As we neared the doorway, a faint glint caught my attention. A nail about five inches long lay on the floor next to the wall. I groaned then sank to my knees with a fake cramp. Christine immediately followed my lead, crouching beside me, her hand on my arm, "Are you okay?"

"The baby's kicking the crap outta me," I covertly pointed to the nail and my friend gently squeezed my arm in acknowledgement.

"Get up," Quinn ordered, annoyed with the delay.

I scooped up the nail as Christine leaned closer, patted my knee, "Sit there a minute and take slow, deep breaths."

"Get up or I'll drag ya by the hair." Anger laced Quinn's voice.

O'Leary bent over my shoulder, "Boss said get up, bitch."

I twisted, swinging the nail and burying it in his leg. O'Leary cried out, stumbled back. Hughes and Quinn moved in quickly and Christine slowed Quinn by booting her foot in his groin.

Quinn lashed out in a foreign tongue I assumed was Gaelic. By the sound of it, it was best we couldn't understand him.

We tried ganging up on Hughes but Quinn recovered fast. His fist clenched to take a swing at me – in the stomach. With no room to run, I ducked instead, letting the blow crush me across the face. I stumbled backward, hit the wall and let myself slide to the floor. My jaw throbbed, my head swam and my ears rang. I literally couldn't see straight for seconds.

Christine maintained a hardy fight for a woman with one good arm to two good legs – until Quinn landed an upper cut to her chin, sending her to the floor beside me. I heard Quinn's heavy breathing, enraged with the two women before him. He stood there, wagging the Taurus .45 in his grasp, his vision bouncing between me and Christine.

Which one do I shoot first, seemed to be his quandary. But I knew Troy Quinn. Despite his anger and apparent haste, Troy Quinn enjoyed taking his time with his victims no matter his busy schedule. His art form consisted of creating unique ways to murder people, why else buy a slaughterhouse with all its heinous machines?

Hughes loomed over us, the muzzle of a .45 aimed at my nose, "I oughta kill you now for stabbing Sean."

Quinn slapped the gun down, making me flinch. With the force he used, the damn thing could have fired, blowing a hole in my forehead. Troy removed the weapon from Hughes's hand only to aim it at my knee, "If ya don't move yer asses inta that room now, I'll cripple ya here and leave ya be for the rest."

I tried to figure out how that was a better deal than what he originally planned for us. Do as he says and die or don't do he says and *still* die. Hmm...

Christine and I took our time maneuvering to our feet. She helped me to a standing position since Quinn's chivalrous side obviously never seeded at conception. He flipped on the office-type room's light – one dim bulb – to guide us as we shuffled inside. The gloomy windowless room contained an old wooden desk, a chair and some metal shelves with boxes on them. It appeared to be a storage area for junk and furniture. At the back wall, a platter-sized concrete support post stretched from floor to ceiling. There were several of the posts throughout the old building, positioned in the middle of the warehouse and some along the walls.

With one hand, Quinn shoved me toward the post, "Stand there an' don't move." He handed the .45 back to Hughes, "Keep yer weapon on Clark. She's as crafty as Mother. Pistol whip the first bitch that moves."

Quinn reached in his pocket for a handcuff key. Mine, of course. He unlocked one cuff then wrapped my arm around the post and locked my wrist in again. Great. Locked to a huge support pillar with no hope of freeing myself.

O'Leary pushed Christine to the same post and Quinn locked her wrists around it above mine. We stared at each other like *now what?* Quinn, apparently sensing our question, answered it for us, "Well, I hate to part on such bitter terms but that's the way it must be. I'll be seein' ya in another life, girls." He turned to O'Leary, his cheerful tone dropping to a calm, ominous one, "Burn it to the ground."

Quinn sauntered out of the room with Hughes and O'Leary limping behind. They closed and locked the big metal door behind them. Moments later we heard clanking and sloshing sounds outside the door, followed closely with the smell of gasoline. O'Leary probably gave the door an extra splash or two for good measure.

Christine, ever so composed, squirmed her hands toward her pants pocket. She grimaced at the strain on her shoulder.

"What are you looking for?" I asked. "Maybe I can reach it."

She moved her hips toward me, raising her left one, "My handcuff key." She shifted closer, painfully inched her left elbow away, "Can you reach it now?"

Pain arose in my belly, first in small waves then larger, harder ones. I swallowed back the discomfort, praying for it to diminish fast. I

had important things to do and collapsing in agony wasn't one of them.
I reached toward her pocket, my hand barely able to reach deep enough
inside, when a key brushed my fingertips. I clasped it between my index
and middle fingers, pulling it out with a relieved smile. God bless this
overly prepared woman, I thought.

I inserted the key, unlocked Christine's wrists. A cramp
unexpectedly closed like a fist in my belly, stealing my breath.

"What's wrong?" She asked with wide-eyed concern.

"Contractions."

"Oh geez. Now?" She freed me from my restraints. "Tell Lily
it's not really a good time."

My arms folded over my stomach with prayers the pain might
abate. "I think they're Braxton Hicks contractions. My water hasn't
broken."

"That's good. So what do you do for Braxton Hicks?"

I rubbed my stomach, tried to retain my focus against the
increasing intensity, "According to the doctor, warm baths and
relaxation. Nice idea, huh?"

Christine approached the door, "Try slow, deep breaths though I
don't recommend that later when the place goes up in flames." She
grabbed the doorknob with her good hand, braced her foot against the
door jamb and yanked. A shriek spilled from her lips. The door held
tighter than a clam with lockjaw. The door seated into a metal frame so
we were stuck unless we Southern Engineered our asses free.

Christine swiped away tears of pain, cradled her bad shoulder
with a blistering curse then muttered, "Shit that hurt." She reared back

and gave the door a powerful kick. The resulting thud divulged the fact the metal door was probably solid, bullet resistant and plenty stout enough to trap two women behind it. It was not moving without serious muscle, a key or a miracle.

"Bastards," Christine growled. "Who the hell installs metal doors on the friggin' *inside?*"

"Besides prisons, apparently psychotic leprechauns."

Christine regrouped, punishing the door with another spiteful kick. It paid her back with another affliction to yelp about so she capitulated, "You got any ideas? Mine suck."

The contractions eased somewhat, allowing me to think clearer. When they led us into the room, I visually searched the room for ways out. No windows. No other doors. The place was filled with shelves lined with boxes. Against one wall sat a desk littered with a hodgepodge of small items. Most of it appeared to be junk. The desk's chair sat across the room with a car battery and attached cables beside it on the floor. I saw a flashlight on one shelf, but no other tools to speak of.

And one locked metal door. The industrial lock showed no exposed mounting screws so we couldn't remove the doorknob. Picking the lock required more expertise than I had and I doubted Christine knew how. I stared at the barrier preventing our escape.

"Hel-*lo*, Savannah," my friend's frustration mounted. "We're in a time crunch here. Got any thoughts on how to avoid being flame-broiled?"

My vision dropped to the door hinges. The door was hinged on the *inside*... "The hinges," I blurted. "Let's try to remove the pins from the door hinges."

"Great idea but how? I've never taken doors off the hinges."

Well, I had. When Ennis and I moved into our new house, the dresser's girth prevented us from placing it in the bedroom. We needed a couple of extra inches of space so we popped the doors off their hinges and presto, instant access. "I need a screwdriver or something similar. That and a hammer."

"Savannah, look at this place," she said like I'd lost my mind. "All we have is a car battery, cables and friggin' boxes."

I scoured the room for tools or implements to use. I looked over the desk, then the car battery. They needed a screwdriver to attach the cables. I hunted behind the battery, beneath it, around it. No screwdriver. I turned to the shelves. Nothing so the desk came next. Papers, an old calendar, scissors, notepad and a silver pen. I eyed the scissors and sterling silver pen, wondering if the latter might hold up to the repeated blows of a hammer. I grabbed it, leaving the scissors in case I needed them for something else later, "Find something heavy to use as a hammer."

The first wisp of smoke wafted in. Faint curls of gray smoke drifted beneath the door. Christine stared at the smoke snaking under the door. The color drained from her face, "Hammer. Right." Then she jumped into action, opening desk drawers, sweeping boxes off the shelves and opening them. "You know, I let Hunter know where I was. Well, I left a message on his phone. He wanted me to tail you and keep you out of trouble. First-rate job, right?"

"We'll get out of here." I sounded way more confident than I felt.

I shoved a box aside and reached for another. So far this search turned out as dismal as our last thirty minutes. "Let's just pray Josh gets the message soon."

"Hey!" She suddenly stood rod straight. In her hand she brandished a black square paperweight about the size of a baseball. She tossed it to me, "Will this work?"

I weighed it in my hand. Solid, firm. "Let's see," I pointed to the door. "I know it's locked but brace the door as best you can."

Acrid smoke stung my nostrils and lungs, launching me into a coughing fit. I sputtered, trying to gain control over the spasms tormenting me while I slid the silver pen into the hole holding the hinge pin. I said a quick prayer for the pen's strength to hold out and whacked the end with the paperweight. The pen survived but hinge pin didn't budge. I hit it again. Nothing.

Christine gnashed her teeth, whether from pain or frustration, "It's not working."

Gee, thanks for noticing. "It's an old door," I defended. "Give me a little time."

"A little is all we got."

I hit it again, as hard as I could. The damn thing refused to dislodge but I wasn't admitting that to her. I held the pen steady, gripped the paperweight. Another solid whack and I saw the hinge pin inch upward. Progress, finally. I hit it again and again until the pin stood tall atop the interlocked hinges. I pulled it free, tossed it aside, "One more. Keep holding the door steady."

"Yeah. My bum arm makes that easy," she lashed out. A

moment passed when she apologized, "Sorry. The pain's getting to me and..." She looked at me. Stark, vivid fear glittered in her eyes as she confessed, "I'm scared."

"I'm scared too," I said. In fact, I clung to what fragile control remained. Panic rioted within me, tearing at hope, clawing at my faith. I wanted to see my husband again – and my daughter when she arrived. To do that, common sense needed to prevail, not thoughts of defeat and death.

Smoke began obscuring the room in a murky gray cloud. Every particle filled with poison, every breath stealing another second of life from Christine, me and my baby. I inserted the silver pen into the bottom hinge, pummeling it with the paperweight until it gave.

My companion heaved a relieved sigh, "Thank God you thought of the hinges. Let's get this door off."

I ran my hand down the door. It felt cool. So far so good, "We can use the chair for leverage but we need a lever."

She scurried to a corner, "How about a broom?"

"Good idea. It might work. Let me do it. Your shoulder is hurting."

Using one hand, Christine manhandled the chair, flipping it upside down then wedged the broom's handle beneath the door. She shook her head, "I'll do it. You pry the bastard open for us."

I hurried to the desk and swiped the scissors. They were good, steel scissors made around World War II, not the namby pamby crap they sold today.

Christine pressed down on the broom handle, lifting the door enough for me to jab the scissors between the crack of the door and metal facing. I shoved, trying to lever the door open enough for decent handholds.

"Is… it… working?" Christine strained through clenched teeth. Even using her good hand, pain contorted her pretty features.

"Yes. Let me check the door –" Coughs wracked me until my ribs and back ached. Smoke burned my lungs and stung my eyes that produced an onslaught of blinding tears. The fire steadily got hotter, the smoke thicker as it spread through the warehouse. Our time ran thin to escape.

I pressed a hand to the door, starting from the top then the middle to the bottom. Still cool. I glanced back, "It's okay so far. If we can pull the door open, we're good."

She surrendered the makeshift crowbar and joined me. Her fingers clawed, trying to grip the door's edge. I kept pushing the scissors deeper, prying as I went. Finally the door gave, clanging to the floor, and releasing us from the small, smoky tomb.

We instinctively ducked as smoke billowed into our once semi-safe haven. We stared into the inky clouds rolling toward us. We now faced a whole new hell to survive and I couldn't remember the way out. The smoke enveloped the entire building in a black cloud, removing landmarks, shrouding every hazard. All I remembered was *turn right out of the office.* After that, I was screwed.

Christine grabbed my hand, "You got us out of this room, I'll get us out of the building. Don't let go of me."

Several feet ahead, flames leapt from the floor. They snaked their way up walls in an undulating hypnotic dance. Orange and red waves crested and rolled along the floor until consuming worktables, machines and equipment. The fire writhed up walls, fighting for freedom as the flames licked the ceiling. How the hell were we going to get out of this unspeakable nightmare alive?

It surprised me how fast and confident Christine traversed the building. Her feet moved swift and decisive past metal tables and equipment I'd have surely stumbled over. Her gait never slowed, her grasp secure and tight around my hand.

Glass shattered overhead and I shielded my head from potential falling shards. The row of skylights along the ceiling busted one after another, sending a shower of thick, deadly glass crashing to the floor. Uncontrollable terror raced through me as my colleague and friend led us to the door.

Another round of coughing shuddered through me. The thick smoke choked my throat and lungs to the point I fought for a mere hint of breath. I felt lightheaded, my stomach sick. "How much further?" I sputtered between my hacking.

Christine battled her own war with breathing, coughing and gasping for air. Doubt crept into her voice, "It's ahead. I know it is. It has to be…"

The inferno's dragon-like roar deafened me, making it hard to hear Christine's words. Heat blasted us like a scorching wind. We navigated around the flames only to have the surrounding heat roast us. Sweat rose along my body not just from heat but nerves. The further we advanced, the weaker I grew. What I remembered as a short trek to the exit felt a thousand miles long with no end in sight.

Christine abruptly stopped which drove me right against her back. Her fist pounded on what I assumed to be a door – the only wall not alive with fire. Maybe there *was* hope. I joined Christine, beating on the door and trying to yell past the burning in my lungs.

"I hear… voices… outside," she said between heaving coughs. It spurred us both to continue yelling for help. Then I heard them. Voices. Voices telling us to stand back from the door.

A thunderous crash caused waves of smoke to roll past us in billowing waves. An exit. Subdued light emerged from the choking blackness surrounding us. Flashlight beams sliced through the murkiness and I took Christine's hand, leading her out.

Firefighters converged on us, thick gloves encircling each arm for support. One spoke three short but infinitely magnificent words, "You're safe now."

Hearing them depleted the remainder of my energy. Tears spilled from my eyes. We made it. I would see Ennis again. I would give birth to our baby girl and Christine would go home to Beans, her Pomeranian.

Another firefighter tended to Christine, leading her away from the inferno. We both leaned into our firemen, using them as physical crutches. Across the parking lot, I saw two men lying on the ground, dead. O'Leary and Hughes sprawled across the pavement, blood oozing from bullet wounds in their chests.

Another body lay beside the silver Audi. Troy Quinn splayed out on his back, his precious Taurus .45 mere inches from his right hand. His chest bloomed with blood weeping from half a dozen bullet wounds.

The Mighty Quinn met his Maker in a hail of 9mm justice, courtesy of the Atlanta Police Department. A hollow victory, considering all the lives he'd destroyed, all the children he'd murdered. I'd take that victory because now I'd sleep well knowing his killing days were over.

More violent coughing spasms stole my breath and strength as my body tried to purge the acrid smoke from my lungs. I smelled and tasted charred wood, scorched metal and burnt insulation. Sheer pain and exhaustion drove me to my knees. My firefighters tightened their hold, caught me, and waved the paramedics over with a gurney. It was a blessing to lie down and a bigger blessing to be safely in an ambulance exhausted but alive.

The firefighters helped Christine climb into another ambulance where she slumped onto a gurney and gave me a thumbs up. I returned the gesture.

Two paramedics converged on me, one slipping an oxygen mask on me while the other chose a more medieval route by poking my arm with an IV. They were all over me, probing, monitoring, listening and asking me questions. I had only one primary concern, "My baby," my voice rasped. "Check my baby."

The first guy pressed a stethoscope to my heart. Reinforcing my request, I moved his hand to my belly. Obliging me, he listened to Lily for several seconds then nodded, "Heart rate is elevated but considering what happened, it's not surprising. The docs will check you both at the hospital. Try to relax."

His words helped but I needed confirmation from an official, card-carrying doctor to *relax*. If I was suffering, my girl was too. I inhaled the oxygen deep, hoping every breath lessened her stress, calmed her down. My hand rubbed the spot she'd been tapping at the last minute or two. I prayed she understood everything was okay now. We were safe.

Outside the ambulance, hell raged as the firefighters battled the blaze. The once pitch black surroundings lit up as flames reached into the night sky, their reflection illuminating nearby buildings, the faces of emergency workers and curious bystanders. Smoke and steam rolled past, surging in enormous dense clouds. Emergency lights from ambulances, fire trucks and police units revolved in a dizzying ballet. The whole scene seemed impossible, almost surreal. I heard firemen yelling, the hiss of water meeting flame, sirens approaching as more units pulled up for perimeter security. I reassured myself – it was over, *really* over. The nightmare of Troy Quinn ended with a trip to the morgue for him and a trip to the hospital for me and Christine.

I drew another breath only to hack myself into a muscle spasm. My eyes still burned and my throat and chest felt like I'd swallowed a gallon of lava. I wanted Ennis there. I wanted to see his handsome face, hear his soothing voice – just as soon as he concluded his lecture about me retiring. A throaty hoarseness replaced the rasp in my voice. I didn't sound like myself anymore and the raw stinging forced me to push the words out, "My husband. I need to call my husband."

The men looked at each other, amused. The oldest, in his late twenties, jumped from the ambulance, ready to close the doors, "Ma'am, just relax for now. We'll contact your husband when we get to Atlanta Medical."

"Hold up!" a man shouted. Josh Hunter sprinted from Christine's ambulance to mine and climbed inside. The paramedic closed the doors, plopped behind the steering wheel and shifted into Drive. My boss sat next to me as we pulled out of the parking lot. For a moment we just looked at each other. I expected a genuine Josh Hunter dressing-down, one promising immediate termination of my employment. He preached almost as eloquently as Georgia, only he used stronger language. That evening, however, Hunter's eyes were gentle, filled with a tenderness I wasn't used to. "How're you doing?" he asked.

"Been better," I started coughing again for a good ten seconds. Once I regained my composure I hitched my thumb at the blaze outside, "But I could be worse."

"And the baby?"

"They say she's okay. The doctor will check her at the hospital."

"I called Ennis and Georgia. They're on their way to Atlanta Medical to meet us. Fair warning though. They're both hotter than that building so you'd better consider maternity leave ASAP." He sighed with what I hoped was relief, "Your dedication to solving murders not only exceeds the requirements for the job, it scares the hell out of anyone who knows you. I mean, *getting locked in a burning building?*" He shook his head, "You and Georgia are day and night. It's unbelievable you're from the same gene pool."

Well, that fell far short of an actual compliment. He knew Georgia as level-headed, calm and sweet. She experienced the occasional foolhardy recklessness, usually when it involved family but it was there. I nearly laughed at his clueless bewilderment. After all those years, he didn't know my sister at all.

He watched the EMT check my heart rate then asked, "Did this penchant for mayhem come from your father's side?"

I couldn't help it. I laughed this time. A round of coughing supplanted my effort and when I caught my breath, I smiled, "As you witnessed with my cousins, mayhem is an old family tradition on *Mama's* side of the family."

36

Being laid up in a hospital made a person reevaluate things. They gained new appreciation for their families, their bed at home, and their freedom from hoses, monitors and wires. It was also when the immense gravity of having a child finally hit. Our baby was less than a month from arriving. A tiny life that relied on Ennis and me. She would need nurturing, guidance, and rational decisions made for her. Most of which I possessed none of. I supposed every new parent feared the worst. Each task aroused a fresh terror – will I accidentally drown this child while bathing her? Does the crying mean she needs changing, she's hungry, or sick? Is she supposed to cry *that* much? How did I expect to raise a child and keep the job I loved? The last question required more than mere days to figure out so for the short-term, I settled for maternity leave. I'd use the time to appraise my life and future. My job was important but if forced into a choice, the baby came first no matter what. That's why when I stood in my office, gathering my belongings, the immense gravity of *that* situation hit. No one expected me at work anymore, not for the next several weeks. Getting up early was optional until Lily arrived. I watched officers pass by the door, their attention straight ahead, no nods or waves acknowledging my presence as before. An acute loneliness swept over me. Business as usual, I thought. My life as a cop concluded for the interim but crime persisted, flourished with or without me. I was no longer part of the team and it hurt.

I retrieved the stack of crayon drawings my niece and nephew gave me over the years. Images of police cars, perps behind bars, and their aunt in uniform. My favorite: one of me holding a perp by the collar, my smile as bright as Vegas. The kids made me feel like a superhero. I only hoped Lily felt the same way about her mama one day.

"Is that everything?" Ennis's glee inflamed my already raw nerves. He helped me collect my nameplate, plaques, books and family photos a tad too eagerly that morning. With mindful yet speedy precision, he placed my belongings in the box he now held, ready to haul them to the car and drive me home.

"No. One more thing." I held the *one more thing*. The pewter 5x7 frame contained a photo of my family taken when I was ten years old. Private Seth Prince stood proud in his army uniform. Sixteen year-old Georgia, her arms draped around her bothersome little sister, beamed with pure beauty – a spitting image of our mother and a young Rita Hayworth. A jubilant smile graced Mama's features as she stood by Seth, her arm linked through his. Daddy, in his best suit, looked dignified and pleased beside his two girls. One arm around Georgia's shoulders, his other across mine.

I placed the frame in the box and saw Ennis's wattage fade a degree. He finally realized how difficult this was for me.

He leaned down, kissed me, "Sugar, you can come back when you're ready. It's just for a few weeks."

The longest weeks of my life, I wanted to say. I looked the place over once more. The day I moved into the office was like moving into a new house. Thrilling and humbling at the same time. I'd made the big league. My own new digs, shiny new gold badge, and the coveted title of Detective. My most fulfilling moment to that date. Now I packed everything and handed the place to another detective – for now.

I nodded, agreeing with him. I ended it with a resigned sigh and a reluctant, "I guess I'm ready to go."

Ennis gave it his best effort. He *tried* to look empathetic on my behalf. Anyone else might have believed the hung-dog expression. Me? I knew his honest opinion about me retaining my job, especially after that hospital stay. By the conclusion of his vociferous ranting, I felt as wrecked as a hit and run victim. No, Ennis Rutherford wanted a regular wife now, one who never carried a gun or badge, or – as he so stylishly put it – came within a gnat's eyelash of death twice a year or more.

"I'll load the car," he bounced out of the office, box in hand and a hint of joy in his voice.

I rolled the chair behind the desk, straightened the books in the bookcase behind me. No need to leave the place in chaos. A sudden rush of fatigue entrenched itself to my bones. I'd been tired all morning. No matter what I ate, drank or consumed in the way of vitamins helped. I leaned against the desk, waiting for Ennis to return.

"I see you survived Ennis's thrashing," Christine joked from the doorway.

I glanced up from the bare desk. Christine stepped in, her arm still in a sling from the dislocated shoulder. She blew out a breath, "He was storming that night. I heard him four cubicles away in the ER."

The whole ER *and* distant galaxies heard him, I thought. "He's determined I retire. I'm determined to have this baby and think about my future. I'm just glad Georgia was there to calm him down. She'd planned on joining the chorus but ended up pulling the reins on him." Now that was a sight. My sister, all revved up to lecture me, had to curtail my husband's temper instead. It rattled her to see him so angry but I commended her on her composed manner. She settled him down after about an hour, much sooner than I expected.

Sadness passed over Christine's face as she traced the edge of the desk, "I'm gonna miss you around here. You're the only real friend I've got in this place. And since Nesbitt's gone, Hunter's assigned me with John Mathis. Great, right?"

I cringed. That would be a disaster. Why in the hell did Josh stick those two in the same partnership? Oil and water. Not good.

She pulled at her black suit jacket to adjust it beneath the sling, "I'm gonna be miserable so don't be a stranger, okay? We can always grab lunch together sometime."

I'd like that, I said. She kept fidgeting with her jacket as if debating to speak. Finally she stepped closer, whispering, "You mind if I ask Hunter to pair me with Ennis? Your hubby is way more laidback than Mathis. Plus he can keep me updated on you and Lily."

"I'll mention it to him before I leave. Don't worry. You and I will keep in touch until I get back."

"So you're thinking of staying on, even after Ennis's tongue-lashing?"

Her hopeful tone made me feel good to know I'd be missed. "I'd like to, yes." I nodded to her arm, "How are you feeling?"

She shrugged her good arm, "Each day is better. The sling got the guys' approval at least. Maybe all that bullshit about being female will slow down now. You and Lily doing okay?"

The mention of my girl's name stirred a smile from me. All the aggravations of pregnancy, the anticipation and fear of mommy-dom, everything came down to bringing another life into the world. To love her and raise her and see her mature into a woman. It truly inspired me, "The doctors gave us both a clean bill of health." I appraised my colleague, giving serious reflection to the past several weeks. Sure, Christine Clark presented herself as a brash, no nonsense female, not to be tangled with. That was the job. Beneath the hard exterior remained a dependable, good-natured, humorous soul. During my hospital incarceration, I considered Christine Clark in a whole different way, "You know, Ennis and I named her Lily Christine months ago. But after the other day, I truly believe my girl has another Christine to look up to." Tears gathered in my friend's eyes. She swallowed me in a giant one-armed hug.

Two loud knocks on the door interrupted our girly moment. "Does your husband know you swing both ways?" the familiar voice sniped. "You two look real cozy."

I looked up to see Matthew Carlisle skulking in the doorway, his evil eye aimed at me. His black eye faded to purple though his nose still shouted *broken*. He'd dressed down for the peasants in jeans and blue t-shirt. I wondered why he ditched the formal wear since he loved strutting in it then I figured the black eye and deformed nose clashed with his medals and commendations.

"You again," my lip curled. "I thought you got the message when we schlepped your ass to jail the other night." The uniforms treated him no better than a perp who belted a cop. That meant no careful handling and if he acquired another bruise or two on the way, so be it. For him to show up again, Matthew Carlisle had more than one screw loose. I mean I carried a gun, for God's sake, and I *had* been known to use it on a few stupid sons-of-bitches.

His jaw clenched and released. Thank goodness Christine's Glock sat safely within reach because his glare felt pretty chilly, "I want to talk to you alone." He transferred his glare to Christine who stood her ground. He waited only moments before hitching his thumb at the door, "I said I'd like a moment alone with Savannah."

My friend's good arm slid across my shoulders, "And I'd like a million dollars. See any stacks of cash around?"

Matthew zeroed in on her arm around me, "You want your girlfriend to hear this? Fine. Your little stunt got me a reduction in rank."

"Well, I made every effort to accurately describe your behavior and the damage you caused."

"Why are you blaming her?" Christine piped up. "She didn't bust down the door and wreck and ruin through Georgia's house. You did."

He ignored her statement, instead choosing to stalk toward me, "I owe you one, Savannah, and I never forget a debt."

As an unspoken caution, Christine's hand slipped from my shoulders to the butt of her Glock, "You need help finding the exit? You can walk yourself out the front or be carried out the back – on a stretcher."

Good one, I smiled.

Matthew harrumphed, "Yeah, and you'd do it too. Cops around here are all corrupt rubes." He stabbed a finger at me, "You want to monkey with my career, Savannah? You'll pay the price. When Georgia and I are back together, I'll make sure you never see her again."

My smile evaporated. Outrage replaced it. I hadn't felt well all morning but hearing that threat tabled any ailment plaguing me. I stepped around the desk to straighten the asshole out once and for all. Christine stopped me with a hand to my arm. "What was your name again?" she asked him.

I replied for him, growling his name between my teeth, "Matthew Carlisle."

She purposefully hindered my access to the idiot. It both irritated and relieved me. I wasn't up to fighting that day. I wanted to go home and rest. Christine squared her shoulders, her tone unyielding, "Mr. Carlisle, since you insist on running your mouth, maybe I should introduce you to our newly remodeled facilities downstairs. Ours isn't as cushy as the one downtown but they have washed the blood off the walls and," she tossed a question over her shoulder at me, "didn't they change out the bunks?"

"Sure did," I played along. "Instead of puke, pee and lice, they only have bed bugs now. You may go home a lowly major, but you'll have lots of little friends to take with you."

Matthew's anger mounted. Christine's hand returned to her gun, "You can either leave Savannah and her sister alone or I'll gleefully pitch you in a cell with all the drunks and raving lunatics until you get lost in the system. Once it gets around that you hurt a cop's sister, lots of things get lost in the shuffle. Even keys to the cell."

The sight of Major Carlisle speechless warmed my heart, especially since my newfound friend figuratively stepped on his neck. He stared at us both, his thunderous scowl promising all manner of carnage – if we weren't cops, weren't armed and not on our own turf. He stewed for the longest, apparently searching for scathing words that might dig in and hurt. All he came up with, "I'm not done with you, Savannah. I'll be back." He turned on his heel to leave.

"We'll still be here," Christine called after him. "With our shiny cuffs and badges *and our loaded guns.*" After he departed our presence, she rolled her eyes and blew out a breath, "Whew. He's a real head case. Where'd Georgia find him, in a crazy farm playing Napoleon?"

"On a book tour. He was a fan of her novels."

"She ever watch *Misery*? She might want to add a home security system to her place 'cause that dude is Kathy Bates with balls."

I couldn't argue with her since it was the truth. Matthew went from hero to stalker in a few short years. Christine's idea rooted with me, "Good idea. I'll tell her."

"If he shows up again, let me know. I'll lock him up and throw the key in Lake Lanier." She looked at me, her brow sank between her eyes, "You feeling okay today?" She scooted the nearby chair closer, "Sit down. You look kinda pale."

I explained that for some reason, I got up abnormally tired that morning. I waved it off to our trauma earlier that week in the slaughterhouse. Christine didn't buy it, "I don't know about that. You need to see your doctor to be safe. Is Lily still moving and kicking?"

She'd calmed down that morning, I said. Her unusually sedate nature concerned me so I agreed to make an appointment with the OB/GYN. Lily never left me alone this long. Now I began worrying. At least I'd called Seth's friend to arrange payment for the Charger that morning. I decided to buy the beautiful car. He gave a fair price – something I figured Seth had a say in.

Christine sat down beside me in the other chair, "I'll stay with you until Ennis gets back. He's just bubbling all over about Lily. Never seen a man so happy about a baby."

I was about to respond when my phone rang. I didn't recognize the number and thought about letting it go to voicemail. Just before it transferred to the recording I answered it.

"Mrs. Rutherford?"

Now *that* was a new one. Even after marriage I was mostly referred to by my maiden name because of the job. Marriage among partners was a no-no but everyone knew I tended to bend and, sometimes, break the rules. Still, the name *Mrs. Rutherford* applied so I answered, "Yes?"

"This is Jamie Johnson, the co-producer of Family Throwdown."

Okay, what was the problem? Were they revoking the money, refusing to pay? I waited for the blow to come. The news saying the only benefit Georgia and I got from sweating our asses off was bragging rights with the family. That *did* have its appeal... I tried to sound casual, "Everything okay with the show?"

"Oh yes. In fact, it's far better than we expected."

That made me curious. What, exactly, were they expecting? I let her continue, "The local ratings were the highest yet. The Cooking Network said they anticipate the ratings will soar considering you and Georgia are celebrities. They wanted me to present you both with a proposal. I know you and your sister have busy schedules but we'd like to film another episode with you. We'd tweak the show's format to fit with Cooking Network's suggestions."

She was kidding, right? Battle my cousins again? Wasn't once enough? "I don't know about that. You're setting yourself up for a lawsuit because my cousins would accidentally poison the public."

"No, it would be a contest with you and Georgia against two new challengers. Would you be interested in participating?"

Absolutely not. But I had one question for the woman, "Have you asked my sister?"

Jamie's voice reached an octave so high only dogs could hear it, "She loves the idea!"

Well, of course she did. "And you can't have one contestant cooking against one challenger, right?"

Now the tone took a nosedive – practically plummeting to alarming depths, "I suppose we could but... The network really wants the two of you again."

I pinched the bridge of my nose. Here we go again, I sighed.

Georgia's enthusiasm was contagious and when she agreed, Ms. Johnson assumed I would too. If I declined, my sister's mood would plummet into an abyss unrecoverable by anyone short of Bob Ballard and his Titanic efforts. "And if we should win again?"

"Then we'd schedule another contest. Of course you'd win the money too. An additional ten thousand dollars, provided by Cooking Network. We were planning on having you and Georgia as returning champions as long as you keep winning."

I swallowed hard. Another ten grand for winning? I quickly did the math, realizing that if I honed my skills, Georgia and I could make a sweet little nest egg. And when one is pregnant, one needs nest eggs that are big, full and firmly packed. "Lemme get this straight. We win an *additional* ten thousand dollars for *every* challenge we win?"

"Every episode, yes. And since the show would air twice a month, you could do really well if you win."

Now I understood why my sister went nuts over the offer. The extra ten grand plus the original twelve, went a long way with anyone – even split two ways. People called me slow but I sure wasn't stupid. "I'd be willing to do it but let me talk to my husband first. If we give the green light for this, we'd have to film around my delivery."

"We will make adjustments as needed. The network is excited about this and they're hoping you agree. Can you have a decision by Monday of next week?"

Oh, I just bet we could. "Pretty sure of it. I'll let you know then."

Okay, so after I hung up I had a long, extensive fantasy involving wallowing in tens and twenties and throwing fifty dollar bills like confetti. Then Lily kicked me back to reality. She finally woke up which eased my mind. I patted my stomach, "You're right. I'm getting ahead of myself. Daddy has to approve too."

I told Christine about the proposal and her jaw dropped, "Need another hand in that kitchen? I'm available."

The phone rang again and this time I hoped it was Publisher's Clearing House. If we'd won a million dollars, *no one* had to cook for their kid's college fund. "Prince," I answered, still gently patting my belly. A strange feeling rolled through it. Not nausea but something I'd never experienced before. Maybe I caught a bug, I thought, praying it didn't affect Lily. I switched to rubbing the area then felt an unexpected pop in my stomach, like an elastic band snapping. What the hell was that, I wondered. Then I decided I'd better have Ennis run me to the doctor before going home. Soon after the pop, I felt a trickle like I was peeing.

"Savannah," my sister barely contained her excitement. It fought for freedom, straining against her good Southern manners until bursting forth in all its glory, "I've got the greatest news! Jamie Johnson from Family Throwdown called. You can finally retire!"

The strange sensation in my belly intensified then the pain roared in and I realized what was happening. "'Fraid I can't right now."

Georgia's tone wilted, "Why not?"

"Because right now I'm having a baby." I looked to Christine for help, "Can you find Ennis? I need a lift to the hospital."

Both my sister and friend went from plain happy to delirious elation. Georgia said she'd be at the hospital within the hour, said she loved me then hung up on me – I didn't have the energy to hold a grudge.

Christine leaned down to hug me, "I'll go get Daddy then I'll drive y'all to the hospital with lights and sirens." She bubbled, "I can't wait to meet Lily."

Neither could I. The day I'd been looking forward to – and dreading – was here. Our little girl kept her own schedule – three weeks early – and for the first time in my life, I was scared witless of babies. The contraction grew harder, more painful and I rubbed my belly again, discouraging my girl of making her entrance before I got to the hospital. I really needed drugs for this, I tried to tell her. No way did I intend to do this the flower child way. I wanted the strongest dope they had and I wanted it in gross.

Christine rushed back into my office with Ennis who resembled a lightning struck owl – wide-eyed and pale with wind-whipped hair. Verging on panic, he pointed to my belly, "Now?"

I nodded, "Now. Nearly three weeks early but now, Lily says."

Both he and Christine helped hoist me out of the chair. We ambled down the hallway while I wore off the remainder of the contraction. It started to ease when we rounded the main area where the desk sergeant and uniforms hung out. The large area usually buzzed with activity and voices. Today it fell stone quiet. We entered the room to see uniform officers shoulder to shoulder, standing pole straight at attention. They simultaneously smiled, every officer applauding and offering good luck as we passed by. The impressive sight brought tears to my eyes.

Their poignant assembly touched and surprised me, considering our tense working relationship at times.

At the end of the extraordinary procession stood the desk sergeant and Josh Hunter. Each gave their good wishes and Josh promised he'd drop by the hospital later that afternoon, then told Ennis to keep him updated through the day.

Tears fell down my cheeks on the way to the patrol car. Christine saw them, "Is something wrong?"

I shook my head, "Just didn't expect such an emotional send off."

"They care about you," Ennis assured, his arm tightening around my waist.

"It's good to have family, the ones that come from the family tree and the ones who don't." And the relatives with the badges were some of the best.

BLACK N' WHITE BROWNIES

Ingredients

3/4 cup all-purpose flour

1/2 cup sugar

1/4 teaspoon baking powder

1/4 teaspoon salt

1 cup quick-cooking oats

1 cup flaked coconut

2/3 cup butter, melted

2 tablespoons milk

CHOCOLATE LAYER:

1/3 cup butter

1 (1 ounce) square unsweetened chocolate

2 eggs

1 cup packed brown sugar

2 tablespoons milk

1 teaspoon vanilla extract

3/4 cup all-purpose flour

1/2 teaspoon baking powder

1/4 teaspoon salt

1/2 cup chopped walnuts

FROSTING:

4 ounces cream cheese, softened

1/4 cup butter, softened

1 1/2 teaspoons vanilla extract

2 1/4 cups confectioners' sugar

1/4 cup chopped walnuts

Directions

1.   In a bowl, combine the first four ingredients. Stir in oats and coconut. Add butter and milk; mix well. Press into a greased 13-in. x 9-in. x 2-in. baking pan. Bake at 350 degrees for 10-12 minutes. Remove from the oven. Reduce heat to 325 degrees.

2.   In a saucepan, melt the butter and chocolate; cool slightly. In a mixing bowl, combine the eggs, brown sugar, milk and vanilla; mix well. Add chocolate mixture; mix well. Combine the flour, baking powder and salt; add to chocolate mixture and mix well. Stir in walnuts. Spread evenly over crust. Bake at 325 degrees for 25-30 minutes or until a toothpick comes out with moist crumbs (do not overbake). Cool on a wire rack.

3.   In a mixing bowl, combine the first four frosting ingredients until smooth and creamy. Spread over bars. Sprinkle with walnuts. Store in the refrigerator.

MACADAMIA CHOCOLATE CHIP COOKIES

Ingredients:

1/2 cup old-fashioned oats

2 1/4 cups all-purpose flour

1 teaspoon baking powder

1 teaspoon baking soda

1/2 teaspoon salt

1 cup unsalted butter, room temperature

1 cup (packed) light brown sugar

1 cup sugar

2 large eggs

1 teaspoon pure vanilla extract

4 ounces English toffee candy (recommended: Heath or Skor bar), finely chopped

1 cup macadamia nuts, toasted, husked, and chopped

1 (12-ounce) bag semisweet chocolate chips

Directions:

1.   Preheat the oven to 325 degrees F.

2.   Line 2 heavy large baking sheets with parchment paper. Finely chop the oats in a food processor. Transfer the oats to a medium bowl. Mix in the flour, baking powder, baking soda, and salt. Set aside.

3.   Using an electric mixer, beat the butter and sugars in a large bowl until fluffy. Beat in the eggs and vanilla. Add the flour mixture and stir just until blended. Stir in the toffee, hazelnuts, and chocolate chips.

4.   For each cookie, drop 1 rounded tablespoonful of dough onto

sheet, spacing 1-inch apart (do not flatten dough). Bake until the cookies are golden (cookies will flatten slightly), about 15 minutes. Cool the cookies on the baking sheets for 5 minutes. Transfer to a cooling rack and cool completely. (The cookies can be prepared 1 day ahead. Store airtight at room temperature.)

SAVANNAH & GEORGIA'S
SOUTHERN BUTTERMILK FRIED CHICKEN

SERVES 6

Spice Rub:

6 chicken leg quarters (leg and thigh separated)

1 teaspoon dried thyme

1 teaspoon dried marjoram

2 teaspoons onion powder

2 teaspoons garlic powder

1.5 teaspoons cayenne pepper

3 tablespoons salt

1 tablespoon black pepper

Buttermilk Brine:

1-2 quart buttermilk

4 tablespoons vinegar-based hot sauce

6 cups all-purpose flour

peanut or canola oil for frying

1.   In a medium bowl, mix all of the dry spices. Add chicken and toss until well coated. Let the mixture stand at room temp (if cooking within 4 hours) or refrigerated in a large bowl for one hour.

2.   Pour enough buttermilk over the chicken to cover completely and stir in the hot sauce. Leave on the countertop for one to three hours, or refrigerate up to 24 hr. Pour chicken legs into colander and allow excess

buttermilk to drain.

3.   In a large bowl, mix the flour with salt and pepper to season well. One-by-one add the chicken pieces, making sure they are thoroughly coated with flour on all sides. Leave them in the bowl with the excess flour while you wait on the oil.

4.   Fill a very large pot 4-6 inches deep with oil and heat to 325 degrees. Grab each piece of chicken and slap it back and forth between your hands a few times to knock off the excess flour before slipping it into the oil. As the legs go into the oil, the temperature will drop. Turn the flame to high to increase the temperature to 350 as the chicken cooks. Cook 12-18 minutes until golden brown and at least 160 degrees at the bone, Remove to a rack to drain and season immediately with salt. Cool a few minutes and serve.

SAVORY FRIED CORN

1 1/2 cups freshly cut corn kernels

1 small sweet onion, finely chopped

2 tbsp. chopped cilantro leaves

1 hot chili pepper, stemmed, seeded, and chopped

1 egg, lightly beaten

1 tbsp. flour

3 tbsp. vegetable oil

salt and pepper to taste

Combine all ingredients except oil in a bowl and mix thoroughly. Heat the oil in a large heavy skillet. Add the corn mixture and saute over high heat for about five-ten minutes or until vegetables are golden brown. If you like onion to carmelize, go a little longer.

J.L. Lemon lives in Texas surrounded by a loving and supportive family, two adorable and devoted puppies, and hordes of garden gnomes.

Before 2002, J.L. Lemon wrote opinions and product reviews for an online consumer guide. When fellow reviewers cited the author's knack for humor, she decided to return to writing fiction. Along with the standalone title Second Chances, she's published 8 books in the Savannah Stories Series.

www.ingramcontent.com/pod-product-compliance
Lightning Source LLC
Chambersburg PA
CBHW020930020726
47495CB00002B/436